Finding Love on Bainbridge Island, Washington

Washington Island
Romance Series

Finding Love in Friday Harbor
Finding Love on Bainbridge Island
Finding Love on Whidbey Island

Finding Love on Bainbridge Island, Washington

Washington Island Romance Series

by

Annette M. Irby

Finding Love on Bainbridge Island, Washington
Published by Mountain Brook Ink
White Salmon, WA U.S.A.

This story is a work of fiction. All characters and events are the product of the author's imagination. Any resemblance to any person, living or dead, is coincidental.

The Team: Miralee Ferrell, Nikki Wright, Cindy Jackson, Judy Vandiver
Cover Design: Indie Cover Design, Lynnette Bonner Designer

Mountain Brook Ink is an inspirational publisher offering fiction you can believe in.
Printed in the United States of America

Dedication

To Angela Premoe, my dear sister-friend. You've been there for me all my life, helping and supporting me in countless ways. I'm certain I wouldn't be where I am today without you. Thank you, Sis, for everything. May God return the blessings to you a hundredfold. This one's for you.

Acknowledgments

Thanks to Douglas and Virginia Monroe, for answering my questions on our family's genealogy and history. What an amazing journey this has been over the past few years as we've learned more about our family. Thanks for being willing to share the stories and for your constant love and support as I chase my dreams.

Thanks to my immediate family for understanding and sacrificing as I pursue my writerly calling, and to my extended family for your support and excitement with each new release.

Thanks to Cheryl Wyatt for your feedback and excitement about this story. I love your mentoring heart, and I appreciate you so much!

Thanks to the following fellow writers or agents. I've benefited so much from your insights and/or our interactions. Specific gratitude goes to: ACFW as an organization, and to Susan May Warren, Rachel Hauck, Karen Ball, James Scott Bell, and Jeff Gerke.

I wouldn't be the writer I am today if it weren't for my McCritters—the critique group who helped shape me as a writer: Ocieanna Fleiss, Dawn Kinzer, and Veronica McCann. Thank you! You haven't seen this story yet because of the timeline for writing it, but I hope you love it and won't need to use your pencils too often. Here's hoping for smiley faces and stars, my friends. More stickers, O!

Thanks to the team at Mountain Brook Ink: Miralee Ferrell, Judy Vandiver, Nikki Wright, and all the others who make this publisher a positive place to publish a series. I appreciate each of you and your efforts. Thanks to Miralee for the opportunity to share these stories!

Thanks to my readers and friends for your prayers and encouragement. The Christian fiction world is a warm and welcoming place, and I'm grateful to be a part of this community.

To Yeshua, my Bridegroom King, thank You for planting a dream in my heart from way back, and for reminding me of those key moments that led me here. I can see Your fingerprints in all of it, and I am writing for You.

In prayer there is a connection between what God does and what you do. You can't get forgiveness from God, for instance, without also forgiving others. If you refuse to do your part, you cut yourself off from God's part.

Matthew 6:14-15 MSG

CHAPTER ONE

Liam Barrett could use some fresh air.

The red-eye from Hawaii to Seattle seemed unending, especially with this snoring guy next to him smelling of curry. Before the flight crew requested that he pocket his phone, he wanted to check on his great-aunt. So long as she kept uploading pictures of her pets or the stormy June weather on Puget Sound, he knew she was okay. But any lag in her online activity and he got worried. His zany great-aunt Matilda was a social butterfly, but she could also be a bit... eccentric. The shorter her leash—and his absences from her vicinity—the better.

A vintage photo of a father, mother, and children was captioned in Auntie Mat's latest upload: *Family is everything. Make peace.* He shook his head, though it wasn't surprising she would post something odd. The point was—he had confirmation she was fine. A relief after everything she'd done for him.

The phone buzzed in his hand as another Facebook notification popped up: *New friend request from Jack Barrett.*

His heart stuttered. Wha—?

An image flashed in his mind of his mother and him alone in the house. She wouldn't stop crying. Preschooler Liam standing at her bedroom doorway, watching. *"You okay, Mommy?"* He'd rubbed his stomach where it hurt. Should he run to her? Hold her hand? Could he hug her and make it better like she did for him? He darted to her side. *"Mommy, are you broken?"*

Now at age thirty-three, his thumb shook as he pressed the power button and turned off his phone. He should've deleted it immediately. Blocked him. Rejection would send a message without having to type a message. He wanted to throw his cell. Or maybe hurl himself off something for the adrenaline fix. How soon could he and his buddies schedule another getaway full of daredevil stunts?

"We are now beginning our descent into SeaTac International Airport. Local weather in Seattle is fifty-six degrees and cloudy with a 70 percent chance of rain this afternoon. Local time is 6:35 a.m." The flight attendant went on to list the various end-of-flight things, like raised tray tables and final trash collection, and Liam tuned him out.

Jack Barrett.

Liam hadn't seen that name for at least two years. Back then, he'd run an online search, as if compelled to track down the man and prove Liam was no longer helpless to fix Mom's pain. Half hating his curiosity, he'd scrolled links. He hadn't done this research as a child, hadn't asked his mom any questions so he wouldn't upset her. The name *Jack Barrett* wasn't uncommon in the Northwest. But, heart thumping, Liam had narrowed it down to those born in Bremerton, Washington around fifty-five years ago.

Best match for the Jack he researched? A felon, busted for armed robbery, grand theft auto, drug possession, and several DUIs. No wonder Mom never mentioned him. Stellar guy. Role model material. Liam didn't drink, didn't use drugs. *He'd* never chased the next high—outside of adrenaline. Or been pulled over by the police. Not even so much as a parking ticket. No, in those ways he was nothing like Jack.

It was the similarities that troubled Liam.

Shake it off, dude.

The plane touched down, and most passengers squeezed into the aisle as soon as the fasten seat belt light went out. Liam let the guy in his row pass, glad to put distance between them. As much as he wanted to bail, he'd be last off today. He and his three buddies would exit after the final passenger—one member of the group moving much slower since the "incident." Poor Hitch.

Liam had a role with his buddies—easygoing. Jack Barrett's name could cancel that part of Liam. The part that had learned to move forward, avoid being too serious.

Around him, his buddies roused. Across the aisle, Isaac "Jinx" Tabor stood and reached overhead. Liam playfully bumped him, though he had plenty of room above his own seat. "Hurry up, Jinx."

Jinx laughed and reached into the compartment. "Shoot, Liam, hang on! I'm grabbing our newly disabled guy's bag too."

"Disabled? Thanks for that. It's only a broken bone." Clark Hanson, known to the group as Hitch since he'd recently gotten married, waited behind them near the lav doors, crutches rammed under his pits. "Flying was sure easier before I needed these." He nodded toward the new accessories.

"We didn't tell you to break your ankle." Liam tugged down his duffel bag. This was good. *Forget the notification.*

"Get a move on, will you?" This from Dylan "Burr" Burgess at the tail of the plane.

Liam marched toward the now-open cockpit. Another adventure in the books. They'd dived with sharks—terrifying and exhilarating—and gone cliff diving.

Out in the concourse, the four of them lined up. Hitch hobbled along and without him asking, the others slowed their pace. The guy's foot must be throbbing after the six-hour flight with no way to elevate it. Still, his buddies teased him about the new *hitch* in his step.

"You're all gonna get it. Line up, and I'll whack you with one of my crutches!"

"Who knew those things made good weapons? Maybe we should alert security." Liam laughed. "You know your wife is going to kill you, right?" Heaven help Liam, but having a wife who could insist he avoid adventures wasn't for him. Good luck, Hitch, and no thanks.

Liam caught his sheepish expression before Hitch answered. "Yes, she is."

"See, that's why I'm not getting married." Burr yanked his duffel strap higher up his shoulder.

"Nah," Jinx joked, "no one'll have you!" He darted away before Burr could punch him. "There's a reason we call you *Burr*."

This earned him a scowl.

The troops went quiet while they waited for the elevator to take them to baggage claim where Hitch's wife and father would meet them. Soon, Jinx and Burr would head back to the Eastside, and Liam would return to Bainbridge Island—something his buddies would never forgive for how posh the island was. Didn't matter that Liam lived in an aged tiny house—not the cool kind—inland, which meant no water view. Or that the roof leaked after the last rainstorm.

At baggage claim, gorgeous Fiona Hanson approached the group. Hitch wore the dopiest of grins. She beelined to him as if she didn't want him to take another step and break something else. "Oh, Clark! Are you all right?" The guys elbowed each other over that name, while Fiona examined him, probably looking for more injuries.

All that fussing—Hitch could keep it. Except, what would it be like to come home to someone? He had a sudden image of Jenna-Shea Brown, the only person he'd ever wanted to come home to. But, she'd made it clear long ago that he'd blown his one chance with her.

All her fuss aside, no one had ever looked at Liam like Fiona looked at Hitch.

"Hey, everyone!" Hitch's dad stepped into the group. Elijah Hanson was a solid guy. He'd personally taken them up in his plane for a few skydives over the years. Seeing Hitch like this, Elijah didn't fret over his son, merely patted his shoulder. "Glad to see you're still with us."

"Hey, Dad." Hitch tilted his head down, but then he raised it and met his father's eyes, as if seeking approval or something, even though he was a grown man. But the looks they exchanged—silent communication from knowing each other so well. Shoot. What was that like? To have someone trustworthy who worked to protect you and build you up?

A dad. Not that Liam would know much about that.

Eli eyed his son's gimpy limb—the cast the Hawaiian doc had put on him, anchoring his ankle to his shin. "You're okay?"

Hitch nodded. "Yup."

"Good. Let's get you home. I'm here to carry this." He reached toward the duffel bag Fiona held, which she happily handed over with a "thanks." Fiona smiled at her father-in-law. Yeah, everyone got along well with Eli. The rest of the guys greeted him, shaking his hand and guy-hugging him with their other arms. He brought respect out of you, and you couldn't object to his warmth or the way he genuinely cared for his son and his family, as well as this foursome who grew up raising Cain together.

They still enjoyed their adventures, but the clock was ticking for Hitch. His days of cliff diving, skydiving, and shark diving were about to end.

A few see-ya-laters after that and Hitch hobbled off with his wife and dad while Liam watched them.

"You coming, Liam?" Jinx asked from several feet away, and Liam meandered in his direction. They fell into step side by side—a faster pace now. "How's your beach-house project?"

Cool, moist air hit as soon as they entered the sky bridge that led to SeaTac's parking structure and the taxi line. Raindrops streaked the tinted plexiglass, rushing down the sides of the elevated transparent tunnel perched over the harried traffic below. Yeah, Hawaii in June beat Seattle hands down.

"Electrical this week. Glad the Browns don't need the house for another few weeks. It's been one thing after another."

Burr nudged Jinx. "Yeah, we feel sorry for you. All that suffering at the beach."

"I don't live at the beach, Burr." *He* could volunteer to trek over and help, but nope. Whatever it was Burr did all day kept him too busy to lend a hand.

Burr grunted again.

For once, Liam was fighting to succeed at something, but all Burr could do was badger him. Enough. "No, I get it. You don't have your life together, so you can't respect that that's what I'm trying to do." Ever since Liam had learned of Jack Barrett's criminal record, he'd determined not to be like him. To keep avoiding brushes with the law, of course, but also to thrive at work, be dependable. To prove he was nothing like Jack.

At the walk-up parking payment booths, Burr stopped. "Yeah? Is that what you think? Working on my sobriety doesn't matter?"

"Dude, it matters," Jinx spoke up—ever the peacemaker.

"C'mon, Liam."

Liam ground his jaw. No matter what he did, Burr always seemed ticked at him, which pushed Liam's buttons and made him overreact. "Knock it off, Burr." Everyone had seen Burr their last night in Hawaii. Nobody said anything, but everybody saw. The guy was spiraling again, without a chute. It wasn't like the four of them to sit around in a circle and spill their guts to each other. So no one really knew what was eating Burr—what secret, or regret, or whatever. The way Burr could push Liam's hot buttons made Liam keep his distance.

Except Liam did owe him.

Burr pivoted away. "See ya, Islander."

There it was. His nickname. Liam clenched his jaw. He didn't hate the moniker, but he knew Burr meant it as a dig—implying Liam was always on vacation or that he was lazy. Burr stalked off. Liam looked at Jinx. "Keep an eye on him, okay?"

A fast sigh. "Yeah. I always do." Jinx lived near Burr, so it fell to him to play babysitter of the tribe's weakest member.

"Jinx!" Burr called from the elevator bank, elbow locked while he held the door.

Jinx was not only the peacemaker, he was the klutz. Eccentric himself in some ways. He jumped, but then shifted into the put-together façade no one ever bought. "Gotta run. Give your auntie Mat a kiss for me!" Because he tried so hard to fake competence in everyday life, he often tripped or sabotaged himself—thus the name Jinx.

But if anyone could figure out what was up with Burr, it was Jinx. For some reason, Burr didn't bark at him.

Liam watched him lope off toward the brooding Burr and felt that sense of aloneness that always followed the high of the guys' getaways. Hitch with his family, Jinx and Burr driving back to the Eastside, and Liam stuffing his parking stub into the automated booth, followed by his credit card, before scuffing toward his parked truck. It was cheaper to leave his beat-up truck here for a few days than to pay a ride service the fare both ways for the distance to Bainbridge from this airport.

He'd head back to his house—alone—and try not to think of how good Hitch had it.

Oh, and Jack Barrett. Liam would rather never think of him again.

Matilda Hartwell held her breath for a second. Liam was going to kill her.

She clicked on the active message box in Facebook and let herself exhale. *I THINK HE MIGHT BE READY TO AT LEAST LISTEN TO WHAT YOU HAVE TO SAY.*

The response was quick. *ALL I CAN DO IS HOPE.*

AND PRAY.

Their conversation went still for several moments, and Matilda wondered if the other writer had stopped to do just that. She'd heard he'd changed, but what if he wasn't a good guy, even now? She wanted to write a new message immediately and demand to know if he'd truly changed. Get him to promise only good would come of this contact attempt. Thing was—Liam was no longer a child under her protection. Not that she would ever put him in harm's way, of course, not even emotionally. Not after all Liam had been through. But something in her gut told her this was the right path—and that it would be hard for her nephew. Plus, the man had found her message, though they weren't friends on Facebook yet.

She wouldn't even consider messaging him today if she wasn't utterly convinced this road was best for Liam. Her nephew carried too much baggage from the past. Too much hurt—and anger, probably—though he covered it well. Most of the time.

Minutes had passed now, and still no activity on the other message-sender's end. Matilda clicked into the message box once more and typed: *IT MIGHT BE TIME TO TRY.* Gulp. *SEND HIM A FRIEND REQUEST. SEE WHAT HAPPENS.*

Again, silence. Had he left his computer, or pocketed his phone? The site's note said he'd "seen" it, but that could just result from an open computer. No guarantees he was there.

She'd take a break and check if her gull friend was visiting her water-side deck. Perhaps he was hungry. She grabbed some berries for him. Sure, part of her knew she should let him fend for himself, but he kept her company while she gardened. For that, he deserved a treat. Plus, she enjoyed singing with him. And he didn't mind performing for an old lady.

Ten minutes later, she returned to her laptop. Still nothing. And then, motion. He was typing.

ALREADY DONE . . .

Matilda's nails clicked as she responded: *THEN, WE WAIT.*

TERRIFYING.

I KNOW.

Liam would have a few choices when he found the friend request. He could delete it right away. He could block the sender. And if God was working miracles at this moment, Liam could consider at least talking to him. Matilda pressed her lips together. No doubt God *was* working miracles somewhere, but Liam had decisions to make and God wouldn't force him.

For as long as Matilda had been Liam's guardian, and even before, she'd tried to teach him the freedom of forgiveness, and how not forgiving brought regret, anger, even rage to the surface. Hopefully, he'd keep those truths in mind when he saw the name pop up in his friend requests. What would he think of her family picture post and the subtle suggestion about making peace?

She clicked on the genealogy site and opened the Search box. She knew the details around Liam's generation and a few names from the previous generation, but the one before that—almost nothing. Later today, she'd try to find Liam's paternal grandparents' names. But for now . . . She clicked into the new family tree she was creating and pressed Liam's name. Then she clicked on Add Father.

There she typed: *Jack Barrett.*

CHAPTER TWO

Jenna-Shea Brown coaxed her tiny car into the gravelly parking stall next to her family's aging beach house on Bainbridge Island's Barclay Spit. She'd made it. Now she had two days to settle in before returning to work at the counseling offices. It may not be ideal to commute all the way back to Bremerton from here—about forty-five minutes one way—but she'd dreamed of living here. That was why, when her roommate needed her house to herself and her soon-to-be husband, and Mom and Dad let Shea know this cottage would be finished by now, she couldn't pack fast enough.

Given how sore her muscles were, it was too bad she couldn't get vacation days this coming week. The remodel should be complete, which meant she'd be the first to live here following all the work they'd had done. This weekend, she'd get as settled as she could, then go back to work on Monday.

Through her splattered car windows, the house drew her attention. Why wasn't the driveway smooth, and the house painted? Where was the usual fresh landscaping? The lawn looked sparse and muddy, rather than laid with fresh sod and interspersed with low shrubs—like rhododendrons and hydrangeas—almost as if a landscaper hadn't worked here yet. Dad had assured her the place was ready for her to rent. So, why the mess?

She'd call her parents, except then she'd have to conjure up her limited vocabulary of French words. Any time they were abroad, they insisted on speaking the language of their location. Shea didn't know a lot of French, and the conversation would drain the last of her mental reserves this busy morning. Instead of dialing them, she'd make a list of bullet points, starting now. She reached for her notepad and a pen while the rain sheeted down. As long as the cottage's interior was ready, she could put up with the waterlogged front lawn until the landscapers arrived.

Wind speckled her windshield with fresh drops and streaks

once the engine—and the wipers—were off. Too bad these waterfront homes didn't come standard with garages. But real estate spaces—lot sizes—were minuscule here. Little room for conveniences like garages, though some of the newer, larger houses boasted them. Many aging cottages crowded this beach like eager summer visitors wanting their place in the sun. No question rainy June mornings weren't anywhere in the mind of the architects of this location on Bainbridge Island. Not for these older homes.

But the view! She flicked the key and swished the wipers a couple of times to see the lagoon. Behind her, Puget Sound rolled in gray waves, but the view in front of her showed the lagoon behind the house. The water was calmer there, though still gray like the skies today.

This spit of land jutted out from the mainland of Bainbridge Island like a hooked finger, creating a half-circle lagoon to the south. That meant many of the houses on Barclay Spit and Point Moore Drive enjoyed a view both of Puget Sound to the north and the lagoon. If she remembered correctly, the master bedroom in her family's cottage boasted both vistas. Oh, she couldn't wait to settle in. But she had to await the movers, and they'd mentioned stopping for coffee on the way here.

During her drive down the spit's narrow road, she'd caught a few glimpses between houses of the Sound's rolling surf, bringing foam and seaweed to the beaches as the tide pushed in. Those waves could be a bit unruly, yet in all the years the Browns had owned property here—both this old family house, and their newly acquired rentals—Shea had never heard of any flooding from the Sound. Low-wake zone laws kept freighters and other ships from causing danger en route to the Port of Seattle, plus most of them sailed safely east of this locale on the island's northern tip.

As kids, the Browns would frolic in the cold waves, darting in and out. She didn't anticipate doing much of that now that she lived here, but she couldn't wait for God to flip the switch and let the weather give over to summer sunshine for a couple of warm months. A few more weeks and the dark rainy season would end, which was good news for her patients suffering from SAD—

seasonal affective disorder.

Shea pictured herself grilling on the lagoon-side deck and having Tia—a coworker and dear friend—and her family over. Maybe her best friend, Mikaela, and her husband, Hunter, could break away from Friday Harbor up north and come visit sometime this summer.

A gust jolted her car, reminding Shea the movers weren't far behind her. She needed to get the house open and ready for their arrival. She'd begin by carrying in the smaller items from her car.

Yanking her slicker's hood over her long brown hair, she snagged her purse and two of the smaller paintings wrapped in plastic she wanted to hang in her new home from the passenger seat.

Blinking against the drops, she darted toward the side door. *Yeah, let's put the parking stall as far from the soaking stoop as possible.* The roof's slight overhang didn't offer much shelter as she jammed her key into the rain-splattered lock. Why hadn't the construction crew finished the exterior? Another bullet point for her email to her parents—a new covered entry and new door.

The warped wooden portal whooshed open to scuffed, bare hardwood floors and the odor of paint from somewhere—though not the living room from what she could see in the dim interior. Blotched paint samples speckled the walls, and the floors looked dusty and unfinished. Dad described a much better situation than this. She schlepped her wet bag and the plastic-covered paintings to the kitchen and laid them on the island—a beat-up slab of aging butcher block. Hadn't Dad promised solid-surface countertops in new condition? A view of the lagoon should greet her here, but the blinds hung haphazardly from the windows as if someone had been in a hurry and these would be the last items to replace. The windows hadn't been washed free of smeared dust and the view was murky—like her future in this house, all of a sudden.

How had this happened? She coughed as another chilled breath drew dust into her lungs. What happened to the heat? The following sneeze trio made her feel ridiculous. That did it. She reached for her phone. Scrap the French-only protocol; she'd conduct their chat in English. Even her parents probably didn't know the French words for *sanded hardwoods* and *granite countertops.*

It was nine hours ahead in France, so she'd catch them at a good time. She probably had ten minutes before the movers arrived. But if this place wasn't ready, where would she go? She couldn't return to her roommate's, and she had to show up at work on Monday. Her stomach churned as the phone rang twice in her ear. *C'mon, Dad. C'mon.*

"Bonsoir, ma belle fille." His nickname for her—my beautiful daughter—did nothing to calm her fears.

She paced the subflooring in the dark kitchen, trying to avoid the long extension cords strung in orange mazes around the room. None of the light switches worked. "Dad, no time for using the *langue française* today. I'm about to be homeless here."

"What do you mean, Shea?" Ah, English. Thank goodness.

She thumped back across the floor, puffing out breaths. "The cottage isn't ready."

Dad inhaled deeply. "Okay, calm down. Help me understand."

Shea sympathized with her dad, not being here to oversee this project. But ire rose inside. "Tell me again—is Liam Barrett the overseer of this remodel?" If so, of course, he had let them down. That's what he did. Why had they hired him again? Maybe, given today's disaster, they would see for themselves why Liam wasn't a good employee *and* they'd stop trying to set the two of them up.

"Sorry, Jenna-Shea, you're breaking up." Her dad's words came through fine. Hopefully they wouldn't lose the connection.

"The house isn't ready." She over-enunciated every word.

"Liam promised me it would be. I even sent him an email last week to make sure."

"Well, he's not here, and the house is a disaster. I could send you pictures if you like. Unfinished flooring. No paint on the walls. Dust everywhere. No landscaping. Old countertops." Her blood barreled through her veins, and her forehead throbbed. "No electricity."

"When I didn't hear back, I should have called him." Regret

edged Dad's words. "I wondered why he never sent me a scanned copy of the final inspection sign-off."

Shea sighed. "Dad, you had to know that trusting Liam Barrett was a risk. I mean, just ask JP." Her brother knew all about his buddy Liam's shortcomings. This was as close as she'd get to lecturing Dad. She preferred to show only respect, so she had to get her irritation under control.

"We wanted to give him a chance. I realize you don't see him as completely reliable, but he is honest. Heart of gold, that man. Since we aren't there, I wanted someone who wasn't going to rip us off."

The last thing she was concerned about right now was Liam's heart, of all things. "But if you can't rely on him, what good—?"

"I'll call him next."

She sighed. "Meanwhile, my movers are due in seconds, with all my belongings from down in Bremerton—you know, not exactly next door. My roommate has no room for me, Dad. She's getting married, remember?" She grabbed a breath and tried to calm down. "Are any of your other properties vacant right now?" *Please, please, please.*

A slight pause. "Unfortunately, all our other properties are occupied."

"Well, then that is a probl—"

"What *arhh ya doin' thar*, Lass?" A screechy voice called out behind her.

She whirled around, her heart pounding hard. "Who s-said that?" The dim living room lent no light.

"What's happening, Jenna-Shea?" Dad sounded as alarmed as Shea felt.

"What *arhh ya doin' thar*?" The strange voice again.

"Jenna? What's happening?" Dad repeated, his voice rising.

"I—I don't know," she answered into the phone. She backed toward the kitchen's exit, ready to flee if needed. Her lungs worked fast as her body trembled.

"Jenna, remember—stay calm. Breathe."

The reminder helped. Well, that and Dad's soothing voice, as if he were right there beside her. *Think.* She had to keep her left brain engaged so her right brain couldn't take her into an emotionally paralyzed state. She clenched her right hand into a fist. *Left brain, engage.*

"Now, tell me what's happening." Dad knew her story, knew how being startled or frightened could set her off, knew to keep her talking.

Focus. "I can't see much in here. But someone said something," she whispered as she stood in the kitchen, hopefully out of harm's way. Someone was in the house with her. She alternated squeezing her right fist and her left hand around her phone. Right... left.

"Do you need to dial 911? We can get off the phone. Or you can find a neighbor."

"Are ye lost, Lass?" The voice was distant. Whoever it was hadn't followed her toward the kitchen door.

"Someone with an Irish accent, it sounds like." This situation seemed more and more odd by the moment.

Squawk!

"What in the worl—"

"Jenna-Shea?"

"Hang on, Dad." Curiosity outweighed fear, and Shea moved back toward the living room where lighting was far scarcer. No life anywhere. She clutched her phone as if holding Dad's hand. "Where are you?" She asked the unseen person. "Who's here?"

"Ach! Pearl is a pretty girl!" *Squawk?*

Pearl? Squawk?

"Jenna?" Dad sounded anxious again.

A flap of wings startled Shea, and she jolted, nearly dropping her phone. She put a hand to her heart. *Deep breaths.* "It's only a—" Filtered daylight leaked in through the murky living room windows, shooting a dusty beam off the pale peach cockatiel that had somehow gotten into Shea's home.

"A talking bird." She stepped closer to the feathered intruder. "Pearl?"

"Pearl is a pretty girl!" The creature cried from her place on the rustic mantel.

"Dad, it's a cockatiel." Shea turned to Pearl. "How did you get in here?"

That's when she noticed the front door was open a few inches. She must have been too surprised by the place's condition to remember to close it. The wind had thrown raindrops onto the dusty hardwoods, making a splattered pattern. The bird had flown in at some point.

She felt her blood pressure ease back toward normal. "It's fine, Dad." Her voice shook. "Just a talkative bird."

"Well, good grief." *You scared me there.* He didn't say it, but she heard the additional words in her mind. "Are you okay?"

Her breathing was still staggered on her long sigh, but yes. She'd be fine. "Better now. Thanks, Dad." No need to worry him. In truth, she'd need a good half hour to bring her heart rate all the way back to normal. With Dad on the phone at least she hadn't dissociated this time. That was a victory.

Dad went quiet. The bird stayed where it was—perched on a skinny slab of wood that wouldn't support her collection of fat candles. That mantel would have to go. Dad took a deep breath. "You're still being triggered."

She tried so hard to hide this broken part of herself.

Shea tiptoed toward the bird as if it were one of her timid, young clients. The house was dirty enough without this bird letting loose out of fear. She found her soothing, counselor's voice. "Where is your owner, Pearl?"

"What *arhh ya doin' thar*, Lass?" Pearl shrieked as if her voice only came with one volume setting, and her repertoire for phrases was severely limited.

First order of business was dealing with this crazy bird. But to send her out into the windy, wet day seemed cruel. What kind of pet owner would let their bird out in weather like this? Some irresponsible, unkind—

"What's happening now, Jenna-Shea?" Even across a continent and an ocean, Dad was a lifeline this morning.

She pinched the phone between her ear and her shoulder and reached toward Pearl. "I need to get this bird out of here." The cockatiel stayed where it was.

"Pearl!" A man's voice at the open front door, followed by a couple of taps on the warped wood. "Are you in there? Hello?"

Shea gasped and spun around. "Who's there?" This time she determined to be strong. She squeezed her free fist and then flexed her fingers holding the phone. "Dad, a man just called out for Pearl from the doorway."

"Be careful, honey." She could tell Dad was going for calm, but that he'd also give anything to be beside her right now.

"Sorry," the voice from the entrance said. Definitely a man, but not one of the movers. They wouldn't know the crazy bird's name. The door slowly squeaked open, and someone stood there, but he didn't come in as if he respected her space. Same get-up as hers—a rain slicker, complete with a hood obscuring his eyes.

"Who's that?" Dad demanded. "His voice sounds familiar."

"I don't know yet." She switched her phone to Speaker.

"I'm sorry," the newcomer said. "I'm looking for my great-aunt's bird—Pearl. Did she sneak in here?"

That voice. She knew that voice too, now that she could think straight. "Liam?"

"Liam, is that you?" Dad chimed in.

The new guy tipped up his head, tugged back his hood, and let his sky-blue eyes meet hers. Those eyes could still get to her, even after all he'd done—or not done. But she was safe, and for the second time this morning, her heart rate slipped back toward normal. Except now, his black hair, blue eyes, and solid build stirred her heart in other ways.

"Shea? I'm sorry, I didn't know you'd be here today." As if she'd done it a million times, Pearl flew to him and perched on his hand. He stroked the bird and murmured to it like he was comforting a puppy. Well. That wasn't attractive at all.

"Is that Liam?" Dad asked. "Let me talk to him."

"Sure thing." She thrust the phone toward Liam. "My dad wants to talk to you." How silly that she felt like a victorious teenager, rather than a thirty-year-old, as she handed him her phone.

"Okay." Liam's expression showed more concern for her than the phone call. But he should be worried about chatting with Dad.

Especially since he'd soon be fired. The one victory she could count on? Her parents would back off and let Shea keep to her current "boyfriend-free" status.

Not that she wished ill for him, but his mistake meant she was now homeless. She strode to the side door and watched for the movers. Maybe she could find a hotel and make Liam pay for it—and then put her things into storage somehow on a moment's notice.

Her life wasn't moving forward after all. Not in terms of this beach cottage, or in terms of her ever getting past the past.

CHAPTER THREE

For two whole seconds, Liam let himself slip into Shea's golden brown gaze and tried not to wince with the impact of seeing her again under these circumstances. Did she remember? Did she care?

How he hated that he'd startled her and that the house wasn't ready yet. But what was happening? Their arrangement was that he had until next month to finish.

Pearl still rested on his free hand. With his thumb, Liam switched off Speaker and held Shea's phone to his ear as he ducked into the unfinished kitchen. Her cell smelled like her—a flowery scent. He liked it. Still.

He'd just gotten back from that Hawaii trip and hadn't seen any emails from Stephen Brown. Whenever he checked during their vacation, there wasn't anything new. "Hello, sir?"

"Is it true the house isn't ready?"

"Yes, but we're still on target for finishing in the next month." So, why was Shea here now? Was she the next "tenant?"

"Month? Didn't you get my emails last week?"

Liam sent Pearl to the butcher-block countertop and yanked out his own phone from his back pocket, pressing and swiping until the inbox came up. Spam like crazy, but nothing in his main folder where his boss's directives usually went. He searched other folders, finally landing on the Junk file. Three emails waited there. Oh, no. "I'm opening them now." He wouldn't make excuses, even though he hadn't seen the messages until now.

He checked a loud sigh. No matter how hard he tried, he couldn't get his life on track. His family legacy followed him, condemned him.

"Well, as you can see my daughter is there to take possession. She says the place is far from ready, and her moving crew is arriving momentarily. But I never received a scanned copy of the final inspection and permission to occupy."

Right. He hadn't gotten that far. His chest went tight. "I'm sorry, sir." He couldn't lose this position. His aunt had landed this job for him, charging him to rise to the challenges. And he'd wanted to. For once, he would prove he wasn't anything like his deadbeat dad. *If* Mr. Brown gave him another chance. "I'm sorry about all this. I will work around the clock to get the place ready as soon as possible." So much for proving to Shea the next time he saw her that he wasn't the same person who'd dropped out of college several years ago or let her down that one last time. "That is, if you give me a chance to make it right."

Mr. Brown went quiet on the other end of the line, and Liam scanned the kitchen making a mental to-do list. Finish plumbing and rewiring house-wide. Then flooring, a few of the walls, two gas fireplaces, bathrooms, appliances, countertops. Okay, yeah. He needed at least one helper and probably two weeks, if they worked twelve- to sixteen-hour days.

He was fired for sure. He sighed and rubbed the back of his neck.

"We've got a serious problem here," Mr. Brown said, and Liam pictured him pacing the floor. "Where is my daughter going to go?"

Liam searched his mind for a solution, and an idea occurred to him. "Maybe I can help with Shea's housing situation."

A truck engine roared outside, and Liam paced the dusty kitchen floors. If his aunt went for his suggestion, he could help. If not, Shea was headed back to wherever she'd come from today. Just the thought of that left an emptiness in Liam's life he hadn't expected. Two hours ago, he had no idea Shea was coming, that she might live on the island, near him, again.

He couldn't let her leave without fixing the past.

"I'm curious." Her dad still sounded irritated, but there was a hint of hope in his voice too.

"As you know, my great-aunt lives next door. She's another generation removed, but I don't usually bother with the 'great.' She doesn't mind. Anyway, she has a spare bedroom upstairs. I could pitch the idea to her and to Shea, see what they say?"

"That's an imposition."

"Honestly, sir, my aunt would probably love having her, and I'd have peace of mind knowing someone was keeping her company—that is, when your daughter isn't at work." Plus, he wanted to solve this for Shea. He held his breath.

His boss went silent as if mulling over the possibility. "You can pitch it to them, of course. I appreciate your trying to make it right for her."

"I'll do everything I can."

Outside of his aunt and his boss, Liam hadn't worried about impressing anyone for years. That had all changed the moment he'd walked in and seen Shea in the cottage's living room. They'd left things a mess in college, and when he'd tried to apologize for letting her down that night, she'd told him to give her some space—hadn't talked to him again. She seemed to overreact, but wouldn't tell him what had happened, and there was no way he could know because he wasn't there. But he'd lost something precious when she'd walked away.

"You can dock my pay. I'd understand."

"Listen, son, just put Shea back on the phone and don't let me down again."

A wave of relief fell over Liam, and he closed his eyes. "You can count on me, sir."

He walked into the living area where Shea waited by the door for her movers to climb out of their truck. "Your dad would like to speak with you." He held her phone toward her. "And I may have a solution to your housing situation. I'll keep the movers talking while you finish up."

She accepted the phone, her expression full of accusations.

As soon as Shea hung up, he'd be nearby to pitch his idea to her.

After finalizing things, Shea disconnected the international call and tried not to worry about how expensive Liam's mistake was going to be. Dad mentioned Liam might have a solution for her, that she should hear him out, but honestly, she'd like to tell him off. He still hadn't changed. Did he even understand the consequences of his immaturity and lack of follow-through?

Lord, I could use a dose of Your grace right now. For both our sakes.

Maybe her brother, JP, could take her in for a week or two. He lived in Poulsbo and her commute would be shorter between his house and work. But could his garage hold all her stuff?

She stepped onto the drenched stoop outside and greeted her movers. How much had Liam told them? "Hey, guys, change of plans. Give us a minute, would you?"

"It's your dime," the lead guy said, shrugging his shoulders and reaching for his coffee.

Inside her jacket pockets, Shea fisted her hands. "Liam, can we talk?"

"Sure thing." He still held the bird under his jacket, out of the drizzle. The tender way he cared for that creature reminded her he had a gentle side, a protective side. That part of him could still disarm her, if she let it.

She stepped back inside and heard him walk in behind her. She was almost to the kitchen when she turned around.

Liam held out his hand. "Before you begin, I have to say how sorry I am. I missed your dad's request to finish the house by today. I had no idea you were coming."

Like that long-ago day, here she was listening to Liam apologize for making a big mistake that concerned her. Back then, she'd vowed never to rely on him again. Then her parents had hired him, and here she was at his mercy once more. He was kind, he simply wasn't trustworthy. Still. If she weren't so chilled and tired, she might be able to overlook his mistakes. What she needed to do was call JP and get the solution rolling, skip whatever Liam was about to suggest.

He'd drawn Pearl out of his open jacket and now stroked the bird, who seemed content, and for once she wasn't accusing "lasses" with her Irish accent. "Let me make it up to you," Liam said.

"How?" She pointed toward the door. "The movers are ready to offload and this place"—she gestured around the dusty space—"isn't livable. I'm going to call JP." She pulled out her cell phone.

"Hang on. Do you remember meeting my aunt? She moved in next door after your family stopped coming here every summer. She may have room for you to live there for a couple of weeks."

Was he kidding? "No, I don't recall ever meeting her. And I could not impose."

He held up a forefinger, his feet shifting. "Give me one second to run over there. Okay?"

His pale blue eyes caught the light slanting in, giving him a sincere appearance. Between that, her parents continued and mysterious trust in him, and the fact that she was desperate, how could she refuse? She shook her head, unsure of everything. "Fine. Go ahead. But I'm calling JP."

Liam started toward the door. "Don't worry. We'll get this solved."

She dialed her brother, hoping he'd pick up. Sure, it was early on a Saturday, but she needed him. Five minutes later she'd learned JP had two roommates and a full house. Her plan B had fallen through.

Now what?

CHAPTER FOUR

"Auntie Mat!" Liam kept his hand on Pearl under his jacket and tugged open his aunt's front door. She wasn't in the living area. Maybe she was out in the sunroom. Rain or shine, she lived in that room. She'd cooed like Pearl the year Liam had enlisted his buddies to help build it. "Auntie Mat, where are you?"

"In here," she called. "I still can't find Pearl."

He came around the corner into his aunt's familiar kitchen. Matilda Hartwell, still thin as a beanpole, wore her usual getup—matching fabric of shirt and pants in a bluish-green with embroidered flowers around the collar. Her short, white wavy hair was in perfect condition, as usual, and her makeup was simple. She'd always had a lot of class, represented in these timeless, elegant outfits. Even her matching flats with their shiny buckle seemed scuff-free, though he knew she'd had them for over a decade. She wore a delicate bracelet and simple heart pendant on a thin gold chain around her neck. Occasionally, when Liam visited she'd be dressed in a costume from her theater days. He hoped today was a good day to ask for a big favor, and that she wouldn't scare Shea off with her eccentricities.

Gently, Liam unzipped his jacket and presented Pearl to his aunt. The escape artist flew to her owner and tucked her head under Auntie Mat's chin.

Squawk! "Pearl is a pretty girl."

"Oh, my darlin' bird! Thar ya be!" Auntie switched into a pirate accent, and Liam smiled. She'd made a career in the local theater and had only recently retired, though she volunteered there a few times a week. Any accent she wanted, she could pull it off. No wonder Pearl sounded like a seafarin' world traveler, what with copying her owner's voice all the time. "I'm so glad you found her," she said without an accent, then she cooed along with her bird.

"Me too. But I also ran into the new tenant." Unfortunately, that tenant was Jenna-Shea Brown, and her vulnerability made him want to wrap her in a hug and help her feel safe. Wasn't she a trained therapist? Why was she unhinged by being startled?

Auntie Mat raised her brows. "I thought the remodel wasn't finished yet."

"It's not." He shifted on his feet. Shea was waiting. But you couldn't hurry things where his great-aunt was concerned. "The worst part is, it's Shea—the Browns' daughter."

She eyed him as if examining the site of her next incision. "Shea is here? Next door? Now?"

His ears went hot, and he rubbed his neck. His aunt had raised him, so she could see through him, knew his heartaches and some of his hopes. Knew how he'd regretted the way things had ended with Shea. Months from now, Auntie Mat would want to have Shea over for dinner, all the time. She'd try to push them together. But maybe he could use what he knew about his great-aunt to his advantage. "Yes. And she needs a place to stay. I wondered if you could help."

Calliope, Auntie Mat's dog, skittered into the kitchen, brown-and-white fur matted from the storm outside. She was a Cavalier King Charles spaniel with wavy ears and lots of spunk, as lovable and goofy as her owner.

Auntie Mat rubbed her cheek against Pearl's peachy head, and the bird closed her eyes and almost seemed to purr like a cat. "What are ya proposin', Son? I take her in with me, now? Look around ye. It's a little bitty space and no question."

He chuckled because he couldn't resist that twinkle in her eyes as she went all leprechaun on him. "How about giving up your pets' room? It's only for a little while." At one time she'd kept a spare bedroom for him, but now she'd turned that room into a pet palace for Pearl and Calliope.

"Knock, knock," Shea's voice called from the kitchen's screen door, accompanied by her raps on the old wood. She'd saved him from another *why aren't you married yet, Son? You're thirty-three years old, and I want to see you settled down* speech. "Is Liam here?"

"Pearl is a pretty girl!"

"Hush, Pearl." Auntie Mat raised her arm and sent her bird toward the sunporch. "Go rest. You've had quite an adventure." Her arms now empty, Auntie Mat searched the immediate floor space for Calliope. The quiet dog seemed to sense it, and came over to be scooped up. "Well, dear," she said to Liam, as she cuddled her pup, "go let her in. We've got a problem to solve."

Shea looked more drenched than a few minutes ago—her fly-away hair plastered around her face. Raindrops clung to her long eyelashes. He had a crazy flash of kissing them away. He shook it off. A noble person would offer her something hot to drink, not imagine kissing her. She stepped back, and he pushed open the screen door for her. Soon she stood dripping on the floor. "I'm so sorry. I'm a drowned beaver in this weather."

Auntie Mat laughed her bell-like sound behind Liam, and he knew she'd found a new soul to perform to. "Oh, no, dearie." Auntie's British accent had made its entrance. "Come in, come in. If you're partial to i', I can whip us up a spo' o' tea."

Liam studied Shea's reaction. Why couldn't his aunt attempt to act normal for one minute while they tried to convince Shea that living with her was a good idea? Over the years, Liam had sometimes let embarrassment about his kooky guardian keep him from sharing her with the people around him. JP had had overnighters with them back in the day, but never with his little sister tagging along.

"Oh, no need." Shea shifted and hugged herself. "I didn't mean to intrude. I wanted to let Liam know I'm headed to Poulsbo. I'll find a cheap hotel and a storage unit, then try again in a couple of weeks." She turned her golden-brown eyes on him. "You'll let me know, won't you, when my house is ready?"

"Don't leave." He reached for her, but then felt silly. "My aunt has a room you could use." He turned to Auntie Mat, pleading with her without saying a word.

"Dear, silly young man," Auntie Mat said in a Southern accent. "He hasn't even introduced us yet."

"Oh," Shea said, her eyebrows bunching. Nope, she'd never met his aunt before. The woman made an impression you simply didn't forget. "I'm sorry, are you from the South, or from England, or where?"

"I'm from right here in Washington, all my life." And once again she sounded like many a Northwesterner—accent free. "I'm Matilda Hartwell, retired actress, pet owner, neighbor."

Shea extended a hand. She still fascinated him. Even her hands. Like her legs, she had long, tapered fingers. He was mesmerized. And not nearly good enough for her.

Sure, she'd been a wannabe tagalong as kids, but in college? In college he couldn't believe the woman she'd grown into. Too bad he could never make a good enough impression to keep her attention. They'd had a few dates, but he'd blown his chance. JP said he should forget about her. She was too focused on her future for a boyfriend. But then she'd dated that one guy for a long time. Her brother kept Liam updated, now and then, so he knew about her breakup with what's-his-name. Something about how the dude wouldn't commit. Loser. Hadn't he known what he'd had?

Now Liam had a chance to prove to her—and himself—that he was reliable. That he wasn't like Jack. If she stayed.

Auntie Mat shook her hand. "You are welcome here," she said to Shea. She swallowed as if his aunt's words touched her. "Would you like to stay?"

Shea shook her head, and Liam worried that she might not agree. "I can't impose. Really."

"I'm sure my Liam will have the place ready in no time. We can make the best of it, can't we, dearie?"

As her attention shifted between them, Shea seemed to debate what to do. Could she see his aunt was safe? "Well, JP didn't have room. If you're sure . . ."

Auntie Mat nodded. "Then it's settled." She turned to Liam. "Tell the movers to bring everything into my parlor. We can fill it to the brim. Meantime, I'll make hot water for tea. We need girl-talk time. And this beauty needs to dry out."

Heaven help him, Liam would get Burr on the phone and beg him to pitch in. Barring tardy inspectors, they would finish sooner with more hands at work.

Yeah, there'd be no escaping his aunt's schemes now. Still, Liam caught Shea's eye—no hardship in that act—raised his eyebrows. *What do you think? You okay with this hare-brained plan?*

Her gaze slipped back to Auntie Mat. "If you're certain you wouldn't mind . . ."

"Of course. I could use the company. And if you're ever home while my Liam is working, we can go over and harass him into hurrying up." She giggled, and Calliope, who'd curled into a sleepy ball, licked her arm.

"I'd be glad to help move things along." Shea gave Liam an impish grin, and he almost choked. He faced his one-time guardian and gave her a grin as she filled the teakettle. *Thanks, Auntie Mat, for stepping into this mess I made, and especially for bringing out that side of Shea.*

He darted out into the rain and directed the moving truck toward his aunt's back door. They reversed into the driveway, complete with all the beeping needed to rouse the neighbors this morning, and whipped open the truck's sliding door. What a heap of boxes. Yeah, the room would be filled to the brim, all right.

Shea was staying. Close proximity. That both excited and terrified him.

Once they were finished clearing away a pet bed and bird cage from the spare bedroom, and relocating Shea's belongings, Liam pulled out his phone. As much as he hated to grovel, he had to call Burr, see if he could come help. Of all Liam's buddies, Burr was the only available one with the know-how. The others had jobs. Plus, his buddy could use the distraction from whatever it was that ate him up.

CHAPTER FIVE

Standing on Miss Matilda's covered stoop, Shea paid the movers for their help and swallowed hard over the total. Yikes. Her savings would take a huge hit. But she'd survive on inexpensive meals for a while if she had to. At least she was here, finally, on the island.

Liam had gone out of his way to help get all her belongings inside, as if he were earnest about fixing his mistake. She'd tried not to notice his muscles rounding out his long-sleeved tee once he'd lost his jacket. Tried not to be affected. But their gazes locked several times, and each time, he'd offer her a reassuring smile as if to say, *you'll like it here. It'll be okay.*

Had he noticed how she'd been triggered over at the cabin? She'd have to hide that part of herself better—redouble her efforts. But soon, she'd live alone and no longer constantly worry about what others thought, at least at home.

She'd simply aim for that day and help his aunt with anything she needed during her stay here, while trying to resist being drawn to Miss Matilda's nephew.

No problem.

"Do you think Burr's stable enough to work with me full time?" Liam had debated this idea in his head, but he couldn't deny Burr was a whiz at carpentry. He planned to call his friend next, but he wanted the lowdown from Jinx first.

As kids, Liam had befriended JP and Jinx first. Then, Jinx had brought Burr into their group. Everyone accepted him. Back then, he didn't seem to hold grudges. He hadn't started drinking until about three years ago, at least as far as any of them knew. And the guy was harmless, though he considered himself a bit of a

Casanova.

"I don't know." Jinx sighed into his phone. "I think he's hiding the drinking."

"He wasn't at the condo in Hawaii." That night, Burr had stumbled back to their room after heading to the on-site mart off the lobby for a six-pack of Coke—or so he'd said. But he'd returned tanked about forty-five minutes later, carrying the six-pack of soda. Somewhere he had found hard liquor.

"Well, not that last night, but he might've been sneaking around before that. He's worked with me a few times. He's a productive alcoholic."

"There's a name for that." Liam searched his memory, not that psychological terms were his forte.

"I think it's called 'functional.'"

Sounded about right. "But it isn't sustainable ..." Maybe he should change his plan right now. Except ... this might be what Burr needed. "I'm desperate for help to finish this project. I even have permission to pay him. And I thought it'd keep him busy, out of trouble."

"You guys fight like crazy. Why is that last part important to you?"

Liam rubbed the back of his neck with one hand. No one knew why Liam should care, and he wasn't up for telling anyone yet. "I'd hate to see him endanger someone else while out drinking or worse—driving. Plus, he's good at what he does, drinking aside." Burr might need babysitting, but he could do the job.

A door slammed on Jinx's end like he was getting into his car. "I think it'll be good for him, Liam. I'd hire him."

"He might not even want to come." Then Liam would have to invent another plan.

"Are you kidding? It's the island. Of course, he will. Right now, his rundown apartment butts up against the railroad tracks—with all the noise and suicide attempts. He'll go."

"But will he help? It's not only for me. It's the new tenant. She's ready to move in yesterday—literally."

Jinx sighed into the phone. "Here's hoping this works then."

Dylan Burgess had barely answered his phone before he heard Liam's voice. "So, are you busy the rest of this month, Burr?" After their oh-so-fun exchange at the airport, suddenly Liam wanted to get chatty? Standing in his dingy apartment, he debated disconnecting the call.

He'd humor Liam for a minute. After all their years of friendship, he probably owed him that much. "Don't tell me—your crazy aunt's dog ran away, and you need to form a search party."

"Watch it. She's not crazy, mostly." Liam barked whenever Burr or the other guys put his aunt down, likely out of respect. But anyone could see she was batty. "Maybe this wasn't a good idea."

A train barreled through Dylan's neighborhood, and he winced, waiting it out. He only hoped no kids were playing on the tracks this time. Took a minute before he knew Liam could hear him again over the racket. "Hey, you called me, Islander." Dylan didn't have time for this. Not that he had anything else going on. Unemployment wore on you. Ironic how an empty wallet could weigh you down. "What do ya need?"

Liam was silent as if he wasn't sure he wanted to tell him. Finally, he cleared his throat. "Remember that remodel I'm doing?"

"'Course." How could he forget, the way Liam always rubbed it in? "The beach job?"

"Yeah, well, we have a new tenant and an unfinished house. I need someone to do the carpentry and finishing work."

"And you assumed I could just jump in?" So like Liam to make that leap. Dylan grabbed another Coke from the fridge and snapped open the top. The soda seemed to shush the room with its noise. "Before you ask, it's a Coke." He hated accountability sometimes, but he'd asked his buddies to watch out for him. And mostly, they were good at it.

Until last week in Hawaii.

He didn't even know what had set him off. He lived for their adventures. They'd had a great time cliff diving. Then . . . something someone had said? Or maybe one of the local girls they'd run into had said something. Correction—women. Liam would tear him up for using that word. He was obsessed with respecting women, said it went back to how his mom had raised him. Dylan chugged his Coke, letting the conversation go silent. What'd he care? He wasn't the one begging for help.

"I didn't ask what you were drinking."

"Yeah, but you heard me open it, and you wondered." A neighbor pulled into the apartment complex, speakers shaking the walls.

"Maybe. Burr, listen, you got something on your mind? You mad at me about something?"

"Nah." Dylan squeezed his soda can until it crinkled in his grip, and he had to ease up so he wouldn't spill any. Liam didn't get it, and Dylan wasn't going to tell him. What good would it do?

"So, we're okay?"

He grunted. *Leave it alone, Barrett.*

"Cuz I really need you on this, man. If you can spare a couple of weeks—maybe a little more..." He hoped it wouldn't take longer, but it might.

Outside, a mom hollered for her son to come in. Dylan moved to the window and watched him scuff up the stairs to their unit across the parking lot. Poor kid. "Where's the *tenant* now?"

"Moving in with my aunt."

"She's letting a stranger live with her?" Crazy old lady. Except, Matilda was cool. She reminded Dylan of Eli, Hitch's dad. Always glad to see you, no matter what you did. Even when you couldn't stand to live with yourself.

"I don't have much room at my place, plus the tenant's a she."

"Hmm, this just got interesting."

"Don't get any ideas, Casanova. She's off limits."

"For you, maybe. You've sworn off dating because of this 'self-improvement' kick you're on." Why in the world did Liam feel like he had to prove anything? He was holding down a job. He was good to his aunt and other *women*—to people in general. As much as he kept worrying about becoming like his deadbeat dad, he hadn't. He wouldn't. So, why worry about it? His life was perfect. "Me—I'm just biding my time till the next girl comes along."

"Woman." Liam paused. "And not her."

Light bulb. "You got designs on her yourself, Islander?"

"No, I'm feeling protect—"

"Protective. Nice." The dig cut because unlike Liam, Dylan *was* like Liam's deadbeat dad. In ways his buddies didn't know. Still, this was a job. "You got money in the budget to pay me?"

"Yes." Was that a sigh of relief from Liam's side of the conversation, as if Burr's question meant he was in?

"You got room in your place for me to bunk, or do I gotta commute from Kent?" That'd be some serious road miles morning and night. And it'd eat up gas and ferry money he didn't have.

"Nah, you can have my sofa. I really appreciate this, man."

"See ya Monday."

"Make it Sunday night—anytime tomorrow, actually. We need to get started early Monday."

"You're killing me."

"You got something better to do?"

No. No, he didn't. And maybe the island life would suit him. Especially given this new *woman* over there. Yeah, this could work. "See ya before the game Sunday, and you'd better have cable."

At her laptop, Matilda clicked into the social media site to see if Liam had added any friends lately. She'd spent Saturday evening getting to know Shea a little bit, and she'd liked what she'd seen—a go-getter who had earned her degree, launched into her career, and found success. A compassionate, rather maternal woman who cared about others. In short, the perfect match for her nephew. The looks he'd given Shea while they moved her stuff in seemed to prove Liam still pined for her. Yes. Matilda was more convinced of that match after seeing them together.

As a teen, he'd mentioned JP's little sister and how she tagged along. Then, suddenly during college he found out Shea attended the same school, and *wow, has she changed,* and *oh, she might even date me.* They had dated, briefly. Then Shea had called things off, but Liam hadn't told her that story. He'd seemed embarrassed.

After Liam shared the plan for Shea to stay here and saved the day, so to speak, Shea had given him a quick glance—something of admiration in her gaze as she peeked at Matilda's nephew. So, the spark seemed to still exist for her too.

He may not know what was best for him, but Matilda had raised him, so she did.

Liam's social media account showed no activity lately—nothing after those pics from his cliff-diving adventure in Hawaii. That kid sure risked his life a lot since he'd come of age. She should probably get to the bottom of that, but she tried not to think about all he was up to when he and the guys went on their adventures. That sky-diving trip they'd taken last fall nearly frightened her to death, even though she trusted Eli Hanson—Clark's father—as he piloted the plane. Over the years, Eli had been a sort of father-figure to Liam. Matilda was grateful. Still, she liked her feet firmly planted on the ground—didn't even enjoy boating because of how deep the Sound was. The only time she liked exploring other worlds or experiences was on stage.

Right now, Matilda was cooking up a role she'd gladly play. A role that would help her nephew settle down. Finally. He hadn't seemed too amenable yesterday morning, but there were two sides to this. She'd simply have to convince the other side to go along. Though Matilda felt rather accomplished about most of the lessons she'd taught Liam, she'd apparently missed a big one. After Shea, he hadn't dated again, which meant he needed help in the area of romance. Matilda would be his teacher.

Liam would thank her later.

She opened the genealogy software on her computer and pressed on the Add Spouse box next to Liam's name. There she typed: *Jenna-Shea Brown?*

Liam would like another five hundred square feet of living space now that Burr had moved in. "There's something you need to know," he said to Burr. Liam didn't want Burr swooping in, thinking he could charm Shea or ask her out. Burr's life was a mess. Liam wouldn't wish that on any woman. Trouble was, Burr wouldn't like Liam telling him what to do.

Burr slouched on Liam's sofa in a wrinkled tee and holey jeans. Hadn't cleaned up even one of his messes since arriving earlier today. "What?" Distracted by the game, Burr shoved the rest of his hot dog into his mouth. The defensiveness in his voice almost made Liam back down. Except, he needed to protect JP's youngest sister.

This tiny rental house, with its kitchen mere inches from the living room, seemed overcrowded what with all Burr's hostility.

Liam rinsed another plate and shoved it into the dishwasher. "Keep your distance from the tenant." She wasn't really a tenant so much as his boss's daughter, but Liam would get to that.

"You act like you know this girl."

"Woman. And I do." They'd see each other the following day, so he couldn't put this off. "You do too."

That got his attention. He muted the TV, twisted his body to see Liam. "Yeah?"

"JP's little sister."

"Oh, her?" He shifted back and unmuted the game. "No worries, Islander. I'm not into cradle robbing." He shoved a handful of crumbling chips into his mouth. Liam didn't consider himself OCD, but he was already planning to fire up the vacuum as soon as Burr was out of the room.

Burr hadn't seen her lately. He didn't know. "She's not a kid anymore."

"Yeah?" Burr studied him, squinting. "You got a thing for her?"

He was trying not to. Not given the way he kept letting her down. "Nah, but we owe it to JP to be cool."

That shut Dylan up. He'd always been almost afraid of JP.

Liam's cell rang, and he scrubbed his hands on the kitchen towel before yanking it out of his jeans pocket. "Burr, do you mind?" He pointed at the loud TV and pivoted toward his room. "Hey, Auntie Mat. What's up?"

"Son, why aren't cha working on the house next door? It's still a wreck."

He walked into his bedroom, heard the June rain pelting the window. "The Browns asked me not to work on Sundays. Said the neighbors deserved one day off from all the noise." Probably a local ordinance too.

"My parlor is packed with boxes and furniture."

"I know, Auntie Mat." Before he'd left the previous day, he'd helped bring the last of the stuff from the truck, jamming that room full. To save time and not have to pay the movers for another hour's work, Shea accepted delivery, and they'd probably left everything in a haphazard state. "Do you want me to come organize it? Make a path through the middle so you can get into the room?"

"Oh, shoot. Pearl!"

Liam dragged the phone away from his ear, too late. His eardrum rang with her shout.

"I may need to hang a curtain over the archway to keep—Pearl!"

"Ahh!" He blinked away the pain of her second screech into the phone. "What's happening?"

Lots of flapping noises on her end. "How soon can you get here?" She sounded frantic now. "Pearl is lost in the stacks of boxes."

He grabbed his keys and jacket. "Where's Shea?"

"Since she needed a few groceries, I asked her if she'd grab a loaf of sourdough bread. I've got soup on the stove. Why don't cha eat here yourself tonight?"

He should invite Dylan if he was going over to his aunt's house where there was real food. "Mind if I bring a friend?"

"I never have. Now, come help me find my silly bird!"

"Be there in a few."

He disconnected and returned to the living room. "Hey, Burr,

I'm headed over to my aunt's. Wanna go? She's got homemade soup and a lost bird."

"She got cable or a dish?"

He yanked on a thin jacket. "Nope. Sorry, man. But she's got good grub. Or you could meet us there after the game. No promises how much soup'll be left." He turned toward the door, but then stopped. "You know how to get there?"

He stood. "I'm in. Mariners are losing so far anyway."

CHAPTER SIX

Anxiety chewed Liam up as he and Burr made the drive, listening to the noisy game on the radio. Shea's car sat in his aunt's driveway now, which meant she'd returned from the grocery store. Liam didn't want to let Burr anywhere near her, but Shea was discerning. In his current state, Burr's usual smarm probably wouldn't affect her. He wasn't a threat physically. He simply considered himself irresistible, and Liam hoped Shea saw through him so she didn't get emotionally involved.

Of course, Liam didn't have any hold on her or say about whom she did or didn't date.

"You ever see JP?" Burr asked when Liam turned off the engine, and the game went silent.

"Not for a few months. You?" He stood from the car, pocketing his keys in his jacket.

"Nah." He headed up the walk behind Liam. "Think your aunt will mind if I stream the game on my phone?" Huh, was that politeness, a smidge of consideration?

"Probably not. But she's likely to make you set the table. I'm sure you remember how she is."

"Crazy as a loon."

"Careful." But Liam chuckled. "Help me find her bird in the storage room?"

"Yeah."

Since Shea was a counselor, maybe she could help Liam with a project, of sorts, over the next couple of weeks—a project that had nothing to do with the remodel next door.

Shea opened the door to find Liam standing in the misty weather with another guy. She couldn't quite place him. One of JP's other friends, probably. She'd only ever noticed Liam. "C'mon in." She held the door and then closed it behind them. "Your aunt's a little frantic trying to rescue her bird, and I feel terrible that my stuff caused the problem."

"Don't worry." Liam stepped farther inside. "We'll fix this." He slipped off his coat and hung it on a hook by the door. "Shea, do you remember Dylan Burgess?"

The guy's name sounded familiar.

Dylan, who'd now lowered the hood of his sweatshirt—he'd traveled coatless in the rain as if he didn't care if he got wet—stuck out his hand, and she shook it. "JP's sister, right?"

She nodded.

Liam seemed torn between sticking around for their chat and getting into the parlor with his aunt. When Miss Matilda called for him, he strode away, waving for Dylan to follow him. But Dylan stayed where he was.

"Liam mentioned you'd be here, but I couldn't quite remember you." He eyed her up and down, which struck Shea as immature, as if Dylan were the self-absorbed type. "My loss."

No surprise he didn't remember her. He always gave her the stink eye whenever she pestered JP for attention. From what she remembered, he'd been kind of a jock and a know-it-all—not her favorite combination. "So, you and Liam—roommates?"

"Nah, I live in Kent. I'm here to help him with the remodel. Get you moved in as soon as possible."

He needn't act like he was doing her any favors, except he was. "Well, thanks for that. Perhaps you could help Liam and Miss Matilda before dinner is ready." She knew the narcissistic type. You shouldn't cater to their yawning need for gratitude and praise.

He shoved his hands into his sweatshirt pockets and then moved toward the parlor, which was now more of a glorified storage room.

She'd join them in the parlor, but Pearl hadn't warmed up to her yet. Instead, she moved toward the kitchen where she'd been helping Miss Matilda, who'd turned out to be quite an interesting and lovable character, prepare dinner. The aromas of cheesy broccoli and crusty sourdough bread filled the air.

Hopefully Pearl was okay. This wasn't a good beginning to Shea's stay. Unlike Burr's need for attention, Liam, with his sparkling blue eyes, had shown up, again playing the hero, only this time to his aunt. He'd complicated Shea's life, but he'd also helped her out. Was that what her folks meant about his heart—this heroic side?

Lord, help me make sense of all this. Standing alone in the living room, she closed her eyes and drew in a long breath. "Jesus," she whispered. His name brought a sense of His presence. She lingered there for a few moments, letting His peace and sweet Spirit pour over her like the rain outside.

"Keep an eye on the soup, will you, Jenna-Shea?" Miss Matilda called from the parlor.

Shea opened her eyes and moved toward the stove. "Of course." Stirring the rich, steaming soup with a large wooden spoon, she pressed her lips together. She should be in there, climbing over her own boxes of junk.

Squawk! Pearl had kept that up, along with lots of flapping, every several minutes for the past thirty she'd been in there. Why didn't she simply fly out? Probably because, as with people, she didn't always do the best thing for her.

Like Shea sorting through her belongings and parting with some of it before the move. The time might be ripe for a purge.

She'd begin sorting this week. Then, she'd have the fresh start she longed for by the time her place was ready. As a concession, given the snafu of not having the house ready for her, Mom and Dad had promised she could choose the final décor—like paint color, tiles, and the finish on the hardwoods—the upside to this whole mess. If she brought less "stuff" with her, she'd have a clutter-free living space over there in a couple of weeks.

Fifteen minutes later, the three of them returned from the parlor, Pearl riding on Miss Matilda's forefinger and Liam rushing to tack a bedsheet across the arched doorway so Pearl couldn't get in so easily next time. Miss Matilda sent Pearl to her perch near the sunroom door.

"You've got some cool stuff in there, Shea," Dylan said from the sink as he washed his hands, per Matilda's orders.

"Careful, Burr," Liam called over his shoulder as he worked above the archway.

Shea turned to Dylan. "Excuse me?" Had he searched her boxes?

"I had to restack a pile of crates and discovered a box of shot glasses. You drink a lot?"

"Dylan!" This from Miss Matilda who carried the soup pan to the center of the old, oval table. Luxurious aromas permeated the room, and Shea's stomach growled.

Strange question, but Shea wasn't offended. "No. Those are a collection my dad is building from his travels around the world." Not that he drank either. She always figured he simply liked their size as collectibles. That box belonged in her parents' storage unit.

She moved away from Dylan and toward the make-shift curtain where she peeked into the parlor. What else had the bird rescuers disturbed?

Liam stood nearby, almost finished tacking up the bedsheet with painters' tape. He held the sheet aside. "Don't listen to him." He kept his voice low.

She shrugged. "I'm not offended. I don't drink."

"Yeah, well, he's trying to stop."

Dylan was an alcoholic? JP hadn't mentioned that. They'd covered addictions in school, though she didn't specialize in treating addicts. Still, maybe she could help.

She stepped into the shadowy room, flipping on her cell phone's flashlight. Funny, she hadn't remembered to use it yesterday morning in the cottage next door. She'd been on a phone call, *and* too frightened to think straight in the dim rooms. Yes, the stacks had been moved, but the rest of the boxes were all still sealed. Not that she had a deep, dark secret. She simply valued her privacy.

Liam stepped around the sheet, bringing food aromas with him. "Everything in order?" he asked her as she milled around.

"Seems to be." Thankfully. "It's kind of your aunt to let me stay here."

"I'm glad you agreed. It'll be good for her too, I think." He paused in straightening the nearest box, as if he meant to say something—perhaps apologize again.

In the past, as a means of letting Liam off the hook, she'd reminded herself of his painful childhood, what little information JP had shared with her. He'd grown up without his parents, which meant he'd suffered a loss himself. Growing up with her family intact, she couldn't imagine that kind of pain, though she had helped patients through the gut-wrenching season of grief that followed such a loss. She'd keep all that in mind as she waded around her piles in this house, rather than next door tonight.

She didn't want Liam beating himself up, so she donned a dopey grin and pointed at the piles. "I think it might be time for a purge."

He snorted. "Maybe." Then, his expression eased back toward relaxed. "I wanted to ask you a question."

"Okay . . ." Would he bring up the past?

"Hey you two, let's eat!" Dylan sure seemed comfortable here already, ordering people around. Shea didn't trust him, nor did she particularly like him, but she'd be polite. He struck her as a player, and, though she'd be civil, she'd keep her distance.

"Maybe after dinner?" Liam asked, and she nodded.

They moved toward the kitchen. "Sounds good."

CHAPTER SEVEN

Stomach growling, Liam followed Shea toward the steaming food. His aunt stopped him at the stove, while Shea continued over to the table.

"Hey, Liam, your phone went off in your jacket," she said in a low voice as she held up his cell. "Hope you don't mind, I peeked. It's a friend request."

Another one? Had Jack reached out to Liam again, after he'd deleted the last request?

Auntie Mat loved social media, but Liam would prefer she not get involved with any requests from Jack. Dylan and Shea stood chatting at the table already, and Liam wanted to get over there. He both hated and needed this conversation with his aunt.

"It's from Jack." She studied him as if he would suddenly charge out into the rain. "I got one too."

She'd heard from him as well? Anger churned inside. Why would Jack reach out to Liam's aunt? He'd do anything to protect her. "You did? When?" During all this stuff with Shea and her beach house, Liam had tried to forget about Jack's contact. But he couldn't ignore that sense of dread that hung over him since the notice came through.

"This weekend."

He pushed out a long breath, angling his body toward the countertop and away from the two at the table. Auntie Mat wasn't the enemy here. And as much as he didn't want to go there, curiosity had eaten at him since he'd gotten the notice. "What'd you do with it?" *Delete it? Block him?*

Accept it?

"It was a surprise to see it come up. He's aged." She'd known him years ago, before he'd abandoned his wife and son. Liam knew that. But he'd never asked her questions—preferring ignorance.

She hadn't really answered him.

"Okay if I dish this up?" Shea called from the table, a ladle and one of the bowls in her hands.

They nodded at her.

"Let's chat later." Liam didn't want to discuss Jack, didn't want to feel forced to decide what to do. He wanted to block him from both of their lives. Forever.

Why now? He sank into his aunt's gaze, so much passing between them, almost as if she'd heard his silent question. Irritation burned in his chest. Her eyes showed compassion—that tilt of her head and the kindness he'd rested in all these years. She reached for his hand. But she didn't say a thing. Didn't need to.

"It's getting cold," Burr whined from the table.

Auntie Mat gestured toward the meal. "Let's eat."

Shea studied Liam when he joined them. "You okay?"

He made himself meet her eyes. Psychologist, psychoanalyzing him, uncovering his hidden pain. But she did have inviting eyes. She seemed trustworthy. As much as he despised therapists and their usual *Get comfortable and start talking,* and *how did that make you feel* nonsense, he was still drawn to Shea.

"I'm fine, but I need some air." He pushed his chair away from the table, stood up.

"Liam." Auntie Mat's don't-mess-with-me-young-man voice. "Eat. . ." She softened her tone. "Then walk."

His options elbowed each other while Burr snickered. For his pride's sake, he should leave. But he didn't make a habit of disrespecting his aunt, so he obeyed and sat.

"So, Dylan," Shea started, as if she sensed Liam needed a minute to pull himself together, "why do your buddies call you Burr? I don't remember that from years ago."

"Yeah, tell us about that," Auntie Mat said as she passed the bread.

Burr jerked his head in Liam's direction. "You tell 'em, Islander."

"Islander?" Auntie Mat faced Liam.

Liam shrugged. At least the last few minutes had been forgotten. The questions about nicknames went unanswered as everyone focused on their meals.

Shea delicately spooned up her broccoli and cheddar soup. In a couple of minutes, Burr was half-finished and reaching for his third slice of sourdough bread. Shea studied Liam as if she could figure out his current state of mind. Soon she turned her attention to Burr as if he were her patient. Then her eyes were back on him, making him squirm, though he tried not to notice her attention.

Because as much as he was attracted to her, he didn't want her to see into his broken life. To witness his struggle to deal with Jack Barrett's reappearance, or his determination to be nothing like him.

But the thing was, Liam needed Burr. To answer his aunt's question without offending his carpenter any further, he'd give a simple reason for Burr's nickname. "Because his last name begins with b-u-r."

Burr grunted from across the table, but he didn't correct Liam. Good.

"And Islander?" Shea asked.

"This one's for you, *Dylan*." Liam deferred, biting into the crusty bread.

"Ah, well, I guess all of you would be islanders." Burr sounded more formal and polite than usual. "So perhaps he needs a new nickname."

Auntie Mat studied their newcomer as she passed the salad. "Or you could call him Liam."

Burr scoffed then shut up. Auntie Mat had a way of making people face a mirror and see what she saw. Tonight, her eccentricities were off duty—no foreign accents. So far.

Yeah, at some point Liam had offended Burr, but he didn't know when or how. And Burr didn't seem willing to tell him no matter how often he asked.

"You have any beer, Matilda?" Burr leaned away from his empty bowl and crumby bread plate.

Liam cringed over both the request and the use of his aunt's first name. He stared down his friend. Then he met Shea's eyes. She'd halted her butter knife over her slice of bread.

"No, I do not, Dylan. Don't keep alcohol in the house." She didn't offer to have any on hand next time Burr came over, and Liam could have hugged her. Liam hadn't mentioned Burr's alcoholism to his aunt, but it was as if she'd guessed.

Shea shifted in her seat. "Is this the time of day you like to grab a beer, unwind?" Her approach surprised Liam. In his experience, the direct approach never worked.

Sure enough, one glance confirmed Burr was close-mouthed, cold. "Sure, don't you?" He slurped the last of his water. "Or do you like a hot bath?" He gave her a cockeyed grin, and Liam wanted to punch him. The train wreck continued with him flirting as he followed the grin with a wink.

"Nah, I take a walk." She gave Liam a glance, and then she focused on her bowl. He could have high-fived her for seeing right through Burr. But was that a hint that she'd like to join Liam later? Sure, they'd agreed to have a chat, but after what Liam had witnessed, maybe he'd change his mind. He planned to ask for her help with Burr—maybe get advice for how to help him, but her direct approach hadn't worked over dinner. So maybe his request wasn't wise.

Burr raised his brows in her direction. "In the rain?"

"Sure. Clears my head."

He stood from the table, reached out a hand. "Wanna walk now?"

What in the world? Liam had specifically told Casanova to keep his distance. And the guy hadn't honored that request for more than two hours. Liam stood too.

Rain pelted the windows in the wind. Maybe Liam would call JP, have him join them this week, drive down from Poulsbo. Keep Burr in line. Shea didn't know about Burr's hair-triggered emotional switch. You said the wrong thing and *bam*! You'd set him off and, within half an hour, he'd be slouched on the sofa, beer can in hand.

Not that Liam wanted to walk on eggshells, but he would like to help him. He owed him.

"No, thanks." Shea stayed in her seat, finishing her salad. After taking a bite, she peered up at Burr. "Don't let me stop you."

"Forget it." Burr spun and headed to the living room, hunched over his phone. Liam wouldn't be surprised if he bailed and found a ride back to the house—even ended up drunk tonight. Sure enough, a few minutes later, the door off the living room quietly clicked shut.

But the way Shea shut him down? Fantastic. JP had been so protective of her in college, but it was obvious Shea could fend for herself. The thought made him grin—head tipped toward his soup—with admiration.

Auntie Mat stood to clean up. "You two go clear your heads. I've got this." When they hesitated, she shooed them as if she had her own agenda tonight.

The logical, psychologist side of Shea intimidated him, but the compassionate, warm side had always drawn him. "Want to?"

Shea smiled and rose. "I'll get my coat. And tomorrow, I'm doing all the dishes, Miss Matilda."

"Sure thing, hon." She wore a grin as she faced the sink. Liam could tell she liked the company. "Don't let that bird escape now, y'all. She's a might sneaky." Her Southern accent had returned.

When Shea went upstairs for a minute, Liam approached Auntie Mat and wrapped an arm around her in a side hug. The woman had her hands buried in the dishwater. "You rock." He kissed her head.

Her gray eyes stared up at him. "Listen, I don't quite trust your brrr-cold friend." She gave him a wink. She'd figured out Dylan's nickname. "Watch him. Especially where Shea is concerned. He thinks he's God's gift, but I have a feeling she's onto him."

"Will do," he said.

"And treat Shea well, Son. She's a gem."

He gave his aunt a sad smile before heading over to grab his coat. Shea was a gem Liam had lost long ago.

Memories from their college days ran through Shea's mind as she and Liam headed out through Miss Matilda's kitchen door and down the steps. Rain splattered every dull surface—the walkway boards, the pebbly road, the distant waves. Foggy mist even blurred the horizon line. The sun wouldn't set for hours this time of year, but dark clouds had tucked the light away, as it had all weekend, blanketing the region in gray. She pulled her waterproof hood closer over her forehead and adjusted the collar at her neck.

They worked their way across the road to the gravelly beach on Puget Sound and found low tide. Mist swept in sideways and the shore was abandoned, except for the occasional small dead crab or half clam shell. Liam huddled into his jacket, seemingly fine with the quiet between them. Maybe he was trying to think of what to say.

Earlier, he'd hinted he wanted to get her help with something, but she could only guess what. Was it about the cottage? Or did his aunt need something?

They had unfinished business. But why bring all that up? He was working on her house, and she believed he was earnest about finishing it quickly.

"Thanks for thinking of a solution for my housing situation."

He walked closer to the water side on her right, and his body blocked part of the wind coming off the Sound. Had he planned that? Such thoughtfulness touched her. The drizzle had let up, but the air was wet around them. "It's the least I could do." He slowed his steps.

This humble side of him, the kind that owned up to his mistakes, made her question her opinion of him. Maybe he wasn't the same guy she'd known in college. Age had only made him more appealing, a fact that unsettled her because that meant *she* had never outgrown her attraction. Every time he captured her gaze with his sky-blue eyes, she had to remember what JP had warned her about so long ago, and what she'd found to be true—at least back then. Two things, really. One, Liam wasn't reliable, which he'd proven this weekend, so he hadn't changed all that much. And two, he couldn't commit. Maybe all his childhood pain meant he couldn't go all in on a relationship. The cause didn't matter. She'd dated a commitment-phobe after him in college and vowed never again.

All she had to do was ignore her ongoing pull toward him. Forget how that spark in Liam's gaze got to her. No problem. As a teen, three years younger than him, she'd found him cute. But then her older brother's warning that he wasn't dependable made her look more closely. In college, Liam had challenged her to see him for herself, not for what JP had told her. She'd tried to do that, and she'd liked what she'd seen—a free spirit, someone who confidently led his life, unconcerned with other people's opinions. She hadn't found that place for herself, even now. He also lived fearlessly, and he made it look effortless.

They'd gone on a couple of dates back then, before that fateful night that interrupted Shea's peace. She craved security, so Liam wasn't for her.

Tonight, she couldn't miss that he obviously still suffered from whatever family dynamic—not involving his aunt—had plagued him as a late teen in college. And though she wouldn't date him, she might be able to help him. Picturing young, broken Liam, wrenched her heart if she dwelt on it.

The noise of the rhythmic waves grew louder as they reached the smoother sand, filling the silences of their conversation. They strolled southwest past a couple of quiet houses along Barclay Spit.

Maybe if Shea kept things light he'd let his guard down. *Please give me wisdom, Lord.* "Your aunt sure is a hoot."

He glanced over, wearing a puzzled expression as if trying to see whether she was mocking Matilda or simply stating a fact. Finally, he smiled. "Think you two can get along for a little while?"

She nodded, looking forward to their time together.

Gray waves rolled in low to their right in Port Madison Bay. "You finished your degree." Was that a hint of admiration in his voice? She liked hearing it.

"Yes."

"So, I should call you Dr. Brown now."

"Nah." She grinned up at him. "No title." A rectangular piece of green sea glass shimmered in her path, and she bent to pick it up. The edges felt smoothed over, so she pocketed it for her collection.

"Counselor." He stopped on the shore, turned, and bowed with a flourish of his arm.

She'd snort over his playful air if his voice hadn't gone sober, intimate. She swallowed. "Sounds rather attorney-ish, don't you think?" She tugged his sleeve, chuckling. "C'mon."

They resumed their walk. "I need your advice, Counselor."

She shook her head, still smiling. "Are you mocking me? I know how you feel about therapists." During one of their college dates, he'd once told her he found them useless—only he'd used more colorful words. Apparently, his experience with them as a preteen wasn't helpful.

He stopped again, and she joined him, blinking away the raindrops in her eyes, studying the water in Liam's lashes. He took a step closer, blocking the northerly wind. "Not mocking you. And I doubt you know how I feel about *all* therapists."

The way he said "all," as if he meant there was one in particular he felt differently about, made her hold her breath.

"Will you help me?"

Finally, they could explore his family stuff. "However I can."

"It's about Burr."

Not where she expected this to go. "Dylan?"

"Yeah. Our buddy, Isaac—do you remember him too?—says Burr has been drinking in secret again." The wind picked up and Liam shifted, blocking the misty wind, taking it on his back so it wouldn't hit her in the face. He inched closer. "I need your advice about getting through to him."

She squinted up at him, several thoughts occurring to her at once. He and Dylan didn't seem all that close, so what did it say about Liam that he was so concerned? And, she thought he didn't respect what therapists did.

He hunched into his jacket and donned a sheepish expression. "I know—it's hypocritical to seek psychological advice when I don't believe in it, right? But I have no idea how to reach him. Isaac doesn't either. And JP lives over here, far from the two of them in Kent. He doesn't get many chances to give advice in person."

Perhaps helping Liam help Dylan would help Liam. "Okay, what can I do?"

They resumed their walk, picking their way over barnacle-covered rocks to smoother sand again. The spit ended at a narrow channel where Puget Sound sent saltwater into the lagoon. The water looked so green here, and it had always fascinated Shea, how it surged in, like a river.

"Well, he asked us to keep him accountable, but he's back to drinking. I hope he doesn't chop off a limb while he's finishing the carpentry jobs."

She shuddered over that image. "I've worked mostly with kids and teens who were struggling at school or suffering an adjustment disorder after a change in their lives." If she'd helped any of them, and she hoped she had, she knew she couldn't take credit for God's part in it. "I love to watch people discover healing." It was too bad that hadn't happened for her, even after all this time. What was wrong with her that God hadn't healed her yet?

"Healing?" he scoffed.

Okay, she'd hit a hot button. She would try to keep things light, even though suddenly she could see his side—counselors and psychology didn't always fix things. "It can happen."

"I'd like to see it." His tone hinted he'd like to experience it himself. He shook his head. "But, with Burr, what would you suggest?" The wind kicked up, rushing at them from the north, chilly and menacing as it stirred up waves in the low evening light. They faced northeast again, and Liam stayed on the Sound side of her. "I mean, I've heard of interventions, but that's so hokey. And Burr would get up and walk right out, *after* telling us that he didn't have a problem."

"He needs to see his behavior for what it is. Get to the root of the drinking. Why does he reach for that beer at five p.m., like he mentioned tonight? What happens at that time of day? What is he thinking before, or when, he craves alcohol?" She paused. "What happened in his past that still gets to him today? If he can deal with those issues, his self-sabotaging and abusive behaviors may lose a lot of their power. He won't need them as much. Eventually, if he faces all these questions and finds answers, he may discover he doesn't need them at all anymore."

Liam shoved his fists into his pockets again as if something she'd said triggered a reaction, but she really hadn't been trying to send a hidden message to him.

"I also pray for my patients, even if they don't know it, but I'm guessing you and your friends are already praying for him. JP probably is, right? And you?"

He cleared his throat as if she'd hit on something else.

"Sorry if I made you uncomfortable." Didn't Liam have a relationship with God? "I thought JP took you guys to youth group weekend after weekend, when I was too young to go."

"You're right," Liam finally said, but she knew there was something he wasn't saying.

They were nearing Miss Matilda's beach now, so she glanced at the house to make sure Dylan wasn't around. She'd heard him leave, but he may have returned. "Okay, well, my advice? Get him to tell you or Isaac or JP what happened that got him 'back to drinking.' It's possible there was one event that kicked this off—a specific regret. Any ideas?"

"Not really. Though, it was about three years ago now. Back when he was dating . . . uh, I can't remember the woman's name."

"My guess is he feels as if he can't cope with something that either happened to him, or that he committed, and he's trying to dull the pain. Once you find the catalyst, you can pray—or hope— he listens to reason and will talk it out with someone. Recommend he find someone he can trust. The more trained, the better. Pastor, counselor, psychologist, psychiatrist."

Liam nodded as he climbed the three steps to his aunt's kitchen door and reached for the handle. Then he paused. "Thanks, Counselor Shea."

She gave him a half smile. "Sure thing."

A blue heron honked as it flew from the lagoon to the Sound, the *whoosh* of those huge wings shooting a shudder up Shea's spine. She jolted and spun in one quick motion, heart thumping. *It's only a bird. Breathe.*

Liam's hand settled on her shoulder. "Hey, what's wrong?"

She tried to get her breathing under control. "Nothing. I'm fine."

She straightened her shoulders and faced the house, but Liam's hand on her elbow stopped her.

He wore a look of concern. "I noticed you startled at the cottage that first day, and now this. What's going on?" His compassion pried loose something in her heart. Aside from her MIA parents, it'd been a long time since anyone had cared to ask her how *she* was doing. Somehow having Liam ask brought warmth into her heart, though her teeth chattered from the jolt and the chill.

If her secrets got out, she could lose everything. Who wanted to work with a broken therapist? Though Liam's eyes were kind, she disengaged and inched toward the door. "It's kind of you to ask, but really, I'm fine." Even as she turned away, part of her longed to let him into her world a bit, to accept his kindness. But that would make her vulnerable, and she preferred to focus on her work with others, hidden and safe.

Shea stepped into the house as Liam held open the door. The man was too discerning. One more reason to keep her distance.

CHAPTER EIGHT

First thing the following morning, Matilda bustled around her kitchen, with Calliope at her heels looking for dropped morsels. Pearl joined Matilda in chatter back and forth, every now and then whistling with her as if they were singing a duet. Pearl could "sing" a solid rendition of "Amazing Grace" in several accents. Matilda whipped up bacon and eggs, and blueberry waffles in the press. Given what she planned to bring up with Liam, the feast should butter him up.

Her dear friend and neighbor, Angie, had sent her an email about getting together soon. Matilda hoped they could. She'd like to catch her friend up, perhaps get some advice, and see how Angie's family was doing.

She and Liam still needed to talk about Jack, and Liam was due any minute for breakfast. Shea's commute meant she left very early to be at work by eight. So, she was long gone before Liam pulled in.

He sighed as he walked through the doorway, looking more bedraggled than when he'd cost his baseball team a win in high school. He wore a plaid shirt over a black tee and his work jeans. Like many folks here, he dressed in layers. The weather had dried out a bit, and hopefully, they'd have sun later today. The temps might even reach into the mid-sixties.

Father's Day was coming up. Did Liam want to make plans? She liked to help him fill up that day. Maybe Eli Hanson could do something with him on the Saturday before. When Liam was growing up, and especially after Matilda's dear niece, Liam's mom, Erin, passed, Eli would volunteer to spend at least part of Father's Day weekend with Liam.

Or this year, Liam could connect with Jack. Her nephew would *love* that idea.

Pushing scrambled eggs around the fry pan, she frowned. He'd never go for that, which was why she had a different plan to pitch to him this morning. "Mornin', Liam," she greeted him using her Southern accent. She strode over from the stove to hug him. "How are ya?"

"Stressed. Hungry. Annoyed." He was tall enough that when he bent toward her, he all but surrounded her with his arms. She was fascinated by how fragile he seemed, even as a grown man sometimes when they hugged. As if he still needed her support, still needed to lean on her. Like he was still the broken boy she'd taken in over twenty years ago when he was eleven.

When he let go, she pointed him to the eat-in kitchen table. "Sit. Food will help."

He grinned at her. "Of course it will."

"Where's Dylan?" She transferred the cooked eggs to a bowl and brought it toward him.

His scowl could peel an onion. "Said he'd drive himself over here and wasn't showing up until nine, at the earliest."

"That sounds less than committed. Does he know this is a real job? That he's getting paid to help you out? Or that you're in a hurry to get Shea settled in?" She carried the platter of waffles to the table.

"You'd think he'd take it seriously, given that." Liam helped himself to scrambled eggs and four slices of bacon. He shook his head. "If he can't do this, I'll have to find someone else."

"Can you do the work yourself?"

"I can, but it'll take longer." Eli had helped Liam learn many trades. They'd spent a few summers together where Eli hired teenaged Liam to be part of his team, which had helped them bond and given Liam skills and productive summers. More official training and licensing followed.

"Well, for Shea's sake it would be nice to finish sooner."

"I'm trying." He spread butter on his thick Belgian waffle.

Matilda liked having Shea around. They'd already enjoyed great conversations. She pulled out a chair across from her nephew and settled in with her mug of cocoa.

"Trying to make a good impression?"

He went still and squinted at her with accusation, plus a touch of humor, in his eyes. "What are you up to?"

As nonchalantly as she could, she sipped her hot chocolate. "Funny you should ask."

"Uh-oh."

"Hear me out, now. Hear me out." She dished up her own plate and then sat back with her glass of OJ in hand. "You know it would do me a world of good to see you find the woman you're meant to marry and make it permanent."

He seemed to relax as if whatever she might say next wouldn't bother him, given the way she'd started. The bacon strip in his hand disappeared bite by bite as he munched it. "So you've said, every time I see you lately."

"You're getting older every day."

His grin spoke of humoring her. "Right . . ."

"And years ago, all you could do was rave about Jenna-Shea this, and Jenna-Shea that. So, since she's back in your life, I think it's time you courted her and then asked her to marry you."

He laughed outright and nearly choked on his bacon. After he swallowed, more waves of laughter came until she feared he might need oxygen. Since she had his undivided attention, she waited for a moment of relative quiet and threw the last pitch at him.

"I want to train you in how to romance a woman."

This time he did choke. He coughed and moved to the sink where she joined him and pounded his back while handing him a glass of water she filled between pats. "Obviously you've had no role model, so you need my help. It's one of my responsibilities as your former guardian to teach you this. And we'll get started today."

"Y-you"—he sputtered—"have got to be kidding me. You've lost your last walnut, Auntie Mat."

When it was clear he was no longer choking, she returned to her seat at the table. As far as she was concerned, this was settled.

He squinted, grimaced, shook his head, leaned against the cabinets, and gripped the countertop with each hand, eyeing her. "What are you talking about?"

"You and Shea. Together." She clasped her hands in front of her and shook them. "Forever."

"You *have* lost your last walnut. What makes you think Shea is going to go along with your plan?"

Mentally choosing her Irish accent for the following words, she clutched her cocoa mug and held it up to breathe the chocolatey steam. "I saw it with me own eyes. That girl is smitten. Or she wants to be. You give her but a single good reason to fall for ye, and surely she will, not a doubt in the world."

He guffawed and followed it up with a few chuckles. "You're serious?"

She nodded. Calm and sure now.

"I love you, but I'm going to miss your mind the most." He rejoined her at the table and sat down.

She reached over and swatted his shoulder. "I have not lost my marbles, my walnuts, or any part of my mind, young man. Thank you very much," she said playfully. Pearl flew over and took up residence on her pointer finger. She patted the bird and fed her a bite of food. "Watch yourself," she said to Liam.

"Yes, ma'am." Finally a sober reaction, as he tipped his head toward his plate. But he still wore a grin.

She gave him a moment to finish his waffle before making more demands. "And I *will* teach you about romancing a woman and you *will* use that advice respectfully with Shea—since you're obviously still smitten with her—"

"I am not—"

She held up a hand to interrupt him. "And we *will* begin today. This morning." She straightened and cleared her throat. "Lesson number one in romancing a woman is to be warm and attentive. You show her warmth, and I guarantee you will get her attention."

Liam stared off toward the floor on his right as if thinking about that one.

"You've already seen that one's true, haven't you?" His head snapped up, and the confirmation encouraged her to keep moving ahead with this plan. "Perhaps on your walk last night?"

His sober expression hinted at secrets. "She's been through something."

Matilda had recognized a few scars as well. Shea needed compassion, and a motherly sort in her life. Especially since her own mother was off in France. "We all have." Matilda pictured the sad little eleven-year-old boy who'd cried on her shoulder more than once after his mom died. She hugged Pearl, who tucked her head under Matilda's chin.

One nod showed Liam understood what she meant, acknowledging they'd all suffered something—perhaps even remembering their history together—auntie and nephew. "For some reason, she's jumpy, and then she overreacts. First, Pearl startling her at the cottage, followed by me appearing at the door when she didn't expect me." He shook his finger at Pearl. Matilda snuggled the bird tighter. "And last night, a blue heron's call about gave her a panic attack. I'm concerned about her—not that I'd know how to help. But when I asked if I *could* help, she got all . . . I don't know. Her face changed—like she appreciated my compassion or something."

"Your warmth." She wanted to high-five him. "That's the way, Liam! You're already on the right track."

He snorted as if she were still one walnut shy of a bushel.

"So, you're ready to add my second guideline to your repertoire."

He grabbed his mug of cocoa and tipped it all the way up, finishing the last of it, as if buying himself time. When he set it down, he gave her solid eye contact, where she read humor in those sky-blue eyes so like Jack's. Not that she'd tell him that. "Auntie Mat, I *have* dated before. For crying out loud."

After a long pause and a sigh, she locked gazes with him. "But you haven't settled down. And that, my dear Liam, is the goal of Auntie Mat's School of Romance."

Another loud chuckle filled the room. She was afraid he'd startle Pearl.

"So, tip number two: do things for her; try to make her happy. Focus on her, not yourself. Ask yourself: what does she need? And then, meet that need, if you can."

Liam had finished his meal. He stood, wearing a good-natured grin. Then he carried his dishes to the sink, rinsed them, and loaded them into the empty dishwasher. "I need to get next door and start working on the cottage—for Shea." He emphasized her name as if showing he was ahead of Matilda's lessons. She doubted he got the romantic aspect yet though. Obviously, she had work to do. "And I hope you're not making brownies later." He opened the kitchen door and took one step out into the chilly morning.

"Why?"

"Because you're all out of walnuts!"

She threw a kitchen towel in his direction, which hit the door as he slammed it shut to the sound of his laughter.

CHAPTER NINE

During a ten-minute break between patients this morning, Shea visited the breakroom to grab a bottled water from the clinic's employee fridge. Anxiety tried to claw at her when she remembered how she kept startling around Liam. For months, she'd been free from her PTSD symptoms. Then, suddenly it felt like someone had switched on a spotlight to highlight her weaknesses. So long as her boss didn't find out, or the parents she served here at the clinic, her job was secure. Imagine learning your kid's psychologist was unhinged. All of her clients' parents would find other therapists, and she'd be out of a job.

Liam's eyes had filled with compassion as if he cared that she was all right. Was he feeling protective because Shea was JP's little sis, and Liam owed his buddy something? Or because he hadn't had her cottage ready for her and now he owed *her* something? Or because he actually … cared? She'd be lying to say his kindness hadn't affected her. Still, she'd like to know his motives. Which was partly why she hadn't answered his questions.

Now, if she could keep more pleasant flashbacks—those images full of a tender gaze and sky-blue eyes shining down on her, or how he protected her from the wind during their walk—out of her mind, she'd have an easier time focusing on the rest of her patients.

On the hour, Shea visited the waiting room and called her next patient back to her office. Seven-year-old Kaden O'Connor bee-lined toward the toys the moment they'd stepped into her counseling office. After closing the door, she settled onto the floor near him. While he played and relaxed, she'd coax him to tell her how he was handling his parents' split. His father had brought him in a few weeks ago because Kaden had lost his appetite. But the boy couldn't tell his dad what was bothering him. He just kept pushing his dinner plate away. He seemed fine with the shared custody his father and mother had in place, and from the interviews Shea had conducted, the parents weren't particularly angry or demonstrative as they worked through this trial. Each of them seemed determined to put Kaden first and make this as easy as possible on him.

His favorite toys were the interlocking building blocks, and he'd already constructed a structure in the few minutes he'd been in the room. "Tell me about your week, Kaden."

"Uh, school. Recess. Home. Same stuff as last time I came in here." His red and blue brick building rose steadily as he avoided eye contact.

She discreetly took notes on a pad. "How's your friend Max doing?"

"He gets to go to Hawaii in October and miss school! I wanna go to Hawaii, but Mom says I can't."

"Have you and your dad talked about it? What does he say?" Right now, Mr. O'Connor sat in the waiting room. They'd catch up at the end of the session when she invited him back in. Sometimes kids opened up more when their parents weren't watching or listening.

"He says a few things have to get settled first. But he still didn't think we'd go during the school year. Maybe we could go during the winter break that's not the Christmas break. I mean that weird one in *Febrary*."

She didn't correct his mispronunciation of February. Grammar corrections shut kids up. "If you did get to go to Hawaii, who would you like to come along?"

"Mom, Dad, my little baby brother. Our dog." On the same large platform, Kaden had started to construct another building, a few spaces from the first. This one was in green and yellow bricks. Interesting. Different colors for each house.

"Remind me of your dog's name again."

"Silly Sid."

She made a note. Kids liked for her to remember the details. They felt "heard," and in kiddo heart language that carried a lot of weight. Helped them trust her. "What a fun name for a dog. Who thought of it?"

"Me." Kaden's hands went still.

A light bulb went off in Shea's mind. "When was the last time you saw Silly Sid?"

"Two weeks ago, I guess. Last time I was at Mom's."

Weren't they exchanging every other weekend? What had happened?

"So, Silly Sid doesn't live with your dad?" Where Kaden lived during the week.

Kaden shook his head but didn't answer. A single tear dripped down his face and onto the yellow and green building. His shoulders didn't even shake. Only silence.

"You miss him."

Kaden nodded, and grabbed a long, narrow platform piece, which he pressed to the green and yellow building. Then, he pressed the other end of the platform piece to the top of the red and blue building. A bridge.

"Whose dog is Silly Sid?"

"He's mine, but then Mom and Dad split up. And you can't split a dog." Kaden added more blocks to the bridge, raising up sides along a central channel. "I guess he's not mine anymore." His voice broke.

Had his parents considered how Kaden viewed their dog? In all the moving and separating, had they thought more than a few minutes about where Silly Sid would go?

"One more question, Kaden, and then I'll get your dad, and we'll pull out the candy jar."

"Mm-kay." Poor child didn't even seem excited about treats.

"Which of your parents lives in the house you all used to live in?"

"Mom does."

That might be why they left the dog there. If Mr. O'Connor lived in an apartment, pets may not be allowed. She might have just landed on what was causing Kaden's lack of appetite.

She reached toward Kaden. "Let's go out to the waiting room and get your dad, shall we?" As they strode down the hallway to the outer room, she felt a sense of satisfaction. Hopefully, today's breakthrough led to solutions. She'd helped another family. She'd discovered the question's answer but hadn't solved the problem. That would be up to the O'Connors.

Sessions like these confirmed she was living her dream, fulfilling her purpose.

Now if she could only overcome her own mental issues.

Sure, she could see a therapist for herself. She had, over the years. But—and she'd never tell Liam this—they hadn't helped. Not like she'd hoped they would. She wanted a magical breakthrough like today. One answer leading to a chain of victories, like she envisioned for Kaden in the coming days as they resolved this issue about seeing his dog.

Her therapists had been able to track her fears back to *the incident*, but they hadn't been able to help her reject fear. She didn't get to a place of exerting control. Fear was a cruel beast. And certain things set Shea off. Given her education, her attempts, and her relationship with God, she should be healed by now. Should be able to leave the past behind. Shouldn't be so susceptible to triggers.

Fear didn't give her a choice. She couldn't simply *choose* to move beyond the past. Couldn't make herself forget and skip through her days without angst.

Like when Pearl startled her, or Liam materialized at the rental house door. She couldn't choose her reaction—that pulse-pounding, sweaty palms overreaction. Sometimes her failure to overcome made her question her line of work and her competence. So she lived for days like today when a patient walked out hand in hand with a smiling parent, who thanked her for lifting their burdens.

So long as she kept up her façade, she had a future. If she dropped it, she'd have a career crisis.

Auntie Mat leaned into the table and studied Liam. "What are you going to do about Jack?"

Only Burr's first day on the job, and he'd dashed off to Winslow as if he needed distance from Liam. After listening to him bang around the cottage all morning, Liam was glad to let him go fend for himself. Meanwhile, he'd crossed the yards and ended up at his aunt's table in her dated kitchen. Trouble was, Auntie Mat wasn't shy about prying.

"You can't avoid your dad forever." As usual she was perfectly put together like she was about to enter stage right on opening night. She wore a blouse decorated in, what did she call it? Some type of needlework. Right—embroidery. Her shirt had a peacock stitched into the front on a teal background, which she wore over black slacks and loafers. She eyed him and crunched a pickle spear. "What'd you decide to do?"

As far as Liam was concerned, he'd been an orphan all these years. He didn't have a "dad." So, this *friend* request—ha!—from Jack was a pesky intrusion on his life. One he didn't have to even acknowledge. But he didn't have to tell his aunt that. Not yet.

Sure, he'd probably crack like a pistachio before lunch hour ended, but first he had a question for her. "What did *you* decide to do?"

"Haven't yet." She seemed to hide the rest of the story, but he wouldn't pry. He had checked her online friends list and not found Jack Barrett's name on the list. That felt like loyalty to him.

He did have a question he wouldn't mind asking her. "How well did you know him?" He held his breath while she prepared to answer. Part of him wanted to hear, and part of him would rather not.

"Well, that's a good question. I didn't really know him. I met him for their wedding, of course, and I tried to learn more about him. I mean he was marrying my beloved niece, but back then, they didn't seem to want input from family."

News to him. "They rushed into marriage?" He'd always trusted his mother's judgment, but he'd been a young kid back when Jack was around, and just after he left, with no gauge to go by.

"Well, not exactly. My guess was always that they each saw red flags—or maybe orange flags—and neither of them wanted anyone to look too closely or talk them out of their relationship. If they shared too much, or had a long engagement, family members might raise doubts."

A sick feeling settled in Liam's gut. "Did he hurt her?" He couldn't remember much about Jack, including any abuse. But what if he'd—what did they call it? Repressed his memories?

Auntie Mat reached for his hand across the table. "No. Not that I know of. And remember, your mom didn't want out. Jack did."

Liam clenched his teeth, making his jaw ache like it had done a lot since that request came through. As if he could ever be "friends" with the man who'd abandoned him and his mother. He'd seen what it'd done to her. Sure, he'd cried himself to sleep enough times, but only because he could hear Mom on the other side of the wall doing the same thing. Any time he checked on her, she'd pretend she was fine and send him back to bed. Then, a few minutes later, he'd hear muffled sobs again. During the day, she'd always told him that he could make things easier if he would simply do what she asked—like be ready for school on time, clean up his breakfast dishes, make his bed.

Yeah, Mom put on a brave face, but Liam knew her heart had been crushed.

And now, he could barely remember the days of their family of three. He'd been about four years old when Jack left. So, there wasn't any way young Liam could fix everything, or somehow make Mom feel better. But even at that young age, he'd wanted to.

"You don't have to accept." Auntie Mat bit into her turkey sandwich.

Right. Facebook. "I know." He pushed his plate away and chugged iced tea. "It bugs me he even reached out to me. Why not leave me alone?"

Auntie Mat studied him, and he could tell she had something on her mind. Sure enough, she drew a deep breath. "Haven't you ever wondered what became of him?"

He had. And then he'd regretted even thinking about him. Wasn't that unfaithful, or disloyal, to Mom? Any type of kind or gracious thought in Jack's—because Liam wouldn't call him Dad—

direction made Liam feel like he'd slammed the door on Mom crying in the other room.

How long would he feel like that? It wasn't as if Mom never recovered. Closer to the end of her life, she'd gone years without crying, found a degree of joy. But no matter how many therapists, little Liam never felt "over it."

If he were honest with himself, he *still* didn't feel past Jack's abandonment. That's why he kept so close to Auntie Mat. He wasn't a kid anymore, but he didn't know how he'd handle it if he lost her.

His aunt had asked him a question—whether he wondered about Jack these days. "Sure, I've wondered." And looked him up on the internet a couple of times.

Her eyes were kind. "He's probably wondered about you too."

"Nah, he's got a bunch more kids now, and he's been married four times."

"You are making that up."

"Yes, I am. I have no idea." He shrugged but he couldn't shake the grief, the weight of being fatherless. Of being rejected. "*I* did not click through and stalk him like he's been doing to me." Which was why Liam made his posts private now.

A touch of fun lit her eyes for the first time during this conversation. "Want me to stalk him?"

Though spoken with humor, something about that suggestion scared him. Liam liked ignorance. "No. Thanks."

"What if he still lives here, near Seattle?"

"So what? He waited almost thirty years to get back in touch."

"What if he's dying now?"

Something cold hardened in Liam's chest, and he crossed his arms. "Nothing new about me being an orphan."

Auntie Mat gasped across the table.

Remorse punched him, and he uncoiled his arms and reached for her hand. "I'm sorry. You know I see you like a mother figure." He'd never want to sound ungrateful for everything she'd done for him, given him, sacrificed for him. She'd provided a home and her loving care. He shuddered thinking about where he'd have ended up if she hadn't stepped in and become his legal guardian when

Mom died.

She squeezed his hand. "I should hope so, Son." The surprise slowly faded from her expression, and she sipped her ice water as if his words hadn't hurt her. But Liam's conscience burned, and he wished he could suck the words back.

Calliope clicked in on the linoleum flooring with her longish nails. Auntie Mat pushed away from the table and scooped the dog into her lap.

"'Allo, li'le pup," Auntie Mat said in her British accent. "And 'ow are we today?"

If she was willing to let him off the hook, he wouldn't harp on his mistake. But he'd watch his words from now on. "You should try out for another role at the theater, Auntie. Volunteering isn't enough for you; I know it."

"I might." His aunt's face went sober again. "Do you want me to friend him and get the ball rolling?" No accent now.

Liam stood. "Not for my sake." He'd never ask that of her.

"So, you're not curious?"

"Nope." He pressed his teeth together. He didn't make a habit of lying to her. But was it lying? No. He didn't want to be curious.

"I've said this before, and I'll repeat myself now and then drop it—for a while. You should consider forgiving him."

"I know . . . I know."

She didn't press him—perhaps she guessed he needed space. His gut tightened. Something didn't feel right. As if he'd just missed an opportunity to do something he was supposed to do. But as far as he knew, as a thirty-three-year-old, he got to call the shots in his life. So he'd get to work and try to ignore the sandpaper scraping at his thoughts that suggested he'd now veered onto the wrong path.

About a half hour after he returned to work, he got a text from his aunt. Burr hadn't shown up yet. Liam figured he'd better call in a reliable carpenter, let Burr go.

HEY, FORGOT TO ASK. YOU HANGING OUT WITH ELI OVER FATHER'S DAY WEEKEND?

This, Liam could get excited about. He tapped his response back to her. YES. BUNGEE JUMPING DOWN NEAR VANCOUVER. CAN'T WAIT. He referred to Vancouver, Washington, not BC up north.

GOING ALONE?

NAH, I FIGURE I'LL INVITE SHEA.

HA! GOOD! I HOPE YOU DO.

TAKE IT EASY, AUNTIE MAT. NO MORE "SCHOOL OF LOVE."

WE'LL SEE ABOUT THAT.

BESIDES GIVEN HER SCARES LATELY, I DON'T THINK SHE'D BE INTO BUNGEE JUMPING.

THEN FIGURE OUT SOMETHING ELSE.

GOTTA GET TO WORK.

SURE THING. SEE YOU FOR DINNER.

TTYL

CHAPTER TEN

Every year, Liam dreaded this weekend. The reminders of dads everywhere he went. The shame, even as a child, of not having a father to celebrate. For years, he'd spent the Saturday before Father's Day with Eli, so riding shotgun next to him this morning felt right. Yet, Liam hadn't been this raw in decades. Something about hearing from Jack opened Liam up. Hopefully, Eli wouldn't dig around in Liam's business too much. It was the promise of the jump that convinced Liam to come today. The adrenaline would dull the pain.

At the southern end of Renton, Hitch's dad merged onto I-5 south from 405, with Liam up front and Jinx in the backseat. Burr decided not to ride along, though he said he might meet them there. At this hour, everyone was downing coffee or Coke to get a jumpstart—no extreme energy drinks allowed in Eli's car, not that Liam drank those.

His day had started a lot earlier because he'd had to commute over to Issaquah from Bainbridge, which included waiting for a ferry. In Issaquah, he'd met up with Jinx at Eli's place. Now, they had about three hours of driving in front of them.

"Too bad Hitch busted his leg. He's always wanted to go bungee jumping." Eli pulled into the middle lane.

"Are you jumping today, sir?" Jinx had a thing about calling him sir, and Liam totally got it. Everyone respected Eli.

"Probably, though don't tell my wife." He chuckled. "Hey, what are you doing tomorrow, son?" he asked Liam, who didn't mind him using the term. He'd been more of a dad than Jack.

Liam shrugged. Every year it was the same thing—no real plans, except to get through that third Sunday in June.

"You could join Hitch and me. The whole family's getting together, and we're grilling out, even if it's pouring. My dad's coming over. He recently turned eighty-six. Keeps pestering Hitch and Fee to start a family and give him great-grandchildren before he drifts off to heaven, as he puts it." Eli smiled as he drove. In his head, Liam could hear Eli's dad, Samuel, saying those things. They'd met on a few occasions over the years, even some Father's Days.

"Thanks for the invitation." The last thing Liam wanted to do was crash the Hanson family picnic and be reminded of the hole in his life. "I'll think about it." And he would. Liam didn't make it a practice to bemoan his lot, but as he worked tomorrow on his roof, he'd be preoccupied by thoughts of the Hanson family having fun and celebrating Eli and Samuel. If he went, and the subject came up, they'd probably try to convince him to give Jack a chance. No thanks.

"But it would be fun to be a grandfather myself and watch Hitch become a dad. You think you'll ever be a father?"

Not with his heritage. Liam would never subject someone else to Jack's genes by having kids. As an only child, the line stopped with him.

Good.

Even he could hear the bitterness in his thoughts. Was that what his aunt had referred to the other day? Was mentioning forgiveness her way of bringing up how cynical he'd become?

He hadn't answered Eli, but what could he say? He settled on, "Only God knows."

Jinx had gone quiet. Liam peeked behind him and saw Jinx had put in his earbuds and tipped his head back. Naptime.

GPS predicted another two-and-a-half hours of driving time, if they didn't stop for food, more caffeine, or bathroom breaks. The monotony of the freeway, even with the traffic at this early hour on a Saturday morning south of Tacoma, could drag a yawn out of Liam too.

"So, Matilda tells me your dad got in touch with you." Eli kept his voice low.

Liam snorted. *And now it begins.* "Of course she did."

Eli gave him a glance. "She means well."

"Yeah. I know." Which was why he wasn't irritated with her. "Truth is, Jack *tried* to get in touch." Liam ground his jaw and studied the passing scenery now that they'd found a slot in the right lane's line of vehicles.

With a glance over his shoulder, Eli probably saw what Liam had—Jinx had checked out. Countdown to fatherly lecture in five, four, three, two ... "These things work both ways." Eli's words challenged Liam, dug around in his thoughts and motives. Eli thought like a father. He probably sympathized with Jack, even though Jack was at fault. How soon could Liam jump off a bridge? They were scheduled for a noon time with the excursion outfit. The digital clock on the dash flipped to 7:47. Maybe Liam would jump from a moving car.

"Did you respond?"

"No."

Eli nodded like he understood. Then, he focused on passing a slow semi with its hazards flashing. "You'd rather he stay out of your life, like he has been doing, huh?"

Liam scratched the back of his neck. Was that what he wanted? Yes. And no ... "I just assumed he would, you know? Lately, with social media, people can find each other." He waved his hand, feeling that bitterness churn in his gut. "What a *great* idea."

Eli chuckled. "It's possible he's known where you were all along." His words came out so quiet, Liam almost had to lean in to hear them.

After letting that sink in a minute, he had to refute it, because, shoot—if Jack had known his whereabouts all this time, where in the world had he been for nearly three decades?

Yet, what would it have looked like if, say a couple of years after he left, Jack had returned?

"It's awful that he abandoned you and your mom, son. That's always broken our hearts." The hint of compassion in his tone spoke of both respect and empathy, without being sappy. For some reason, Liam felt honored. He cleared his throat. No need to get emotional. The decision to reconnect with Jack was not an emotional one. It was about deserving. Did Jack deserve a response from Liam? No. No, he did not. Jack had abandoned his wife, and she was long gone now. So, if he'd meant to apologize to both of them, he was around twenty years too late. The soundtrack of Mom's tears ran through Liam's mind, and he fisted his hands.

Jack deserved to be ignored, as if he didn't exist. That's how he'd treated Liam and his mom. *That* was fair payback.

"Change of topics, son. Matilda also told me you're really stepping up with this job for Stephen Brown and his properties." He used his free hand to squeeze Liam's shoulder and then got back to gripping the steering wheel, studying the road, and checking his mirrors and dashboard. "I'm proud of you for that."

Those words undid Liam too. Shoot. Was Eli going for tears? *Let's see how long it takes until Liam is bawling this Father's Day weekend. My money's on before we even reach the jump site.* Maybe he would put his own earbuds in and check out for a couple of hours. He cleared his throat. "Thanks."

Besides, and he wouldn't announce this to Eli, Liam *hadn't* been successful at his job. He'd let Shea down. He'd missed the emails and failed Stephen. It was a miracle he still had a job. That failure was another reminder that, though he didn't want to be, he was, in many ways, like Jack. There was no way to outrun genes. Why should he even keep trying? Maybe he was destined to be a deadbeat, just like Jack.

Eli seemed content to drive without talking for a long while, so Liam stretched out as much as he could, rested his head, and closed his eyes, letting the miles pass and pushing aside unwelcome thoughts.

"Dark skies ahead."

Liam's eyes snapped open to a view toward the south. Ominous clouds full of wind and rain. He wasn't given to believing in omens, but the impending storm might argue with him.

"So, son, you still go to church with Matilda?"

A weight sunk into Liam's gut on a long sigh. When Eli wasn't prying around in Liam's personal life, he was usually digging around in his spiritual one. This time Liam felt less equipped to handle all that curiosity with the ease he usually used. "Sometimes." But not lately. His boss preferred he take Sundays off, for the sake of the neighbors, so Liam had focused on his own property, mowing the lawn or trying to repair the leaky roof the landlord didn't seem too inclined to fix.

"You know God's just looking for an opportunity to speak, right? Then, our job is to listen." Outside of Olympia, lightning flashed, and Eli chuckled. "See?"

"Ha-ha." Maybe Liam had grown distant from God lately, but even he knew God wasn't only about lightning and anger and judgment. He missed the gentler nature of the God he'd known as a small child. The One who smiled at him. The One who could do anything.

The sky darkened overhead as they drove directly into the storm. Rain pelted the truck, slowing traffic on I-5 to a crawl. Winds slammed the line of cars from the west. The weather report this morning had suggested possible passing thunderstorms this far south of Seattle. Maybe this thing would pass. Would the bungee outfit still permit them to jump in about two hours if this storm kept up? Standing up there on a bridge, the jumpers would make rather effective lightning rods.

Liam often got a high from beating death. Still, he'd rather not be an idiot about it.

"I have this friend at work, says he has a challenge relating to God as a father because of his own father's failure to be loving and kind and protective," Eli was saying. "*He'd* probably think the lightning was the perfect expression of God's 'fathering' heart."

Liam scoffed. No matter how much Eli pried, Liam couldn't hate him. But he didn't have answers to the questions Eli wasn't asking. So, he kept quiet in the midst of the pounding rain and sea of red brake lights ahead. The wipers thumped back and forth in a quick rhythm.

"I'm only looking out for you. And I get it. Believe me."

If he turned the tables, would Eli stop asking him questions? "Tell me about your dad," Liam began. "What was he like while you were growing up?"

The GPS announced a ten-minute slowdown due to an accident ahead, and the rolling traffic stopped.

They'd get back to Eli's dad. "Think they'll still have us jump, in this?" Liam pointed to the dark skies and pulled up the radar image on his weather app. Then he zoomed in on the southern-most section of Western Washington. Their destination was outside of Vancouver, in the forest.

"We'll get a call, text, or email if they call it off. And a refund or a chance to rebook. But they said they rarely cancel." Eli tapped his thumbs on the steering wheel, inching forward every now and then. Good thing they'd padded their timeline this morning. "You asked about my childhood." He took a quick break from gazing out the windshield and faced Liam with a knowing expression as if to say *I see what you did there—distracting me.* "Fair enough. My dad was a military man and as we were growing up, he was the angry sort, and you couldn't always tell why. He's mellowed a lot. You've met him. He isn't intimidating anymore."

"How'd he treat you? Your mom? Your siblings?"

"Nothing physical, but not a whole lot of affection either."

Jinx stirred in the backseat. "We there yet?" His voice sounded gravelly like he'd been asleep for miles.

Eli waved at the sea of cars with swishing wipers all around them. "We are stuck."

Liam was glad to leave the conversation alone. Given Eli's childhood, how did he interact with God? How did he see Him? Obviously he hadn't let his father's failures overshadow his desire to be a good dad.

But how did Eli trust God?

I will never leave you nor forsake you.

Liam sat back and sighed deep, pretending to patiently wait out the traffic, but he'd definitely heard a gentle voice in his mind. Auntie Mat kept a plaque with that Scripture from Hebrews on the wall in her upstairs hallway, had for years. So the words were familiar to him, but in this context—the context of God and Jack and Eli's words about abandonment … Liam had a feeling this wasn't an ordinary moment.

I will never leave you nor forsake you.

The words repeated, and Liam studied the sky through the window. *Are You trying to tell me something?* It sure *felt* like God had left him, or that He wasn't all that interested in whether things were hard for him. But the verse seemed to say God didn't abandon His people. Liam studied a building visible from the freeway and swallowed. At some point, he'd decided that not only could God abandon people, He *had* abandoned Liam.

Maybe he was equating God with his deadbeat dad.

Apparently today, God was back, making sure Liam knew it, and cheerfully siding with Eli.

Wind whipped sideways at the SUV, bullying them and tipping the RV in front of them. The sky darkened even further, and if Liam didn't know better, he'd worry about a tornado. But Western Washington didn't have many of those. This was earthquake and volcano territory, not a region given to tornadoes.

Their three phones pinged at the same time, and since Eli was driving, he didn't reach over, but Liam swiped his cell to life and read the text that had come up from the bungee jumpers: EXPECTING STORMS THROUGHOUT THE AFTERNOON. LOTS OF LIGHTNING AND HIGH WINDS NOW AND MORE PREDICTED UNTIL AROUND 11:00 TONIGHT. CANCELING ALL JUMPS TODAY FOR THE SAKE OF SAFETY. TEXT BACK: REFUND OR REBOOK.

Jinx groaned from the backseat like a teenager missing vacation.

Eli glanced at Liam and then in the rearview mirror. "I take it that means we're headed back up north without getting to jump today, right fellas?"

"Yup. More storms incoming for the next twelve hours." Liam shook his head. At least if they'd been able to jump, he could clear his thoughts. Fill up on adrenaline. For a few minutes, maybe, shake the hovering cloud full of questions and second-guessing himself.

Eli threw on his blinker, so they could exit the freeway. "Then, that calls for lunch. There's gotta be a diner around here somewhere."

Sure enough, a few miles of back roads to the east, Eli found them a mom-and-pop diner complete with red checkered tablecloths and sticky floors.

"While you were out cold, sleeping beauty," Eli said to Jinx who crunched ice from the soda the server had brought minutes earlier, "Liam and I were talking about dads. Tell us about yours."

Jinx launched into story after story of fishing escapades and camping trips—stuff Liam didn't even know, though they'd been friends forever. Jinx's dad was cool. Never raised his voice. Didn't hit anyone. *Stayed.*

Anger worked Liam over, and he wanted to pace. If it weren't for the drenching rain … But maybe that's what he needed. Lightning flashed, and thunder immediately followed, rattling the windows and scaring the kids at neighboring tables. So much for a stroll.

The server brought their burgers, fries, and onion rings, and Jinx dove in.

Eli eyed Jinx. "You think Liam should reconnect with Jack?" Eli had guts, Liam would give him that. He never had been one to pull punches, especially when he felt strongly about something. Liam respected that, even when it made him squirm. Like now.

Jinx shrugged. "None of my business." He knew about the contact from Jack, of course, because Liam trusted him. And Jinx never preached.

"Well, okay. In his shoes, would you respond to the dad who left your family?"

"I might."

Liam forced himself to take a huge bite of burger, even though he wasn't hungry, so he'd have something to focus on.

Eli's food sat untouched. He leaned his elbows on the table and got comfortable. "This is how I see it—as a father and a man who's lived a lot longer than you two. If I made big mistakes in my past, and they involved my kids, I'd be eaten up with regret, especially if I'd grown up a little since then and had a change of heart. So, if one day, I had the chance to get back in touch and apologize, I would take it. Any of us could die anytime." Lightning split the sky and thunder roared overhead. "Especially if we were to bungee jump today." He grinned. "Nah, if I had a chance to try to fix it, I would. I'd at least want to tell my kids I was sorry and ask for their forgiveness."

Liam dropped his burger and faced off with Eli. Maybe not going toe-to-toe with a father all his life had made him bolder. Or stupider. "He doesn't deserve it."

Eli tipped his head. "None of us do." His voice came out quiet. Then, he doctored his own burger with additional ketchup and even a few of those onion rings between the meat and the bun and took a huge bite.

Liam tried to act like he wasn't seething. He wanted to curse this storm that kept him from running away from this conversation, kept them from jumping, made him feel trapped.

That's what he'd been doing his entire life—running away from the ache inside. Racing to jump off the next cliff, or dive into the nearest shark-infested sea. All these challenging words from Eli and there was no place for Liam to run.

He choked down the last bite of his lunch and set his phone beside him on the table. As a rule, out of respect, he kept his cell in his pocket when they ate with Eli, or when he ate at Auntie Mat's. Today, he had three things to do: reinstall that social media app on his phone, sign in, and accept someone's friend request.

Then, he might find peace, get Eli and his aunt to back off. Maybe shut down the sander grinding away at his conscience. *See this, Lord? I'm trying here. But for the record, I don't think this will end well.*

CHAPTER ELEVEN

As much as Liam hated to confront Burr, his friend had made it necessary. "Burr you can head back to Kent now. I'll find someone who can fill in for you." Should Liam add anything else? "Sorry things didn't work out." Not that Liam hadn't tried. He'd given Burr chance after chance. But he'd been here for a week and hadn't stepped up. Liam could often smell alcohol around him, and he didn't have time for Burr's nonchalant attitude. He'd staggered into the Brown's cottage an hour and a half late today, already sloshed. The final straw.

"C'mon, I-Islander. I need the w-work." He tried to straighten as he teetered in the unfinished kitchen.

"Were you this tanked on the trip up here?" Where was Burr hiding his alcohol? In his vehicle? Liam didn't keep any in the house.

He shrugged. "*Meh-be . . .*" He looked around. "Hey, Liam. I'll get my act together. Give me another ch-chance."

Liam headed for the cottage's side door, closest to his aunt's house. "I'll be right back. Do *not* touch any tools. You're too soused to work."

Burr raised both hands. "All right, all right." He spit out an expletive as Liam was shutting the door.

Storming toward his aunt's house, Liam knew he still had to fire Burr. But where would that leave his *frenemy*—part friend, part enemy? Back at home, drinking. No income. No future. No hope. Yet, if he didn't want to get better, who could reach him?

"Hey, Auntie Mat," Liam said as he stepped into her kitchen. "I could use your help."

His aunt stood there in a bright magenta cotton pantsuit, misting the plants in her bay window. "Sure thing. What's up?"

"Burr is drunk. I've had it. He needs to go."

"*Where* will he go?" She darted around the kitchen, and Liam stayed out of her way.

"I can't fix him. He's a mess." Liam didn't need this. After he'd accepted that ridiculous friend request from Jack, the guy had immediately direct-messaged him and asked if they could meet up. Yeah, he wasn't satisfied with taking things slowly. Auntie Mat said he should meet him, hear him out. Eli would probably say the same thing. But Liam couldn't. Back to Burr. "He doesn't want help. He says he wants this job, but he hardly ever shows up. When he does, he's late and already toasted." He shrugged. "I can't help him."

She'd pulled leftover quiche from the fridge, nuked it, and poured a tall glass of water. "I don't think you should give up on him."

"You wanna take a crack at him?" As soon as he said the words, heard his own anger, he wanted to reel back the words. "Sorry. It's just, I've tried everything. Nothing works with him. Giving him this job was supposed to provide a lifeline. I can't make him grab the rope."

"I hear you. Listen, send him over here to sober up. I'll chat with him."

"You sure? He's a nice drunk, but I still don't want you to see him this way."

"I can handle it." She held the door for him. "Send him over."

Of all the people in Liam's life, Auntie Mat was the only one who knew why Liam was so motivated to help Burr. The fact she respected that desire, meant a lot to him.

Did Burr remember? If so, why wouldn't he let Liam save *his* life?

The loaded paintbrush glided over the canvas, leaving a solid line of sky blue as Matilda painted on the sunporch. *Lord, if You don't get through to him, who will? I know Dylan matters to You. What can I do to help You help him when he doesn't even want to help himself? We're throwing him lifelines, like Liam said. He won't take them.* It hit her then that Dylan might not want to live. He might feel he had nothing to lose. Why? What was he running from?

Currently, unless he had ducked out, Dylan sat in the living room guzzling another glass of water. She'd given him space and food, and time.

She heard a shuffling sound behind her and turned from her easel to the doorway from the kitchen. Dylan leaned there, his eyes clearer than when he'd first arrived over an hour ago.

"Feeling better?" she asked him. The guy was likely dehydrated, but she had sports drinks with electrolytes if he needed them.

"Yes, thanks. Sorry about this." He pointed at himself as if apologizing for being alive.

"No judgment here, young man. Now, how can I help?" She went back to smearing blue paint across her canvas.

"No help for me, I'm afraid."

Ask him what he's running from.

Matilda knew that Voice. She faced Liam's friend. "Dylan, tell me something."

He nodded, seemingly willing to listen. For now.

"What are you running from?"

He put the glass to his lips and upended it then swallowed and cleared his throat. "Regrets, I guess."

She dipped her brush into the midnight blue paint on her palette and mixed it with white. "We all have those, I'm afraid."

He scoffed. "You took in Liam. You gave him a home and a good life. I mean, he's had a better life than I did, and I had both parents."

She studied him, noting the bitterness in his tone. "Well, I'm sorry to hear that."

"That's where I picked up my love of liquor."

"You regret their mistakes—your parents', I mean?"

"Nah. I regret my mistakes, of which there are plenty." He lifted his glass in her direction as if offering a macabre, empty toast.

God nudged her to ask more questions, to keep digging, and since Dylan still seemed engaged, she continued. "Like what? I bet you can't surprise me. I've seen a lot of life."

His gaze locked with hers. "Oh, yeah?"

"Try me."

"You know all this hubbub about Liam and Jack?"

She nodded, keeping her expression open and warm. "Of course."

"Well, I am Jack."

She squinted at him, her brush still. "Come again?"

"Or, I may as well be. I am the villain in some kid's story."

Oh . . . "And you don't think there's hope for you because of that choice? That your life is pretty much over now? You're what? Thirty-three or so, like Liam, right?" When he nodded, she continued. "So, this is the end?"

Dylan shifted his weight, stretched. Didn't answer.

Tell him I love him and that I want to redeem this situation.

"You know why Jesus is called the Redeemer? Because He can't help Himself. He *loves* to redeem—people, situations. Our regrets and mistakes and choices, and those of others." She took a long, slow breath. "You don't have to let the enemy win. If you ask Him, God can rescue you and fix even this."

He shook his head. "I'm way past that."

"No one is 'past' asking God to rescue them. Not Jack, not you."

His eyes crinkled when he squinted. "You think Liam should make nice with him, don't you? Pretend all is well?"

"What would you do, in Liam's shoes?"

Dylan scoffed. "I can relate more with Jack."

"So, like him, why don't you try to make it right?"

"There is no way they'd have me back. I blew it." He turned and headed through the doorway to the kitchen, setting his glass in the sink. "Thanks for that. I've gotta run." The kitchen door closed softly behind him as he stepped outside.

She'd tried, and hopefully, he'd heard what she'd said about God.

If anyone could help him, God could.

Don't give up on him, Lord. She slid her brush across the canvas, adding a touch of midnight to the sky. "I know You won't."

CHAPTER TWELVE

Warm sunshine heated Liam's neck as he stood on his aunt's deck, facing the Sound. Why had he stopped to chat again? She had one agenda lately, and out of respect, he had no choice but to listen.

"Have you decided how to help Shea, Son?" Auntie Mat was still on her school-of-romance kick. With a bucket next to her feet, she worked at deadheading the flowers she grew in the pots on the deck. Now that July had arrived, summer came with it.

Liam rubbed his lower back. He'd finished a ten-hour day next door. What he wanted was a hot shower and a meal, which he'd help with. What he didn't need was another lecture on romancing Shea. He tipped up the watering can over her snapdragons. "Her cottage is coming along. Got the floors refinished. Tile's going in for the kitchen floor. Then molding throughout."

"Good. But I'm talking about what you can do for her personally."

"I know you're on this whole 'I'm your guardian, so it's my job to teach you how to romance your future wife' thing, but I'm good. Thanks anyway."

"You need to settle down. I won't rest until you do. Humor me?"

She had no idea how often he humored her. He recoiled the hose from watering her hydrangeas. Now that the rains had let up, they had to wet everything down every couple of days.

"Shea's due home any minute and could use help with the purging she's been doing lately. Those boxes full of giveaways have to go somewhere. Why don't you help?"

"Of course." Is that what this was about? Clearing out the clutter, and carrying a few boxes? That he could do. "I'm happy to help with that. I thought you meant romantically."

Auntie Mat straightened her back and then her straw gardening hat. "Son, I don't understand. If I remember correctly, you pined for Shea for years. Yes?"

That was before he'd given up on ever being married, given up on having a family. Given up on . . . himself. He wanted to tell his aunt he didn't deserve Shea, but he knew what she'd do—preach to him about how God had created him with purpose and then she'd ask him when he'd decided he was worthless. That wasn't how she'd raised him.

So, like when he was twelve, he only shrugged.

Shea pulled into the driveway between the two houses, and Auntie Mat excused herself to finish prepping their dinner. Liam had grilled burgers and corn on the cob, and she'd sliced watermelon and whipped up potato salad and chocolate chip cookies. Her disappearance right as Shea appeared didn't surprise Liam. She probably figured leaving them alone would lead to wedding bells by Christmas. Sure thing.

"Hey, Liam." Shea climbed from her car, sunglasses in place. She looked gorgeous in a sundress with her long golden-brown hair falling in waves over slender shoulders, and her feet in strappy sandals. He'd always liked her classy sense of style. But they were friends. He should stop noticing those things about her.

Easy, Barrett. "Hey. How was work?"

"Good. Tiring." She reached into her car and grabbed her bag. "I've noticed a big difference now that the sun makes a regular appearance. My patients are less sad."

"I'll bet." He didn't suffer from SAD, but he knew plenty of folks who did. He'd heard light therapy helped during the darker seasons. "Hey, my aunt mentioned you have a load of giveaways to haul off. Can I help you do that tonight?"

Her head tipped up as if she hadn't expected the offer. "Thanks. That'd be a great help. Especially if we could use your truck."

"Absolutely." He used a broom to sweep away the sand from the deck.

"How's the cottage coming along?"

"Wanna see? We're getting there."

She followed him. "Is Dylan still helping?"

"For now." Liam had tried to find a replacement, but so far, no luck. Since threatening to fire him, Burr had risen to the job.

When he drank, Burr became a kinder version of himself. He'd make promises to be more responsible or dependable. He'd beg for forgiveness and do a rather good job on his work, so long as he wasn't too unsteady.

Liam could barely remember Burr sober—except he didn't miss his irritability. And he still couldn't get Burr to tell him why he was so angry with Liam, or why he'd gone back to drinking. One battle at a time. Liam had enough trouble trying to keep him from driving intoxicated.

"I'm still open to suggestions on how to help him," Liam said as he held the door of her house open for her. "Although, I don't know if I'd try that direct approach again."

"Thanks." She passed him and stepped inside. "Sometimes, direct works, especially with adults." She spoke quietly. "Is he here?"

"No. He took off for the day." Liam still worried how much alcohol Burr had drank after he left and how much he had hidden in his car.

In the living room, Liam tried to see the progress through Shea's eyes. The floors gleamed, and though they hadn't washed the windows yet, light poured into the kitchen on the lagoon side of the house, and even brightened up this room, with its view of Puget Sound.

"We need to talk fireplace tiles soon. Your countertops are due this week for the bathrooms and kitchen."

"Ooh, it looks so good in here!" Her excitement over Liam's progress as she wandered around did something funny to Liam's chest. Maybe his aunt wasn't crazy. "I can tell you've been working hard." She faced him, met his eyes. "Thank you. This means a lot to me." Something zinged between them that Liam couldn't—wouldn't—name.

"My pleasure." His voice cracked. Shoot. *Settle down, Barrett.*

He showed her the bathrooms, which had fixtures but no paint, countertops, or tile flooring.

"This is great. Let's do sky blue walls—like your eyes. It'll complement the seafoam green countertop and backsplash." She turned to him.

He went still. "Come again?"

She shook her head. "I just meant . . . sorry. Forget it."

Shea stepped back into the living room, and he followed her. What was that? Had she meant she wanted rooms painted in his eye color? Since when had she noticed his eyes? And why did her mentioning it hit him square in the chest?

"I'm sure we can find a similar color." He let her off the hook and then gestured to the fireplace. "Let me show you these tiles. When I was looking at them again, it occurred to me that they might be a bit too dark for your taste."

A box waited unopened next to the gas fireplace. Liam pulled out one of the twelve-inch-square tiles. Their fingers touched, and she caught her breath. Maybe he wasn't as dense as his aunt thought, because he was picking up on signals today. Again and again.

Once she held the tile, he put space between them and approached the wall. "Those will serve as both a fireplace surround and as a false hearth on the floor." He pointed as he talked.

She seemed unsettled but determined to focus as she gave her full attention to the brown tile. "Oh, no, no, no." She turned the square into the light, tilting it this way and that. "These are far too dark. You were right. Let me guess—Dad's choice?"

He nodded. "They were a good match for the hardwoods, before you chose to go lighter." The floors were a gray-wash, which would look great with cooler colors, but not with warmer dark-mahogany tones like the marble her dad picked out.

She stood close again, and she smelled good. Her sunglasses held her hair back and when she looked up at him, nothing got in the way of his view into her golden eyes. Why did he have to keep noticing things like that? She was talking about decor, and he tuned in again.

". . . I'd much prefer something lighter, maybe white with striations of blue. Or, what about glass mosaic tiles in blues, greens, whites, possibly grays? That would be perfect. Especially with a white wooden surround." She tugged her phone out of her bag and typed in something, then waited. Soon, she had a photo to show Liam. "Like this."

The photo showed mosaic glass tiles in the colors she'd described and a white glossy wooden surround and mantel. The same tiles served as the hearth. "We may be able to find that locally, but we'll probably need to order it. Maybe take a couple of weeks."

She sighed. "Another delay. But I couldn't live with that." She pointed at the box of brown tiles.

Her disappointment prompted him to make promises. "How about we head to the local home-improvement store and see if we can find any you like? We can make it an evening of errands. They're open late, and we can drop off your giveaways while we're out. Sound good?"

Hope returned to her eyes. "Yes." Her stomach growled. "But first, perhaps dinner next door."

He chuckled and followed her out of the cottage.

If Liam gave himself permission to just be her friend—no expectations, no flirting, he could relax. He'd simply have to ignore her signals and how attracted he was to her.

Oh, and he'd have to convince Auntie Mat that her so-called School of Romance was a waste of time.

What is wrong with me? Thoughts tumbled in Shea's mind. She'd compared her wall color to Liam's eyes! He walked behind her now, closing up her cottage on their way to dinner at Miss Matilda's.

She'd been going through the motions so far this summer— commuting to work and staying focused on the future. Meeting her obligations. Keeping herself from unpredictable situations. Thankfully she hadn't been triggered lately.

And she was determined not to date, not to let Liam's nearness affect her. Then, she'd gone and invented a paint sample of his eye color.

He held the door open to Miss Matilda's kitchen and the aroma of fresh-baked chocolate chip cookies wrapped her in a homey feeling. She'd be able to create that next door soon. She passed Liam on her way into the house. He smelled of sawdust and sunscreen. Electricity zinged between them, and a part of her—probably the one that was tired of repressing so many things—didn't want to deny it.

She called for Calliope, who scampered in, glad to see her. They'd really bonded. Away from the table now, Shea scooped up the dog and snuggled her. Then, Shea glanced over to make eye contact with Liam. He let the screen door thump shut, and his sky-blue gaze snapped to hers as if magnetized.

Yeah, that color would work perfectly for her walls. In fact, she may want her master bedroom in this shade. It was restful. Peaceful. But right now, there was a challenge in his eyes. And questions. She could swim in that gaze. Unable to resist, she let herself fall in and smile.

"And how is the cottage comin' along?" Miss Matilda asked as she buzzed around the room.

Liam shook his head and broke their connection before striding to the sink to wash up.

"Your nephew is a hard worker," Shea said, finding her voice. "Especially since he's on his own, and Burr is hit or miss. The place looks good." She may be able to move in soon, except now the tiles could delay things. That wasn't Liam's fault.

At the counter, he turned, drying his hands on a towel, letting his focus come back to where she stood nuzzling Calliope.

"Did you hear that, Son? Our lovely neighbor has paid you a compliment."

His grin curled Shea's toes, and she didn't mind. Yeah, all that repressing of her mental issues and triggers had exhausted the part of her self-control that cared about not letting on that Liam's maturity, his commitment to see this through, to make a good impression on her dad, and his heroic traits all made him even more attractive to her—as if his black hair and blue eyes weren't enough.

"What do we say?"

Shea chuckled at Miss Mat's prompting of Liam, as if he were five years old. Playing along, Shea raised her eyebrows at Liam and waited.

"Thank you, Shea." His voice came out intimate, especially paired with that grin.

Miss Matilda nodded at him. "Good boy."

Shea half-forced a laugh, and Liam's neck went red as he busied himself with glasses of lemonade for dinner. She could use a drink.

She didn't want to send him mixed messages, but she was weary of working so hard to push everything down. So, they'd run their errands tonight and shop for tiles, and she'd relax. Not hold so tightly to this area of her life.

And his aunt Matilda? Shea was already in love with her.

When Liam dropped Shea off that night, he came in for a second to say good night to his aunt. She seemed to be waiting up for him, and after Shea went upstairs, she coaxed him into the living room with her. "So . . . how's it going?" She kept her voice low.

He settled onto the sofa adjacent to her favorite wingback chair and crossed an ankle over his other thigh. "We found the tiles she prefers for her fireplace, so she'll have the look she wants without the delay of ordering them. And we dropped off her boxes of stuff."

"How does it feel to help her?"

He gave his aunt an I-know-you're-up-to-something face. "Good . . ."

"Great! Let's move on to step number four." She held up four fingers.

He sighed. Why hadn't he just left for the night and asked Shea to give his love to his aunt? Thinking of Shea and love in the same sentence, he swallowed. They'd continued their nonverbal flirting all evening, though he wasn't going out of his way. Really, it was all Shea. She wasn't overt, but she definitely seemed... different toward him, if he could even entertain such a thought. And her gratitude for all his efforts—her eyes lit up, she'd squeezed his forearm after the last box landed with a thump at the thrift store's donation stand. Yeah, that didn't get to him at all. Not that he'd tell his aunt any of this.

"Lesson number four: discern her love language—you know what that means, right?"

He barely kept from rolling his eyes. "Of course."

"And learn to speak it."

Peering toward the quiet stairs for a moment, he shook his foot up and down and pressed his jaw together. "Seriously? Listen, Auntie Mat, I love you. I get what you're trying to do, but I do not want to toy with her."

"You aren't interested in her?"

After noticing her hair, eyes, scent, laugh, heart—she'd oohed and aahed over a teacup Yorkie in the next cart at the home-improvement store—he'd be lying if he said he wasn't interested. She'd changed since college. Matured. Unless she was startled, she seemed calmer than back in school. Even maternal. That was a crazy thing to notice, he knew, but that part of her—reaching out with a gentle touch and delighting in the pup—gripped his attention, and maybe his heart, if he was honest.

He zeroed back in on his mischievous aunt. "You're not going to let this go, are you?"

She pressed her lips together and shook her head side to side. "I can't believe it took me this long to realize I had failed you in this area."

He chuckled at how absurd that sounded. "You have not failed me."

Her expression went sober. "Something else is going on here."

He planted both feet on the floor and prepared to stand, but when she spoke again, he shifted to rest his forearms on his thighs and leaned toward the coffee table, ready for a quick escape, but respecting her enough to stay and hear her out.

"You don't think you're worthy of her."

A lump filled his throat. She'd caught him.

"You know her parents think you're a good match, right?"

A good match? Seriously? "What is this, the dark ages? You and the Browns have an arrangement between you?"

She shook her head and leaned toward him. "Listen, Son. I'm saying if they think you're good enough, and she's their princess, then perhaps anyone who thinks differently doesn't see what they see."

He scoffed. "I'm sure they *see* how messed up I am." He pointed toward the cottage next door and tried not to raise his voice.

"You think one failure disqualifies you?" She *tsked*.

An uncomfortable thought flitted in like a hornet and tried to land. "You put them up to this, didn't you? Like with my job."

"Aw, Liam." Sadness glistened in her eyes. "You really can't see it."

Her sincerity made his throat burn, though he couldn't say why.

"Yes, I put in a good word for you about the job. But all on their own they noticed something in you, something that makes you good for their daughter, in their opinion." She paused for a second, and he swallowed against that burning sensation. "I pray you discover what that is."

CHAPTER THIRTEEN

The triggers got to Shea more regularly this week. A slammed door down the hall, or a person yelling outside, and she startled.

Vanessa Stratford ran the counseling center, overseeing all the therapists in her office. Tia Hadley and Shea Brown worked mostly with children and teens, and Vanessa and the other three counselors worked with adults.

Of all the people in Shea's life, she had to impress her boss. There were plenty of psychologists vying for a job at the Stratford Counseling Offices. Shea had seen Vanessa fire counselors before, often without giving an explanation to the rest of the company's therapists. In Shea's experience, her boss was fair, but neither could she let anything risk the well-being of the clinic's patients. And Shea couldn't blame her.

"Lunch today, Shea?" Tia met her in the hall between clients at almost ten. Each of them had clients on the hour, for forty-five or fifty minutes. Then a break again before the top of the next hour.

Shea had been in her late teens when she'd met Tia at Fay Bainbridge Park during that summer before Shea started college. The Browns had come to their cottage to spend July and August, as they'd often done during the sunny season as the kids grew up. That summer, JP had already been gone, out on his own since he was six years older than Shea. His schedule didn't allow him to be there both months, but he did visit for a couple of weekends. And Jewel-Kate, their sister who was smack dab between them in age, was off studying in France. Shea had been jealous, and she'd hoped to study abroad, but it had never worked out for her.

Barclay Spit jutted out toward the west from where Fay Bainbridge Park occupied a northern spot on the island. The park was walking distance, but since the Browns' cottage was near the farthest end, the stroll could be intimidating in the wrong shoes. Couple that with how narrow the road was, and Mom and Dad hadn't wanted the kids to head down there often, until they were much older.

One afternoon, as an eighteen-year-old, Shea decided to walk to the park. Her parents had told her she could choose a location for her own study abroad, so she'd gone strolling and dreaming. Where would she go if she could?

She hadn't known then that fear and PTSD would keep her home when the chance finally came for her turn to travel.

Along the way, she caught glimpses of water views on both sides of the narrow spit. Her legs were tiring by the time she reached the curve in the road that led up the hill, toward the rest of the island. But there, across that same road, was a wooden fence with a gap for pedestrians to enter the park's property.

Soon, she was crossing the large parking lot, with an expansive view of the Sound and the mountains beyond the water to her left. Few cars dotted the pavement that day, yet there were plenty of campers in the sites to the right. She was headed for the pathway that led out to the beach when she glanced toward the playground. That same teenager she'd seen earlier in the summer slumped in the tire swing, head bowed, shoulders hunched like life simply weighed too much. As with earlier times when Shea had seen her, she felt a nudge to talk with her. Until that day, she hadn't complied. But for some reason, that day twelve years ago, she did.

She approached the tire swing. "Hi." There weren't any other swings, or she'd have sat nearby. Instead, she pretended there was something interesting in the sandy gravel at their feet.

The girl didn't even look up.

Shea pointed toward Point Moore Drive. "I live down there, during the summers. I keep seeing you here. We might be close to the same age."

That got the girl's attention, and finally, she turned heavily made-up eyes Shea's way. "Hey." Shea read depression in the girl's dark makeup and drab clothes.

She would try to keep things light. "I'm Jenna-Shea."

The other girl just grunted as if she didn't want to speak.

Shea stayed near the left post of the structure that held up the swing. She faced the water, trying to be nonthreatening to the other girl. From here, she saw more grasses and driftwood than water, especially up close. JP was due at the cottage for the weekend, and she could only hope he wouldn't bring the rowdies over. "My brother's coming today, so I decided to find someplace quiet. Ugh. Brothers!"

Gaze toward the ground, the younger teen pointed at herself. "I *wish* I had a brother."

"Yeah?"

"I'm Tia, by the way," she said, barely moving her swing.

"You can have mine."

This earned a snort from Tia.

Shea let their conversation go silent, shifting sand with the toe of her sandal so Tia would know she could talk to her.

Tia finally stirred. "My family's moving. Again." Such a bitter note in her voice.

Shea turned back to her from studying the families playing on the massive driftwood logs several yards away. The sun shone, all sparkly on Puget Sound, but the tide was way out, letting families play quite a distance from the park in the cool breeze of summer at the Sound. Not a whole lot of people splashed in the waves, that she could see from here, though some souls braved the cold water.

"Military family?"

"Yeah. One summer here on this island, then off to somewhere else." She paused. "Story of my life," she muttered.

"Leaving friends behind?"

"Mm-mmm. And my sister is off to college, so—ha!—I'm on my own now with dear old dad."

"Your mom's in the Navy?"

"Yup."

Shea thought of Jewel-Kate, her older sister. "My sister is studying in France right now. I miss her. What's your dad do?"

"My dad gets to start over in every new city, like me and Sloane—my sister—finding any odd jobs he can. No one wants to hire someone who can't commit to working there long-term." She finally tipped her face up, and the sun hit her caramel skin, painting her amber. Tia was beautiful.

"Okay, let's dream for a second. When everything is outside of my control, I use my imagination and come up with my perfect world." Warm sun shown on Shea's closed eyes. "What's your perfect world?"

"To be settled somewhere—for as long as I want. To have roots in a place and do what I love. Without anyone telling me I have to leave it all and move."

"I want that too." Shea peered down at her again.

Tia eyed her, something sincere in her expression. "What's your dream job?"

Shea shrugged. "I like helping people. So maybe a teacher or something." She wouldn't confess she'd always wanted to be a counselor. That might scare Tia off. "What about you?"

"Art. Maybe a tattoo artist? I don't know. But I also love kids. Maybe I can work with them one day. Especially military families. Help all the kids who keep having to move every other year. Like me."

"So, live for that day. Consider today, and the next move, a mile marker until you get to the life you're dreaming about." Shea smiled at her. "One day, you'll make it."

Tia sighed. "I do feel like I'm only marking time . . ."

"But it's valuable. And what you want to do—help kids—that's valuable too. Noble, even. You could make a difference."

"That's what Mom always says." She swallowed, eyes downcast again. "I don't have anything to give."

"Yeah, you do. You're strong. You've learned how to survive life in a military family. *That* is what you can offer. Advice. Help. Hope." She gestured toward the swing. "Want help getting this to spin?"

"Sure."

Shea grabbed the chains and worked the swing around, faster and faster. "You're a good listener, Jenna-Shea." Tia squealed as she spun on the tire. "And I'm never gonna forget this conversation."

That same Tia had grown up, gotten a degree in psychology, and moved back to Bremerton with her husband and two-year-old daughter, Princess, whom they called Cessy. She had gorgeous caramel skin like her parents and the brightest green eyes, like her mom. Now Tia worked with military families, helping kids in transition. And she was good at it.

Shea and Tia settled at the long breakroom table with their sack lunches and bottled water. The breakroom looked out over the parking lot and busy street. Normally, the blinds were slanted closed for the sake of patient confidentiality as clients passed by here in the hallway, but today they were angled to give a clear view of the bright July day. Shea didn't mind. She loved sunshine.

"How's it going?"

Tia finished eating a bite of her egg salad sandwich. "Okay. You know how it is. Some of their stories crack your heart open. But then you get a glimpse of someone's breakthrough, and it keeps you going."

Shea was already nodding. Tia worked with older kids, teens mostly. But the dynamic was the same. "Plans for this weekend?" She crunched on a carrot stick.

"Thought we'd drive up and see you at the cottage. You know, kayak and paddleboard and wade in the water—lagoon side, of course. Much calmer than the Sound."

Sometimes the lagoon was smooth as glass while Puget Sound threw waves at the beach on the other side of the road.

"Great idea, except my house isn't ready yet."

"What? I thought . . ."

Shea made a face. "I know. It's been almost three weeks. Liam's getting there, and Tia he's so committed. It's like he's trying to impress me, or his aunt, or my parents. It's kinda cute."

"Interesting."

"Now, don't read into that. Anyway, I'm living at his aunt's house, for goodness' sake."

Tia put down her sandwich. "You used to crush on him."

She waved off her friend's words as if they were pesky flies. "Yeah, yeah. In another life."

"It's still funny, by the way, that you won't even say what's-his-name's name." She referred to Shea's old boyfriend.

"He doesn't deserve it."

"True. He didn't have what it took to make a commitment. No strength of character. That's what you need. Like my husband. But I'm not afraid to say his name—Brooks."

Shea had a flash of Tia as a lost teen. "I'm glad you found each other and have a beautiful family now. I am. But that doesn't mean I'm ready to settle down."

"Oh, you've been ready. You just don't know with whom." She finished her sandwich and started on her apple. "What if it's Liam?"

"Now you sound like my parents—"

A horrific screech filled the air, and Shea's eyes flashed to the street outside where a car slammed into another, sending it over the curb and into the clinic's parking lot. She jumped out of her seat and pressed her back against the wall, her heart pounding as the car came to rest a few yards away from the building.

"Wow. We better call 911." Tia glanced over. "You okay?" A pause. "Shea? Shea, you're white as a sheet!"

But she couldn't answer. Her mind flashed to the worst-case scenarios. Her limbs shook, and her eyes wouldn't blink as terror gripped her. *Shake it off. Come back!* But fear held on to her.

Tia was right there. "Shea, listen to me. You're safe. Look at me."

Shea couldn't turn her head. All she could do was study the scene of the accident outside. People gathered, sirens blared. A few of the clinic's staff rushed outside. But Shea couldn't move.

Tia took hold of Shea's face. "Shea. Look at me; it's Tia."

Her eyes darted over to Tia's face but didn't stay. Tia took her hands and gripped first the left, then the right, over and over. "Come back, Shea. You're safe. You're perfectly safe. It's over."

Shea blinked, several times. Her thoughts cleared, little by little. Tia's pressure on each of her hands registered in her mind, stimulated both sides of her brain, and Shea swallowed. "I'm okay. I'm okay."

"Yes. You're okay." Tia studied her. "Your pupils are less dilated."

The door burst open, and Vanessa shot in. "Everyone okay in here?" She glanced at them and then at the large window where several people gathered around the wreck now. Then her gaze came back to Shea and Tia. "What's going on? Shea, you're very pale. What's happened?"

Tia kept up the pressure to each hand in turn. "She was startled. That's all."

"Let me have a look." Vanessa was very tall, especially in her heels. She walked over in her business suit and peered down at Shea. Tia let go and moved away. "Mydriasis. Pale skin. Dissociation. Tia's using bilateral stimulation—EMDR. You've been triggered."

Oh no.

Her expression softened from assessment phase to concern. "Why didn't you tell me you were suffering from PTSD?"

Shea feared two things in her life. The first was a repeat of that violent night at the minimart where she'd witnessed the attack. The second was her boss ever finding out she was a broken therapist.

Today one of her worst fears had come true.

CHAPTER FOURTEEN

Liam heard the cottage's side door close and glanced over to see his aunt step into the Brown's kitchen. Ah, she was here to harass—*ahem*, visit—him while he worked on installing the fireplace tiles. The colors were certainly beachy. Hopefully, Shea would love it. He'd finished the hearth and was beginning on the bottom of the right "leg," of the fireplace, facing the unit.

"Any ideas on her love language yet, Son?" Auntie Mat's day off from volunteering meant she could busy-body herself into his workday.

Shea's love language. He had a few ideas. The biggest hint was how, whenever he did things for her, she would brighten. That seemed like a strong clue that her love language might be acts of service. Did he want to tell his aunt that? She'd task him to test it out and follow up with romantic moments.

"Still unsure." Shea had lit up when he'd promised she could see the mostly finished product by tonight, and he could hardly wait. In fact, he looked forward to those moments after she returned from work every evening.

For some reason, doing things for her made him feel good. He experienced satisfaction when he mowed his aunt's lawn or power washed her deck, and he was glad she was pleased. But doing things for Shea was different. Maybe his aunt was onto something with her School of Romance.

Not that he'd ever tell her that.

He needed to change the subject. "I got a message from Jack the other day."

"You did? What'd he say?"

Using a trowel, Liam spread adhesive onto the cement board at an angle. Maybe this topic wasn't better than discussing Shea. But who else could he talk to about Jack? Jinx didn't relate. Eli had, it seemed, only one position—open the gateway and let Jack in! Sure.

Not a problem. "He wants to meet up with me. Which is exactly where I thought this was headed." He tacked the tile sheet onto the wall and grabbed his grout float to press it into place.

Auntie Mat stood nearby but didn't touch anything. She seemed out of place here, as dressy as she looked. "You're right. That's not surprising. He probably has a few things to say to you."

"I'm not meeting him. You and Eli strong-armed me into accepting the request, which I've regretted since." Though if Liam had to guess, God Himself agreed with his aunt and father-figure.

"Hey, I never pressured you."

"Ach. You're like my conscience." He let a smile soften his words. "I can't hide either my anger or my motives from you."

She crossed her arms over her chest. "Good. That's worked in my favor all these years."

He couldn't be angry at her and just laughed off her words. The sheet of mosaic tiles in place, he ran his rinsed sponge over the top to clean them until they shined.

"That is looking good. Great colors. Shea will love it." She clapped her hands as if this was part of her master plan.

He glanced at the blue, green, gray, and clear uniform rectangular tiles that made up each sheet. "Shea loves these colors."

"She has good taste. And the fact you're the one doing this for her? All the better."

Don't take the bait. "She likes seafoam and periwinkle, with white as an accent color. She's doing most of the rooms in those colors." She'd schooled him on their proper names.

"Well, if you don't know her love language, then figure out what she likes to do and do it."

Liam sighed. "I'm working as hard as I can." Nowhere in his aunt's School of Romance did she ever mention whether Liam, or Shea, for that matter, had a choice. Or that Shea might reciprocate. Plus, this couldn't go anywhere. He needed to set his aunt straight, but she'd left the room. "Auntie Mat?"

"In the kitchen," she called. "I'm digging around for cold water. You look like you could use a glass."

She brought him a bottled water from the fridge. "This'll help."

He unscrewed the top and took a few long swigs. Exactly what he needed. "Thanks."

"So, what do you want to do about Jack?"

"Ignore him?"

"You know, Shea's a therapist. She might have advice." Auntie Mat opened her own water bottle and downed a few sips, then tipped the bottle in his direction. "Hope you don't mind I grabbed one for myself."

"Not a bit. But, I think it'd be bad form to invite Shea into my past and have her swim around in there."

"Does she know about your—Jack?"

Once again, he appreciated she didn't call Jack his dad. "I don't think so."

"Well, one way to build intimacy is to share your heart with her."

He stood from his crouched position next to the fireplace. He only had a minute because his adhesive was drying as they spoke. "I don't think you understand—"

"Oops, I hear Calliope. I'd better go see what she's doing. Probably playing in the Sound for all I know." She trotted toward the door, and Liam shook his head.

"I'll see you later."

Intimacy? Right. He'd get right on that. Love language, no problem. And Shea's interests? He lifted another sheet of mosaic tiles. Apparently, she had a thing for seaside cottages dressed in their beachy best.

He dropped back into a crouch to resume his work. She'd be home in a few hours, and he wanted these tiles all in place. If he finished here, he'd tackle the kitchen. She was using a larger subway tile in there, still seafoam, as a backsplash. Not necessarily masculine like he'd prefer. But she did have an eye for beauty.

An hour later, the cottage's front door opened and Shea snuck in. He jolted. She wasn't due home until evening. Why was she here at two in the afternoon? "Hey," he said, deciding not to ask too many questions. He was the guest here, after all.

"Oh, hey Liam." Her voice sounded odd—nasally. Scratchy. "I

was hoping . . ." She gave a shuddering sigh, and that's when he saw the tears. He dropped his sponge into the bucket of murky water and stood, on alert.

"What happened?" He walked a little closer, carefully, as if she were a doe in the yard and he might frighten her off.

She shook her head, swallowed hard a few times. "I only need a private space."

"Um . . . nothing's very comfortable in here right now." He scrambled. If only her bedroom were finished. "I can clear out, though, if you want."

"No, no." She finally glanced around. "The fireplace looks great. I don't want to interrupt. It's just, I saw your aunt's car. I know she's off today from the theater."

Liam understood. Bless his aunt's heart, but she was very inquisitive, and a sorrowful Shea would bring out all of Auntie Mat's one million questions. "How can I help?" He wanted to ask her what had happened but didn't feel it was his place to ask or how she'd respond. "Have you eaten? We could go to Madison Diner, get a burger. Sit outside. We don't have to talk, if you'd rather not." He didn't want to leave her alone, but he'd respect her choice if she'd prefer he not tag along.

Madison Diner was a converted 1950's train car that'd been trucked in from Pennsylvania several decades back. It was a local favorite, and a well-known, food-related network TV star had visited in 2007, giving the place his seal of approval.

She studied Liam as if considering his proposal. "You know what? That sounds good. I could use a friend to talk to."

Something about her needing him accessed that same place that helping her did, and made him want to lean toward her, offer her the world. "I'll clean up a bit, and we can head out." He'd put in more hours tonight after they got back. No problem. The adhesive was dry by now, anyway.

"Don't worry about all that still needs to happen here. I suddenly have"—she took a shaky breath—"time on my hands." She crossed her arms over her chest. Was she hugging herself or protecting herself? "I can get started on the painting later."

Giving her a minute, he carried the bucket of dirty water to the kitchen and returned. "Shea?"

She swayed back and forth on her feet as if rocking soothed her. A cloud had settled over her.

He stepped closer. What would his aunt say to do right now? Wait. He only needed to trust his instincts. He put a hand on her shoulder, squeezed lightly. When she didn't cringe or pull away, he tried to make eye contact. Her eyes were red.

"What happened?"

She gave a deep sigh. "I blew it."

He tipped his head. "Blew what?"

"My job. My career. My life." She spun and headed out toward her car, and he grabbed his keys and darted after her. No way should she drive right now. He'd volunteer to take her, even if they had to drive her tiny econo-car. But she beelined to his truck.

And he'd listen. Scrap his aunt's School of Romance. He would be a friend, which she obviously needed. No reason to notice how light her eyes were when she was sad or the way her hair glowed in the sunlight over her tan arms in that sleeveless burgundy top. And those strappy sandals? She wore a different pair nearly every day, and he loved every single set.

All he had to do was listen and keep himself from falling for her.

CHAPTER FIFTEEN

Losing her job made logical sense to Shea. Then, she reminded herself that her worst fear had come true, and she faded out of the present again.

Liam gave her space on the drive to Madison Diner, but maybe she'd ask him to keep her talking. That way, she could stop dissociating. Her fears were coming true. What was next?

No. She wouldn't think about that night. It hadn't happened to her, but for all her PTSD symptoms, one would never know. Tia had talked with her, outside of their counseling offices, a few times about it. She'd assured Shea that she wasn't crazy. That lots of people would have had a hard time processing what happened.

Today's car accident replayed in Shea's mind, and she gasped, suddenly wanting to be anywhere but inside a moving vehicle.

"You okay?" Liam focused on pulling into the lot, then found them a parking stall.

"Better now." She got her breathing back under control. Yeah, she was a nutcase. Vanessa was right to let her go. She'd be no good to her patients until she could find relief for her own mental illness.

Even though she worked in the field of psychology, knew the value of getting help, knew labels for psychiatric illnesses and could diagnose patients, she hated the stigma attached to that phrase: mental illness, especially when it was aimed at her.

"Let's see if we can distract you, okay?" Liam escorted Shea directly to the outside seating under the awning. A breeze blew through this alley, between the end of the old train car and the hedges bordering the property, while Liam pulled out a chair for her. "I'm going inside to let them know we're out here, okay?"

She sat and tugged her chair up to the table.

"You all right?"

"I will be." She had to hold on to that hope, because what else did she have? Yet, now, she had a hard time remembering her own name or where she lived.

"I'll be right back." He strode toward the side entrance and stepped inside. She began counting seconds until his return as a means of grounding herself in the present. In just over two minutes, he reappeared with a pitcher of ice water and two plastic cups. The server followed him. Shea blinked at them, feeling disconnected. *Lord, help me. Please.*

Another light breeze stirred the overhead leaves, and Shea breathed deeply, trying to engage her vagus nerve. She may need to use every tool in her box in order to land on reality.

At the table, Liam poured them glasses of water, starting with Shea, which he handed to her and encouraged her to drink. The water soothed her throat, and Shea focused on the sensation.

At the edge of her awareness, she heard Liam order a Coke. Then the server left them in quiet. Shea stared up at leaves reflected in the awning overhead—maple, green, rustling in the wind.

"What do you like to eat here?"

She squinted at him, making eye contact for the first time since they'd sat down. The server stood there as if she'd reappeared from thin air.

When Shea didn't answer, he continued. "I always get the mushroom and swiss burger."

The server scribbled on her notepad.

Shea's stomach rumbled, prompting her answer. "BLT. Fries." She shook her head and focused on him as the server walked away. He had the purest gaze. "Thanks for this, Liam."

"Of course. Please tell me how to help." His tone suggested he'd do anything for her.

If Shea couldn't keep a handle on reality, she might have Tia give Liam and his aunt a call. Maybe it was a good thing she wasn't living alone right now. Her PTSD hadn't been this debilitating since it first set in.

Shea reached for his hand on the table and took hold. He startled and made eye contact. "Thank you," she said again, feeling her smile shake. "This is very kind. And it's exactly what I needed."

He threaded his fingers through hers as if it were the most natural gesture. "Of course. What are friends for?" He gave her a minute before asking his next question. "You wanna tell me what happened?"

She bit her lip, but no words came out. Then she squinted at him. "I'm on an unpaid leave from work, effective immediately." She kept her voice low and glanced around. No sign of anyone she knew.

"Unpaid leave, meaning . . . ?"

"My boss saw what you saw and now, exactly as I'd guessed would happen, she's let me go. Temporarily, or until I'm not a nutcase anymore."

He squeezed her hand. "You are not a nutcase. And what do you mean, 'saw what I saw'?"

"Me. Startled. Triggered."

"Triggered?"

"You know, how I react when I'm frightened. Sort of recede into another place and time." She gripped her water cup and downed another few gulps. He used his free hand to fill the plastic cup when she set it down, but he didn't let go of her hand.

"I knew this would happen if she ever saw me like that. I knew it." Her mind replayed today's events that had kicked this off. To keep herself planted in the present, she focused on where her thumb stroked Liam's hand. His gaze darted to the contact and then back to her eyes, and there was an instantaneous and minuscule tightening in his hand, like a flinching muscle. His gaze was tender, so she took that to mean he didn't mind.

"There was a car accident at work." She fixed her attention on his fingers, his rough skin. "A car swerved, skidded over the curb, and slid to a stop in the clinic's parking lot, smashing into a few cars along the way."

"Were you hurt?"

The fear in his voice brought her attention to his face. He scanned her.

"No. Just . . . alarmed. My coworker, Tia, and I were in the breakroom for lunch. We saw it all happen."

"Where's Tia now?"

She waved her free hand. "Still at work. I flipped out, and that's when my boss came into the room." She shook her head. "I knew this would happen. I knew it." She was repeating herself.

Their meals arrived, and Shea reluctantly let go of his hand. The crisp bacon and sweet tomato prompted her to eat faster than she normally would, especially when out in public. The crisp, salty fries vanished almost as quickly as her BLT did. Liam was half finished with his mushroom-swiss burger as Shea pushed her plate away. She felt better able to control her thoughts. Finally. Maybe it was the timing—it'd been a few hours now. Or maybe it was the fact her stomach demanded her body's resources and sent nourishment to her brain. Either way, she thanked God for some lucidity.

"I owe your aunt so much."

He blinked as if confused by her sudden conversation shift. "For what?"

"For letting me stay with her. Especially now that I'm without a job. I'm a mess."

"Whether you're gone all day at work, or not, she's happy to have you. And I'm glad you're there, keeping an eye on her. She's not as young as she'd like to think. Left to herself, she'd be out on a twelve-foot ladder painting the house, or up on the roof with a power washer, hosing off debris."

She pictured his seventy-something aunt out doing those things and laughed. "I believe it. Still, I owe her. Can you think of anything I can do to repay her?"

"I'll think about that, Shea. But I'm sure she'd say you don't owe her anything."

She spun her sweating cup around on the vinyl tablecloth. "This really helped. Thank you."

The corners of his eyes crinkled. "My pleasure."

Her mind felt clearer, which prompted an idea. What if she and Liam gave his aunt what she wanted? Matilda was always hinting that she'd like to see Liam settle down—how good that would be for her heart. Sitting here across from this version of Liam, the suggestion didn't seem too far-fetched, though he'd probably never agree to playacting. Plus, she didn't want to confuse their friendship. There was no way she'd get into a *real* relationship right now. She was too sick. This was the time to work on herself. She shook her head. Nah, she wouldn't even pitch her idea and add more confusion to her muddled mind. Maybe she wasn't thinking as clearly after all.

"What are you considering?"

She met his eyes and recalled the feel of his warm, calloused hand in hers from before lunch, how he'd come to her rescue today as soon as she'd gotten home.

He leaned in. "I don't mind brainstorming ideas."

Well, he asked for it. "I do have one, but it'd involve you and I'm not sure you'd go for it." Or that it was wise.

He finished his last fry and pushed his plate away. "What?"

"She's always talking about wanting to see you settled down."

He rolled his eyes. "Tell me she has *not* brought that up with you."

"Says she wants to see you settled. After all, and I already knew this but, you are thirty-three. Gasp." She grinned with that number. As a kid, she'd been unhappy with their three-year age difference; now it was something she could tease him about.

His grin curled her toes again. "I know your age too, but I wouldn't, gasp, say it in public."

She squinted at him but didn't try to hide her smile. Spending time with him had turned out to be more than a good distraction. She wasn't sure why, but she felt encouraged. Either way, maybe this idea could work. "I think it'd do her good to see you in a caring relationship. She carries a heavy burden for you. I hope you don't mind my saying that."

"She does? I mean, I could believe that when I was a kid, and a teen, but now? I'm making something of my life. I'm living independently. She raised me well."

"I'm sure she'd agree with you, that she raised you well. You're a good man, Liam." She paused, letting those words swirl between them. Something about his expression said he didn't quite believe her. "Miss Matilda has mentioned to me a couple of times that she hates how lonely you are."

"Seriously?" He cringed.

Oops, she'd pushed a button. "And that you've smiled a lot more since you've been working on the cottage."

"It's enjoyable work. I will finish soon, I promise."

"And since I've been around." Her face went warm, and he looked away while fighting a grin. "See? That's what she's talking about."

He grunted. "So," he said, meeting her eyes again. "This is what you two do, sit around the breakfast table at six in the morning chatting about me?"

All she could do was shrug. The man was right. "A bit."

"Tell me she hasn't talked you into anything."

"She mentioned your love language."

He groaned.

"Words of affirmation."

He jiggled his leg, which made the table tremble, and studied something behind her. Did he pick up that she'd used words of affirmation a couple of minutes ago, in this conversation? His attention shot back to her face. She gazed at him without looking away. Electricity snapped between them while thoughts zipped through her mind.

He took a breath. "I know I'm going to regret this, but what are you suggesting?"

She swallowed, again unsure. "Do you wanna date?"

CHAPTER SIXTEEN

Liam was going to kill his aunt. Well, okay, not harm, exactly, but sternly lecture. What was she thinking?

Shea hadn't waited long for his answer, especially when he didn't—couldn't. Instead, after a minute or two, she'd pointed toward his truck with a question in her eyes. She didn't have her purse, so she'd promised to pay him back her portion of the bill. But he'd taken care of it, while debating how he was going to respond. Did she still expect him to?

She couldn't be serious. Date? Him? Auntie Mat *had* gotten into her head. Exactly like she'd gotten into his. Nutty, but lovable old lady.

Except, if they went home and announced they were dating, Auntie Mat might finally lay off pressuring him *and* Shea, as it turned out, to get together. She'd probably let it go, let their relationship play out. In a short while, when they "broke up," because they would, she'd have to relent. Right?

At the truck, Shea stopped near the driver's side door. He'd forgotten, until recently, how gorgeous she was.

She peered up at him with those golden-brown eyes. "You don't have to go along with it. I didn't mean to make you uncomfortable." Head down, she walked to her side of the truck. Shoot. Had she taken his lack of agreement as rejection? If he wasn't such a screw-up, he'd have said yes before she could have asked the whole question. *Would you like to—? Yes! Anything you ask, the answer's yes!*

He scurried to her side of the truck and used his key to unlock the door, which he opened to let her in. This truck was the base model, and it was old with manually operated everything—windows, locks, the works. Like his life, he wished he could offer her something better. She climbed in with a thanks and he closed the door, taking his time to cross back around, so he could think about his options.

Did he want to hurt her feelings? Nope.

Did he want to encourage his batty great-aunt? Not one bit.

Did he want to lie to his aunt? He tried to never do that.

How about confuse himself or Shea? No thanks. That was the type of thing a deadbeat did. Not someone who was trying so hard to be an honorable man.

He climbed into the truck and put it in Reverse. Out on Madison Avenue, he glanced at her. The road wasn't too crowded as they headed away from town. "Sorry if you felt . . . rejected." That's the last thing he wanted to do. "This isn't about you. Auntie Mat's been pressuring me too. I don't want to hurt anyone's feelings."

"I get it." She tapped her fingers on the door's arm rest beside her, as if she couldn't wait to get out. "You don't want to date me. Message received. No problem."

That wasn't at all what he thought. Should he tell her? "The more time I spend with you, the more I like spending time with you." He held his breath after the words came out, wondering how they'd land.

She turned, and he could feel her gaze on his face. "You do?"

He drove them farther from the bustle of town, out toward highway 305, letting himself take shallow breaths. "The thing is, I can't date right now. My aunt doesn't understand timing. It's not you."

"You 'can't' date?"

"My life's a mess."

She snorted. "Mine too."

"Well, then let's be friends. I'm here for you."

"You know, we never talked about that horrible night."

Horrible? "The night I didn't show up?" He caught her nod in his peripheral vision. "For the record, I was on allergy meds then and took a nap that lasted too long. I had every intention of keeping our date. I never meant to stand you up. I wish you would've let me explain."

No response. Where had she gone? This felt like those moments under the awning at the diner. She seemed distant, as if her thoughts or memories had carried her away. He turned north onto forest-lined 305. "Earth to Shea." He kept his voice gentle. "You all right?"

She shook her head. "I was just thinking. I never told you."

His burger settled like lead in his gut. "Told me what?"

"About the attack."

Violent memories flashed across Shea's mind, and she made a fist with first one hand and then the other. *Come on back.* The last thing she needed to dwell on today was that awful night. Would she ever be able to gear up to tell the story without getting lost in it? After several moments of battling the images, she was finally able to string her thoughts together. "You know what? We'll be home in a few minutes, and I don't want to keep you from your work. Plus, I need to talk with your aunt. I hope you don't mind if we talk about this later." Or never at all.

"Well, now I'm worried about you." He pulled onto Point Moore Drive and eased down the hill. Views of Puget Sound appeared in front of them. Fay Bainbridge Park came up on the right beyond the wooden fence, while the road curved left giving them a view of the lagoon at low tide on that side. The sun shone over all the glistening beauty, but those dark images vied for her attention.

"Hold on. Could you let me out here? I could use some time at the park." Maybe God would send her an angel to talk to today, like she'd talked to Tia so long ago. How silly. She could simply talk to *Him.*

Liam stopped the truck. No other cars approached in either direction. "Sure. Want me to pick you up a little later?" He gestured toward her feet. "Those sandals might be uncomfortable for the walk back to the cottage."

"I'll be okay."

He rested his arm across the top of the bench seat. "I wish you'd talk to me."

If we were dating, I would. The thought hit her. Exactly what had possessed her to offer to date him for his aunt's sake? Obviously, she wasn't thinking straight this afternoon. "I'm sure we'll talk sometime. Good luck at the cottage this afternoon." She climbed down and slammed the door shut before stepping away. When he'd slowly driven off, she strode toward the opening in the fence and passed through onto the park grounds.

Through tree branches, the sun felt warm on her skin as she paused to take it in. *Oh, Lord, what am I going to do?* She hadn't exactly lost her job. Vanessa had probably done Shea a favor—giving her time to get treatment for her PTSD. But she'd also reminded Shea that she wasn't healed and would never heal. All her efforts hadn't helped. And events like today . . . she shuddered. That vehicle barreling toward the window, only stopped by a row of parked cars. . . Thankfully no patients had been out in the lot at that moment.

Lord, what's wrong with me? Why won't You heal me?

She listened as a breeze rustled the leaves overhead but didn't hear God answer.

She crossed the parking lot and headed down the boarded walkway toward Puget Sound and its sandy beach. Maybe she could find peace among the seashells and salty waves.

Maybe her best friend, Mikaela, was available to chat.

At the end of the boardwalk, Shea climbed over the huge driftwood logs to get to the more level sand. Then she headed away from the clusters of people. The park boasted a long beach, so she'd simply keep walking until she came to a semi-private place. A kid screamed nearby, playing tag with the incoming tide. She peeked over at the children and caught herself before she reacted. *They're just kids. No one's in danger.*

Several yards up she found a section of beach where few people lingered. Smooth, bleached white logs lying on their sides made perfect perches for beach-goers, and Shea took a seat on one. She faced the incoming waves many yards away and took a couple of deep breaths, focusing for a moment on the Cascade Range and its snowy peaks.

After snapping a few shots of the view with her phone, she opened her texting app to send a message to Mikaela up in Friday Harbor.

HEY MIKS, ARE YOU FREE?

In a few moments, her phone pinged.

JUST SAILING AROUND THE ISLANDS, HUNTING CETACEANS. WHAT'S UP? Mikaela was a marine biologist serving on her husband's whale touring vessel. Naturally, she'd use whales' scientific name.

I GOT FIRED TODAY. SORT OF.

Surprise-faced emojis followed in a long string. Then, SHOULD I CALL YOU?

NOT IF YOU DON'T HAVE PRIVACY.

WHAT HAPPENED?

MY BOSS SAW ME IN FULL PTSD MODE.

:/ SO SORRY.

AND LIAM'S AUNT WANTS US TO DATE EACH OTHER.

HA! WELL, THAT LIVENS THINGS UP. HOW'S YOUR COTTAGE COMING ALONG?

MIGHT BE ANOTHER WEEK OR TWO. That was the least of her worries, so long as Miss Mat didn't mind a freeloader. It wasn't as if she'd been paying rent. But now that she didn't have a job, she felt much less respectable. And she'd tried to pay rent, but Miss Mat wouldn't accept money.

She had to find a way to repay her kindness.

AWW, TOO BAD. MORE TIME WITH LIAM IN CLOSE PROXIMITY.

Shea knew Mikaela was being sarcastic. Since no response came to mind, she'd wait her out.

Sure enough, another ping. WITH THE BREAK FROM WORK, MAYBE GOD'S GIVING YOU A CHANCE TO GET SOME THINGS FIGURED OUT.

I DID NOT ASK FOR THE SUMMER OFF.

BUT NOW YOU CAN GET HELP. OOPS! WHALES! GOTTA RUN. YOU GOING TO BE OKAY?

SURE. THANKS, MIKS.

<3 TALK SOON. HUGS.

Shea couldn't decide if she felt better for chatting with her BFF or not. From their earlier conversations, Shea knew Mikaela supported a romance between her and Liam. Of course she did, the newlywed. Shea grinned. She couldn't hold Mikaela and Hunter's happiness against them. They'd overcome a lot to get to their HEA.

Lord, do I get a happily ever after?

Here in the privacy of her thoughts, while the sun poured over her with the salty breeze, she had a choice to make. Well, a few choices. Her boss had given her time off from work. The trick now was to find someone who could walk her through the process, someone competent in EMDR treatments. Vanessa had suggested someone named Natalie in Winslow that Shea could check into seeing.

She'd make the call. But she didn't have a lot of hope. If the previous therapists couldn't help, why should this time be different?

In truth, she wasn't in a condition to date. Miss Mat had mentioned the situation with Liam's dad. Maybe she could help him, like he'd helped her. As friends.

He'd have to make time to talk with his aunt when Shea wasn't around, but right now Liam wanted to work on the house. He found Burr's truck in the driveway and Burr at work on the living room window trim. He had much of it finished.

"Hey, you're back." Whenever Burr greeted him cheerfully, Liam knew he'd been drinking. But he didn't seem unsteady as he used the nail gun to pin the next board into place.

He inspected the progress. The white trim looked great. "Good work." What a timesaver to have Burr doing his job. "Thanks for this."

"It's what you're paying me for." He paused. "I hope." He attached the final trim piece, and then straightened from crouching. "I know I've blown it. Sorry for that. If I'd been on it, Shea could have moved in by now. I'll apologize to her when I see her."

When Burr got like this—all kind and apologetic, Liam

wondered if he should ask Burr what ate at him. Liam still owed him, though his buddy wouldn't appreciate the reminder. They'd never talked about it.

"Hey, take a break," Liam said. "Let's get cold water from the kitchen."

Liam led the way and pulled two ice-cold bottles from the back of the new fridge. He handed one to Burr who guzzled two-thirds of it at the first gulp.

He hadn't had the courage for this conversation, and still didn't think he did. But he wanted to try. "Do you remember that dive in Kauai when my O_2 tank malfunctioned?"

Burr nodded. "Of course." He didn't bristle, so Liam continued.

"Well, I never thanked you for what you did that day."

Burr shook his head and held up his hand as if he couldn't bear to hear Liam's speech. "Don't worry about it. That was a long time ago."

Maybe a year and a half or so. Not that long. "Well, thanks to you, I'm still here."

"No big deal." Burr finished his water and squirmed. He was either irritated with Liam bringing up what happened, or he was uncomfortable with whatever he had on his mind. "But there is something I wanted to say."

Relief and triumph settled inside Liam because he'd done what Jack never would. He'd thanked the guy who'd saved his life. Didn't let pride get in his way. Didn't act like a slacker or a no-account. Maybe this was how he proved he wasn't like Jack. One decision at a time, he chose the opposite of what he figured Jack would do. "Okay. What's up?"

"Matilda mentioned you might go face your da—Jack."

He groaned, though he shouldn't be surprised. His aunt was super busy lately, telling everyone about Liam's life. She needed another hobby!

Burr shifted his stance as if still uncomfortable. "I really respect that. Takes guts." He squeezed the empty water bottle in his hand, and the loud crinkling noises filled the empty house. "I couldn't do it," he scoffed almost as if mocking himself. Why would Burr relate with this part of Liam's life? What was he facing?

Thing was, Liam hadn't decided to go see Jack. In fact, he'd been pretty sure he *wasn't* going to go see him. But having Burr respect him . . . Maybe Liam could inspire Burr to face whatever it was that kept him drinking. He still owed him one. Simple gratitude didn't satisfy his debt. He had to figure out what was eating Burr, get him to talk about it so he could move forward. Whatever the secret was, it probably wasn't as powerful an enemy as Burr thought.

Huh, is that what therapists, like Shea, were trying to do?

Burr tossed his empty water bottle in the box they were using for recycling. "So, when are you going to see him?"

"We haven't set a time yet." Though Liam knew Jack would agree to just about anything, based on how desperate he sounded when he'd begged Liam to meet him.

"I think it's cool. Let me know how it goes, okay?"

Burr had never met Jack, so it seemed odd that he should care so much, or sound so impressed, or invested. But Liam wouldn't dig for information right now.

"I gotta get back to work." Burr headed toward the next box of trim pieces.

Shea showed up an hour later and worked on painting. She seemed quiet, thoughtful. All three of them labored until dinner at Auntie Mat's. Since Burr was treating Shea respectfully, Liam headed over a little early, hoping for a second to talk to his aunt.

CHAPTER SEVENTEEN

Standing in the kitchen, sneaking avocadoes from her salad, Liam yanked back his hand so Auntie Mat wouldn't smack him. Then he sobered. "I can't do it."

She gave him *the look*—the challenging, I'll-hear-you-out sort of look that reminded him of his childhood escapades.

"How do you know what he wants in this situation, Liam? What'd he say?"

"It wasn't direct or anything." Liam watched for Shea or Burr to come in from next door. Strange how Burr was acting more like himself than he had since his breakup with his last girlfriend, Seneca. What had ever happened to her?

"My dear aunt." He walked up to her and gave her a side hug. "Have you been talking to Burr and Shea about me?"

She smiled, caught, and hugged him back. "Well, Dylan did stop by for coffee. I may have mentioned you were considering meeting with Jack."

"Yeah, he told me." He pulled back far enough to shake his finger at her. "And Shea?" He drilled his great-aunt with a look.

Auntie Mat shrugged, turning from the counter with a salad bowl covered in plastic wrap. "I may have chatted with her about a certain lonely *somebody* who's thirty-three, has zero plans to settle down, and whose love language may be words of affirmation."

Liam rubbed his forehead and leaned against the counter near the sink. "Auntie Mat . . ."

She set the salad on the table and moved toward the fridge. "Have you discovered her love language yet?"

He grabbed the kitchen towel to strangle in his hands. "You are so determined about this."

At the refrigerator, she reached in and grabbed the lemonade. He abandoned the towel and took the pitcher from her and set it on the table. "Back to Jack. You should go see him."

He grunted. Never. "I don't think so."

She pressed her lips together. Of everyone, she knew what Liam had faced all these years. She'd held him as an eight-year-old who hated Father's Day. Talked him through the sports tryouts of high school. Pointed out men of integrity in their lives that Liam could emulate. She knew the size of the hole in his chest.

So it was difficult to stay angry with her. "Burr said he respected that I was considering it."

"He's a mess, isn't he?"

"Hard to say how far gone he is."

Jack's request played through Liam's mind as he brought the barbecued chicken to the table. Maybe he was approaching this from the wrong angle. This meeting could be a time for answers, *if* he had the guts to carry it out. There were plenty of things he'd like to say. So far, Liam had seen the possible get-together as one-sided. But who said it had to be only that? Or that he couldn't ask his own series of questions?

It was also possible Auntie Mat knew more about Jack than she'd let on. Before Burr and Shea arrived, Liam would see if she'd spill any more information. "Okay, if I'm going down this path, you're going to turn the streetlights on." He smiled at her, gentled his voice. "Tell me everything you know about Jack Barrett?"

She squared her shoulders. "Fair enough." She sat at the table, leaving the chicken wrapped in tinfoil until the other two arrived. The aromas of barbecue sauce, baked potatoes, and sliced muskmelon wafted toward him making his stomach rumble. "Sit, Son. This'll take a minute."

Liam joined her at the table and released a long slow breath. Like thoughts of seeing Jack, he both wanted to hear what she had to say and didn't want to hear it. She'd shared a little already, but he had the feeling he was about to learn a lot more.

"Jack and your mother met when they were in high school. They married right after graduation. Jack went to college, but he demanded Erin not go."

This wasn't news. "Mom told me. Which was why she wanted me in preschool so young, and then kept drilling into me how important earning a college degree was, even though I was a kid." A degree he'd never earned. That fact burned his gut.

"Well, he was controlling. He didn't understand respect or kindness or honor. Eventually, I think he left because he thought you and your mother would be better off without him." She paused and let that sink in.

Liam hadn't considered that possibility before. That made Jack's abandonment sound almost . . . noble. But had Liam and his mother been better off without him? What kind of creep did that make Jack, that he'd want to protect others from himself?

"What do you remember of him?" she asked Liam.

He shook his head. "I don't."

She gave one nod. "I don't blame you."

"No, I mean. I've tried to remember. I've tried to think back to being a preschooler. There's nothing there. It's blank." Everything out into the open tonight, he forged ahead. "Do you think that means he was a monster? Since I pushed all those memories away?" He kept forgetting the word for that. Shea would know. Liam held his breath. Would his aunt tell him a different story from the last time he'd asked?

"No. He wasn't. Like I said, not that I saw," she answered, and Liam exhaled. "He was just . . . incapable. I think he sincerely wanted to do the right things, but he couldn't. He didn't know what was wrong with himself. See, the thing about society back then is that everyone believed therapy was for losers, and getting mental help wasn't considered a viable option. People called psychologists, psychiatrists, shrinks. And if you went to them, especially as a man, you were considered weak. Unable to keep your stuff together. Knowing how prideful Jack was, he didn't want to be seen that way."

Liam could easily judge that pride, except was pride keeping Liam from facing Jack? That thought could humble him. Cliff diving didn't scare him. Facing Jack terrified him. "How often did you have one-on-ones with him?"

Auntie Mat's eyes held gentleness. "I didn't really, only a couple of times. A few Christmas Eves when we'd get a second in the kitchen. I always tried to check in. I cared about my niece and how her family life was. Sometimes he carried a look like his life hurt, and he didn't know where to turn. Frankly, I thought sometimes he might be clinically depressed or . . . suicidal."

This was another picture of Jack that Liam hadn't considered. He could have compassion on a depressed man, and more easily set aside his condemnation for a suicidal one.

"That's why, as soon as I could, I got *you* into counseling." She reached across the table and covered his hand with hers. "Especially after your mom passed." Her voice cracked, and Liam felt his own throat burn.

Her words explained a lot. Auntie Mat had been determined that he see a therapist when he was eleven. His mother had died of cancer, though she and Auntie Mat tried to tell young Liam everything would be fine. He could see her fading more every day. By the time she was in the hospital, he knew, deep in his chest, that Mom wouldn't be there through the next Christmas. They probably thought they were protecting him, but Liam had a fear that something bad would happen to his aunt and he'd be outside the loop. Not that he was eleven anymore.

At this moment, he didn't want to tell his aunt the sessions hadn't helped. He'd never known why. It wasn't as if he hadn't tried to cooperate. But how much had he understood about himself back then? Who could read a kid's mind?

"What age of patients does Shea treat?" Auntie Mat moved to her kitchen window and misted her indoor plants. Yeah, she didn't fool him. She got a sparkle in her eye whenever she saw Liam and Shea together. And it wasn't lost on him that whenever possible, she would leave them alone together.

He wouldn't tell his aunt Shea was on a break. "I don't know. You could ask her." Didn't matter. He sure wasn't hip to letting Shea psychoanalyze his mind. Or his heart.

CHAPTER EIGHTEEN

A moment later the front door clicked open and then closed, and Liam hoped his aunt would let the conversation drop.

"Hey, you two. I'm here." Shea appeared under the kitchen archway from the living room. "Something smells good." Paint splattered her clothes.

"Work hard over there?"

"Yes, I did. And the walls look great. Burr's on his way." She seemed to have recovered from her troubled day.

Auntie Mat poured lemonade for every place setting on the table. "Hey, Shea, when you're finished at the sink, Liam had a question for you."

"Thanks for putting me on the spot," he murmured to his aunt.

Shea turned from the sink. "What's up?"

He stepped closer. "First, how are you feeling?"

"Better, thanks." Her smile was tender and open, and he stepped a little closer. Auntie Mat busied herself on the sunporch with Calliope and Pearl. "I also told your aunt about it. She was very gracious."

He smiled. His aunt was a port in a storm, when she wasn't stirring things up.

Shea put a hand on his forearm. "Thanks for listening today."

He couldn't find his voice at first, what with the zinging sensation running up his arm where she touched him. "My pleasure."

"I wish I could do something in return for everything you and your aunt are doing for me."

He studied the gold flecks in her eyes. "Consider us friendly neighbors."

A moment later, she stretched up to hug him. No hint of distrust with this embrace. He wrapped his arms around her slim body and breathed in her floral scent, closing his eyes. Maybe he should change his decision and reconsider dating her, especially if it meant they could share more of these hugs. At the edges of his mind, the word *friend* lingered, but he didn't grab on to it.

She pulled back. "Please let me know if you ever want to talk about anything. I respect that you don't trust therapists, but I am a good listener, and I'll try not to go all Counselor Shea on you," she murmured, only for his ears.

He ducked his head and grinned, wishing for her back in his arms.

When Burr didn't arrive in the next fifteen minutes, Liam called his cell. No answer. He checked outdoors, and Burr's truck wasn't in the driveway. "I guess Burr's eating elsewhere."

"I hope he knows he's welcome here," Auntie Mat said, gesturing that they should all have a seat at the oval table.

"I'm sure he does." Shea joined her, and Liam did as well. "You are a warm person, Miss Matilda. Thanks for your encouragement earlier."

"Of course, dearie. Of course." She used her British accent, and Liam knew she was feeling playful and trying to keep things light. "Plus, I know it won't be long now until you're back there, helping more people."

"Thank you."

Auntie Mat passed the bowl of salad to Shea, then she turned to Liam. "Did you ask her yet, Son?"

"Ask me what?" She dished up a pile of greens with cranberries and avocado pieces.

Liam squirmed as he peeled the tinfoil from the chicken. "Well, my *aunt* was wondering what age group you work with, primarily—kids, teens, adults—the elderly?"

Auntie Mat swatted the air in his general direction. She probably thought if Shea answered that she treated adults, Liam could sign up for some sessions. Yes, because that was exactly what he'd do.

Shea handed the salad bowl to Liam. "Children, mostly. Especially kids in transition."

He wasn't a child now, but somehow, her specialty unnerved

him. Auntie Mat gave him a pointed look, and he set down the dish and adjusted the pitcher in the center of the table. Ice. They needed more ice in here. He jumped up and darted to the fridge.

"Why do you ask?"

"Oh, we were chatting about this and that." Auntie Mat said, and Liam worried she'd blurt out his life story any second. Or that she already had. "So," she began, and he held his breath, "if, say, a child lost their father and then a few years later they lost their mother, what kind of help could you give them?"

Liam faced the open freezer, letting the cold air blast crystalized oxygen against his hot face. He ground his jaw and slowly reached for the tray. No matter how many times he begged his former guardian to keep his personal stuff private, she was determined to spill it all out for examination.

"Oh . . . well," Shea slowly began, as if trying to respect Liam's discomfort.

Liam pulled the tray from the freezer and gave it a hard twist. The plastic cracked, and the cubes popped loose.

"Liam, do you mind talking about this?" Once again empathy carried through in her words, and he melted, though he wouldn't let the matchmaker see his reaction.

He glanced at each of them. Auntie Mat faced him, unashamed. Shea looked so compassionate and honoring, he could kiss her. He swallowed. Maybe she had an insight he could learn from.

Deadbeats were prideful, right?

Liam straightened. "No, go ahead." Then, he softened his tone. "Please."

"Okay." Her voice was soothing, gentle. "First I'd try to help the child trust me. We'd talk about whatever she wanted. Then, after some time, she'd probably open up about what she was thinking and feeling. Thing with kids is they each perceive the world in their own way. And different kids are confused by different things. So, you have to figure out how they're perceiving life, which is individual, to get the bigger picture. Then, zero in."

"They probably can't tell you what they're thinking a lot of the time." Even at eleven, he didn't always understand himself. Still didn't.

"You're right. It takes digging and lots of patience to help people trust you." Her unspoken message—that he should trust her, maybe?—made him uneasy. Was she analyzing him? "Plus, a good therapist can draw information out of a child. Then, we make deductions."

"So, you'd say that it might be the therapist's fault if the sessions weren't . . . fruitful or helpful?"

"It's no one's fault." She picked up her glass from the table and took a long drink, as if giving him time to think.

All his life, Liam had blamed Jack for his mom's and his problems—not enough food? Jack abandoned them and never sent support, that Liam knew about anyway. Bad genes and poor choices? Must have come from Jack's side of the family. Liam wouldn't blame him for everything that was messed up in his life, but he'd sure blamed him for a lot.

He wanted to be angry that Shea was showing him a different way to look at his own situation, at therapists, even indirectly, at Jack, but all those warm fuzzies earlier tamed him. Still, he hefted the pitcher from the center of the table and tipped up the tray, dumping the cubes inside and giving himself a breather.

What would his life look like if he didn't place blame?

"I can see you really know your field," Auntie Mat said lightly.

Not dumping all the guilt at Jack's feet meant Liam had to overcome the past, and—gulp—consider forgiving Jack for his mistakes, which he was not ready to do.

He set the pitcher on the counter. "I need to run an errand," he announced and bolted out of the house, toward his truck.

No wonder therapists hadn't ever helped him. They'd only poured more confusing tidbits into his world and let those swirl with the rest of the chaos.

He eased down the one-lane private drive that led to the slightly wider paved road, taking him off Barclay Spit.

Shea was exactly like the rest of them, though he'd hoped she wouldn't be. Speaking in riddles. What could she mean, implying that Jack was somehow innocent? How *crazy* was that?

And Auntie Mat was convinced they should date?

As drawn as he was to Shea, he knew they'd never see eye to eye on this. Her words didn't help. So dating her, like Auntie Mat wanted? Wasn't going to happen.

CHAPTER NINETEEN

The house went still after Liam left, except for Pearl's occasional squawks from the sunroom and the clicking of Calliope's nails on the floor. Shea worried about Miss Matilda, who wrung her hands at the table. "I think I pushed him too hard." She'd tried to call him back in, but he'd said something quiet to her outside the house and then driven away.

Shea sent him a text, apologizing if her words were harsh, and he'd responded: No WORRIES.

Pearl flew in from the sunroom and landed on a perch near the kitchen door frame. There she preened and oversaw the conversation, now and then making a chattering sound.

"Nah, it was my words about no one being at fault. I should have stopped to think." Maybe he blamed himself. "You'd mentioned to me about his dad abandoning his family when he was a kid. I remember JP telling that to me too. The story makes my heart ache for him."

Miss Matilda, sitting there in her matching top and cotton pants with all that embroidery around the collar, called the dog over to her and pushed back her chair to hold her. Matilda looked up, met Shea's eyes. "He cares for you. He's just had a rough time lately."

"Think he'll meet with Jack?"

"I'd love if you two could discuss that."

"We are talking more lately." But she doubted he'd want to open up after this train wreck.

"Good, good." She nodded, then gestured toward the table. "Please eat. I can hear your stomach growling from here."

After they'd finished filling their plates, they ate in silence for a few minutes.

"So, what's next for you? I mean, during your break from work."

Her "break" felt like a suspension without all the negative connotations. "Try to find someone who can help." Not that she expected it to make a difference. Liam must have felt that way. If he ever spoke to her again, she might point that out, so they could find common ground again.

She relived one of those moments in the kitchen earlier—how kind and open he'd been. He was all-in on that hug, and she'd breathed in his scent not wanting it to end. She was drawn to both his brokenness and his attempts at living a better life, not to mention how badly he wanted to help Dylan. In his arms, she could throw away her anti-dating decision and stay right there, staring up into gentle, sky-blue eyes.

"He just needs time. I'm trying not to push him where Jack is concerned. But he knows what he has to do." Auntie Mat hadn't eaten much. She leaned back and rubbed her pup's fur. "Everything will be all right. Better, in fact, for all the growth in this season. Like my snapdragons who weathered 'June-uary' and came out into the sunshine of this month." Matilda referred to the weather pattern that often hit the Seattle area in the month of June, keeping temperatures in the fifties and low sixties, rainy, and dark—like wintertime. "If there's any way you can help him, Jenna-Shea, I'd appreciate it."

She'd been thinking the same thing, but obviously, she wasn't the right one to address his issues. "I'll do what I can."

"Thank you. As stubborn as he is," Miss Matilda said with the hint of a grimace, "I'd really like to see Liam feel better. He's carried all this around with him for too long."

Letting go seemed impossible. There had to be a trick to it. One Shea hadn't found yet. "Think he'll be okay tonight?" she asked as she forked up a cube of juicy cantaloupe. Her appetite had faded, but she'd honor Miss Matilda by finishing.

"He'll probably find an adventure and come back with a tale to tell."

"No doubt." It was interesting to Shea how he thrived on thrills. Did he have a death wish, or was adrenaline simply his drug of choice? Or was a different problem driving him? Did the abandonment make him feel unwanted, unlovable? Was that why he worked so hard to get her cottage done—to prove something about his worth as a person, not only his value to her dad's team?

Oh, man. No wonder words of affirmation spoke love to him. She winced picturing the sad, confused boy he must have been. Had he blamed himself for Jack leaving?

Maybe his quest for thrills was a cry for help, for attention. For someone—like a father, perhaps—to bravely say that they cared about him and to *please, please don't get hurt.*

"What do you think about Liam's adventures, Miss Mat?"

She sent Calliope off her lap and then stood to wash her hands. Perhaps she was hungry now too. "Well, he's been taking off on his adventures for years. Even before I was ready to see him do them, Eli Hanson—do you know him?" Shea nodded. "Eli would take the boys up in his tiny plane or go paddle-boarding in the Sound, kayaking under the Tacoma Narrows Bridge with the strong currents under there." She settled at the table with clean hands and worked on her chicken leg. "I have not always been comfortable with the whole thing, I tell you. Not at all."

"Have you ever asked him to not go?"

"Nope. Not once. I knew, somehow, that was what he needed: to be surrounded by other guys his age, taking risks." She grabbed a slice of melon. "Don't ask me how I knew, I just did."

Still, Shea wondered if part of him was silently begging for someone to ask him not to risk his very valuable, very lovable self.

There were only so many places you could go and so many things you could do on this island without planning ahead and without a lot of cash. Liam didn't have a kayak, a paddle board, or scuba gear with him. He could get on the ferry over to Seattle, but that was a peaceful ride on a still night like tonight. Maybe he could jump off the Agate Pass Bridge. Except he didn't have permission to bungee jump here. His palms sweated thinking about it.

He'd bug Burr to hang out, but Burr probably had drinking on his mind, and honestly? Liam didn't need the weight of Burr's issues tonight.

Where could he take all this anger, all these words, all this *blame* burning inside?

He pulled off 305 at the corner of High School Road, into the McDonald's and parked his truck. Then he yanked out his phone and opened his messaging app. He found Jack's name and typed out a short message. Suddenly he had a lot to say to him, and he'd prefer to do it right to his face.

YES. I'LL MEET YOU. WHERE? WHEN?

Several minutes passed, and no answer came. Liam hit the drive-thru and ordered a burger, fries, and a chocolate shake, his hands clutching the steering wheel hard while he waited.

GREAT. DOES TOMORROW NIGHT @ ALKI BEACH IN SEATTLE WORK FOR YOU?

There was a certain tone to his response, a sort of humility, and Liam was reminded of feeling sorry for Jack earlier tonight when his aunt talked about him possibly being depressed or even suicidal. But, Liam's anger was justified. And he'd let Jack know exactly what he thought tomorrow night.

YES. TIME?

LET'S SAY 7. SOUND GOOD?

OK

Liam focused on choking down his food. He was really going through with it. In less than twenty-four hours, he was going to come face-to-face with Jack.

And probably burn a bridge neither one of them would be able to cross again.

CHAPTER TWENTY

The following morning, noises told Liam that Burr was already up, dressed, and in the kitchen when Liam schlepped in for something for his headache. He'd ended up swimming in the Sound after dark, despite how he kept finding clear, sand-dollar-sized jellies washed up on the beach. He'd taken the risk, and tolerated the cold water, to get relief from the pressures on every side.

"Man, you look like *you* had too much to drink last night."

"Ha-ha." Liam's head pounded harder. He reached for painkillers and tap water. Burr must have put the dishes away and reloaded the dishwasher like the guy was doing penance.

Burr leaned against the farthest counter, a hand on either side, relaxed. "Okay, what happened?" So unlike him to dig around in—or care about—someone else's issues. What was up with him?

Liam couldn't back out of the get-together now. He gulped water, chasing the pills down his tight throat. "I'm going to see Jack, tonight after work."

"Dude."

He scoffed. "Right?"

"He lives in the area?"

"I don't know. Seattle was his suggestion."

Burr gave him a second. Then, "Was he happy to hear from you?" He sounded almost . . . timid about asking, like he had a stake in Liam's answer.

Liam mixed hot chocolate with microwaved water, wishing it had more caffeine. "I don't know. I'm meeting him at Alki. I didn't wanna tell him I'm living on Bainbridge. Let him think I'm in Seattle. Close enough."

"Dude, if he knew enough to suggest Seattle, he knows enough. I'm guessing he lives near here." Burr studied Liam as if he wanted to say something.

"What?"

"I just gotta give you props. This whole thing takes guts, man." He snorted in self-deprecation. "I wish I had 'em."

Liam eyed his friend. "Something's different with you lately."

Burr squirmed, but he didn't walk away.

"I think you're stronger than you think." Liam grabbed a water bottle from the fridge and headed toward the door. "I have a stop to make before I get to the beach house today. I'll meet you there."

Maybe Liam was right. Maybe Dylan could reach out to Seneca and let her know he was thinking about her. Ask when might be a good time to come meet his daughter.

He ground his jaw. What kind of man didn't even know his own kid, eight months after she was born? It wasn't like he was in the military or something. He had no excuse for not seeing her, not seeing them.

But despite Liam's pep talk, Burr couldn't face them now. Not after all this time. Not when he still didn't have his life together.

At his truck, he reached into the cooler in the back and pulled a beer from the water that had been a bag of ice last night. Another drink before work wouldn't hurt.

Liam was wrong. Dylan wasn't nearly as gutsy as he thought.

At the cottage, Shea yanked painter's tape from the roll. Something was eating Liam this Friday morning. His aunt had hinted at family stuff Liam had to deal with tonight but hadn't said what. At breakfast, Miss Matilda recommended Shea talk to Liam about it. Was he still mad at her for their conversation over dinner?

While Liam banged around in the cottage's kitchen—she was giving him space—Shea finished taping off the main bathroom so she could paint. Aqua tiles accenting a periwinkle wall color. She could hardly wait until she finished, the hardware was installed, and she could put up the artwork she'd found in Winslow—seashell paintings. She'd also found a beachy shower curtain to span the tub—featuring a palette of aqua, periwinkle, and light sand in an abstract wave pattern. The sand-colored floor tile and granite vanity top would bring it all together. This might be her second favorite room in the house for how beachy she pictured it.

She strode to the kitchen where all the paints were stored on mats to protect the hardwoods. Liam worked in here installing the crown molding. Wasn't that Dylan's job? He still hadn't arrived today. At the risk of poking the bear, she'd like to help Liam if she could. She stood over the paint cans with thumbprints of color smeared over the top. Many of them were the pale sand color for the main walls throughout the house. She'd chosen that warm tone over anything gray given the skies offered enough gloom almost year-round here. Some of the paints were a seafoam green, but where was that periwinkle? "Hey, Liam. Have you seen the blue paint for the main bath?"

Standing up on the ladder, he turned toward her. "Should be there. I know I brought it home." His voice sounded calm, which seemed to take effort.

She lifted a stacked can off the one underneath. Maybe her blue was hidden. Not there. She circled the collection.

"I guess it might be in my truck."

Two more gallons were stacked together on this side, and when she removed the top one, a smear of blue greeted her. "Got it." The handle dug into her palm when she lifted the heavy container to carry it to the doorway. They'd have plenty of this color left. She paused near his ladder. "Hey, are you okay today? You seem upset. Are *we* okay?" She gestured between them, her heart fluttering.

He climbed down and stepped from the last rung, stopping near her. His expression of irritation melted away to show a tender gaze, and she swallowed, holding her breath. "I'm sorry if you thought I was upset with you, Shea." After brushing his dusty palm on his shirt, he laid his hand on her forearm. "I'm not. At all."

She gave him a smile and used her free hand to exaggerate

wiping her brow. "Well, whew!"

He let go and chuckled. "Nah, it's just the pressures from all around, you know?"

She did know, very well.

He reached for another section of molding stacked on the floor. Carpentry work fell to him today.

"No sign of Dylan, huh?" she asked.

Liam grimaced. "I wanted this to work out. Still, we're almost finished."

She glanced around, mostly seeing dust. The granite countertops would go in soon and then, Liam would do the tile backsplash. The new fridge hummed. "Someone should wash those windows. I can probably work on that. First floor, anyway."

"I can hire it done, but it'd cost less if they only do the outside. There's room in the budget."

"I'll get to it after I finish painting." Beyond the deck, the lagoon glistened in blue-green water. "Can't wait to see the view unobstructed."

The appliances and much of the counter space hugged the left wall if you were facing the huge windows looking out at the lagoon. A kitchen island ran parallel to that left wall, filling much of the center of the room. Then, an eat-in area would occupy the back, right corner, leaving a pantry in the closer right corner.

Shea could hardly wait for gleaming surfaces and clean windows so the sunrises could stream in from the eastern sky.

"You're picturing this finished." Liam stared at her, his voice soft.

She shook off her musings and grinned. "You caught me."

"I hope you like it." His voice held an intimate tone, which touched her. Had he guessed her love language was acts of service? Didn't matter. He'd been clear about not dating.

She'd keep things light. "I do. It's going to be beautiful."

"Like you."

She peeked at her over-sized pink tee covered in paint, and her denim cutoffs that went to almost mid-thigh. "Yeah." She gave a snort.

His turn to grin. "Most of the time. And you might be surprised how attractive you are in that." He gestured toward her getup but then shifted as if uncomfortable with his own confession.

How *attractive*? Maybe they needed a little chat, so he knew how those kinds of phrases affected her. "Sure." She pointed at the paint can. "I'm off to work on the main bath."

"I didn't answer your question." He remained near the bottom of the ladder. "Want a snack?" He strode to the island. He'd picked up a box of donuts earlier in the morning, and as he passed it across the counter, he flicked open the top.

Was he about to tell her what was bothering him?

She ambled toward the island as a waft of sugary glaze scented the air.

"Sorry it's not a fruit salad." He wore a devilish grin, which didn't make him look sorry at all.

"I think I'd better be the one to pick up the snacks tomorrow." She chuckled. The box contained two glazed donuts and two maple bars. Her mouth watered despite the fact she preferred to avoid sugar, most of the time.

He watched her as she studied the treats. "Deal."

Right now, there wasn't anything else to eat, and she had worked up an appetite. She reached for a round glazed. "Halvsies?"

Another snort. "Sure. But I'm having one of the maple bars too."

"You go."

Maybe she'd hike back to the park this afternoon, roundtrip. Twice. Still, she broke the donut in half, returning one section to the box. The sugary pastry melted in her mouth, and she closed her eyes. It'd been a long time. "Definitely getting fruit tomorrow morning," she said around the mouthful.

He watched her and took a big bite of his maple bar. "Good."

She laughed. "I like working with you." Oops, that sounded personal. "I mean, since I must give up my day job for a while, we make a great construction team. What's next for you? Mom and Dad have another house in need of TLC?" They owned four on this island and had plans to buy more. They were constantly watching the market.

"Your dad's been great about everything, letting me keep my job with him. There's a property in Yeomalt that's up next. Outdoor work, so I shouldn't bother the tenants much. By the way, I think it's cool your folks don't mind renting to you while you're … on leave."

Oh, no. She hadn't considered how they'd take the news.

He went still. "Uh-oh. You haven't talked to them yet, have you?"

She used her sugar-free hand to rub her opposite shoulder. "Well. . ."

He moved around the end of the island, coming a bit closer, but not into her personal space. "I'm sure they'll understand. That's one of the things I like about them. Makes for great parents." He tipped his water bottle at her as if offering a toast.

"They can't afford for me to mooch off them, especially in such prime real estate. As it is, my monthly rent was only going to cover their mortgage payment. With weekly renters, they'd make a lot more, even after paying their cleaning staff and lawn maintenance crew."

"Your dad seems easygoing." Liam raised his brows, his face full of concern with a touch of hope. "I'm sure it'll work out."

He let things go quiet between them for a minute as if mention of her dad brought to mind thoughts of Jack. He finished his maple bar and ran his hands under the water in the sink before he faced her again, paper towel drying his fingers. "Speaking of dads."

Would he tell her? "Yeah?"

Liam took a deep breath and let it out on his words. "I'm meeting with Jack tonight. You know, my bio dad. Auntie Mat's probably mentioned him."

Suddenly his earlier mood—all that noise he was making this morning as he banged around the cottage—made sense.

"I think that's brave." Curious how he called Jack his "bio dad." Was that so he could keep his distance and not use the words "my dad"?

He dipped his head, sadness pressing his lips into a frown. Then, he shifted and drank about two-thirds of his water. Finally, he peeked up at her. "Do you say stuff like that because my aunt brought up 'words of affirmation'?" He used two fingers to make air quotes as if he didn't quite buy into that concept.

The air went still around them. She could deny it. But she always tried to be honest. She settled on saying, "Maybe," because she couldn't really explain—even to herself—why she kept affirming him. But his acts of courage drew respect from a deep place inside her. Should she tell him that?

Besides, she liked speaking his love language. She'd analyze why later. "For what it's worth, coming from me, I'm impressed by what you're doing, and I respect you for doing it."

He stood close now, and she could see the royal blue circle around his irises as she met his silent gaze. He swallowed. "You do?"

She gave a slow nod as his eyes traced her face with admiration. How he could appreciate all the paint smudges and dust and crazy hair in a high bun she had no idea. When he eyed her lips, she licked sugar from them.

Okay. She needed to redirect. This was all too confusing.

"Thank you for saying that. I think you mean it."

She gave him a warm smile. "Of course I mean it." Then, she headed back to her paint gallon. "I'd better get to work."

CHAPTER TWENTY-ONE

That night, Liam's heart pounded as he waited in the ferry line to cross Puget Sound to Seattle. He'd drive onto the ferry, buzz to Alki Beach, fire his questions at Jack, and then escape as early as he could.

Why was he doing this again?

Auntie Mat had wished Liam well. Even sent him off tonight with a sandwich and a prayer.

The ferry arrived on time, and offloaded pedestrians and then vehicles. The sun hung high in the sky as if it had no reason to hurry toward the horizon this time of year.

His turn came to board, and he followed the car in front of him. Maybe once he landed, he'd head the opposite direction, let his—Jack—feel what it was like to wonder, to wait, to hurt.

After parking on the lower level, Liam climbed the stairs to the ferry's passenger decks. People milled around. Body heat warmed the space. The smells of popcorn and burgers from the café filled the indoors area. But Liam needed to stand outside. Instead of walking to the back of the boat and breathing diesel fumes once they got underway, he walked in the direction that would be the front of this two-sided vessel for this voyage. The wind would blast him, but that's what he wanted right now.

Overhead the announcer came on as the ferry pulled away from the dock. Liam tuned out the familiar words about life boats and life jackets. Wind gusted at him as he stepped through the wide, swinging door. Families lingered out here, but as the boat got up to speed, they ducked back inside. Newbies. They didn't understand the headwind. Maybe didn't need it as much as he did right now.

His phone buzzed in his pocket. Burr? Auntie Mat?

A message notification. Burr better not be messing with him. He knew what Liam was in for tonight.

Jack Barrett.

Now that Liam had conjured the guts to make this trip, would Jack duck out?

Liam turned his back to the salty wind and hunched over his phone. Sunlight hit him in the face, and he squinted.

RUNNING LATE. SORRY. STILL COMING.

Sorry. The word stabbed Liam in the chest. *Sorry.* He faced the headwind again, let the gusts scrape past his ears and gouge into his jacket. He pocketed his phone and drew in his shoulders, shoving his hands into his pockets. His throat burned.

Sorry. For . . .? What? For everything? For traffic?

Why was Liam doing this? Charging over to see Jack as if this had been his idea? His chest ached. How could he face him?

His phone buzzed with a text, and Auntie Mat's face showed up on his screen. THINKING ABOUT YOU. AND PRAYING.

He pressed the phone symbol to call her, then he ducked into an alcove just inside the swinging door, away from the swarms of a Friday night trek to the city. "I can't do it." He faced the slanted plexiglass and kept his voice low.

"What happened?"

"I'm on the ferry. He sent a message to say he's late. To say he's—get this—*sorry* he's running late."

His aunt's weighty sigh came through the phone connection as if she knew what Liam felt. Maybe she did. "What if he's gearing up to apologize for more than a bit of tardiness?"

Against his will, Liam's chin trembled, and his eyes burned. "This is killing me."

"Liam, Son, I don't think you remember this, but there were several nights you told me you wished you could see him again . . . that you could talk to him. Even as a kid, you had all these questions."

Liam remembered feeling that way. He stared through the window, watching the Seattle skyline grow on the horizon.

"Now's your chance. What do you want to say?"

"I haven't really let myself think that through." His voice scraped out. "I've been too focused on hurling my anger at him." His heart thumped. Less than an hour now. Why couldn't he shove his emotions down? He'd been successful all these years, for the most part, in stuffing them. Today—when it really mattered that he keep himself together and not show a hint of weakness—today, the pain boiled up, and he couldn't get the lid to stay on. His conversation this morning with Shea hadn't helped. She believed in him, yes, but if he bailed now, she'd know. And he couldn't live with disappointing her again.

"My dear Liam," Auntie Mat said, her voice full of compassion. "It's going to be a tough experience for sure. But this is your chance. No guarantee you'll get another. I wouldn't verbally attack him, but you should feel free to say whatever you need to."

"Part of me doesn't want to give him a chance to defend himself, or explain." Shoot. That sounded petty.

"Because if he did, you'd have no more excuses for holding his past against him."

"Right. I'm so used to being angry with him, I don't want that to switch over to anything like mercy." And that sounded like the type of guy who rejected kindness and held grudges. He groaned.

He'd been trying so hard to *not* be like his bio dad, to be a solid guy, and yet here in this situation, he wasn't—he couldn't—all he wanted to do was run. He squeezed his free hand into a fist and debated punching the plexiglass.

"So, knowing the details might make you feel compelled to let him off the hook."

"It might. Especially if he has a good reason."

"And if he doesn't?"

Liam groaned again, still glad no one stood nearby. People milled around, and a few even headed out into the wind beyond the doors.

Auntie Mat took a deep breath and exhaled. "Liam, you have to forgive him either way."

Always with that message. Ever since his aunt had taken in his mom and him, and Liam had shared two-way conversations with her, she'd brought up forgiveness where Jack was concerned. "So, we're back to the beginning—I don't think I can do this."

Auntie Mat gasped as if she'd thought of something. "You know, this could have happened a whole other way. What if, instead of hearing directly from him, you had heard from his new wife, or maybe he has another kid or two and twenty years from now you had heard from them. And they told you Jack was this way or Jack said that thing. But here's your chance. Straight from the man's own mouth." She paused. "That's worth something."

She had a point. Until now, he hadn't had this chance, and he may never again. Maybe this was God's grace, somehow. "You're right." He closed his eyes and debated praying. Right now he could use a lifeline and a dad like Eli, who hauled you in on the rope without judging you or shaming you and who talked you through the situation. Was God like that?

"Part of you is afraid you won't be able to handle what Jack says. But you're an adult, not a little boy. Son, you've got this."

Her words sunk deep, and he relished the belief in them. "I hope so." Seattle's Great Wheel dominated Pier 57 as the ferry neared its terminal. Liam still hadn't ridden the Ferris wheel. He didn't spend a lot of time on this side of the Sound.

"Listen, Dylan just walked in," she said in a quiet voice. "He's staggering through the living room."

"Really?" Liam's gut sank. "I'm sorry, Auntie Mat."

"Hey, I can handle him. Don't worry. You do what you need to do. I believe in you."

The ship's engine cut back as the ferry lined up with its dock. "I need to go. Pray for me?"

"Always."

Liam disconnected the call and weaved between the rows of seating and the tables to the aisle, so he could get back to his car. A river of people joined him. An older guy watched him from one of the tabled booths, and Liam had a sudden jolt to his chest as he passed. The stranger wore a big plaid shirt as if he'd come in from the Midwest in the fall. Something about him hooked Liam's attention. Liam was halfway down the stairs before he spun and switched to the right-hand side and worked his way against the crowd to march back up the stairs.

He passed through the propped-open door.

The guy was gone. Stupid, how Liam kept wondering if any of the fifty-something men he saw could be his father. Maybe seeing Jack today would finally put that to rest. Stupid, stupid, stupid.

He skimmed the steps down toward his car.

Yeah, he wasn't messed up at all, or powerless to change it. Did he want to be messed up? No. Did he want to be like Jack? No! Did he want to search for Jack in crowds everywhere he went? Or feel all the pain the mere *thought* of this little get-together caused? No. Didn't matter. He couldn't fix it. Praying for God to fix it wasn't enough. Liam was missing something.

Shea had been forced into a season of healing. Was that what God was up to with Liam too?

Fantastic.

CHAPTER TWENTY-TWO

Lovers strolled along, and kids played with their parents as Liam paced near the Liberty statue replica at Alki. Western sunlight glinted above, making the place glow. Families gathered and splashed in the Sound's cold, blue water, which glistened with yellow diamonds only a few yards away. Normally, saltwater soothed Liam, but not tonight. No further messages from Jack. Was he still coming? Maybe he was driving and couldn't send a message. They never exchanged phone numbers because Liam preferred not to, but maybe they should have.

His phone buzzed, and he jolted.

Jack Barrett.

All his life he hadn't seen that name as often as he had this week. He ground his jaw.

Almost there.

Liam's heart thumped hard while he thumbed his response. I'm here. Near the statue.

As soon as he'd sent the response, his phone rang. *Shea Brown.* Her beautiful face on his screen made him smile. She never called him. He could use her calming way right now. He was the one who jumped out of planes, and she sometimes startled at noises. But most of the time, she seemed so peaceful, while inside his gut churned day after day. He only *pretended* to be fearless. Not that he'd tell her, or anyone else, that.

"Hey, Shea." He was going for nonchalance but couldn't quite hide the tremor of fear in his voice. "What's up?"

"Hi. Any sign of him yet?"

"Not yet."

"He still coming?"

"Says he is." For whatever that was worth.

"I called to say I'm rooting for you."

Such kindness, on a night like tonight, sent warmth through his chest. "Thanks, Shea."

"And if you want to talk, I'm here to listen."

Maybe it was time for him to seek advice. He moaned. "What would you tell someone in my situation?" His shoulders tightened, and he rolled them.

"Well . . ." She paused. "I recommend you try to remember that he's probably as scared as you are. There is a lot at stake. Each of you has expectations. You both could use a bit of kindness." She let those words sink in, then added, "And mercy."

Mercy. Would God grant that if Liam asked Him to? He didn't deserve it, not when he wasn't willing to extend any to Jack, even in his own thoughts.

"Also, this type of face-to-face encounter is powerful, emotional. You might even see yourself in him—for better or for worse. So, brace yourself. And if you feel like you can't go through with it, you can. Don't run. You *are* strong enough. I believe in you."

Her words struck him in the gut.

I believe in you. The ultimate affirmation.

His aunt might be onto something with this whole love language thing because every single time Shea said stuff like that, he pictured her linking them together with another knot. Then her gentleness tugged that chain, drawing him closer to her. "Aw, thanks, Shea."

Was it crazy he wanted one of her strong hugs right now? Thing about her—she didn't hold back. When she hugged you, you felt appreciated, cared for. Was that the maternal side of her?

A car pulled into a recently-vacated parallel slot out on the road, and Liam turned. The vehicle looked run down and the guy who emerged from inside, even more so. And when the man faced Liam, he knew he was looking into the pale blue eyes of his father.

He's here. Liam caught a sob in his gut, but he pushed it down. He would *not* cry, not about this.

"I need to go, Shea. Thanks . . ." His voice came out raspy as if he'd regressed to being a crying child. If he did, did that mean Jack would regress to the same age he was when he left Liam? He'd read about that dynamic somewhere, but now he was living it.

"I'm praying for you."

"Thanks."

They disconnected, and Liam pivoted to face the water and collect himself. He hadn't expected to feel such a wave of sadness, or grief, wash over him. He couldn't watch Jack approach. He shoved his phone into his back pocket and his fists into his front pockets. Then he waited. There'd been no sign of plaid, so the ferry guy wasn't him. That stranger behind him was his actual father. Liam shifted so he could see with his peripheral vision. With rounded shoulders, the man shuffled closer.

"Liam?" A familiar voice from almost thirty years ago, like a ghost. Familiar, but scratchier.

An emotional wave hit him again, and Liam couldn't speak. Instead he nodded and gulped against the burning in his throat.

Jack stopped a few feet in front of him. "Liam ..." He studied him, and Liam used the time to do the same.

Jack looked older than the age his mother would be right now—mid-fifties. They'd graduated high school together, so Jack was close to Mom's age, give or take a year. But he looked twenty years older. He was tall but beaten down. He wore a jacket over faded jeans and had shoved his hands into his pockets too. Almost as if he wasn't sure if he should shake Liam's hand or what.

They stood there facing each other for long moments. The wrinkles at the corners of Jack's eyes worked with every blink. Those eyes—pale blue, matched the ones that stared back at Liam from the mirror every day.

"Thank you for meeting with me." Jack's voice sounded over-used. Like it was wearing out.

Liam nodded once. He still couldn't speak. Didn't even know where to begin. Maybe he should have prepared better. Right now even the words he'd imagined yelling at this man back when he was a kid wouldn't materialize. Not one syllable.

"I know this took guts, and I'm grateful."

Silence. A gull squawked in the distance behind Liam, whose back was to the water. People strolled by. Kids yelled down the beach, begging their parents to "watch me!"

Liam had never had a dad around to yell "Watch me!" to. Well, not after preschool. His gut tightened.

Jack pointed at the nearby bench. "Can we sit?"

The man looked like he needed to. Liam gestured for Jack to go ahead. But Liam couldn't. Too much nervous energy. Adrenaline that needed to go somewhere. Maybe a jog around the park. Or he could dive into Puget Sound's balmy fifty-degree water. Take a little swim.

From his spot on one end of the bench, Jack turned watery eyes on Liam. "You're not going to say anything? Or sit down?"

The bench looked short. Maybe if Liam were a kid, he'd fit. But if he sat there now, he'd be leg to leg with Jack. And nearly face-to-face. Couldn't do it.

He needed distance. He needed a minute. He needed . . . out. He grunted, turned, and walked away. His walk morphed into a jog, and his jog became an all-out run down the pathway. The sidewalk went for almost three miles, if he remembered correctly, with bicyclists and runners zipping past. The words *I can't do this, I can't do this, I can't do this* played in his mind. Why had he thought that after all these years, he could stand toe-to-toe with his dad and not, what? Explode?

Hold up, Liam. God's voice.

Huffing, Liam slowed his steps on the path.

Don't run from this.

He braked to a walk, tried to ignore the people around him. *Help?* He kept moving away from that statue back there. *I know I haven't talked to You in a long time. Would You tug my lifeline in, haul me up into Your boat, and walk me through this? Please?*

A breeze blew against the sweat on his forehead, and Liam closed his eyes for a moment. He sensed acceptance. Peace. Maybe a bit of hope. And a challenge—not quite a command.

Hands on his waist he spun around, back toward the Liberty statue. Couldn't see the bench from here. Would Jack still be there when Liam returned?

Now that he'd gotten the adrenaline out, maybe he could endure this. He'd lean on God, on purpose, and see what happened.

He crested a rise and saw the bench. Jack was still there. He sat hunched over, elbows on his legs, focus on the water. He seemed tired. Broken. Humbled.

Liam marched in Jack's direction. He would face this, and he would prevail. He owed it to Mom. And to himself.

And then, he'd be glad if they went their separate ways for the rest of their lives.

CHAPTER TWENTY-THREE

Sweat ran down Dylan's back as he stretched. Liam's aunt had needed a few rocks moved from one side of her beachfront to the other. Dylan's steps had weaved a little, but he'd tried to help her out. That was his repayment for her fantastic peach cobbler. Every time he came over, she fed him well. Liam had it so good. An aunt who cared what happened to him.

Half an hour later, he went for his truck. Shea wasn't home—she'd mentioned something about a walk to the park.

Liam was off chatting with his messed-up dad. Matilda had told Dylan that she felt like God wanted Liam to talk to Jack. Dylan wondered about that. Did God care at that level? Enough to direct someone to talk to someone else? Probably not, right? And had God told *Jack* to get back in contact with his son?

Dylan reached for the hidden vodka bottle under the truck's bench seat and, while still bent over, so he was out of view, he downed a long swig. Then, he recapped the bottle and hid it again with old hamburger wrappers and other trash.

Nah, God didn't tell people who to talk to. Didn't make people face their mistakes. That would imply a God who knew all the details of your life. God had more important things to do than keep tabs on Dylan Burgess.

Shea returned from her walk and stepped up onto Matilda's deck to rinse her feet at the outside shower.

Liam had suggested that Dylan face his demons. Ha. That would take another bottle of vodka. Had Liam drank tonight before going over? Probably not. He was too *good* for alcohol. He never drank, and he'd never used. Well, Dylan didn't use drugs either. So, at least he had that to brag about. God might even give him a high-five for that.

His head was fuzzy as he sat behind the wheel, his vision blurry as late-evening sunlight slanted through the windshield. It would set after nine, but it wasn't quite that time yet. Where were his shades? Eyes closed, he slapped around on the passenger side and checked the glove box. Nothing. Ah, he'd just squint all the way back to Liam's house. No problem. It wasn't far. Except, Dylan didn't want to be at Liam's when he came home with tales of how things went with dear old Dad. Or, worse, more of Liam's pep talks about Dylan facing his stuff.

Matilda had taken Dylan's keys, and he'd promised her he wouldn't drive for a while. Then, he'd found the key ring hidden in the sunroom when she'd been in another room. Now, with her inside the house, he could take off without her scolding him or trying to keep him here.

Window down, he threw his old junker into Reverse and backed up without looking at the quiet street. Someone screamed. His pickup thumped into something hard, and he stomped the brake pedal, squeezing his eyes shut. His head pounded. *What—?* He put the vehicle in Park and jerked open his driver's door. If only his vision would clear, or that blasted sun would set. There. As he stumbled around his truck, the shadow of Matilda's house helped block the light.

He couldn't see what he'd hit. Had someone been parked here? Was there a fencepost or mailbox he didn't remember? Stupid fuzzy head.

Several people came running out of their houses, Matilda and Shea included. Why? A bunch of them were on their phones, snapping shots. Frantic voices made calls. He weaved around to the back of his truck.

There, bent at an odd angle, a woman lay on the ground. Not moving. Not talking or screaming.

People shouted. "What happened?"

"Did anybody see what happened?"

"Are you the driver?"

Dylan gulped and backed away. Shea and Miss Matilda gawked at him, fear written all over their faces. Matilda called something to him over the noisy people about how he shouldn't have his keys. He had to get out of there. Nowhere to go. Couldn't hide. Couldn't escape. The crowd seemed to sense how desperate he felt because two big guys blocked his path. And the rest closed the circle on the other side right before sirens blared in the distance.

Jaw tight, Liam approached Jack, who stood, eyes crinkled with concern. "You all right, So—?"

"Don't!" No way did Liam want Jack to call him *Son.*

Jack lifted both of his hands, palms down in front of him as if steadying a wild horse. "Sorry. I'm sorry."

The apology hung between them. Saltwater waves hit the beach. Kids shrieked as they played. Parents redirected.

And Liam's dad said he was sorry.

Liam's chest burned hot.

Jack squirmed, shifting from one foot to the other. Did he realize his words sounded like an admission of guilt for everything Jack had done wrong where Liam and his mom were concerned? Would Jack leave this time?

Urgency hit Liam. He couldn't let the man get away before he'd said what he needed to say. "Did you know Mom died?" He fired his first question at him, not waiting long enough for Jack to answer, but the news hit him somewhere in the gut, judging by the flinch. "Yeah. I was eleven. Considered myself an orphan." He crossed his arms over his chest. "We were homeless for a while after you left. Church people took us in." Then, Auntie Mat gave them a home when she lived in that larger house away from the beach. "But you didn't care where we ended up because if you had, you'd have stayed. Do you know about that? Staying? I'm guessing the answer is no."

Hands in his pockets and shoulders hunched, Jack seemed to absorb the words and the pain as if he knew this was his penalty for all the years of agony he'd caused.

A sob jerked in Liam's chest, and he gulped against it. "Why?" The broken-voice question lingered in the air between them. Liam was glad Alki's other visitors were far away. "I was only a kid. And Mom needed you. We both did. Why did you walk out on us?" Another sob and Liam barely caught this one. Part of him felt four years old, demanding answers with clenched fists.

Jack freed one hand to rub against the back of his neck. But he didn't respond.

Because what could he possibly say? There was no way he could account for his decisions, no way could he justify abandoning Liam and breaking his wife's heart.

Mom. The grief clawed free and seized Liam as if she'd just died this moment. Now that he'd accessed the cavern, years of misery climbed up his chest. He didn't know where to take this unimaginable ache. What to do with the burning. That's why he kept pushing it down all these years. But tonight, it wouldn't be contained.

"I'm sorry." Jack's voice sounded even hoarser, as if the pain Liam felt had gotten to *him.*

Well, Liam didn't need his pity.

"Everything I uh"—Jack cleared his throat, his whiskery chin trembling—"practiced sounds so hollow in my head right now. No excuse can fix this."

"But I want a reason!" Liam said, hearing how juvenile he sounded as anger seared hotter than sorrow inside. He fisted his hands and leaned in. "When you walked away that day, while I was at school, what were you thinking?"

Jack let the accusations behind the words sit for a moment. "What was I thinking?" His voice was so quiet, Liam could barely hear him over the seagulls' squawks overhead. He gave a long sigh. "What a failure I'd been to you, to your mother. How I couldn't see a way to change. I—I had a picture in my head of the kind of dad I wanted to be, the kind of husband, and I failed every single day. I didn't want to be like my dad—so messed up. I was tired of that. Hated that I couldn't give you both something better. A better version of me."

Liam shook his head, trying to process Jack's answer. Mostly nonsense in his words, except that one phrase: *I didn't want to be like my dad.* "So you keep trying. You don't give up."

"I thought you'd be better off without me." Just like Auntie Mat had said.

Liam's chest opened up. "Better off?" He scoffed and pointed at himself. "This huge cannon-sized hole in my chest—this aching hole. You put that there. You failed me, and Mom, because you wouldn't even *try*. And there's no fixing that now. She's gone. And I'm through with this little chat."

Liam marched back to his car, huffing at the tears on his face.

So, he'd gotten a few answers. Confirmed Auntie Mat's guess that Jack wanted to apologize, that he hadn't felt up to the task of being a decent dad or husband, not that it did any good.

This little get-together hadn't solved anything. Instead, Liam hurt more now than since the day Mom died.

Tonight, he had to see clearly enough to drive and go back to the island. He'd put this behind him. Get on with his life.

His eyes burned, blurring his vision as he pulled away from Alki en route to the ferry. His phone buzzed, and he reached for it but didn't read the screen. He pulled off and answered. "Yeah." His voice came out wobbly, and he cleared his throat.

"Liam, honey." Auntie Mat's voice. "Something awful has happened. How soon can you get here?"

She didn't even ask about his night. Must be pretty bad. Was she hurt? His heart thumped. "Are you okay? Is Shea?" He sniffed and ran a fist under his nose, checking his mirrors. No sign of Jack pulling out of his parking stall.

"Dylan hit someone with his car. We don't know if she's going to make it. This is really bad, Liam. We need you over here."

The news slammed into Liam like a freight train. "Are you safe?"

"Yes."

"Where's Burr now?" He'd probably run off. He didn't like dealing with life's tough stuff anymore than Liam did. But this? This was unbelievable.

"The police arrested him and took him away." She sounded so worried, as if Liam had been the driver.

This night kept getting better.

Vision clearer now, he put the phone on Speaker and the car into Drive.

One victory tonight? That Liam faced Jack and could put that behind him. He'd never have to do that again. Never have to hear lame excuses or pathetic—

"Are you still there?"

"Yeah. I don't know when the next ferry is. I just left Alki . . . I'm on my way to the terminal on the Seattle side."

"Got it. Well, get here as fast as you can and plan to spend the night at my house tonight. We need to pull together."

"Of course."

CHAPTER TWENTY-FOUR

Seneca Hawke couldn't get her baby to stop crying.

"C'mon, Breeze, baby. It's going to be okay," she soothed. Seneca bounced her, sang to her, rocked her. She checked her diaper, tried to burp her. Of course, at almost eight months, Breeze didn't need help burping as often as when she'd been a newborn. Oh, if they could only sleep. Breeze had been a content baby, until lately. Even teething hadn't been as hard as Seneca had feared. But this? Now Breeze's cries scared Seneca. She was in pain, at least it seemed like it from the urgency, the anger, the pitiful sniffling after hours of crying.

Breeze wouldn't eat. Wouldn't sleep. Wouldn't let Seneca sleep. How many nights had it been in a row now?

And Seneca's mom was at work tonight. She couldn't come over and help like she often did, though she wasn't getting much rest either.

Since Seneca was pretty sure Breeze's cry was one of pain, she laid her in a safe place and went to find infant acetaminophen. If she could get Breeze to swallow it, maybe the pain would let up. And they could have quiet. She hated to see her daughter suffering. They'd been through enough already.

Her phone buzzed with her mom's number.

"Hey, Sen. How's it going tonight?"

"Breeze is screaming. Can you hear her?" She spoke loudly. The medicine was in the cupboard. But where was the oral syringe?

"I can, but from far away."

"I set her down in her crib for a second. I'm kinda scared. She hasn't done this before. But no fever, and no new teeth."

Mom went silent.

"Mom, what's up?" She must have called for a reason, though it was kind of her to check in.

"I'm covering the desk tonight." Seneca's mom worked at the

county jail. "They just brought someone in, and generally I wouldn't call you, but you needed to know about this case. Since it concerns Breeze."

Seneca's hands were shaking now, but her baby had quieted a little, so she could focus on her mom. "What happened?" She walked back to where Breeze was bouncing in her crib. "Hang on a second, Mom, could you?" Pinning the phone between her shoulder and her ear, she grabbed a few tissues and tried to squirt the medicine into her baby's mouth. Probably half of it came back out.

When Breeze swallowed the remainder from the dropper, Seneca scooped her up and went in search of Breeze's bottle. "Okay, I'm back. We'll see if Breeze will let us talk."

"They brought Dylan Burgess in tonight."

"What? Why?" Not another drunk-driving offense. It wasn't as if Seneca kept tabs on him. In fact, hearing his name was like ripping tape off your skin. Startling with a sharp sting. But bearable. Kind of.

"There are rumors of vehicular homicide." Her voice went quiet.

Seneca's knees gave way, and she dropped onto the sofa. "What? Somebody died?"

"Those are the rumors, but I don't know for sure yet."

Breeze let loose another cry, and Seneca reached for the bottle the baby had been nursing for most of the last half hour. The clock read ten, and the sky was still navy through the broken blinds. Breeze took the bottle, sucking hungrily, and Seneca sighed deep. Maybe this would work. She stroked her baby's face.

The sofa's spring jabbed her, reminding her she could use new furniture. But where would the money come from for that? "Mom, what happened?"

"It's another DUI, I think. I can't share details, of course. But I wanted you to know."

Tension settled on her shoulders. "I shouldn't be surprised, I guess."

Mom didn't answer. She knew all the details. Dylan hadn't been the type of boyfriend, or father, Seneca had hoped he'd be. She pulled her sweet baby in tighter.

"Thanks, Mom."

The thought of Breeze's father behind bars—again—made Seneca hurt for him. He wasn't a bad guy. He just couldn't seem to get his act together. Half the time, Seneca was relieved they weren't dating anymore. The other half . . . she missed him. She could use his help with their child. His financial support. But last time she tried to get in touch with him, he took off in the opposite direction.

She felt a nudge in her spirit.

What do You want me to do about this, God? He doesn't want to see us. Not that she'd take her daughter to the county jail. *He walked out, remember?* Another nudge poked her in the heart. She stood, and this time she paced and prayed for Dylan instead of letting the anger build. She prayed Dylan would see what he hadn't seen yet—God loved him. That he'd be able to do what he hadn't been able to do—act like an adult and face his responsibilities. That he'd find true freedom and become a respectable man.

Seneca kissed the top of her sleeping baby girl's head. She may never get to know her daddy.

What Seneca couldn't decide right now was whether that was a good thing or a tragedy.

Only the Lord knew the answer to that.

CHAPTER TWENTY-FIVE

Two hours after leaving Alki, Liam pulled into the driveway at Auntie Mat's place, his gut in a knot. She met him outside the kitchen door on the wide top step, and after catching all that agony on her face, he opened his arms. She walked right in. "Are you okay?" he asked her. Frogs croaked a chorus nearby in the dim summer light.

"Better now that you're home. What a night." She clung to him. Her trembling got to Liam. She was always the strong one.

He stroked her shoulder and let her stay right where she was. "I'm really sorry this happened." He'd been dreading something like this all summer, as Dylan spiraled further and further into his addiction.

She shuddered. How much had she seen? Should he change the subject? Shea and other therapists would probably say to face the feelings, as challenging as that always seemed in the moment. For once, he'd try that.

He couldn't imagine witnessing a car accident where the car hit a pedestrian. Maybe it'd be wise to give her the choice to discuss it or not. What did she need? He loosened his arms a little. "Do you want to talk about it?"

She pulled back and opened the screen door for him. "C'mon in, and we'll chat. I need to find out how your evening went too."

Inside the house now, he moved to the archway and scanned the living room. "Where's Shea? Was she here when it happened?" He kept flashing back to images of Shea being startled on her first day at the cottage, how pale she'd gone. Her leave of absence from work following the car accident outside her clinic's window, and now tonight? What if she'd been a witness?

"She was here. Out on the deck rinsing sand from her feet."

"Oh, no." His heart squeezed tight, and he longed to look into her eyes and see if she was okay. To hold her close and reassure her.

"Now, she's upstairs."

A salty wind carried in off the water, cooling the house after the sunny day. As Liam moved closer to her, Auntie Mat turned from the stove where she'd been fussing with the teakettle. "I'm really concerned about her." She kept her voice low. "She's in the bathtub, hopefully relaxing a bit. Oh, Liam ... you should've seen her. I met her outside in the driveway after I heard the scream. We moved toward Dylan's truck. Saw the woman behind it—*underneath* it."

Liam swallowed against an empty stomach and moaned, leaning on the counter.

"She went white as a dove. Her eyes got a sort of glazed look." Auntie Mat scooped up Calliope after she scampered down the stairs. Pearl was asleep under her draped towel by this hour every night. "It reminded me of my brother—your great-uncle—after Vietnam. He used to, I don't know, 'check out' for a few minutes whenever we heard something loud. Like when an engine backfired or if someone was hunting on their wooded acreage and fired a rifle. Or fireworks." She shook her head and Liam gave her a side hug, patting Calliope. She handed off her pup, and Liam took her, nuzzling his nose into her soft, wavy ear.

Auntie Mat poured hot water from the teakettle for herself. Still no sign of Shea.

"So, they just hauled Burr off to jail?" Liam asked her. "Was he drunk?"

"He was stumbling all over the place."

Of course he was.

She dropped a teabag into her mug, nodding. "You know," she began, "I put him to work on a project—moving rocks for me. Then, shortly after he left, I heard the woman scream. At first, I was afraid it was Shea. But then I saw her on the deck."

Liam closed his eyes. What if it had been Shea? He wanted to punch Burr. Except, now it was too late. He couldn't help him now, either. That realization sunk like a heavy rock thrown into the Sound.

And then, there was the victim of Burr's selfish foolishness.

"What about the woman? Is she okay?"

"Reports are she's in bad shape."

Someone wasn't going home to her family tonight. "Was it a neighbor?"

"I think she was here on vacation and out for a walk. No one in the neighborhood knew who she was. Probably renting one of the beach properties for a few nights."

Nausea churned in his gut. If it would help her to tell him the whole story, he'd listen. "Tell me everything." Calliope sighed in his arms, and he was glad to hold her right now. Auntie Mat led him to the kitchen table and poured ice water for him.

"I don't know everything that happened after he finished helping me out on the beach." She joined him at the table, placing a plate of shortbread cookies in the center. "He mentioned he was, I don't know, proud of you for going to see Jack. He kept bringing that up. And the rest I already covered."

Liam's gut tightened. He wasn't any kind of hero. Still no sound came from the stairs or the second floor. "How long has Shea been up there?"

"I suggested a hot bath about forty-five minutes ago. She just didn't seem to . . . come back, after the police drove Dylan away and we returned inside."

Liam would run upstairs in a minute. Maybe he could help, not that he had any training. But he'd do what he could. "Do you think Jinx or JP or Hitch know yet?"

Auntie shook her head. "This is probably something you should tell them."

Ten minutes later, Liam hung up after talking to Jinx, who promised to call Hitch, JP, and Eli first thing in the morning. Now Liam had two things on his mind. One, Burr, given his history and what had happened tonight, was in for a world of hurt.

And two, Liam needed to check on Shea.

Her vision blurred as Shea rocked on the edge of the tub, which was barely wide enough for her. She'd drained the water, stood, wrapped herself in a towel and now she balanced here, arms and legs still wet, clumped hair dripping water onto her lap.

Mumbled voices rose from the kitchen below. Liam must be home.

She needed to pull herself together.

Counselors shouldn't let things get to them. A therapist should be able to overcome, properly catalog what she sees or hears. Process. Move forward. The phrases played in an endless loop. Still, she couldn't shake the cloudiness, the disconnect.

In a moment of clarity minutes ago, she'd self-diagnosed—dissociation brought on by a new trauma, which reminded her of earlier this week and that day long ago. Sitting here in a trance wasn't going to help her shake this any sooner. She had to try to bring herself back.

The past is behind me. I'm safe here. Focus on Jesus.

A glass dish containing polished, heart-shaped stones with a pillar candle nestled in the center sat on a tiny nearby table. She chose a green rock, ran her thumb over the smooth texture and took a deep breath, which she held before releasing. Holding the heart closer to her face, she eyed the speckles, counting them. *Be in this moment. Focus on your five senses.* She sniffed the rock. As she'd guessed, it smelled like the candle centered in the same dish—vanilla.

An image slammed into her mind of Dylan's face from tonight. That moment he'd staggered around to the back of the car and finally seen what had happened. The horror in his expression.

Come back to this moment.

She willed herself to exchange the smooth, polished stone for the rough, waxy unlit candle. The bathroom's steam had slicked its surface, but the pocked texture still drew her attention. Holding the candle to her face, she inhaled deeply.

I'm safe. Not standing in that minimart during college. Safe. Not watching the car accident at work. Safe. Not standing outside a few hours ago. Safe . . .

She breathed deeply again. Word association. Vanilla. Another long inhalation. Vanilla beans. White. Beauty. Perhaps purity. Sweetness. Recipes. Baking.

The work kept her mind busy, as she'd hoped. Bringing herself back from dissociation was hard work. The trance faded more with each minute that she fought it, though.

A light tap on the bathroom door drew her attention. She focused on the sounds out in the hallway—shuffling followed by two more taps on the door. "Shea, are you okay?" Liam asked. His voice was deeper than JP's. Something about that had always drawn her. Soothing. Comforting. Like someone she could lean on after what had happened tonight.

"Just got out of the tub," she said and cleared her throat. Why had she told him that? "I mean, I'll be out in a few minutes."

"No hurry, Shea. My aunt and I were wondering if you wanted to join us on the sunporch." *So you don't have to be alone right now.* He didn't add those words out loud, but that was the invitation she heard.

The idea of finding comfort together—the three of them, like a family—warmed her. Gave her hope. She'd like that. "Thanks. I'll be down soon."

Except right after she made the promise, panic crept through her veins. She'd rather they not see her like this. Maybe if she kept engaging her five senses, the dissociation would fade completely for the night.

She finished drying off, focusing on the towel's texture. Her jasmine body lotion soothed her skin. She tugged on shorts and a coral-colored T-shirt. The comb pulled on her hair as she dragged it through, the sensation keeping her grounded in the moment. No need to concern herself with makeup. It wasn't as if she had to impress Liam. He didn't want to date her, and though she shouldn't want a relationship with him—she did. Heaven help her—*Lord, help me—I do.*

More minutes passed as she tidied up the room, hanging her towels and wiping up water droplets from the floor. She couldn't stay in here forever.

Let them help you, dear Shea.

Jesus.

Hand on the doorknob, she went still. *Oh, Jesus.* He'd started calling her "dear Shea" after that horrible night. Every time He said it, her heart melted, tipping toward Him. Opening. Reaching.

Why was it so hard to seek help? Perhaps because she didn't believe it would make a difference. That was why she hadn't made the appointment with the new counselor yet.

I'm here. Such gentleness in His voice. In her spirit, she leaned into Him, closing her eyes, sighing.

You're my Counselor, my Prince of Peace, and I need You.

Dear Shea. That was her identity. A truth to ground her tonight. Every night. As "dear Shea" she was cherished. Imperfect, but accepted.

And yet, still broken.

CHAPTER TWENTY-SIX

Finally, Liam got his first glimpse of Shea as she descended the stairs, and her appearance confirmed his fears.

He'd been waiting on the enclosed porch with Auntie Mat, windows open to the screens, night falling around them. As late as it was—about 10:30—the skies were still blue above the Sound. Incoming waves provided background noise while they stewed, worrying about Shea, rehashing the night in silence. Well, Liam was. From the way she wrung her hands off and on, he guessed his aunt was too.

Shea appeared in the doorway, her eyes red and somewhat dazed. Her damp hair hung limp over her shoulders, wetting the short sleeves and collar of her T-shirt. She used a hand towel to wring it out. He'd never seen her so undone. Natural. Vulnerable. He counted it a privilege that she let them—him—see her like this.

He wanted to wrap her in his arms, reassure her. Carry what weighed her down. Didn't matter that he already hefted his own load. He kept picturing Burr in a jail cell. Catching himself before he grimaced at the image, he took a deep breath. Shea was the focus right now. He stood and shoved his hands into his pockets while his aunt opened her arms.

"Are you okay?" Auntie Mat asked her from near the doorway off the kitchen.

"I will be." Her voice sounded weak. Had she known the woman? That would make tonight even harder. Auntie Mat gave her a long hug.

A heron cried outside in the twilight.

The best thing he could do for her, like he'd done after the accident at work, was to listen. Or perhaps give her space to chat with his aunt, woman to woman. Maybe he should excuse himself.

The women broke off their hug while he debated, standing there next to the love seat. Shea ran her fingers under her eyes, draping the hand towel over the back of one of the wicker chairs on that side of the room. Then, she seemed to notice him for the first time. "Oh, Liam." She darted over and threw her arms around him. Gasping, he caught her, and his balance.

"Shea," he whispered, emotion hitting him, though he didn't understand it. Tonight began with seeing Jack, and then learning Burr had hit someone . . . How could all this be happening? Emotion swamped him like a tidal wave, and he barely caught another sob. No matter how irresponsible and, okay, selfish, Burr could be, there was no way he'd meant to hurt anyone. Though that was a risk he took every time he got behind the wheel after drinking.

She held him tight, and he gave himself over to her compassion. "I'm so sorry about Burr." Shea stayed right there in his arms, running a hand over his back as if she could hear his thoughts. As if she wasn't suffering, and only he was. Ridiculous that he'd felt put together until her compassion undid him.

He'd been trying to comfort her, for crying out loud.

"I was hoping we could help him," she said, her tone hoarse.

Liam could relate and that hurt even more. No matter what Liam had tried, nothing kept Burr from sabotaging his own life. "So not your fault, Shea." He squeezed her tighter, barely getting his voice to work. He'd felt her compassion, could she feel his? That sounded corny in his head, but he'd skydive without a chute right now if he thought it could help Shea.

"Ah! I'm getting your shirt all wet!" She pulled back and braided her damp hair.

"Don't worry about me." His arms felt empty and cold. He pocketed his hands again, his vision still blurry with tears.

Auntie Mat let Calliope in from a late-night trip to the yard and then snuggled her, as if glad for someone to love on.

Liam didn't know what to do. He wanted Shea comfortable, to somehow ease those lines around her eyes tonight. Relieving even a part of her pain would make him feel less useless right now. "Please"—he gestured toward the loveseat—"sit. Do you need anything?"

She sat, shaking her head. Then, she used a hairband from her wrist to hold back her long side braid. "I'm okay, thanks." She studied him. "You're kind; you know that? That's one of the things I like about you." The words came out almost under her breath, but he caught them. He marveled at how open she seemed. He liked this side of her, a lot.

"Please, Liam. Sit." She patted the spot left of her on the love seat.

He'd planned to pull up an ottoman, try not to crowd her. He raised his brows. *Really?* He'd be close if he sat there.

"Yeah." She answered his silent question aloud. When he still hesitated, she pointed. "Sit." Her command got a noise out of Calliope, and Liam obliged like a pup, chuckling. Shea laughed. "I like how you can lighten a mood too," she said to him. It's as if she were adding up a checklist of his better qualities. That felt good.

He'd spent a lifetime creating the opposite list.

Sitting beside her, their shoulders kept bumping as his aunt asked her questions. He needed a place for his arm. He shifted, and then his leg bumped her knee.

Shea faced him. "You can put your arm over the back of the love seat," she murmured. "It's okay."

He stretched out, sighing. "Thanks." He clutched the wicker near her shoulder, tried to tune in to what his aunt was saying. But Shea's fresh-from-the-shower scent distracted him.

"I love seeing the two of you together," Auntie Mat said from her spot near the kitchen door. "It does my heart good. I'm glad you found each other." She snuggled her dog, eyes closed as if in her own world. They still hadn't discussed Jack, but there'd be time for that after Shea was feeling better.

Liam tensed, ready to set her straight. The last thing Shea needed tonight was pressure to date him. "Um, Auntie Mat, we're not—"

While he spoke, Shea raised her left hand, crossing her arm over her chest, taking his hand from the back of the love seat, and threading her fingers through his over her right shoulder. Her skin felt smooth. What was happening? He gulped. "I'm glad too, Miss Matilda. Really glad. And I know it puts your mind at ease, which we appreciate, don't we, Liam?"

He blinked, held his breath, searched the shadowy corners of the room as if they might give him answers.

Her elbow nudged his chest, and he met her eyes—so close to his own. "Right?"

He was glad they were friends now . . . Before he could answer, Calliope hopped from his aunt's arms and chased into the kitchen, barking. "What in the world? Calliope!" His aunt followed the dog. "Quiet! You'll wake Pearl."

Moments later, Shea released his hand and turned. He left his arm behind her and pulled back enough to clearly see her face. "What's going on?"

"Sorry." She stood, walked toward the windows, then pivoted to face him. "Your aunt mentions her desire to see you settled down almost every evening. And now, with her news, I thought, well . . . now I wonder if I've rushed things. I'm not thinking straight tonight."

Liam stood up, his mind catching on a certain phrase. "Her what now?" *Please don't let Auntie Mat be sick.* Like Mom.

"Oh, no. She hasn't told you yet . . . I *did* blow it." Shea rubbed her lower back as if the day's tension had lodged there. When she finally tipped up her head again, she watched him as if diagnosing him. If only he could bail. But his feet wouldn't move. Words didn't form.

"Are you okay?"

No. No, he wasn't. Suddenly he couldn't remember his own name. He dropped onto the love seat. What was happening to him?

She dragged the ottoman closer and sat near him. "It's too much at once," she said as if addressing his confusion. "You need time to process all of it. Someone safe to talk to about each event, one after the other with time in between." When she went silent, the only sound was the rhythmic waves outside, as if God Himself were reminding Liam of His faithful presence with a whispered *I'm here.*

Liam's thoughts wouldn't line up, like he was checking out or something. Was he losing his grip on reality?

Shea tipped her head, gained eye contact. "How can I help? I know you met with Jack tonight. Do you want to talk about it?" Her golden-brown eyes sparkled in the pale light from the corner lamp.

"Wait . . ." He shook his head. Why wasn't his mind working? "I was trying to help *you*."

"I think you're the one who needs help right now." She reached toward his arm. "May I?"

He blinked at her. "Okay."

"Here." She took his hand. Her eyes were clear. But Liam feared his were now glassy. "Try to stay in this moment. Set aside everything else that happened tonight or before. There will be time to get to each incident. Squeeze my hand, then release. What do you notice? Use your five senses."

He tried to follow her simple instructions, squeezing her hand.

"Tell me what you notice," she encouraged again.

His gaze darted between their joined hands and her face. "Your skin is smooth."

"Okay, good. Keep going. What else do you notice about this moment, right here?" She leaned closer as if holding him prisoner with her gaze.

"You smell like some type of flower." Where had his oxygen gone? Had the breeze off the Sound stopped?

"Jasmine."

"Jasmine . . . I like it. I've always liked it on you." Her eyes met his, and he studied them. "Your eyes are brown with gold. I've never seen anyone else with that color."

Her face broke into a grin. "Not even my big brother?"

"I have no idea." A chuckle came out, and the fog thinned. "Why would I notice that about him?"

"Of course." She grinned. "Keep going."

"Um, I like holding your hand." His mind was clearing. Words formed. "And I like being close to you. A lot."

She went still.

He shouldn't have said that, even though it was true. Wanting to date her and being free to do so were two very different things. And he wouldn't risk it. But he also didn't let go of her hand. He ran his thumb over her knuckles. "Thanks for bringing me back."

She looked away, swallowed. "Well, you've done the same thing for me a few times, so perhaps we're even."

He didn't want to be even; he wanted a relationship. "And thanks for being an easy person to talk to."

"You're a safe person too. Like when you gave me space at the cottage that day—standing outside in the rain until I felt comfortable. Or lunch at Madison's."

With all this openness tonight, maybe he could bring up what he'd been wanting to ask her. "Why do you startle so easily?" She hadn't explained what she meant about "the attack," and he feared the worst. He'd never forgive himself if something horrible had happened to her because he'd never shown up.

She let go of his hand, straightened her shoulders, and dragged in a deep breath. "That's a topic for another day." Her smile was kind, though her words were firm. When she stood, he joined her. "I hope you sleep well tonight. Don't rush things, but do take time to process and don't worry if it *takes* time. The human mind is a complicated place."

No kidding. He'd had no idea. All this hitting him in one night almost threw him into the loony bin, whatever that meant. Okay, so even now he wasn't quite forming logical thoughts.

Maybe he'd been wrong about therapists after all. "Can you answer a question for me before you head upstairs?"

She stopped on her way toward the kitchen. "Sure."

"What just happened? I mean, we need to talk about the whole dating thing," he said, keeping his voice low. He gave her a momentary grin, and she returned it. Then, he pointed at his head. "But with me, what was that? Do you know?"

She eyed him as if trying to discern if he was serious. Finally, "You were dissociating because you've been through a lot tonight. You were slipping into a bit of a trancelike state. Don't worry—perfectly natural. Everyone does it. If you've ever daydreamed by letting your sight go blurry and 'staring off into space,' you've been in a trance. It's God's way, I think, of giving us a chance to catch our breath mentally, emotionally, even physically, because it forces us to take a break from everything around us."

"But I couldn't even think straight." The lack of control was unnerving.

"That's partly how I know what it was. Again, perfectly natural. Take time to think through, or better yet, talk through, what happened tonight. Soon. But sleep first. You need it."

"Yes, ma'am, Counselor Shea." He let affection come through in his words, because he no longer meant them in a teasing way. "You should talk to someone about your stuff too."

"Oh, I will." She sounded more convinced than she had before tonight.

"Thank you."

Her smile was open and gentle. "You're welcome, Liam."

After saying good night to his aunt, Shea disappeared upstairs. He had a million questions for Auntie Mat, plus a whole story to tell her, but he was too tired to think. They'd have to talk later. Fatigue washed over him as he hugged her in the kitchen.

"Sleep here tonight, Liam." She didn't seem in a hurry to talk about everything right now either. Plus, what if Liam dissociated again and Shea wasn't there to bring him back?

Ten minutes later, they'd made up the sofa bed for him, and he crashed.

CHAPTER TWENTY-SEVEN

Somewhere around 5:30 the following morning, Liam rolled off the sofa, smacking the floor with a thud. He groaned as he righted himself and then perched with his back to the sofa, rubbing his shoulder where he'd landed. Sunlight shot across the sky outside the east-facing windows over the lagoon, brightening the living room. Someone bumped around in the kitchen. Auntie Mat? Or Shea? After hitting the bathroom, he padded out there to see.

Shea stood near the sink, pouring orange juice into a glass.

"Hey, Shea." His voice came out scratchy.

She didn't startle this time. Maybe he was becoming a normal part of her life. That realization felt good to his foggy brain.

"You okay?" She reached for another small glass and held it toward him, eyebrows raised with the silent question of whether he wanted some too. He nodded. "I heard you fall," she said, pouring him a glassful, "but when I peeked in, you were in the bathroom."

He rubbed his shoulder, rolled his neck. "Yeah. I'm fine. Stupid couch."

She frowned as if picturing him falling off the couch. "You sleep at all?"

"Four hours, maybe." He accepted the glass and let the citrus burn his throat, but the coolness felt good.

"Me too."

He met her gaze, held her there. "Are you okay?" *I'm safe. Talk to me.*

She broke eye contact and her attention slipped over his face. He reached up and scratched a palm over his scruffy skin. Seeing her at this early hour, hair piled high on her head in a type of looping, gorgeous knot. Without makeup. Loose-fitting sweatpants and a tee under her open robe. Yeah, she distracted him too. Was she thinking the same thing—that this morning felt right, and intimate, all at once?

Shea stepped back and reached into the fridge for a bowl of strawberries. "I'll cut these up, if you'll work on the cantaloupe." She handed him the melon.

"Sure." He'd prefer bacon and hash browns with scrambled eggs, but fruit was fine too. Especially with Shea smelling like— what had she called it? Jasmine—and standing so close as they worked at the counter. *Sleep on, Auntie.*

"Sure," she said, echoing him and using a low voice.

"Hey!" He set down his knife and nudged her left side with his elbow. "What's the matter?" He spoke as deeply in his range as he could.

She giggled, and he relished the sound. Then she chopped more fruit. "So, you do, or you don't, like the idea of dating me?"

He almost choked on the juicy bite of muskmelon he'd popped into his mouth. "Come again." Suddenly he wanted to buy time. What had he said last night?

Her shoulders rose and fell, remaining a bit hunched as she bent over her strawberry slicing chore. "I mean it's fine if you see me like a sister."

He snorted before he realized she was serious. He did *not* see her as a sister. He never had. Her attention shot to his face, and she studied his eyes before redirecting to her growing pile of red strawberry slices. So much hurt in her expression.

Knife still on the counter, he touched her shoulder, tipping his head toward her own knife until she set it down. Then he gently turned her to face him, lightly taking hold of each shoulder. "Seriously? That's what you think?"

Those shoulders tried to shrug again under his gentle touch. When she dipped her head, he did too and caught her eyes. "Oh, Shea... I have never seen you as a sister. Why do you think I wanted to date you in college?"

Her hands flapped between them. "Well, that was a long time ago. Now, I'm all damaged and jittery. I jump at every—"

He tugged her close, and she stepped into his hug. Had he overstepped? Her arms wrapping around him showed he hadn't.

Then, she gave a long sigh as he rubbed her back. This idea that he'd reject her—how long had she thought that?

"You've seen me all anxious, and broken. Who wants to date someone who's freaked out half the time?"

He leaned away and waited until he had her focus again. This close her eyes reflected his image up to him, about six inches taller than she was. "I care about you."

She swallowed.

"And you are not broken." *I am.* But he didn't say that aloud. This moment was about her.

"Really? You don't think I'm too messed up?"

"We're *all* messed up."

She went still. Was she replaying their conversation? "You care about me?"

"I always have."

"Then, why . . .?"

He tilted his head. "You think Auntie Mat," he whispered, "should determine if we date or not? I'd like *us* to decide and then tell her, if we do choose to try again."

"I might not be good at this."

"I *know* I'm not good at this." But could he be?

She squeezed his bicep. "You don't give yourself enough credit."

He took a deep breath and watched her do the same. "Do you want to try again?"

She nodded up at him. "Do you?"

He shifted on his feet. "I don't want to let you down like before."

"If this is about the house—"

"It's not."

"Oh."

"You never told me what happened that night in college."

"I will. Soon."

He studied her lips and then her eyes. "I guess we have a few things to figure out first, then."

"Okay."

"For now, one more hug. Because we could both use one." Shea pulled him closer and tucked her face against his chest where his heart thumped. He held her tight. "Thanks, Liam. And thanks for last night. Hanging out with you and your aunt kept me from getting too lost." The images still came at her, but today she had more distance and more control.

She inhaled deeply. Liam smelled of something she couldn't identify, but it was masculine and inviting.

"You're welcome. Anytime I can help, let me know."

He was pulling away, if not physically, then emotionally. Why? If she tried to meet his gaze right now, he'd no doubt walk away with an excuse about getting to work on the cottage next door.

And how good did it feel to know he didn't see her as broken? He may not have meant it, but those words rooted around in her heart and sought a soft spot to grow into something. Paired with *I care for you* and *I've always wanted to date you.*

"I'm sorry I implied to your aunt that we're dating." She said the words quietly. His back muscles stiffened. Maybe he was concerned about lying to Matilda. Or maybe he was about to let Shea down easily. "I can set her straight this morning, if you want."

He loosened his hug, and she tipped back. Helping Auntie Mat had been on her mind with this fake-a-relationship plan. But then she'd seen Liam's kindness again last night. His compassion. She valued that in others because, in her experience, very few people exhibited empathy. He also seemed rather humble, and he was always watching out for his aunt. That nobility demonstrated a strong character more than any words could. Plus, he was working very hard at the cottage—her cottage. He kept doing things for her, and goodness, but that thoughtfulness touched something deep in her heart.

"You need to understand the reason I'm concerned about this, Shea." Liam's gaze hooked hers. Could he see all her doubts? "Shea, I want to date you. I always have."

"Great!" Miss Matilda breezed into the kitchen, catching them. "That's what I wanted to hear. And now I've heard it from both of you. Finally!" She wore a flowing robe over shiny, modest pajamas, all in pink, and walked straight to the countertop toward the fruit. "Looks good."

Shea didn't know what to do, so she fell into place beside Liam, with one arm around his back. Wonder of wonders, he circled one arm behind her back too. She peered up at him. What was he thinking?

"You may be onto something, Auntie." Liam squeezed Shea's side and instinctively, she pressed her face to his chest, against his shoulder as if the small hollow space were meant for her head. "Plus, when you find someone as ... precious as Shea, or as beautiful inside and out, you want to make sure she knows it." He gazed down at her with open adoration, and her heart thumped.

Wearing a big grin, Miss Mat clapped her hands together, which brought Calliope from the sunporch. "Yay! Then it's settled."

She may never have this chance again, so Shea decided to seize it. While Miss Matilda's back was turned, Shea reached up on tiptoes and pressed a kiss to Liam's scruffy face, lingering for a moment when he melted against her lips and leaned into her. His hands came up to her elbows and held her for a second before she lowered herself and pulled back. Then he met her gaze, wearing a hint of a grin like he knew what she was up to and he didn't mind one bit.

CHAPTER TWENTY-EIGHT

How was Liam supposed to concentrate after Shea kissed him? Sure, it'd been a couple of days, but he kept replaying the way she'd stretched up to catch him by surprise. *Focus, Barrett.* Now that the countertops were in place, he could install the backsplash in the cottage's kitchen and the two bathrooms. That was almost mindless work, which meant he had a lot of time to think.

Shortly after Auntie Mat caught them chatting Saturday morning, Shea had excused herself. That left him alone with his aunt, trying to tolerate her giggles and gloating. She whipped up bacon and hash browns for him, as she'd done many times before. "I knew it. I knew it!" She kept saying the phrase while Liam tried to piece together what had happened.

Shea seemed willing to attempt a relationship. He wanted that too, but he didn't want to hurt her.

That was something Jack would do.

Jack.

"So, let's talk about last night," Auntie Mat invited as she joined him at the table. "About your get-together."

He gave her the details, even confessing that he'd run away at first. If she was disappointed, she hid it well. She studied him peacefully, with love in her eyes. Acceptance. And empathy. When he finished, she gave him a moment. "It's possible you're assuming too much about Jack. How do you know any of what you believe about him—good or bad—is actually true? You might have to get to know him to sift through all of it."

What, did she have an agreement with God to push Liam out of his comfort zone and into Jack's vicinity? Liam wasn't planning to ever see him again. He'd said what he needed to say.

"Any word on Dylan or the victim?" she asked him.

"Nothing yet."

Then, he remembered Shea's words about Auntie Mat. "How have you been feeling?" His mother had died of cancer. Was it possible his aunt hid such a secret? That thought could bring him to his knees.

She reached across the table and covered his hand. "I'm fine."

"Remember, we have a deal."

"I know. I won't forget."

"If you get sick, you tell me. None of this, 'Keep it from Liam. He'll never know.' It didn't work when I was eleven, and it won't work now." He'd known Mom was sick and had never understood why they weren't straight with him.

"I got it," she assured him. "But I'm fine. Truly."

Should Liam tell his aunt what Shea had said? He didn't want to break Shea's confidence. Maybe he'd fish for a minute and see what his aunt might reveal. "Shea tells me you've mentioned to her you don't like that I'm not married yet."

"Oh, I dearly hope she didn't feel pressured." She used a Southern accent and put a hand to her chest as if she wasn't guilty.

He laughed out loud. "You, my dear aunt, are *not* innocent. You've talked her into dating the son of a deadbeat. Not a good idea." He'd been kidding, wanting to keep things light, figure out what news his aunt might have, but those words he'd just spit out didn't lend themselves to keeping things light.

Her face contorted into one of pain and sadness. "Is that how you see yourself?" No accent now. "The 'son of a deadbeat'? Aw, Liam."

Her tone brought a lump to his throat. She'd always been too perceptive where he was concerned. Always one step ahead of him, seemingly knowing his motives and ill-advised plans before he carried them out. He pushed back from the table, and she caught his hand again. "Son. Stay."

He resettled and studied his plate.

"You are *not* 'the son of a deadbeat.'"

His eyes burned, and he couldn't look at her.

"Hey." She dipped her head, trying to meet his gaze. "Hey," she whispered again, making contact. "*You* are the son of a beautiful woman, my niece, who gave everything to see that you had a good start in life. And you're my son"—eyes shining, she put her free hand on her heart—"since I never had my own children. You are my son," she repeated, "and I am not a deadbeat."

His chin trembled. "No, no you're not. And neither was Mom."

She gave one sharp bob of her head. "That's right. And we raised you. So, no more of this deadbeat talk."

He nodded, wanting to see himself the way she did.

"You got it?"

His jaw felt tight, fighting all this emotion. But she deserved an answer and judging by the way she wasn't letting up—all that intensity in her forward-leaning posture and unblinking gaze—he'd better give her one. "Yeah."

"You might find, as you're dating Shea, that she doesn't see you the way you see yourself either. Please, let our positive opinions matter where your value is concerned, your sense of identity." She didn't defend Jack again, and he could have kissed her for that. In fact, he did before he headed out to work on the cottage next door.

"Love you," he said, his voice still tight.

"You have my heart, Son."

Now as he worked on the backsplash at the cabin, he tried to plan what he'd say to Shea.

She'd seen herself as broken, but Liam knew she wasn't. She was only wounded, and given time and good help, she'd probably feel better, startle less. *Lord, if therapy ever works for anyone, let it work for Shea so she can be happy again.* Like during their early college days.

And His name will be called Wonderful, Counselor, Mighty God, Everlasting Father, Prince of Peace.

The Scripture ran through his mind, and he paused from pressing the tiles into place. "Counselor?" He whispered to the ceiling. God had made people, and God called Himself a counselor. Maybe people sometimes needed help, for the sake of strong mental health, or in the case of trauma, as a means of getting past the ordeal.

He hoped she found the right match for her, someone who knew what they were doing and could help her.

CHAPTER TWENTY-NINE

Shea knew the process. She'd worked with tactile pulsers before.

Her new counselor, Natalie Patton, used EMDR—eye-movement desensitization and reprocessing—therapy like Shea had sometimes done with her patients. But Natalie had been in practice much longer, since she was probably twenty years older than Shea. The two-piece palm-sized handheld device was wired together to a central control, so each device could be adjusted as to intensity and pulse duration. The device would alternate buzzing, first left, then right, back and forth. The patient held the pulsers in her hands, and they vibrated alternately, stimulating both sides of the patient's brain while they talked.

If you could stimulate both hemispheres of the brain, you could overrule the emotional portion and keep the logical left side engaged to think through, and discuss problems, and help catalog—or process—trauma. This was the same technique she used on her own whenever she was triggered, when she alternately squeezed first one fist and then the other. Having an instrument do that for her, meant a more consistent stimulation of her brain, and one she didn't have to concentrate on.

Her therapist recommended they meet twice a week for a month and reevaluate at that point. They'd been working for nearly forty minutes already, and today they were only setting the background for working through the violent event.

As Shea drove back to the cottage, she longed for a peaceful place to review the first session. Her boss had recommended Natalie, and she'd been right. The therapist did seem like a strong fit. And she'd affirmed Shea, telling her that she shouldn't feel ashamed at not finding healing earlier, that now was the right time to seek help again.

Still, Shea worried about her own patients at the Bremerton clinic in her absence. She knew Tia would help as much as possible, and Vanessa would take some of the kids. Yet Shea felt like she'd abandoned them. Hopefully, they didn't feel the same.

She pulled into the cottage driveway to bright sunshine in her eyes this late morning. The lagoon lay before her car, calm, deep, peaceful. Liam could probably use her help painting the living room at the cottage, but she wanted to take a kayak into the lagoon and paddle around for an hour. The tide was in, filling the inlet with calm, almost still saltwater. If she followed through and headed out there, Liam would be able to see her. She'd seem lazy. Good mental health sometimes required a break. Isn't that what she'd told Liam earlier? Still, guilt poked her for needing downtime.

Without debating any longer, she climbed from her car and headed for the shed. Mom and Dad kept four kayaks here. Hopefully, they weren't full of spiders. The shed probably harbored more than bugs. She'd never looked too closely.

Her patients would likely relate, but she felt vulnerable after her appointment. Exposed. Breakable. She'd probably dissociate at the first sign of being startled. Natalie had reiterated what Shea already knew about bringing herself back whenever she was triggered. But she hoped for a restful afternoon. Natalie had also said to take time for herself; that was part of the healing process.

Liam stepped out of the cottage just as Shea was crossing the small yard to the shed. "Hey."

His smile was welcoming, almost careful like he knew where she'd been. Or was he thinking of their interactions earlier and all their talk of a relationship? Nonsense. She couldn't even imagine that now.

"Hi." Being polite meant making small talk, but she didn't have the energy. "I hope you don't mind. I need a break from everything. I'd be happy to help in the cottage later. Right now, I thought I'd kayak around the lagoon for a bit."

He grinned down at her. "What? No attempts to tame churning Puget Sound for you?"

She had noticed the Sound was throwing foaming waves at the shore. As usual, one view showed rougher waters than the other. "Not today." She opened the shed door and stood back when a huge spider web blocked her. Of course, Liam would be up for any type of adventure in the Sound. Paddle-boarding clear to the other side of Port Madison. Uncaring about the depths of the bay or what he might run into.

Miss Mat appeared in her yard near the property line. "Oh, are you two headin' out on the water?" She used her Southern accent.

"Um . . ." Liam hedged. Of course, he had work to do, and Shea needed a bit of space. He didn't have to join her.

"I'm sure Shea won't mind you takin' a half hour off from work to spend a little quality time together." Miss Mat faced Shea. "Right?"

"Okay . . . why not?" *Note to self: next time, visit the park.* But she sincerely wouldn't mind the company, if Liam kept looking at her like he had that morning—all tender and concerned. Like a friend.

Liam stood closer than Matilda, and he leaned in. He smelled good. "Are you sure you don't mind?"

She snagged a breath and nodded. "I'm sure. Let's grab the rowboat. We can go together." She closed the shed door on the spider web and turned her back. Like her past, and nearly everything else in her life if she had her way, she'd deal with that later.

They waved at Matilda and pulled the rowboat from its spot where it leaned against the deck. She scanned for spiders and snakes. It wasn't unusual for a garter snake to curl up in a boat and sleep.

"Everything okay?" Liam asked when she hesitated.

"Just checking for critters."

"Oh, of course." He set down his side and circled the whole rowboat. "I don't see anything." He came to a stop beside her and ran his hand under the boat's lip—how did he do that? What if there were creatures under there? "I think we're clear."

She offered him a weak smile. "Thanks."

He studied her for a moment longer then shifted the front of the boat. "Shall we?"

She nodded and hefted her end.

"I'll row," Liam volunteered, and Shea wouldn't mind just riding along, so she didn't object. An accusation went off in her mind again—lazy! But she shushed it. She'd advised her patients plenty of times, sometimes you had to let others do things for you.

Saltwater flowed into the lagoon now as the tide pushed in. Once they'd positioned the rowboat halfway into the water, Liam motioned, and she climbed in and scooted to the forward bench. Rocking the boat side to side, Liam pushed off and jumped in to sit on the rear seat. Then, he reached for the oars in turn and threaded them through the loops, securing them with the rings.

She held on to the edge with her free hand while he worked. "I'm glad we're not in the canoe." Not that it was deep here, right?

He watched her closely. "You need a life jacket? Please tell me you can swim."

"I can swim. I just don't like getting wet when I didn't plan on it." He was close in this small craft, and their knees kept touching.

He rowed them toward the center of the lagoon. "I know this isn't your speed, Liam. That you love adrenaline and thrills. But thanks for coming out here."

"Sorry about my aunt. She is rather . . . pushy sometimes."

"Nah, it's fine."

"You seemed preoccupied. How'd your meeting go?"

Last weekend, God had nudged her to share her struggle with both Miss Mat and Liam, to let them help her. Over the past few weeks, she'd discovered Liam made a rather good friend. He'd been trustworthy, so far. "I saw the counselor my boss recommended this morning. They're old acquaintances. She fit me in on a moment's notice, and she seems like a good match. We'll see each other again in a couple of days." Shea sighed, dreading the next meeting when they'd rehash that first traumatic event.

Like today, they'd use the pulsers for ABS—alternating bilateral stimulation. The strategy of Cognitive Restructuring was to walk through the traumatic event, minute by minute, speaking every detail she could remember. The ABS device would keep her left brain working to help her think as clearly as possible. Getting the event out into the open would rob some of its power, clear up any misconceptions about what really happened, and give her a chance to reframe it. Her counselor would then have her imagine herself as the strong, capable woman she was today joining herself in that situation with reassurance, wisdom, and words of hope. She may even have Shea imagine rescuing herself. It was a long, emotional process. One Shea had never gotten to in all these years, even though she knew the science behind it.

Sometimes God didn't choose to heal. What if—maybe for the sake of her remaining compassionate with her own patients—He planned to let Shea deal with this all her life? What if this, her final hope for any kind of healing and relief from the PTSD, didn't work?

The rowboat glided through the water, and Shea shifted her weight to get more comfortable, while Liam worked at moving them across the calm lagoon. "I hope—well, I'm praying it works for you this time."

She raised her eyebrows. First, that he'd believe in a therapeutic approach seemed like a breakthrough. But that he was praying again? Wow. "Thank you, Liam. That means more to me than you know."

He looked away. Was he embarrassed? She wasn't in a mental place where she could filter her words or her actions right now. One wrong move and she didn't know what she was capable of confessing or doing. If he kept acting heroic, being considerate, helping her, she was liable to do more than kiss his face.

He shifted, and their legs touched, and she didn't pull away. No other residents were out on the water right now. They had relative privacy, though each of the houses on this side of Barclay Spit had a clear view of the small bay. "Wanna discuss anything?" He seemed uncomfortable as if there was something *he* wanted to bring up.

"Like . . . ?" She hoped he didn't want her to share her thoughts, muddled as they were.

"Oh, I don't know." He grinned at her. "There was that moment Saturday morning when you snuck up on me."

She laughed at his tone and his expression. "I did not."

"Oh, you did." He nudged her with his knee, and she playfully knocked him back.

"Okay, we can talk about that." Why not? The topic of kissing

Liam was more enjoyable than her therapy appointment. "Let's see, it's hard for me to resist a few things in life."

He snorted and seemed to fight a grin.

She held up her forefinger. "One, a man's scruffy face—especially yours."

His eyebrows rose.

"Two"—she held up two fingers together—"a man who is respectful to his former guardian and other women, and is considerate."

His gaze went more serious, thoughtful, as he slowed his rowing. They were near the center of the small harbor now.

"And three"—she raised her ring finger with the other two—"someone who had had a rough night himself, but who comes home and makes sure everyone *else* is okay." She still couldn't get over the fact he'd done that. Selflessness, another quality she admired.

He swallowed, and the oars went still.

"What?"

"You're killing me with your speech. Do I get a turn?"

She pressed a palm to her chest and gave him a dopey grin, just to keep things light. "I don't think I can take it."

He leaned toward her. "It's only fair."

Pressing one hand to the rowboat's seat, she locked her elbow and decided to humor him. "Okay, fire away."

"First, it's easy to respect you because you're full of dignity and grace." He didn't count off on his fingers because his hands were occupied holding those oars. "Second, you are beautiful inside and out—that needed repeating from Friday night. And third, I hope to one day return the gesture."

She froze. He was planning to kiss her?

Keeping eye contact, he let his words sink in and then started rowing again. Houses lined most of this D-shaped cove, but trees obscured the houses' windows on the mainland side. Liam steered them toward that stretch of land.

His grin slowly faded, though his expression stayed open and kind. "But I did want to ask you about something. Getting back to our chat at the diner—about the attack, what happened?"

Feeling more relaxed now, Shea decided she might have the courage to finally tell him. "This won't be fun to hear." Or say.

He stilled the oars and gave her a nod. "Warning received." Was it her imagination or did his muscles tighten, even though he wasn't working?

This was the story she'd share with Natalie during their next session, but she didn't need to go into as many details today. Like their rowboat, she'd skim the surface.

At her sides, she squeezed first one fist and then the other. She'd try to keep the accusation out of her voice, because those events still affected her, and it was challenging not to place blame.

Though she still dealt with the consequences and always might, maybe it was time for her to forgive Liam for his part in what happened.

CHAPTER THIRTY

Across from Liam, Shea tensed and made alternating fists. Was she gearing up to punch something? That wasn't like her, so he pushed the crazy thought away. What was she doing? And hadn't he seen her do this before?

Her tanned legs almost glowed in the sunlight as she sat across from him wearing shorts and a flowy sleeveless top. Anklets circled one lower leg and drew his eyes to her sandals, and bracelets jangled on one of her wrists. Without sunglasses, she squinted, and so did he because of the bright skies around them. Many Seattleites, in his experience, squinted when the sun, and the mountains—due to cleared visibility—finally came out.

"Remember that night we were supposed to go to the theater?"

"Sure ..." He tipped his head, waiting for her. He'd wondered about that night a lot lately, especially after she mentioned an attack. But he'd try not to let his own angst show up in his actions. The last thing Shea needed was his reaction making her feel worse.

"I have PTSD, because of what happened that night. Do you know what that is?"

His muscles went tight, though he tried to appear relaxed. "Post-traumatic stress disorder." *Please tell me* you *weren't attacked. Please, Lord ...*

"It means I have flashbacks and that I startle easily, dissociate—disconnect from reality. Some sufferers have recurring nightmares, or anxiety, or depression. We can't break out of the flashbacks, while sometimes we wish we could go back and relive that moment again and do something to achieve a different outcome. Not everyone responds to trauma with PTSD, and some people take a long time to process, get through treatment, find healing or any semblance of peace."

"What happened?" He barely had the courage, or the breath, to ask. His back went tight, his shoulders and arms tensed as he squeezed the oar handles with a profound urge to protect her. Or avenge her.

He'd known that area of town wasn't very safe, but he'd wanted to surprise her, so he'd asked her to meet him at the minimart. His plan was for them to walk together to the theater, which chronically lacked parking. But, he'd fallen asleep. "Did someone hurt you?" *Please say no.* He didn't know how he'd live with any other answer.

"Not physically." She sighed, and he barely let himself breathe. Their boat drifted off toward someone's dock, so he rowed them back toward the center where she could talk without worrying about being overheard. He'd love to hold one of her hands, given how challenging this seemed for her. But he kept his grip on the oars as they dripped over the water and made himself meet her gaze as often as possible. Whatever she had to say, he'd face it straight on. And he'd own up to his side of it because that's something a solid guy would do.

"The following day, do you remember anything in the news about that minimart?"

Nothing came to mind. "No." His heart pounded.

Her fists worked faster now, one and then the other. "Well, I parked there, didn't see your car. Decided to go inside and grab a drink, because I was thirsty. While I was inside, a group of—I don't know, gang members?—showed up in the parking lot. They all rode motorcycles, had greasy hair, tattoos, leather vests, muscles. They were cussing each other out, goading each other." She trembled, though the sun beat down on them in this exposed lagoon. If they were on land, he'd ask if he could hug her and somehow soothe away the memories. What would a counselor suggest he do for her in this moment? And what did she mean she wasn't hurt physically? He'd been finally able to fill his lungs with those words, but confusion settled in.

He crossed the oars in front of himself, held them with one hand, and reached for her. She'd have to give up on the fist-making, so he wasn't sure she'd let him take her hand. But she did.

"I kept waiting for you. When you were about forty-five

minutes late, and I couldn't reach you, I decided you weren't coming. But I couldn't leave the minimart with those thugs out there. Eventually, I told the clerk that I was going to try to get to my car—the men all surrounded it by then. And I asked her if she could watch me because we both knew I was taking my life in my hands." Shea straightened. "But I was also angry because I didn't want to be afraid or intimidated."

Their boat drifted north, but he couldn't let go of her now. He gulped. Guilt pounded him. "How did you get out of there?"

She gave a sad shake of her head. "The clerk on duty that night was female—poor woman. I hated that she had to work in that area alone at night. I could tell she was scared, like me. She pointed me toward the phone, but there was no dial tone as if the number had been disconnected. When I called the police with my cell phone, the operator sounded bored and annoyed since no crime had been committed. She said she'd notify dispatch but couldn't promise we'd see the authorities for a long time since they were tied up with priority calls. It was getting dark, and I couldn't stay there all night, so eventually I marched toward my car, rehearsing my self-defense training and clutching pepper spray in my fist. The clerk went out and distracted them. I got into my car. Then, one of the guys grabbed a rock and bashed it against my window, trying to get in. He said if I didn't let him in, he'd hurt the woman. I was terrified."

She gulped and stared off toward the floor of the boat. Liam held his breath, squeezing her hand. "I started my engine, and the man yelled at me, but then he strutted over to the woman. That's when I escaped. She couldn't get back inside to lock the doors." Shea wouldn't tell him everything. She couldn't. "Last thing I saw in the rearview mirror after I pulled away was a couple of the thugs standing over her as she lay on the ground. One of them kicked her, and the rest gathered around. I—I couldn't go back and put myself in danger again. Shaking, I honked like mad at the closest stoplight, frantically pointing, and two pickup truck drivers turned into the parking lot. Then, I drove to a nearby urgent care clinic, and they called the police, who sent officers and an ambulance. That poor woman." Another shake of her head.

What would he have done? It was hard to imagine that kind of vulnerability. He'd never been a woman or been in that situation. "I think you did the right thing." He could guess what they'd have done to her if she'd opened her door, and there was no guarantee they wouldn't still have harmed the clerk.

"She sacrificed her safety for me."

"Do you know what actually happened?"

"I think they beat her up." She took a long, shaky breath.

He rubbed her smooth skin. "I'm sorry I wasn't there." Not that he could've taken on a whole gang, but he'd have done whatever it took to protect Shea. "No wonder you didn't want to see me after that. You needed someone you could trust." Liam did not fit that bill. No matter how hard he tried.

She gripped his hand tighter. "But I'm learning that you *are* someone I can trust. Now."

He shook his head. She'd suffered so much because he'd been unreliable. "I didn't have your cottage ready for you on time." He let go of her hand and made a Y with his thumb and pinky and shook the "hang-ten" sign like a surfer in Hawaii. But he couldn't even muster a smile. Then he slowly rowed them back toward Shea's cottage.

She shrugged. "Honest mistake. Plus, you've worked really hard every day to get me closer to moving in." Was that a hint of admiration in her voice? Admiration he didn't deserve. Maybe Auntie Mat was right, and Shea didn't see him like he saw himself. All her compliments in the last few days couldn't overcome his self-condemnation, no matter how he wished their opinions were true.

Her hair was falling out of its ponytail, framing her face in wisps that begged for his attention, but he remained focused on his job of getting them back to her dock.

"I feel horrible about what happened to you and that clerk." *That I wasn't there to help.*

"I have to admit—I did blame you for a long time. But then I realized that it wasn't your fault the gang chose that night to intimidate us. You don't deserve the blame."

"Still, you decided not to date me."

"My brother hinted you weren't—" She stopped suddenly, cutting off her own words.

"I know, I know. One girlfriend to the next." That morning in Auntie Mat's kitchen, Shea had feared he didn't see her as good enough for him, but it was he who wasn't good enough for her.

"Liam, you're different since then. Sure, you still go off on adventures—risking your life, chasing adrenaline highs. Then, you come back to your responsibilities, and you meet them." She shrugged and leaned back as if she'd gushed too much. But she finally relaxed once more. "Like I said earlier, I admire that. Plus, I haven't seen you dating anyone lately." After a moment's pause and a glance around, she faced him again. "Are we finished with our tour of the lagoon?" She may have meant to sound light, but her voice came out disappointed.

Houses crowded in on either side, now that they'd docked, but they stayed in the boat, and he'd keep his voice low. "You mentioned not feeling good enough for me, but I'm the one who isn't good enough. You don't have to fake date me for my aunt's sake. I understand. We'll clear it up with her." After Shea's story, he couldn't imagine she'd want him in her life, beyond friendship and her cottage work. Didn't simply being with him remind her of that violent night? In her shoes, he'd want space. So he'd make it easy for her.

Shea opened her mouth. "I don't want—"

"Oh, you're back!" Auntie Mat seemed to appear out of nowhere lately. "How was your little trip?"

Perhaps Shea felt she owed his aunt something for letting her bunk in her house. All they had to do was sit her down and tell her the news, then she could harass only Liam and let Shea be.

Liam jumped out of the rowboat and carefully hauled it up onto the shore, with Shea still inside. Then, he reached over and helped her step onto the sand from the rocking craft. She walked right up to his side and wrapped one arm behind him like she had on Saturday. Hadn't she heard what he said? He was letting her out of the charade. She should run while she could.

"Miss Mat, could I chat with your nephew for a minute?" Shea said as Liam reflexively drew her close and breathed in her jasmine scent. He'd go along, but as soon as his aunt left, he'd repeat himself and set things right.

"Of course." Auntie Mat waved at them. "I don't want to get in the way of anything." She giggled as she headed toward the Sound side of the house.

Alone again, he dropped his arm and gazed down at Shea. "What are you doing? You don't have to carry out this pla—"

She moved to face him head on and stopped him with a finger to his lips. He froze. Then she shifted her hand to the side of his face, which he still hadn't shaved—why bother? Her fingertips felt soft as they ran over his whiskery skin. And, once again, he leaned into her touch, closing his eyes.

Why did he have to be so needy? So broken, himself? His aunt knew him better than he did, and he hadn't even realized he was lonely until she'd told him. Every kind, tender act Shea showed him got to him, had him lapping it up. Were all his life-endangering stunts a cover so he wouldn't feel this vulnerable?

She left her hand on his face, stroking her thumb over his jaw. He opened his eyes and stared into golden-brown pools. "I don't think you're listening. I want to spend time with you. No façade. No playacting. And not because I feel sorry for you or owe a debt to your aunt, though I do."

Her hand held him there, but he shuffled his feet. "*I* want to jump off something."

She pressed her lips together and stroked his face again. His skin hummed with her touch. "If you do, I hope you'll be very, very careful. *You* are important to me, Liam. And to your aunt. And a lot of people. We don't want anything bad to happen to you."

He swallowed and tipped down his head. That sounded like she cared about him, like he mattered, like his life mattered. Her words burrowed into the knot of pain in his chest, prodding moisture into his eyes.

Using her fingers, she tilted up his chin, and he cooperated. "What if we gave it a trial run?"

"A trial run? I don't want to hurt you."

"Then don't turn me down." She grinned, and then she eyed him as if searching for something deeper. "Plus, I believe you won't hurt me. Or at least not on purpose."

He couldn't even imagine that, though he wished he had her faith in himself.

"And I'll try not to hurt *you*." She gave him a small smile. "But you'll have to put up with my stuff for a while. I'm in a confusing season right now."

She had no idea how easy it was for him to "put up with her stuff." Her flaws, her problems and battles, weren't barricades for him. He cared about her and none of those things could overshadow his affection.

Yeah, he kept coming back to that word.

It scared him, and more than a little. He was used to failure, used to letting people down. Succeeding, being reliable and competent never mattered more.

But he'd try because he couldn't reject her. "Okay, I'm in. We'll take it slow."

Her face broke into a smile like the sun from behind spring clouds, and he mirrored her before covering her hand, still up at his face, with his.

They should seal this agreement somehow, but it was far too early for much more than a hug. Unless . . . He did owe her a kiss. He released her hand and opened his arms. "Deal?"

She walked into his personal space, wrapping her arms around his neck. "Deal." From real close, she gazed up at him and seemed to go still. Did she suspect his intentions? Could she read the heat in his eyes?

He bent down and gently pressed a kiss to her temple. This time she leaned into his touch, which shot flames through him.

For one moment, he let himself linger there, like she'd done, then he straightened his back and pulled her in close.

Lord, help me not to hurt her.

CHAPTER THIRTY-ONE

Alone with his aunt, Liam followed when she motioned him out to the breezy sunporch. Shea had excused herself after lunch to go find painting clothes for the afternoon of working in the cottage.

"It's time for our next lesson in my School of Romance, Liam," Auntie Mat said.

He groaned.

"I see things are moving along. Good job. My lesson plans are working!" She buzzed around the space, watering her corner plants like some type of gardening pixie in an animated fairy tale.

A chuckle rolled out of him. "You're impossible." Plus, part of him didn't want to give her credit for this ... odd situation they found themselves in. But when he allowed thoughts of Shea in his arms to cross his mind, electricity shot through his chest. Maybe it wasn't all bad.

His aunt opened the porch door and motioned him out to the deck. Then she peered up at the house, as if checking to see if Shea's bedroom window was closed. "First, I want to say how proud I am of you for stepping up. Well done."

His throat went tight, so all he could do was nod. Her approval weighed a lot.

"Now, next lesson: kiss. I thought you were going to get ahead of me out there on the rowboat this afternoon. That was good, by the way, taking a romantic moment together." She produced a fist for him to bump, and he obliged but shook his head. Loony woman. But he loved her, and he owed her everything.

"Find a place and a time," she said. "You'll know when it's right." With that she flitted around to the pots on her deck, tending her flowers. "And there will be a quiz: I will be asking if you followed through, though you can keep the details to yourself."

This "lesson" wasn't necessary. It wasn't like he'd never kissed a woman. He and Shea were determined to take this trial run slow, so who knew if they'd ever get there. *If* it ever happened, there was no way he'd be sharing any details with his aunt. Still, he humored her and let her think he was taking this seriously.

"Now, off to work with the two of you. I'm headed to volunteer at the theater for the evening, so you're on your own for dinner. Remember the earlier lessons: Be warm and attentive. Learn her love language and speak it. Do things for her out of consideration. Woo her." She opened the house door again and took one step through as he held the door for her. "You have my blessing."

At the cottage a half hour later, Shea taped off the opposite wall in the kitchen where Liam was still finishing the backsplash. He'd keep things light and easy, and he'd try not to think about his aunt's orders. Why did her lessons keep getting in his head? She may have an agenda in this relationship-coaching thing she'd designed, but so did Liam, and his was much more cautious.

That look of rejection on Shea's face when they spoke earlier was what convinced him to give this a try. He couldn't risk her thinking she somehow wasn't lovable. Oh, she was lovable. Maybe he should tell her. Over and over. Or find more ways to show her.

"Can you help me move all these cans away from the wall so I have room to work?" Shea tore off the last piece of tape from the roll.

"Sure." He hadn't mixed the adhesive yet for the tiles. This was the perfect time to help her.

She seemed content to act like coworkers, and he was fine with that for now.

But his attention kept landing on her mouth.

Several cans of paint lay stacked near the wall she planned to tackle. He shifted them across the room, leaving one can of Sandy Shore for her to use as she got started. She snapped open the tarp to lay on the floor.

"You're good at this. I should take you to all my jobs."

She smiled at him. "I hope to be back at work soon, but thanks."

"I finished the bathrooms this morning, so when I'm done with this tile, I can help paint."

"Sounds good."

Liam got to work mixing the adhesive and then applying it before pressing the seafoam green tiles into place. They talked about Dylan and decided Liam might go see him, when they allowed him visitors, but Shea wouldn't. She had too much going on and had no real relationship with him. Shea's brother, JP, however, would.

What was Burr thinking right now? Would the woman be okay? How long of a sentence would Burr get?

A tap at the cottage's street-side door surprised him. So she wouldn't be startled, Liam waved at Shea, and she pulled the earbuds out.

"Someone's at the door." He was already headed in that direction. "I'll get it."

"Sure."

He felt her eyes on him as he crossed to the living room entrance. He wasn't expecting any deliveries today. He caught a glimpse of Auntie Mat's friend's car in her driveway through the window as he walked to the door. Good. Angie was a great support to his aunt and vice versa. They'd been good friends all these years. He thought his aunt was due at the theater, but maybe her plans had changed.

Outside the Brown's cottage, a woman stood holding a baby in her arms. She was about Liam's age, if he had to guess. Gorgeous with her blonde hair and green eyes and caramel skin. Mixed African-American and Caucasian, like Hitch and his wife, Fiona. The baby was beautiful, with paler skin, textured black hair, and blue eyes, like . . . Burr?

Liam pulled open the door and smiled. "Can I help you?"

"Are you Liam?"

"Yes."

"I'm Seneca." She hiked the baby higher on her hip. "I wondered if you and I could talk."

He knew that name—Burr's last long-time girlfriend. How had she found him? "Of course." Generally, he didn't allow strangers into the worksites. This house wasn't his, after all. But this place was nearly complete, and Shea was here. Plus, Seneca didn't seem threatening, so he invited her in and closed the door. "No furniture here yet, or I'd offer you a seat. About all I have is bottled water. Would you like one?"

"Yes, please."

The baby cooed in Seneca's arms. "This is Breeze, by the way."

In the kitchen, Shea approached, rubbing her fingers on a rag. "I'm Shea. This is my family's house." She held out a dry hand.

"Seneca." They shook, and then Shea smiled at Breeze.

"Beautiful baby."

"Thanks." Standing next to the island, she faced Liam at the fridge. "I didn't mean to interrupt the work here."

With a smile, Shea took the water bottle Liam held toward her. "I can head next door," she said to them.

"Are you friends with Liam or Dylan?" Seneca asked Shea.

She nodded, uncapping her water. "Liam and I are . . . together."

A zing ran through Liam with her admission, and it felt something like pride or anticipation.

"Then, feel free to stay. Dylan spoke highly of Liam, so I know he's trustworthy."

He had? Burr could barely be civil to Liam, unless he'd been drinking.

Seneca shifted Breeze on her hip. "So, if Liam trusts you, I will too. I only need a couple of minutes."

They stood next to the island in the kitchen, Seneca still holding her baby. Good call given all the paint and dust everywhere. Not a baby-safe zone.

She faced Liam. "Breeze is Dylan's daughter."

Shea gave a little gasp. Liam was floored, though the puzzle started to make sense. Burr had never said a word. "Does he know?"

She huffed and sipped water. Breeze batted the plastic and caused her mom to spill on her top. Seneca turned her face and sipped anyway, distancing the bottle from her baby's reach. Finally, and with no lack of resentment, she said, "Yeah. He knows."

Was this why he drank so much? And why Liam's delinquent dad tale got to him? Was Burr *living* what Jack had done?

"Did he ... I mean, was he helpful ... with uh ... Breeze?" Talking about Burr made Liam uneasy.

Breeze fussed, squawking like Auntie Mat's bird in a way. What did Liam know of babies? Shea seemed to want to hold her, but she was covered in paint and didn't volunteer. Still, she cooed to her and Liam liked the sound.

"No. He wasn't. He's never even met her. Didn't want to." Seneca set her bottle of water on the new granite counter and pressed her yawning daughter's head to her shoulder. Then she bounced up and down with her knees, and the baby's eyes fluttered closed.

Burr wasn't here now, but Liam was. "What can I do?"

"I needed to hear from one of his friends what happened." Seneca's appearance was so striking, Liam could see why Burr had dated her. She seemed almost too beautiful to believe. Still, no one compared to Shea. "And when Hitch told me it had happened out here, on this street, I decided to come over. Hitch also mentioned you were working here. So, I figured I could see for myself and ask you about it while I was here. The news hit me hard, I guess. And I had to see for myself." She repeated herself, and Liam wished he could offer her a chair considering how this accident had affected her.

Shea froze at the mention of the car accident she'd witnessed. "Excuse me for a minute." She gave a gentle smile before slipping out of the room. Liam didn't blame her. He'd make sure she was okay in a few minutes.

Liam focused back in on Dylan's ex. "Forgive me, but it sounds like a rather ... sad errand."

"Indeed." Still bouncing from her knees, she patted her daughter's back. Breeze looked asleep to him. Maybe Seneca kept moving so she'd stay that way. "Do you know what's next for him?"

That's what Liam wondered too. "Not any more than Hitch does." Liam clutched the countertop. "Honestly, Seneca, it's probably not good." She must know his history with the law. But if she didn't, it wasn't Liam's place to tell her.

"I'm afraid you're right." She nodded and stared off toward the murky windows. "I love him."

Her words hit him. Sincere. "I wish I could help."

"If you're like me, we tried. Right? It came down to Dylan making decisions for himself. He's an adult. He understands consequences."

"If it helps, I think he regrets how things went with you." Should Liam continue with his train of thought? He was only guessing.

"Regret is a killer." She sighed. She'd stopped bouncing now. "Thanks for talking with me. I'm glad we could meet."

Shea returned and quietly listened, which he assumed she did most days at work.

"It's odd that Burr never brought you around." What had motivated him to keep her a secret? Liam couldn't recall . . . Wait. Had Burr been dating someone else at the same time? There was that one woman—Jess. But did the timelines overlap? "You know what? Next time Hitch and his wife, and the rest of us get together, you should come." Maybe the whole crew could make up in part for the loss of Dylan from her life.

"Thanks. I'm girlfriends with Fiona, but it's been a while since we hung out." For the first time, she broke a bit of a smile and her countenance brightened. "Her stories of you guys sound terrifying." She gave a soft snort.

"Hmm." He grinned. "So, no skydiving for you?"

She kissed her daughter's head. "Nope."

Liam took a deep breath. "Has Fee met Breeze?"

"Yes, but I only recently told her who my baby's father was."

"Well, if there's anything I can do, let me know." He pulled out his phone. "Can I text you so you'll have my number?"

"Sure." She rattled off her phone number, and he sent a message with his name so she could save his contact info.

A few minutes later, she left. A wake of sorrow lingered.

Shea faced him. "That was something."

He stepped close, studying her eyes, cupping her elbows. "Are you okay?"

"Yeah," she said in a breathy voice. "It's still fresh, you know?"

"I do. I wish we could get an update on the woman."

She loosed a long, slow sigh. "Me too."

"I never expected to meet her," Liam said, referring to Seneca. "But their history might explain a few of Burr's choices."

She nodded. "My heart hurts for all three of them."

"Mine too."

Liam went back to work with several people on his mind: Shea, Jack, Burr, and his family—Seneca and Breeze. Would Burr ever see them again? Or in the case of his daughter, meet her for the first time? If he had the chance, would he want to?

Both Jack and Burr, apparently, had abandoned their families. What kind of person did that?

And could Liam avoid becoming that kind of man? He liked to think he was above it. But he truly didn't know.

CHAPTER THIRTY-TWO

In two hours, Matilda would report to the theater. Right now, she mixed fresh strawberries into her homemade lemonade as ice cubes clinked in the glass pitcher. Her neighbor and dear friend, Angie, should arrive soon for a long-overdue chat this fine July day. A fresh breeze off the Sound would make sitting outside a delight. She carried the pitcher out to the round table under the umbrella on her front deck. In the spring, she'd filled the space with planters and grew petunias, pansies, vincas, snapdragons, geraniums, and begonias in a variety of bursting colors. Her rose garden thrived on the south side of the house in reds, whites, and pinks.

She adjusted the foil cover around the pitcher's top to keep out bugs and strolled back inside for the snack platter she'd put together with cheese, grapes, crackers, apple slices, and chocolate-covered peanuts for a treat. Hopefully, the warm summer air wouldn't melt them.

A light tap rattled the kitchen door, and Angie's smiling face peeked through the window. Matilda waved her in. "Welcome, welcome!"

Angie wore a light sweater over a long cotton sundress with sensible shoes because, in her words, "at my age, I can use the stability."

They'd been friends for over fifty years. They'd lost touch a few times over the years, what with moves and career shifts. But now that each were widowed, they'd settled into their beach homes on Point Moore here on Bainbridge. Angie volunteered for several charities, trying to fill her time, so they hadn't seen each other much lately.

"It's finally summer." Angie shifted her sunglasses to the top of her head.

Matilda stepped up for a big hug. "So good to see you."

"I'm glad we were both free. I'm just back from running errands in Poulsbo, so I have my car today." Angie pulled away. "It sounds like you have something heavy on your mind."

"I thought we'd snack outside and chat. Sound good?"

"Oh, yes."

Matilda led the way out to the deck on the Sound side of the house.

"Oh, your flowers are lovely." Angie looked around, then walked over and inspected a section where Matilda had planted mostly purple blossoms of various types.

Matilda busied herself with removing aluminum foil and plastic wrap and pouring her friend a drink. "Container gardening—very little bending, weeding, or tough digging, and easy replacement of dead plants."

Angie received her lemonade from Matilda. "No argument from me. If I didn't have a crew coming in to tend my flower-garden patch, I wouldn't have one."

They chuckled over the familiar chatter.

"Grab a snack," Matilda invited as she poured herself a glass of strawberry lemonade.

Glass in hand, Angie raised hers. "To the white-haired women at your house today!"

Matilda chuckled. "Cheers!" Oh, they'd had big dreams. Big crazy dreams. And some of them had come true.

Angie stared toward the water. "I'll never grow tired of that view."

The tide was out, leaving a long stretch of gravelly beach between the quiet waves and the highest part of the shore.

"Me either."

Matilda breathed the salty air and closed her eyes, glad for the shelter of the umbrella over them. "Thanks for checking on me that night." Angie had texted Matilda when she'd seen her bedroom light on.

After Dylan's accident, Angie had seen the commotion and rushed over to stand next to Matilda and Shea. She even came in for a bit but had been fighting a headache, so she'd excused herself for a spell of quiet and rest.

"Of course. I'm so sorry that happened, and right in front of your house." The compassion in her voice urged Matilda to raise her eyes. "Tell me again how you know the driver?"

"He's buddies with Liam. They've been working on the house next door, the one the Browns own. But he's got a drinking problem."

Angie stacked a cheddar cheese square onto a cracker, but she left it on her small plate. Matilda didn't have much of an appetite either. "I feel really sorry for the woman's family. How scary."

"Any more word about her?"

"Last I heard she was in critical condition."

Birdsong filled the air around them, joining the distant wave noise. Calliope scratched at the sunporch door, and Matilda let her out to join them on the deck. She had a small grassy spot for her with a fence around it, so the pup had plenty of places to explore, and she loved Angie.

Calliope and Angie greeted each other and then the spaniel was off, sniffing the deck and grass. "How are things with Liam?"

Matilda glanced toward the cottage next door. The windows were open in the living room over there. A car pulled into the drive, and she didn't recognize the driver or her baby. But she could be a friend of Shea's. Either way, they'd be busy talking so they weren't likely to overhear Matilda seeking advice. "He's having a hard time with the reappearance of his biological dad—Jack."

"I remember him. I met him once or twice, if I recall correctly. Back when we all lived near Bremerton."

"Yes. He recently reconnected with Liam, but I've been ... talking to him for years." She whispered that last part.

"You have?"

Matilda nodded. This secret had been eating at her for a long time.

"Like, phone calls? Letters? What?" Angie kept her voice low too.

"All of the above, plus emails. And now, social media. That is, since he got out of prison."

"Oh gravy, my friend."

Matilda grimaced. She knew Angie would understand the challenges here.

"And your nephew doesn't know?"

"He'll kill me."

"Possibly . . . But I'm curious—why all the chatting between you and Jack? I didn't realize you were close, especially when he chose to leave his family."

Matilda glanced toward the Browns' cottage. "Wanna walk?"

"Yes."

They tidied up by returning all the food inside, so the gulls and crows wouldn't get to it and let Calliope back into the house. Matilda didn't want to wrangle her curious dog while she was trying to concentrate on her conversation with Angie. Cleanup complete, they sauntered across the narrow dirt road to the beach.

With the tide this far out, they could find a smooth walking area and stroll far enough away from everyone's property that they wouldn't mind. For the most part, residents understood folks were harmlessly ambling, and though the owners officially held title to their beachfronts for a certain number of feet, when the tide was out you could legally walk near the water's edge without concern of trespassing.

They'd head left, or southwest, first, to the end of the spit because there were far fewer houses in this direction. They picked their way slowly to the finer gravel, offering each other a hand as needed. Gulls cried over the bay, which sparkled with a diamond-studded sea of blue. The water lapped at the shore gently as if not striving to take new ground for the moment. "We live in a gorgeous area."

"Yes, we do," Angie agreed. She seemed content to wait Matilda out. Northwest of them, the mainland rose out of the water, and directly west, Bainbridge's Agate Point stood tall, with houses and large evergreens poking out of the hills.

"To answer your question," Matilda said as they passed a huge dead tree trunk on its side where the tide had left it long ago. Thick root "branches" fanned out probably seven or eight feet in all directions. "I started chatting with Jack right after he got out of jail the first time."

They strolled past more houses, saw the crab traps anchored in the sand way down the beach at this minus tide. "What was he in for?"

Glad for her sunglasses, Matilda adjusted her cap to tame the brightness. "Various stuff. Some of it was being in with a bad crowd, and in the wrong place during a crime. He contacted me, humbled. I took his calls for a while. He said that being in there had made him want to reach out to family, lots of time to dwell on his regrets."

Angie held her dress hem above her sneakers with one hand. "Makes sense. But why didn't you ever tell Liam?"

"At first, I wanted to protect him. I mean, what if Jack turned out to be dangerous? Then, as Liam grew up and could handle himself more, I didn't want him to feel betrayed."

"Makes perfect sense to me." Angie had her own family. She understood one generation looking out for the next. "What is the latest?"

"Jack's changed. A lot." They neared the end of the spit and the green channel came into view. Matilda paused on the beach. "I encouraged Liam to go see him."

Angie's eyebrows hiked above her sunglasses.

"That didn't go well. Liam's still angry. Feels that holding a grudge makes him loyal to Erin, his mother."

"That's understandable." Her friend nodded. "It's too bad he can't talk with Erin about it." She stopped to pick up a half oyster shell that glistened in the sun. "He has to choose whether he wants to forgive."

"I hope he does. Maybe then he can move on. I've been tempted to ask Jack over for dinner and surprise Liam, but I think that'd be taking it too far."

Angie chuckled. "You're probably right about that."

"So, all I can do is encourage Liam to search for peace." They turned to amble back to the house. "Meanwhile, I'm teaching him about romancing a woman."

Angie guffawed. "You are not!"

"Aw, don't worry. He loves it." Matilda giggled. "And better than that—it's working."

CHAPTER THIRTY-THREE

His buddies might razz him for showing any weakness, but Dylan knew when he'd been beaten. And ending up back in jail had drained his soul of hope. Worst of all, while he was in here, he couldn't drown the pain in alcohol. So, he'd checked into meeting with the local prison chaplain, who made visits to the jail. First time for everything.

The man seated on the other side of the desk from him didn't come across like a tough guy, though he looked strong. He seemed like at one time he may have even served on this side of the desk—as a prisoner himself. If he had, he might understand Dylan. Now that he sat here, he didn't look forward to feeling exposed.

"So, Dylan, thanks for coming in here today. How can I help?" The man's gray hair and matching short beard, along with leathery, wrinkled skin, made him look old. Maybe he was nearing retirement.

Dylan leaned back in the hard chair in this almost empty room. Even here, the space was dank and hopeless. "Have you served time before?"

The old guy nodded his head. "I have. A few minor infractions, a felony. I know what it's like to walk prison halls, marking time. Wait for visitors who never come."

That hit Dylan in the chest. He couldn't have visitors yet, but when he could, would anybody come? He'd rather gut things out than whine aloud, but the loneliness here mocked him. And the one person he wanted most to see would probably never show up.

He blamed himself for that. Even with his buddies, he acted like they owed him and that he owed them nothing. It was a wonder they kept inviting him on their trips. Liam went out of his way, ever since that one dive, to help Dylan when he could. But Dylan had rejected him. Resented him because he didn't know how good his life was. Maybe if Dylan tried to be a good guy, others wouldn't reject him so fast. Ha. As if he could simply make that choice and watch it happen.

What good were all these thoughts now? He was locked up. He couldn't see his job through with Liam. He couldn't get into rehab—again—or try to reach Seneca. What did it matter if he all of a sudden started caring about life and people? He couldn't do a thing about any of it.

"I'm not sure why I came in here." He shifted, raised himself up toward standing.

"Sit, sit." The chaplain acted as if he didn't care either way. "I don't have another appointment for an hour. We may as well chat."

Hanging out in this room beat anywhere else in the jail, so he resettled in the chair. "Fine."

"Ya know," the old guy began, "when I was in prison, I started having all these regrets." He pointed his index finger at his temple and spun his hand. "Thoughts went 'round and 'round in my head, like a movie reel of all the stuff I'd done wrong. Where my decisions had taken me."

Dylan could relate with that, but he wouldn't let on. Where was this guy going with this?

The guy's face filled with sorrow, making him look even older as he slouched over the desk and linked his hands, resting on his elbows. "I walked away from my family too." He shook his head and even now, who-knew-how-many years later, Dylan could read the regrets in the lines on his face. "And there I was, alone."

This chaplain guy had left his family? That made three deadbeat dads Dylan knew of, himself included. He hung his head, and then remembered where he was. "The warden must trust you now. You must've turned things around."

He nodded. "I did, but it was a decision I had to make. It's like AA. Are you familiar?"

Dylan grunted and shifted in his chair. The guy was reading his mail. "Yup."

"The advice I got when I was in there was that we couldn't fix everything or every relationship, but we should try wherever possible—to make amends with people, to ask forgiveness, to make things right." He leaned back in his chair. "It all begins with one decision, even a small one. One right decision can change your life."

While he spoke, Seneca's face flashed into Dylan's mind. "There is no way the people I've hurt could forgive me." And no way he deserved it.

"Let me tell you, I know what you're fighting. My own son can barely spend ten minutes with me. Wouldn't listen to anything I wanted to say. Will probably never forgive me."

"Then, why even try?"

"Because once we've tried, maybe then we can forgive ourselves. Find a way to move on. Until we try, guilt beats us over the back with regret and pressure. Like the bullies around here."

Dylan had run into several of those.

"There's always hope."

Dylan stood and though part of him wanted to believe this pastor-type guy, he couldn't.

"Listen, sometime this week, reach out to that one person you feel you have hurt the most. Write a letter if you aren't allowed calls yet. Try." He waited for a response from Dylan, but he wasn't making any promises. "Remind me of your name again," the pastor said as he reached for his hand.

"Dylan." Anyone who worked here could look up his last name. No reason to hide it. "Dylan Burgess."

They shook. "I'm Jack Barrett, prison chaplain. I hope we can meet again."

CHAPTER THIRTY-FOUR

Jack Barrett? Liam's dad? Dylan still couldn't believe it. Liam's father ended up being the prison chaplain—a pastor!—at the prison where he'd served for a felony. They hadn't chatted about which crime, but it didn't matter. Jack, as beaten down and humble as he seemed now, didn't look like the type to commit anything violent. But who knew what kind of man he'd once been? Maybe he was guilty back then of armed robbery or another felony.

Today, Dylan was finally allowed to call out. He considered dialing Liam, to tell him the news. Dylan had never heard from Liam how the meeting went. According to Jack, not well. Again, Dylan could see both sides.

He settled at the table with the push-button phone and pressed familiar numbers he hadn't used in a long time.

"Hello?" Seneca's voice impacted him like a punch in the stomach. He hadn't heard it in too long. He didn't deserve to hear it now.

He wished he could answer, but instead he listened as the operator's voice spouted the usual spiel about how this was a collect call from the correctional facility, that Dylan Burgess was calling, and would the recipient mind paying any applicable fees. He held his breath. Would she accept the charges? He knew she wasn't rich, and he certainly hadn't contributed to her or his baby's welfare. Shame kicked him in the chest. *Deadbeat. Failure.*

A click followed and then a dial tone. Now the life ring around him seemed to have snapped, and there was nothing to keep him from sinking.

She wasn't willing to talk to him. His gut hardened. Of course she wasn't. He couldn't blame her for hating him. Couldn't blame her for never wanting to hear from him again. He'd wrecked his life. And Seneca wasn't the kind of girl—Liam would make him say *woman*—to enjoy getting calls from a *correctional facility*. Had she even known he was back in here?

The officers didn't make him walk around in shackles on his ankles or handcuffs, but he felt bound just the same. Bound and gagged. The one person Pastor Jack recommended he reach out to wouldn't even listen.

Why hadn't he tried to talk to her, or gone to see her and meet his daughter, when he was free? Not that he was a great guy then, either, but at least he'd been free to go where he wanted. Now he couldn't even call someone whenever he wanted. Or get a stiff drink.

He shuffled back to his cell. Maybe he'd write her another letter. See if he could get her to understand how sorry he was. All he could do was try. And maybe one day he could forgive himself.

I probably should have taken the call.

Seneca poured warm water over Breeze's back in the tub, watching her baby splash and giggle.

What could Dylan want with her? And why reach out to her now? Because he'd blown it? Protecting Breeze was her number one priority. Who wanted a prisoner for a father? If the phone rang again, she'd answer on the first ring. This time, she'd accept "any applicable charges," hope they weren't too high, and at least hear him out.

Or tell him off.

Ideally, she wanted Breeze to know her father, but Dylan would likely be in prison a long time. And he wasn't setting the best example of responsibility, safety, protection, or integrity for their daughter.

What if his victim didn't survive her injuries? What if Dylan was actually guilty of vehicular manslaughter? The thought made her sick inside. She caressed her daughter's skin. Yeah, maybe it was better for Breeze, and Seneca, to keep their distance from Dylan.

She pulled Breeze from the bath and laid her on the mat so she could wrap her in a towel. Seneca was now almost as wet as their daughter.

Listening to whatever Dylan had to say couldn't hurt her more than his abandonment and rejection had. If he tried again, next time she'd hear him out, say what she needed to say, and move on with her life—her and Breeze on their own and finding their way. Without Dylan.

CHAPTER THIRTY-FIVE

Auntie Mat was still working at the theater tonight, so Liam grilled hamburgers for Shea and himself. He stood over the searing meat, his mind full. The inspector had cancelled at the last minute today. Since it was summer, they may not even sign off until next week. Meanwhile, Shea was getting antsy about moving her stuff over there and "letting Miss Matilda have her house back." The calendar read mid-July, and though Shea didn't seem angry, Liam still beat himself up that it had taken this long to finish.

He'd gotten a phone call today and needed to talk it over with her when she came back from her shower. Two phone calls, actually.

Considering everything happening with Burr and his ex, and Jack reappearing, Liam was tired of his own thoughts. He was weary of second-guessing every decision—should he talk to Jack again? Why couldn't he forgive him? Would he ever forgive him? What was going to happen to Burr? Would Liam end up like Jack?

So tonight, he was going to take a break from thinking and rather than skydive or bungee jump to avoid his anger, he would try relaxing.

And he would enjoy spending one-on-one time with Shea.

He brought the burgers in on a plate and pulled tomato, lettuce, pickles, sliced cheese, and condiments from the fridge. They could build their own sandwiches and then watch a movie since the temps were sweltering outside this evening.

Wearing modest cut-offs and a tank top, Shea padded down the stairs, washing the room in her jasmine scent. He wanted to make a beeline to her but held back. Just what were the rules in a trial relationship?

"Hey, Liam. That smells amazing." Her stomach rumbled, and she clutched her trim middle. "I think all this work at the cottage has been good for me."

"You look great."

Her face darkened, but she didn't look away. "Why, thank you."

Forget his rules. He walked over and laced his fingers with hers. "We both have a zillion things to worry about, but how about tonight, we put all of them aside. Sound good?"

"Absolutely." She squeezed his hand and then let go to reach for a plate. "So glad it's cool in here."

He stood back to let her reach the food on the counter. "Me too." The window air conditioner blew cooled air into the room. "I wanted to update you about two things before we relax."

She slapped a large leaf of lettuce onto her plate and reached for the tomato. "Fair enough. Chat while we prep."

"I called the hospital." He'd get to his own plate in a minute.

She stilled and faced him. "And?"

He could stare into her eyes all day. "This part's good news. The woman has been downgraded from critical condition to serious condition. She's doing much better."

Shea sighed. "That is a huge relief. I wonder if Dylan knows. I wish we could simply text him or something."

"Speaking of him. I heard from him today *before* I got the latest on his victim." Burr had kept the conversation short as if he only had time to explain what was happening and how often he could reach out.

Shea took his hand. "What'd he say?"

Her palm felt warm in his, comforting, like she was offering him some of her strength. "He's only allowed to talk to about three people. We all had to be approved. And each call can last no longer than fifteen minutes."

"Can you see him?"

"No." So his plan to visit, along with JP, was now on hold.

She grimaced. "When's his arraignment?"

"Tomorrow. He said pleading 'not guilty' seemed ridiculous to him because he knows he's guilty."

"A 'not guilty' plea only means they have to prove the case and provide evidence."

"Yeah, but he said it felt stupid, and that he's tired of hiding from his screw-ups—he used a different word, of course." Burr had been far less amiable today on the phone than when he'd been drinking. "And he mentioned that he ran into someone I knew in there but wouldn't say who." That was a relief. Liam didn't need another prisoner to worry about. He shook his head. "I can't help him."

"I don't wish anything bad on him, or the woman he hit, but God might use this to motivate Dylan to get help. He's already detoxing from the alcohol."

"True. That's been hard." Burr mentioned vomiting, sweating, shaking, especially at first. He'd told him the medical staff brought up using benzodiazepines, if Liam remembered that term correctly, but no word whether the medication eased his symptoms.

"I'm sure it has." She had probably studied the medical stuff in school. Liam's stomach growled this time, and Shea pointed to the cooling burgers. "Shall we work on this?"

Side by side they created their own masterpieces.

She crunched a baby dill while she worked. "I'm curious about something."

Sharing all that with her made him feel lighter. "Shoot."

"I know you, my brother, and the guys are all buddies, but why do you seem so concerned about Dylan's life?"

Liam tilted his head down toward her. "Long story."

She dropped extra carrot sticks onto her plate, and then reached for the chips. "I've got time."

He waited until she finished crinkling the bag and faced him again. "Do you know what buddy breathing is?"

"I think so. Remind me."

"In scuba diving, it's when one person shares their O_2 with someone else. On one of our trips, during a dive, my tank malfunctioned off the coast of Kauai. The guys and I were ascending. I swam up to Burr, signaled what had happened. Without a hint of hesitation, he motioned back what he wanted to do. The others were way ahead of us. I was trying not to panic." The moment came into focus in his memory with such clarity, he paused to fill his lungs with oxygen before continuing. "I act like I'm all about the next death-defying act, but *that* was terrifying because we had to pace ourselves. Try holding your breath off and on, over a thirty-minute time period." That was a lesson in trust. And Dylan had saved his life, without any fanfare.

"I can't even imagine that. Like claustrophobia, of sorts." She paused, her expression brightening as if a thought had just occurred to her. "I think I've misjudged him."

"Easy to do when he acts like he does." He piled chips onto his own plate. "We didn't talk about it afterward. Burr didn't give me a hard time. He didn't razz me about not having a working tank. Didn't tell the others. And I was too ... I don't know—humiliated?—to make a big deal, or even to thank him, until recently."

"Maybe after the arraignment, they'll let you see him."

"Here's hoping." Liam needed to lighten the mood again. "*You are a very good listener, Jenna-Shea Brown. What kind of jobs are there for people who like to listen?*" He tapped his chin with one finger. "Let me think ..."

Her elbow smacked into his ribs.

He grunted and lifted his full plate. Then he nodded toward hers. "Ready?"

She gave a nod as she picked up her own meal. "Yes, and I have the perfect movie in mind."

Fans circulated the air in the living room as they carried in their food. Shea had a plan she hoped Liam would like.

At least once a year, she tried to watch this movie. She wouldn't tell Liam what it was, would simply queue up the DVD player and let it roll. Who didn't like a Keanu Reeves film? She liked his character in *A Walk in the Clouds*. He was honorable, heroic, and self-sacrificing. A bit like Liam, though he probably couldn't see it.

They parked themselves in front of the coffee table in the living room, burgers in front of them, sharing the sofa.

Tonight, they were hanging out as a couple, and it'd been a long time. What were the rules? She'd never attempted a "trial relationship" before.

Though the sofa was plenty long enough for three adults, she settled near him. He didn't seem to mind. Liam, somehow, held his plate in one hand and the fat burger in the other and inhaled his meal. Miss Matilda's DVD player remote didn't work, so they'd have to tolerate five trailers while waiting for their movie to begin. But they played them on mute.

After she finished her dinner, Shea relaxed beside him. He lifted his arm, and she curled herself next to his side. He smelled good, though it'd been a hot day. Maybe that was pheromones. As a psych student, she remembered studying those in biology. She didn't care right now as it was certainly drawing her to him.

This movie may be too intense for their first real date in over a decade. There wasn't any nudity, and there were only a couple of make-out scenes, yet sensuality infused more than a few of the scenarios. What had she been thinking? Maybe it wasn't too late to pop in a comedy or a Disney film. She tightened her muscles as if ready to stand, and Liam eyed her.

"You okay?"

No worries tonight.

She nodded. They were both adults. They could handle this. Plus, she liked the movie's theme of family. She relaxed against him, and he ran his fingers over her upper arm.

Oh, and they'd mute the war scenes. She didn't need that stimulation. As the film got underway, she reached for the TV remote. "I may need to mute some of this."

"That's fine." He gave her a gentle smile, one she loved seeing this close up.

So far, their first date was going smoothly. Would Liam be okay with her movie choice, or cut the evening short?

Liam tried not to squirm or sniff. Why hadn't Shea warned him how emotional this film was? All that talk of no longer being an orphan, and the tough-guy father who acted gruff, and who separated himself from his family? He'd seen Keanu in action flicks. But here his character was quiet and noble. Liam wanted to be noble. Come across like that to Shea. She shifted against him and wrapped her arm around his middle. This part of the story had gotten intense as the family worked to save their vineyards by warming the vines. Shoot. She snuggled deeper into his side. From this angle, he could see the outline of her lips, her eyelashes fanning her cheek whenever she blinked. He swallowed.

Focus on the movie, Barrett.

He glanced back at the screen, but couldn't miss the way Shea pressed against his ribs when she breathed. Or her lean legs stretched out on the sofa. He wondered if they were as smooth as they looked.

Maybe watching a "chick flick"—there must be a more respectful phrase than that—with Shea on their first real date this summer wasn't such a good idea.

When the fictional family sat at dinner, the father mocked the newcomer for growing up in an orphanage. Liam identified himself as an orphan. Outside of Auntie Mat, of course.

Jack has returned.

Was that God's voice? Liam stilled as certainty clicked into his chest. Why would God remind Liam that Jack was back? Because of the context of his thoughts? *Lord, I don't see him as my . . . anything.*

You have Me.

Liam swallowed, eyes on the screen, mind processing God's words.

The story regained his attention when the grandfather walked Keanu's character up the mountain and made a declaration: *You are an orphan no longer.*

Those words punched Liam square in the sternum.

Keanu's character had a choice—stay or leave the vineyard. Did Liam have a choice? Was that what Auntie Mat had been trying to tell him? If Jack wasn't a monster, if he really had changed and he sincerely wanted back into their lives, is that what Liam wanted?

No.

But something strange had happened since his conversation with his aunt about being her son. Liam didn't feel like an orphan anymore. Maybe he was making progress.

The grape crushing scene forced Liam to excuse himself and offer to bring Shea a glass of lemonade. He came back into the room, two icy tumblers in his hands, right as Keanu's character took a stand against dishonoring Victoria, like a hero.

Shea received the plastic cup from him and took a long drink. She gave him a gentle smile and it occurred to him, she knew the father themes in this movie.

"You set me up."

"Why," she said, mimicking Auntie Mat's Southern accent, "whatever do you mean? I am innocent." Then she patted the seat next to her and, chuckling, he rejoined her on the sofa.

He got comfortable and stretched out his arm, making room. "C'mere."

She giggled and tucked herself back into his side, sighing. "I like this."

"Me too." And because he'd decided to let his worries go tonight, he wouldn't think too much about dating or not dating or taking things slow.

Near the end of the movie, as the family faced their losses on the screen, the story zeroed in on the teary father as he apologized for not loving well. Liam tightened his stomach around the emotions. Shoot. Shea probably figured this would force him to sympathize with the broken father. He stiffened and debated heading back to the kitchen, or out to the Sound for a frigid swim. She reached across his stomach and stroked his side. Now he was stuck.

Could Liam sympathize with Jack?

The credits rolled, and Shea muted the TV, but she didn't move to get up. Instead, she quietly stroked his forearm and avoided his eyes, which he appreciated since they burned.

"I hope you'll forgive me for springing that on you," she said, quietly.

He snorted and then sniffed. "You are full of shenanigans tonight."

"Maybe." She toyed with the long hairs on his arm, and he noted her skin was smooth. "I hope you don't mind too much."

Did he? It seemed every area of his life forced him to face this Jack thing. "You think I should make up with Jack?" Genuinely curious, he kept his voice gentle.

"I didn't say that."

"Do you understand what it's like, carrying something like this all your life?"

She sat up, met his eyes. "No. And I feel for you."

"Thanks." He gave her a tender hug. With images of the romance playing in his mind, he'd better excuse himself. "I'm going to head out. I'll be back tomorrow for the inspection at your cottage."

"Sure thing." She pressed her hands to each side of her and locked her elbows, shoulders poking up outside her tank top. Her hair cascaded down, rumpled and gorgeous.

The door opened behind Liam, and he scooted out of the way as Pearl squawked a hello to Auntie Mat. Calliope scrambled off her napping pillow and barreled toward her owner. "Oh, hi, Son. Hi, Shea." Auntie Mat strode inside, patting Calliope's head. She studied them and then gave the living room a once-over. The DVD had queued up to play again, leaving the menu on the screen. "I see we've been on a little date. Good. Good." She nodded and turned toward the kitchen. "Well, kiss her goodnight, Liam. We'll see you tomorrow."

When his aunt was out of the room, Shea stepped right up to Liam and pressed that tank top into his space. He could barely breathe.

"You heard your aunt. You'd better obey." She drew his arms around her and then placed her hands behind his neck where she feathered his short hair with delicate fingers. He shuddered. "Unless you'd rather not."

The hint of rejection amidst her playfulness begged him to refute all her self-doubts. They probably had a minute before

Auntie Mat returned and kicked him out—after patting him on the back for acing her latest School of Romance lesson.

Shea's leaning into you, Barrett. Stop thinking about your aunt for a minute.

He tugged her closer. "Shea." Then he closed the gap between them, and she let out a little gasp when his lips touched hers. He was going for caution, but when she pressed in, he locked his arms around her. Maybe his kisses could silence any sense of rejection.

If only he could tune out the not-so-subtle clapping in the kitchen.

CHAPTER THIRTY-SIX

Seneca's phone rang on the kitchen counter, and she reached for it. "Hello?" She stood over the stove, stirring the pot of boiling macaroni while she talked. Breeze banged a plastic spoon on her highchair tray a few feet away.

"This is a collect call from Kitsap County Men's Correctional Facility. Dylan Burgess is calling. Do you agree to accept all applicable charges?"

The chance she'd been half dreading, half wanting. She'd hoped Dylan would try at least one more time before giving up. It'd been a few days since she'd rejected his first attempt, and she'd feared he wouldn't call again, even while wishing he would. Did that make her a nutbar? "Yes." She eyed her baby and bit her lip.

The line clicked. "Hello?" Dylan's voice sounded uncertain, yet masculine and oh, so familiar.

"Hi." She kept her tone cool. She wouldn't let her guard down. She'd protect her daughter.

"Thank you for taking my call."

Compassion hit her at hearing the defeat in his voice. "I was sorry to hear how things . . . happened."

He sighed over the line. "I'm sorry for a lot of things." He sounded older. Sober, for once. She didn't answer for a while. What did he want? "You still there?" Desperation came through in his voice as if he worried she'd hung up.

"Yeah."

"How is, uh . . . our daughter?"

Anger burned inside her at his question. He'd never checked in about Breeze—not once since she'd been born. Seneca's attention went to Breeze's beautiful face. She would protect her with her life if she had to. "Do you even know her name?"

"Breeze Serene Hawke."

Wow. He did know it. Something about that dug deep into

Seneca's heart. "Yes, she has my last name." Let him try to defy her.

Breeze threw the spoon to the floor, and Seneca handed her an orange. So long as Breeze didn't try to bite in like an apple, she'd be okay. Breeze rolled the fruit around on her tray as if it were a ball, babbling.

"Okay," he said as if maybe that barb didn't sting. "Is she all right?"

"Seriously? *Now* you ask?" She hadn't planned to get irritated, would prefer to keep her emotions in check. But, ugh. Pinning her phone between her ear and her shoulder, she crossed the room to the stove, picked up the pot of water, and dumped it into the colander in the sink. Steam billowed up along with the smell of salty noodles.

"I didn't mean to tick you off. I've been ... rethinking everything." He'd never sounded so hopeless. So—broken.

Rethinking? *That* she could understand. What else did he have time for now that he was in jail? After she returned the pasta to the pot on the stove, she mixed the cheese sauce in, then the milk, stirring. Breeze loved mac and cheese, and this was easy to prep for the two of them. And cheap.

"I should have gotten in touch, helped you out more. Been there for you." She could almost see him cringing. Normally, he was only kind when he'd been drinking. Since he couldn't have alcohol in jail, this was a new side to him. Maybe he was changing in there.

"We're doing fine." She'd made it this far alone. Well, with the help of her mother who worked at the jail. Though she didn't mean to sound bitter, resentment still knotted in her stomach. She pressed a hand to Breeze's head, caressing. Worrying. Hoping for a better future—one that didn't include living in this dump in the bad part of town and working twenty-five hours a week at minimum wage. "We're going to be okay." That last part may have been more for her than him.

"I wish I could see her."

"Well, I sure ain't gonna bring her to see you in there."

"Didn't ask you to."

She forced out a long, hard sigh. They were volatile together.

Better Breeze never meet him than that Seneca and Dylan fought the whole time, or that Seneca exposed her daughter to the type of life Dylan was leading and couldn't seem to break free from. "You know what? It's better this way."

"With me locked up so I can't come over?"

"Yeah, maybe." She sighed deep. The whole reason she took this call was so she could get closure. But their conversation only irritated her. "You're in trouble, aren't you?"

He snorted a confirmation. "A lot depends on how that woman does. They're holding me over for trial. And that's not for like six months."

She grimaced, which of course, he couldn't see.

"I know. You think I brought this on myself."

"You did." She spooned steaming mac and cheese onto a paper plate and spread it out in a thin layer so it could cool.

"I tried to get sober. Never worked."

"Is it working now?"

He scoffed at her question.

She tried not to revel in her small victory, like a small person. She didn't wish him ill. "Do you know anything about the woman you hit?" Seneca had chatted with Liam and found out the woman was doing better. Did Dylan know that?

"No. For all I know she may have died already, which means the charges change, and my sentence goes from bad to worse. But I'm hoping she's getting better." Maybe Dylan was evolving. He never used to care about others. Was prison humbling him?

She could offer him mercy, maybe at least ease his mind a little bit. "I'm surprised your public defender didn't tell you, but the woman is doing a little better. She may survive."

He released a loud breath as if the news lifted a heavy burden. "Thank you for telling me that." He paused, and she wondered how much time they had left before the line cut out. "Listen, Sen, I just wanted to let you know I'm sorry."

In the past, she wouldn't make him spell it out. But letting him off stopped today. "For . . . ?"

"Everything."

She shifted on her feet. "Are you looking for forgiveness or something? Because that's not--"

"I understand. I'm just sorry, okay?" He paused for a second. "Like how I left things, how I left you." Not long before Breeze's due date, but Seneca wouldn't remind him.

Something about finally hearing the apology reached a deep place in her heart. Maybe it was a good thing she'd answered the call this time. "Well, thanks for saying that."

He swallowed hard over the line. "Sorry I wasn't brave enough before I was locked up."

"It wouldn't have changed anything." She tried to keep the judgment from her voice. Defeat washed over her now too.

"Okay, fair enough. But, I have to ask—will you forgive me? I mean, not today maybe, but someday?"

She couldn't answer. Caring for Breeze kept her so busy and sleep-deprived, she hadn't spent much time thinking about forgiving him. Would she feel less defeated if she could? "You sound different. Whatever you're doing in there, it's working."

"I've been talking with the chaplain. He's helping me see things differently, own up to my mistakes. Try to make amends. Sen, you won't believe who the chaplain is."

She knew their time was about out. "Who?"

"It's—"

The line went dead before he could finish his answer. She peeked at her phone's End Call screen. Well, maybe he'd call again. Until then, she'd work on that whole forgiveness thing because it wasn't healthy to live with all that bitterness inside.

Sitting across from the chaplain, Dylan leaned back and draped one leg over his other thigh. "She took my call this time."

The old man's gray eyebrows rose over eyes like Liam's. "She did?"

Relief soothed a place in his gut that he hadn't known burned before their conversation. "Thanks for suggesting I call her and try to make things right."

Chaplain Jack nodded. "Of course. We have to make amends where we can."

"I think the reason I left her was that I feared I'd fail her, and with a baby on the way, I'd fail the baby too. I couldn't risk it. I'm not a responsible man."

"Hmm, you are not alone feelin' like that. In fact, you've summed up why I did what I did in my past." He shook his head, shame once again etched into the lines on his face.

Dylan still hadn't told Jack that he knew his son. And Liam didn't know Jack was the chaplain here. Strange to see this side of the infamous Jack Barrett. But rather than feeling triumphant, Dylan felt understood.

Jack leaned forward, hands clasped on his desk. "Is she still angry?"

"So angry. But she listened to me apologize." He swallowed, almost tasting the pride he'd had to overcome to get the words out.

"Did you ask for forgiveness?"

Dylan squirmed in his chair. Jack didn't seem afraid to talk about the humbling things. Liam probably had no idea his bio dad was like this—nothing like Liam imagined, no doubt.

"I did, but she needs time."

"All we can do is ask; her response is up to her."

"I admit, I feel better, but my life is still a disaster."

"One step, one day, at a time."

He nodded. He'd certainly heard that before. The need for forgiveness burned in his gut so much lately, eating away. But maybe he could meet Breeze sometime—a dream he'd keep to himself.

For now, he'd dig around in Jack's past because Dylan was forming a plan—something else he'd keep under wraps. "So, you met with your son this summer?"

"Around Father's Day, I contacted him." Jack leaned back in his chair, crossing his arms over his chest. "I don't know what convinced him to meet with me, but I'm glad he did." His eyes teared up, and Dylan squirmed again. *He* wasn't the counselor here. But maybe Dylan could learn from him. Jack had already taught him so much.

During the guys' getaways, Liam was always such a clown. But he'd lost his dad, through abandonment, at a young age. The guys didn't talk about it. Dylan saw Liam as a solid guy. He made an effort. He cared for his kooky aunt. He held down a job, and he didn't use drugs or alcohol. Then, Liam had decided to go see Jack—to face him. Dylan shook his head, still impressed. That took guts.

Now, Dylan had to give props to Jack for reaching out to Liam for a meeting where, no doubt, he had asked for forgiveness himself. "How did it go with your son? I mean when you told him you were sorry for what you'd done?"

"About like it went with your ex-girlfriend, I'm guessing. Anger. Resentment. I don't know what he was expecting, but"—he pointed at himself, all scruffy and old and knocked around by life—"probably not this. And we didn't reach that place of forgiveness yet either."

"What do you think it'll take?"

"Time. You're marking time in here, until your trial and then afterward."

True enough.

"Well, every day any of us goes without choosing forgiveness is a day we're marking time in our own lives. Unforgiveness is a prison of our own making. Let me show you." Jack reached into the drawer of his desk and drew out a scuffed-up brown, leather-bound Bible.

This was the first time he'd brought out a Bible during their chats, but Dylan didn't mind. He could use all the help Jack offered. And if God came into it, then maybe Dylan could use His help too.

Jack flipped through the pages. "First, you know how heavy the burden of your mistakes is. I don't need to remind you of that. But I will say that God calls those mistakes, sin."

Dylan's poor choices stared back at him in the mirror every day and constantly beat him over the head. They pressed down on him, made him second-guess himself, his decisions, his life. Tormented him without mercy.

"God offers us forgiveness. You can have relief from those heavy burdens and that accusing voice that reminds you of your sins and tells you you're no good."

Dylan was very familiar with that voice. Only alcohol could dull it.

"God has an abundance of forgiveness, which we all need. He's not picky about who He gives it to. But there is one catch."

Dylan leaned forward in his chair. He didn't care about appearances in here. Only Chaplain Jack and God were watching. And maybe the person monitoring the security cameras in the corners. If there was a way to acquire mercy, Dylan wasn't going to miss it.

"You have to ask Him. I highly recommend you find a minute to do so."

He swallowed on a dry throat. "All I have is time right now."

Jack nodded, then opened the Bible, flipping pages until he found a certain place. He spun the book around on the desk so Dylan could read it. The columns lined up—two on each page. Strange. And the print was rather small. Was this what a Bible looked like on the inside?

Pointing with his index finger, Jack said, "This is Matthew, chapter six. Read verses fourteen and fifteen. Right there."

Dylan pulled the book closer to him and found the tiny number fourteen. "*In prayer there is a connection between what God does and what you do. You can't get forgiveness from God, for instance, without also forgiving others. If you refuse to do your part, you cut yourself off from God's part.*"

"So another side of this is you need to ask yourself if there is anyone *you* need to forgive. It's all part of the same process. When we don't forgive others, we live in jail." Jack pointed around them at the office's walls. "Holding other people's sins against them, means we don't get the benefit of feeling forgiven ourselves." He let those words sink in. "That's the choice for you, for my son, for your ex-girlfriend."

Given everything, Dylan couldn't imagine Seneca ever letting him off for what he'd done.

"And we have to forgive ourselves."

Or him letting himself off.

"I don't know about you, but I could use deliverance from this heavy burden, couldn't you?"

"I don't get it—all this 'God forgives you' stuff." But he wanted to. He needed it. Maybe he needed Him.

"It's about recognizing we've made mistakes we can't make up for."

"Ha." That one was easy. "Check."

"And that God is sinless and demands we be sinless too."

Who could live up to that standard? "That disqualifies everyone I know."

"Absolutely."

"So why bother? We're all destined to carry this heavy load around with us forever. No hope."

"Except God saw our situation and did something about it."

Dylan had a feeling this was the part where Jesus came in. He'd heard about Him. Eli Hanson always brought Jesus into conversations on their trips. But he never dug for more info because Jesus sounded too good for Dylan.

"No doubt you've heard of Jesus, God's Son?"

Dylan nodded.

"He is God, but He came as a baby and lived a sinless life to show us a pattern for life. Like we said earlier, it's not possible. So, God made provision. He took out His punishment for everyone's sins on Jesus. And that's where the crucifixion comes in."

Dylan swallowed. He'd heard about that—a horrible way to die. Miserable, loaded with agony and horror. He grimaced picturing it.

Jack watched him closely. "Yeah, you've got a scene in your head. Now, think about this: He did that for you. For me. So no one—*no one*—had to be left out. Not even convicts like us, behind bars."

Everyone was included? "What's the catch?"

"You have to overcome your pride and humble yourself to ask

for His forgiveness, ask Him to save you from yourself, your sins, your past, and all the mistakes you'll make in the future. Ask Him to be your Lord, and then out of gratitude for all He's done for you—some of which you probably won't even know about until Heaven—you live for Him as best you can. Don't worry about that part. His Holy Spirit—another part of God—helps with that if you ask Him."

Sounded too good to be true, but if everyone could be included by simply agreeing with what God already did, by simply humbling themselves, it was worth trying. Especially if it meant he could be free. "And I can get rid of this burden?"

Jack nodded, tears in his eyes again. "That you can, son. That you can."

Dylan's throat clogged up. "I want that."

"So, tell Him." Jack pointed toward the ceiling as if God lived up there, and then he leaned forward again, hands clasped on the desk.

Dylan lowered his head because that seemed like the right thing to do. A wave of something new hit him, like fresh air. But when his head shot up to look around, he didn't see a source for the breeze—no fans. And the AC had been running on low as if they couldn't afford to fix it.

Jack glanced at him and nodded. "Tell Him. He's here."

"Out loud?"

"Your call. Remember you have nothing to be ashamed of in this decision."

Dylan lowered his head again and took a deep breath. "God, I need You." Saying those words aloud brought emotion to the surface, and Dylan swallowed against it. "I need Your help, Your forgiveness, Your Holy Spirit. Please, would You forgive me for all of my mistakes?" Something told him he didn't have to name every single one, so he didn't. What else had Jack said? "Would You be the Lord of my life? It's a heap, but I'm hoping You can do something with it. Please, help me." His throat burned so when the words stopped coming, he remained like that—chin almost touching his chest. Jack didn't seem in a hurry to kick him out of his office.

That breeze blew over him again, and then he felt something new stirring inside where no one could see. Weightlessness. A hint of joy as if part of him was coming alive. He raised his head, not even fighting the smile that formed. "Something's different."

Jack looked back at him, his face shining. "It sure is. That's what God can do. And you're only getting started."

CHAPTER THIRTY-SEVEN

Shea took the pulsers her counselor, Natalie, offered and sat down across from her. Once she was settled, she adjusted the intensity of the vibrations and the speed at which they pulsed in her palms so she'd be less distracted and more assisted by the stimulation.

"Let's begin by talking about your week," Natalie said after giving Shea a chance to take a long, slow breath.

Shea shared what was happening with her move into the cottage and how being without a job was an adjustment.

After hearing the updates, Natalie nodded. "Try to get comfortable. Remember you're in a safe place."

Shea's breath froze in her lungs as Natalie geared up to guide her into those moments. With Liam, she remained at the surface. Now she would dive in.

"When you're ready, close your eyes, and take me back with you. Describe what happened. Share details that you think are key. You're a psychologist; you know the routine. If at any time you need a break, open your eyes and we'll pause. You're safe."

Shea nodded and closed her eyes. Today, she had to share the worst part. Even now she wasn't certain she was brave enough. But she'd come this far, found a therapist she could trust. So, she opened her mouth and relayed the story.

JP had tried to warn her. And he hadn't even told her very much—just that Liam wasn't the type to commit, which she now knew meant he couldn't be trusted to keep his word.

Tonight she might pay for her misplaced trust with her life. Her heart thumped hard in her chest as the gang of men circled her car out in the parking lot. The yellowish outdoor, overhead lighting cast foreboding shadows on the gang's greasy hair, black leather vests, and visible arm-length tattoos. Wearing muscle shirts and scruffy beards, the mangy crew shoved each other, swearing and roughing each other up. They were obviously looking for trouble and didn't expect anyone to interfere—at least not effectively. Somewhat safe, for now, Shea waited inside the convenience store. But at some point, she'd have to go outside.

The middle-aged woman behind the counter paced and wrung her hands. Why was she managing the store at this hour, alone? Given how alarmed she was, maybe this wasn't her usual role.

Shea could barely breathe. She perused the snack options again, her eyes not really focusing on the chips and nuts. Chances were no one would visit this minimart tonight so long as the gang members hung out in the parking lot. So, her hope of a diversion was slim.

Liam was supposed to meet her here. Where was he? As the sun set this evening, the minimart seemed even more foreboding than it had minutes before.

You can't count on him, especially when it matters. JP's words ran through her head. Tonight proved he'd been right. She shook her head. How stupid to sneak around with Liam the past few weeks, trying not to let JP see them. They hadn't crossed any lines, but they'd grown closer, developed a degree of intimacy, had several dates. And the chemistry between them? Even her best friend Mikaela had mentioned it. She'd had a touch of envy in her eyes when Shea and Liam were together.

But none of that mattered if Shea never got back to campus.

Liam wasn't a particularly big guy, but he had a way with people. He could charm folks. She'd seen it several times—a feisty waitress, or even an angry brute of a drunken guy on the city sidewalk. The staggering man had blamed Shea for bumping into him, and she'd tried to challenge him, but Liam had stepped in front of her and said something—she couldn't remember what—and the man had smiled, *apologized*, and weaved off.

Yeah, Liam could get her out of this alive. If he were here. The criminal element leaned on her lonely car out there in the lot. Her rusty little college car. It was as if the hoodlums were waiting for the owners, so they could hijack their vehicles, or at the very least terrorize them. She would not be going out there until they lost interest and left.

Using broken English, the clerk led Shea to the office in the back where a phone sat on a cluttered counter, but there was no dial tone as if the business didn't make enough to pay the bill. She'd used her cell phone to try Liam's number, repeatedly, but no answer. And she wouldn't put her brother or other friends in danger by calling them.

She paced near the beverage coolers, grateful none of the thugs had decided to come inside. The clerk walked over and locked the door, which wouldn't be good for business, but neither was the criminal element terrorizing them. They hadn't made any threats, but Shea was tired of feeling trapped, so she dialed 911. Her heart galloped.

"911, what is your emergency?"

"I-it's not an emergency, yet. I'm in a minimart and there is a gang outside. I can't get out."

"Ma'am, slow down. Give me the address." The operator sighed as if she didn't have time to deal with Shea's nerves.

Shea gave her the address and described the situation.

"Have they hurt you?"

"No."

"Have they made any threats to you or anyone else?"

"No."

"So, there hasn't been a crime. Ma'am, this is a busy call center." Phones rang in the background, proving her point and shaming Shea. "I'll have a patrol car drive by, *when* one becomes available, but they're all out on calls relating to actual emergencies right now."

"Um, okay. What should we do until then?" And how would Shea and the clerk know when the police had driven by? Would they stop in if they didn't see any "criminal" activity?

"Ma'am, if there hasn't been a crime, I need to get to the next call." The phone went silent as the line was disconnected.

Maybe she didn't need the police or Liam in order to be safe. Growing up with Dad and an older brother, she'd gotten used to a protective force around her. She'd wrestled with JP, and Dad made sure she had a few self-defense skills. She could face this. She marched to the front counter. "Hi," she greeted the woman as warmly as she could, though her hands were shaking, given her plan. She could wait for the police car, but who knew when or if they'd drive by. And how would she see them from here? She set her bottle of lemonade on the counter and handed the woman cash. "I'm going out there. Could you keep an eye on me until I drive away?"

The woman, her eyes wide with fear, nodded almost frantically, though her utterances weren't English, as far as Shea could tell.

Shea would arm herself with pepper spray and stride to her car, ignore the catcalling she knew would follow her, get in, lock her doors, and drive away. And she'd never speak to Liam again. If anything happened, the woman could serve as a witness. She faced the clerk and mimed that she should lock the front door after Shea.

"Lord, we could use Your protection tonight—both of us," she murmured. Then she straightened her back and walked to the glass exit door where she flicked the lock.

Those twenty-five feet to her little hatchback were the longest stretch she'd ever crossed in her life. As soon as she stepped outside, the men all turned, howling like a pack of wolves. A siren approached, which seemed to keep the men from getting too close. Had the police decided to patrol the area? Or were they headed somewhere else? One brute blocked her car door. That's when she heard a crash of glass shattering by the front of the convenience store. All eyes turned as the men startled, and she saw her opportunity to jump into her car.

Once inside, hands shaking, she locked her door. Then, the nearest monster yanked on her door handle. When he couldn't get in, he grabbed a rock and bashed it against her window, demanding she let him in. He threatened the clerk if Shea didn't cooperate. There was no way she'd open her door. Fearing for the woman and feeling helpless, she flipped the ignition, heart pounding as she sped away.

In the rearview mirror, she watched the woman smash another glass jug of something as she held the shop's door ajar. The men surrounded her and yanked her outside before she could lock herself in again. She yelled at them, fist raised. She'd helped Shea make her escape. "Lord, help her." *Thank You for getting me out of there.*

Out on the main street, her hands shook as she tried to catch her breath. This traffic light, directly in view of the mart, ran long. What if the men came over here? Right now, they circled the woman, who was on the ground, raising her arms over head. Had they knocked her down? Someone kicked her. Desperate, Shea honked her horn, and when the other drivers around her noticed, she pointed toward the store. Two of the trucks pulled into the lot.

The light changed to green, and Shea drove down the street, her whole body shaking. What were those men doing to that clerk? Unsure where to go, and fuzzy headed as if she might be in shock, she found an urgent care clinic. Inside, she reported what she'd seen and someone called 911. The staff studied her. Perhaps they didn't believe she wasn't injured somewhere.

Once they knew the police were on their way to the scene, they convinced Shea to be seen in the back. She'd been diagnosed with acute stress reaction, and they'd had a psychiatrist check in with her before releasing her. He'd suggested she follow up with a therapist. He mentioned dissociation and PTSD and told her what to watch for. Then, he'd asked if she had family or close friends who could check up on her over the next few days.

But it was the following day when she'd learned the truth. That clerk had died.

The pulsers in her hands brought Shea back to the counseling session as she finished the story. The room grew quiet. Tears soaked her face. This was the part she hadn't told Liam. She hadn't even admitted it to herself for the past several years.

"You can open your eyes now, Shea," Natalie said, her voice soft. "I think we've just discovered why it's been difficult for you to move past that trauma."

Shea nodded, her chin trembling despite the bilateral stimulation to her brain's hemispheres. Her logical left brain couldn't overcome the right brain's deep emotions in this moment. She breathed deeply and focused on the sensations of the pulsers.

"It's time you let yourself off the hook, for both not feeling healed yet, but especially for what those men did to that woman. You are not to blame. We have more work to do with this today, but later, I want us to address survivor's guilt, okay?"

Shea nodded, swallowing. Of course. Finally, the root.

Natalie studied her while Shea blinked several times, feeling disconnected and disoriented.

Natalie gave her several seconds, then spoke again. "Now, let's go back to the beginning. This time, you're going to go with yourself. Back in college, you didn't have a degree in psychology. You felt powerless. This time, you're safe."

Shea's mind felt fuzzy.

"Stay with me." Natalie reached into a bowl of beach items and grabbed an oyster shell. "Let's try this. Put the pulsers under your legs. They'll still vibrate and stimulate each side of your brain in turn. Then, hold this in your hands. Study it. Tell me what you notice. Use as many of your senses as you can."

Shea settled the pulsers, one under each thigh, and then she took the shell. Her vision was a little blurry as if her mind wanted to check out.

"I think this is hard because you were an adult when it happened, and you struggle with the fact that it still bothers you."

Shea nodded. "I wasn't even the one they hurt. What kind of therapist am I that I'm still stuck, after all these years?" *And what kind of person am I that I drove away?* "I feel so guilty," she made herself admit.

"But you couldn't have protected the clerk, or yourself, by putting yourself in more danger. The key here, and I'm guessing part of you knows this, is to remember that we don't have to make sense of the whys. We only need to do the work. Sometimes there are too many variables for us to pinpoint the whys. Make sense?"

Shea nodded, still holding the seashell, studying its veins and textures, the colors and size. Her thoughts grew clearer. Perhaps those questions had been stalling her ability to process.

"And you're not responsible for what that gang did. They made that choice. Not you."

Shea eyes wouldn't even focus, as she fixed her attention on Natalie for a moment, and then off toward the windows.

"Let's study the shell for a second. Tell me what you notice. Use your senses."

Shea needed to cooperate, needed to find healing. She lifted it to her nose. "Smells like the sea."

"Good. What else?"

"Lots of edges. Several iridescent colors. Smooth on the inside where the animal lived. Rough ridges on the outside for protection."

"Good. Great work."

Seeing more clearly Shea tipped up her head and gave her counselor eye contact, because that's what she'd like if she were the therapist right now, so she could see if her patient's eyes were growing clearer.

"Drink some water."

Shea complied, sipping from the bottle at her side.

"Now, sit back and breathe deeply. Close your eyes. Focus on the shell in your hand. Feel the peaks. Keep breathing. Picture a peaceful place."

Like in Shea's old office, Natalie had a small fountain running. The sound registered with her, and she pictured a mountain brook up in the Cascades. A getaway.

"Okay," Natalie said, bringing her back. "Let's return to that night, and this time, we'll equip you to have victory. You survived. Again, we'll deal with the survivor's guilt later."

As Shea retold the story, Natalie interrupted and guided Shea in picturing her current self in the minimart, coaching her younger self through the scene with plenty of reassurances.

When Natalie talked her back to the present, Shea had clarity. She no longer felt like a victim or a failure. If she hadn't left the minimart that night—hadn't driven away—she may have been killed too. What were the odds she could take on seven thugs and win? By leaving, attracting attention through honking and waving, and then calling the police, she may have kept the gang from doing far worse to more than that poor clerk.

She had additional work to do, but for now, she no longer needed to dissociate. Her thinking was clear.

And she knew exactly what she needed to do.

CHAPTER THIRTY-EIGHT

He hated this whole thing. After the last time Liam had visited a jail to see Burr, Liam figured JP, Jinx, and he wouldn't be back. Of course, that was over in Kent, but it didn't matter. Here they were again and all because Burr couldn't, or wouldn't, change.

They'd finally cleared security and been led to a room where the officer would bring Burr to see them. He'd only recently been arraigned, but someone must have put in a good word for him, because suddenly they were allowing him visitors.

Hitch had opted out of this visit today since he was still hobbling around. JP, who was a little older than Burr, was quiet like he was brooding or something. And Jinx seemed anxious as they sat on one side of the table and waited for Burr. None of them had said much since they arrived.

Liam didn't even know what to hope for, but he'd do what he could to help. He owed Burr that much.

When the officer opened the door, Burr came in looking different. Sure, he wore the orange jumpsuit so you could pick him out if he escaped, but he also seemed . . . happier. How was that possible?

"I'll be right outside," the officer said and closed the door.

The guys didn't wait for permission. They walked over and shook Burr's hand, giving him one-armed guy hugs.

Normally, Burr wasn't a hugger. "Hey guys," he said, subdued. What was going on? Had he gotten hold of alcohol in here?

Liam's turn. He hugged Burr and then stepped back.

"I'm glad you came." Burr's voice was quiet.

This sincerity made Liam clear his throat.

They caught up on the news Burr could share and made sure he knew the latest about the woman he'd hit—that she'd been downgraded to stable condition and though she had a long road ahead of physical therapy, her prognosis was good. When JP told

Burr that news, he tipped his head back to the ceiling and mouthed something as if he was . . . praying?

"They'll go easier on you since she's getting better," Jinx said, ever the optimist.

They settled around the table, and when things quieted down, Burr leaned forward. "Liam," he began, not using his nickname. "Remember I told you I'd run into someone in here? He's someone you know. And he's been a big help to me."

"Okay . . ." Liam searched his memory for people he knew who might currently be in jail, and like before, no one came to mind.

"Yeah, he encouraged me to talk to Seneca."

"What's your ex got to do with anything?" JP asked, his brow creased.

"I'll tell you later." Liam turned to face Burr again. "I met her. She came to see me."

Burr made a face like he might cry. "Was Breeze with her?"

Seeing all that raw pain, Liam could only nod. First time Burr had appeared this cracked open.

"Don't know what she looks like. I've never even had a picture of her." Regret weighted his hoarse words. Then he shook himself as if remembering the clock. "I need to ask for your forgiveness. I've been really angry at you for a long time." He paused, and the atmosphere shifted toward reverent. "I was jealous."

Liam sat back. "Of what? The fact I was an orphan who had to live with my aunt? You grew up with both parents."

"Your aunt is the best, as unusual as she is. And I hated that you complained about not having a dad. Dads aren't always awesome. My dad was a mean drunk. You had it good with your aunt. She paid attention to you. Tried to help you through life. I resented that you didn't understand what you had in her. But not anymore. I'm sorry for that."

Liam hadn't expected that kind of humble confession from Burr. He shook his hand across the table. "Forgiven."

Burr made a sound somewhere between a scoff and a sob, and his eyes went shiny. "Thanks." He took a moment, got himself together. "Before they kick you out, I need to tell you something,

Liam—the guy who helped me reach out to Seneca, to try to start making things right with her and anyone else I've failed—he works here."

"Okay." Liam drew out the word, waiting to see what Burr was getting at. JP and Jinx sort of hung back, watching, keeping a respectful distance. Strange that Burr didn't ask for privacy for all his confessing. Maybe they were next to hear from him, if there was time. The old Burr would have walled himself off and mocked any display of emotion, except anger. Something had gotten a hold of him.

Burr strode toward the door and knocked twice. The officer opened it, but the man who came through wasn't a cop. He wore a gray uniform with a clerical color, and he had pale blue eyes, like Liam's.

Jack?

Liam shot a glance at Burr. "What's going on?"

Burr put out a hand as if trying to calm Liam. "Chaplain Jack Barrett is the man who's helped me with Seneca, and he's helping me with my new relationship with God too." Tears glistened in his eyes.

Standing now, JP grunted, though with more shock than judgment. Jaw hanging open, Jinx stared at them in turn.

Liam hadn't expected to run into Jack here, of all places. "You work here?" He perched a hand on each hip. "As a pastor?"

Jack nodded his gray head.

"And you helped Burr—Dylan—find God?" Liam knew Burr had been meeting with someone here, but Liam's father?

Without speaking, Jack gave another nod and swallowed.

Liam couldn't process all this. He felt himself slipping into that dazed place that Shea called, what was it? The trance?

Jack stepped forward as if trying to hold Liam's attention so he couldn't check out. "Liam, I know you're angry. I don't blame you." His voice sounded scratchy, exactly as it had at Alki that night. "But, I am sorry for what I did to your mom. To you. I'm sorry for leaving and not coming back." The old guy's bearded chin trembled. "I wish I could relive it, do the right thing. Get the help I needed, so I could try to be the man I wanted to be in both of your lives—a good husband to Erin. A good father to you." He shook his head. "I can't. So I'm asking you"—he met Liam's eyes—"can you forgive me?"

Liam felt the stares of his friends as they shifted on their feet in this awkward moment. Burr stood off to the side, head bowed a bit, though he peered up at them. Jack had put Liam on the spot in front of his friends.

"No." Liam went for the door and pounded until the officer opened it. Then, he barreled down the hall.

Away from Jack.

Away from Burr.

Away from the past.

CHAPTER THIRTY-NINE

Don't run. God's voice. But what did He want Liam to do? Rush back into the jail and say all was forgiven? Fat chance.

JP caught up to Liam in the parking lot. "Dude." He grabbed his arm. "Slow down."

Huffing, Liam stopped at JP's car and paced. Where was Jinx? "I need to get out of here."

Liam knew running away made him like Jack. So what? He obviously couldn't escape his own genes.

Jack wasn't *allowed* to show Liam another side to himself—a softer, repentant side that Liam could pity.

He left Mom. He left me. He's the villain here. And I'm just like him.

That thought compelled him to punch JP's trunk.

"Dude!"

"I need to jump off something or find a shark to swim with." Would the bungee jumping outfit take Liam without an appointment?

JP shook his head. "That's not what you need."

His chest burned as he paced and scowled up at JP, who was a few inches taller than Liam.

Jinx joined them, his expression cautious. "What's next, guys?"

JP turned his back on Liam, who continued pacing like a caged puma, and spoke out of the corner of his mouth. "We talk Liam down, Jinx. Think of something." He probably thought Liam couldn't hear him, but he did.

This was the reason he couldn't be trusted. This reaction. He couldn't trust himself. He didn't know why he still ran off at these moments. Something simply compelled him.

And this was why he needed to break up with Shea and end their trial relationship. He was a lost cause, sired by a deadbeat. He'd never stop running. And if they were to get married, he'd only end up leaving her when things got hard—like job losses or adjusting to new babies in the house. His aunt couldn't help him, though she'd tried. His mother wasn't here to help him. There wasn't any help for him.

Liam would never escape Jack's mistakes. Instead, he'd spend a lifetime duplicating them.

But one thing he could do—let Shea go and protect her from himself.

CHAPTER FORTY

Shea needed to talk to Liam.

Miss Mat was volunteering in the theater tonight, leaving Liam and Shea to visit Mora Iced Creamery—a local and well-loved ice cream shop. He'd mentioned wanting to tell Shea something, which scared her a little. He'd come back from the jail looking angry, and he wouldn't say how it went or what had happened.

Shea hoped they could find some privacy for their conversation.

At the shop, the evening line was long, but the staff was competent. Shea ordered her usual dark chocolate, one scoop, in a waffle cone. Liam went for the coconut in a sugar cone.

They settled at a table outside near the Eiffel Tower replica. Now that the line out the door had dwindled, they had a little privacy.

"Seems like you have something on your mind," he said, giving her a gentle smile, though it looked a little forced. Funny how she'd been about to say the same thing to him.

A breeze ruffled the maple leaves overhead, dappling the ground with sunlight. "I had my intensive appointment today."

"Oh, I'd forgotten that was today." Concern lit his eyes, and he leaned toward her. "How did it go?" She noticed his melting treat and pointed, which convinced him to work on his ice cream, catching the drips on this warm evening. "Was it helpful?"

"Absolutely." Already she felt somewhat lighter, less like a victim, more like an overcomer. As a counselor, she'd often tried to get her patients to see themselves as victors. Yes, she still had to address the survivor's guilt. They'd discovered the root— something she'd repressed. But she didn't need to get into that with Liam today. "Natalie helped me not regret that I didn't find relief sooner. I *thought* time would heal the wounds, resolve the PTSD," she said, keeping her voice quiet. "But time wasn't enough. I knew better." She shook her head, trying to dislodge the condemnation that wanted to settle.

"You're getting help now; that's what matters."

She gave a strong nod. "Yes. But while we were talking and came to the end of our time, it hit me. I needed to follow up on another side of this situation." She paused to focus on her own dripping ice cream, letting the rich dark chocolate cool her throat.

"I still feel awful that you suffered all that because I didn't show up." He shook his head like he still blamed himself, like he hadn't let it go.

Her plan could wait. Clearly Liam needed relief too. "Natalie offered me a new perspective. I told you how this therapy works— using my imagination and her guidance, I walk through it with myself. Doing that gave me a new outlook. I saw that my decisions that night made sense and actually helped more than if I'd stayed at the minimart and put myself in harm's way too. I also saw how much I've changed, and that strength got me through the session today. I'm not the same person I was then." Shea leaned forward, her long, highlighted curls spilling over her shoulder. "You are not the same person either."

He crunched into his cone. "I see what you're up to, Counselor Shea." Was he back to calling her that? He almost sounded bitter. She tried to picture their romantic moments, remember him kissing her. But the guarded expression he wore now and the anger rolling off him pushed those memories aside.

A family stepped through the door—Mom, Dad, three kids all around seven to eleven years old. The two boys chased each other into the parking area, and the dad scolded them. Once they moved on, Shea zeroed in on Liam, who had finished his cone.

"I wish you could see it. You've nearly finished my cottage, nearly met all your obligations. Dad's really pleased." She finished her cone too and wiped her fingers on her napkin.

His brow wrinkled, and she sensed he was battling something he hid from her. "What's wrong?" she asked him. When he didn't answer, she tugged him up to stand next to her. "Let's walk."

He joined her and held her hand, though she sensed he was far away. "I need to tell you about this morning—our visit to the jail."

"Okay." They crossed the parking lot toward Madrone Lane and the other shops. A few round tables with umbrellas dotted the pedestrian-only area.

"Remember I mentioned Burr saw someone I knew in prison?" He let go of her fingers, and she had a feeling he meant to distance himself from her, possibly more than only in this moment. She let out a long, quiet breath.

"Of course."

"That person was Jack."

"Jack's in jail?"

"Nope, and you won't believe this." Liam waited until a couple passed them, then drew close to her again as they arrived on Winslow Avenue and headed east. "He's *Chaplain* Jack now."

She peered over at Liam as they strolled and watched him clench his jaw. "Really?" *Thank You, Lord. That's good news.* Why then, was Liam so angry?

"He had the gall to ask me—there in front of JP, Burr, and Jinx—if I would forgive him for everything." He snorted. Then he shook his head. "Unbelievable."

"If Jack is now the pastor there, doesn't that mean he's changed? That he's not the same man he was years ago?"

"Oh, you mean when I needed him? When Mom depended on him? That man?" He stopped on the sidewalk and other visitors had to weave around them. "Don't tell me you're on his side."

There was no reasoning with this Liam. "I'm only saying the past is the past. Forgiveness wipes away the sting of it, like me forgiving you for that night we never made it to the theater."

His expression softened, and she caught a glimpse of the man she was starting to fall for. The revelation felt like a brook gurgling inside.

"And now"—she took his hand and swung it between them lightly—"we can move forward having learned from the past, but not harboring harsh feelings or being stuck there."

He shook his head as if he didn't agree. "No, no we can't. The past isn't wiped away that easily. I confirmed today that I'm a lot like Jack. I can't guarantee I won't become more like him the older I get. I can't promise you"—he swallowed and grimaced like his throat burned—"I won't run if things get hard. And I can't promise if I do run that I will return. Jack ran and never came back—well until last month, when it was too late. And I can't outrun Jack's genes."

He let go of her hand. "I'm afraid our trial relationship is over." He touched her shoulder, but he seemed to want to touch her face. "I'm sorry."

No, this couldn't be happening. "Wait. Wait a minute. You shared that long speech, and I don't get to say anything?"

A group of five teens passed them, pushing and swearing and laughing. Liam nodded his head toward his truck. "C'mon, I'll take you home."

That was it? "Hang on." She grabbed his arm, and he stopped so suddenly, there in the middle of the sidewalk lining the diagonal street-parking stalls, that she ran into him. "We can't be over. We're only getting started."

He did reach for her this time, threading his fingers into her hair near her ear. His expression broke into a tender, agonized gaze. "I will not hurt you."

She swallowed against her own sore throat. "You're hurting me right now."

He studied her face, slowly, as if taking inventory or committing her features to memory. His palm grazed her jaw, and her eyes closed on their own. She leaned into his touch and made a small sound. He answered with a sigh. This time his thumb brushed away her tear when she opened her eyes. He wore a mask of misery.

She reached for his chest and laid a palm over his heart. "I'm not going to give up on you, so don't give up on yourself." Was it a reflex when he covered her hand with his? Maybe he wanted to believe what she said about forgiveness erasing the sting of the past, about believing in him.

His Adam's apple worked up and down, and his eyes glistened. This was killing him, so why was he doing it? "Too late."

She knew this wasn't about her. That his decision was rooted in his own battle to become the person he wanted to be and outrun the man he worried he may already be. But his declaration still felt like rejection, digging deep and hollowing out her heart. Maybe he wasn't saying it, but what if her brokenness really did disqualify her from having a beautiful life? Her lungs went tight, and her throat burned.

As she drew away, her hand dropped from his chest. The war in his eyes when they darted to hers said he already missed her touch, and maybe he wasn't even sure of his choice. But he'd made this decision.

Now they both had to live with it.

CHAPTER FORTY-ONE

Liam's legs burned as he hiked the Tiger Mountain trail in Issaquah. His backpack weighed about fifty pounds, but adrenaline carried him up the trail to the staging area.

"Liam, slow down!" JP huffed behind him. "I don't know why I'm even here—except to keep you from jumping without your paraglider."

Liam had hurt Shea, something he'd hoped to never do. That heart-wrenching look on her face, moving from surprise to acceptance, about killed him. Especially since, in order to quietly accept his decision, she must have agreed with it.

Liam was beyond help. Hope couldn't reach him, and it sure couldn't save him. He left the trail. They'd get there faster if they used a more direct route.

JP had fallen behind again. "Dude!" he puffed, several yards back, from the sounds of him banging around in the brush and cracking twigs. "You know I'm not used to all this legwork. I've got a desk job now, designing buildings. Hang on!"

Liam didn't even slow his steps. He couldn't outrun his past, no matter how hard he tried. He couldn't escape his genes. Maybe flying could make him forget for a few minutes.

At the wide staging area, Liam had his gear pulled from his pack before JP even appeared.

"You'd better wait for me."

A few other jumpers worked in their own space, gearing up, prepping to drop off the mountain.

The instructors timed the jumps so people's wings didn't get tangled with each other. But Liam didn't care about protocol or safety or rules. He wanted freedom. He wanted to escape everything burning inside him: The directive—because God had been rather clear—to forgive Jack that nagged at him day and night, kept him from sleeping. The hurt he'd caused Shea. She didn't understand it yet, but he'd saved them both from a lot of pain in the future by ending things now. The conviction he would always be Jack's son who let people down. Who ran. Who failed the people he loved.

The instructor came over to double-check Liam's harness and to test the lines.

"I've done this before," Liam lied as the guy tugged various straps.

"We do this for everyone." He finished his inspection. "You remember how to twist up and untangle?"

"Of course." Liam had no idea. He'd figure it out. How hard could it be? He'd parasailed in Hawaii behind a boat; this couldn't be much different.

"Remember your training." The instructor looked him in the eye. He was probably in his mid-forties, fit, and wise. He didn't seem convinced of Liam's claims.

"Got it." Liam had watched plenty of videos online, and he'd sat through part of a class. He knew the basics.

"You signed the waiver?"

"Yup."

Apparently, they bought it, because they waved him forward.

When they gave him the all-clear, Liam raised the lines and his wing spread open. He spun like he'd seen in the video and the chute lifted him, then, like the two that launched before him, he positioned himself and prepared to run off the edge of the cliff.

"You're supposed to—"

Liam didn't hear the rest of JP's shouted warning as his feet cleared the cliff edge, and his body lifted into the air. Now, he just needed to get the hang of steering this thing and figure out how he was going to land.

Evergreen treetops passed beneath him, and Mount Rainier stretched in front of him as part of the Cascades. Glorious. A thermal lifted him, and he climbed higher. This weightlessness, *this* is what he needed to forget his problems.

He figured out how to turn slightly, and he glanced around at the others who'd launched before him. They seemed to be aiming for the landing zone off Issaquah-Hobart Road, equipped with huge windsocks. Rather than give JP a heart attack, Liam would shoot for that field and slowly start to bring himself down. He pulled the brakes and lost altitude, hovering and circling the forested mountainside. No problem.

Suddenly he was dropping too fast. What was he forgetting? The landing zone that had been beneath and in front of him, right in his path, was now behind him, and he was plunging into the forest. He yanked the lines and his right shoulder gave a sickening pop. A blue spruce came up fast and he slammed into a Douglas fir, which halted his movement. His wings deflated around him, contorting before tangling in the dense trees. Without the lift of the chute, gravity mocked him, yanking hard against his hold on the high branches that cracked under his weight.

Body aching, shoulder screaming, and face stinging from the impact, he shook off the fear and pain and glanced down. The safety of the ground waited for him, about sixty feet below. Agony shot through his shoulder and into his back. All his adventures, and he'd never broken bones or dislocated anything. Not so today. To get free, he'd have to slowly lower himself, using only one arm—his right was useless—and working around the branches poking straight out on all sides. But twenty feet down, his lines caught. He'd have to detach from his chute if he was going to get back to the ground.

How long until JP or the paragliding team came looking for him? Had anyone seen where he'd crashed?

Shea's words came back to him, something like, *If you do decide to jump, I hope you'll be very, very careful because there are a lot of people who care about you.*

He heard sniffling directly below in this deserted section of mountainside, far from the trails. One glance confirmed his guess. A black bear shuffled beneath him. He held his breath, afraid to move. Bears could easily climb trees. He wouldn't even work on his lines right now because the bear—make that two bears—would hear him. If they looked up, he might become their target.

He could radio for help if he could get one arm free, but if he lost his hold on this branch, he could end up hanging here—dangling without a guarantee that something wouldn't give. He knew the lines could hold him, but there was no guarantee the trees would.

The branch he hung from cracked, and the bear froze and looked up.

Lord? Help!

Something wasn't right.

Working out on her western deck with the morning sun tucked behind the house, Matilda couldn't disregard the feeling that her nephew was in trouble. She'd known he might head out for another adventure but wasn't sure where.

The intensity of the sensation pressed in more, and she paced. *Lord, please protect Liam. He's in danger, I know it. You may be about to use this situation, whatever it is, to convince my nephew to let go. If so, so be it. Your will, Lord.* Her stomach churned. *Have mercy.*

Shea appeared in the lawn between their properties. "Hi, Miss Matilda. Have you seen Liam?"

"No."

"I have a bad feeling." She joined Matilda on her deck.

"You too?"

"Yeah. I know he and JP were headed off to Issaquah to paraglide, but JP also told me Liam never finished the training."

That confirmed Matilda's guess. "Well, we could race over there, but I think I'll try calling him."

"Good idea."

The phone rang three times, and then Liam answered. "Son, I'm worried about you. Are you all right?"

"I am now."

Matilda switched him to Speaker phone so Shea could hear, then she clutched the young woman's hand. "You're on Speaker.

Shea's here. What do you mean, you're fine *now*?"

He didn't answer for several seconds. "I—" He sighed. "I may have pushed God a little too hard."

Matilda closed her eyes. "Are you okay?"

"A little broken. Mostly good. Now. That bear is going to have a headache when it wakes up."

"Bear?!" Shea's first contribution to the conversation sounded more like a shriek.

"Well, two bears. Here, talk to your brother."

"Jenna-Shea?" JP said into the phone.

"Yeah, what's going on?"

"Islander tells me he broke up with you because he's too blind to see what he has."

Shea's face went sober.

"Broke up?" Matilda whispered to Shea. "Since when?"

"Long story," Shea said quietly.

"Well, he didn't say that last part," JP admitted. "But he is. In fact," he continued, "he's stupid about a lot of things."

"Thanks, JP." Liam sounded a little farther away than before. "I'm the one in the ER bed. Really enjoying this Liam bashing."

"You deserve it," JP added. "You're an idiot."

If he'd only forgive. But Matilda had told him again and again. Liam would probably say she blamed every single one of his problems on unforgiveness. He missed that she was right about several of them. Unforgiveness drove Liam to take chances he shouldn't take. To risk his life.

Lord, help him see clearly. Please.

"Should we head over there? Which hospital are you in?"

"No, they're going to release him. I'll get him back to you safely, Miss Matilda," JP promised.

CHAPTER FORTY-TWO

Liam's face hurt where the tree scraped away a layer of skin. They'd popped his shoulder back into place—super comfortable procedure—and splinted his arm. And they'd wrapped his ankle. Yeah, he was fine.

"What is wrong with you?" JP had carried on with this high volume of frustration for a couple of hours now as they headed to the ferry terminal in Seattle. The lines were long, so Liam had been trapped in the car with JP, while boat after boat filled before they got a turn. Sunshine heated the car, which didn't help Liam's discomfort. Between ferries, people milled around the waiting lot, shooting selfies with the Sound behind them or the city rising adjacent to the pier with its glimmering skyscrapers in blues, grays, and gold. "All this because you can't let Jack off the hook. So he blew it. So what? You've never blown anything, and then later regretted it? You act like you're perfect and he's not, that he's to blame for every evil thing in the *world*. Get over it."

Ankle throbbing in the cramped space, Liam seethed. "Easy for you to say; you and Shea had both parents and nobody left or died."

JP pressed his lips together. A bee buzzed through the open car windows. "I was there, okay. I remember when your mom died. I'm sorry about that. Sooner or later you have to move on. Do you have to have Jack in your life? No. Do you have to start calling him Dad? No. Do you have to love him for the rest of your life? Probably not."

Liam scoffed.

"But for the sake of everyone around you who is watching you destroy your life just as surely as Burr destroyed his, get a grip, dude. You are headed toward a cliff without a chute, and I don't wanna watch that destruction. None of us do."

Shea's words again. All the people who cared for him. Liam didn't like all the attention. Maybe he should just live alone and stop calling his buddies for adventures. He could get by on his own, right?

You'd sentence yourself to isolation. Is that preferable to forgiveness?

God's voice, but Liam couldn't dwell on those words right now. "If I 'let Jack off the hook,' I'm betraying Mom. I won't do it."

"You think your mom held a grudge against Jack all her life? You think she never came to terms with his selfishness? You have to chalk Jack's failures up to his own weakness and stop this." JP paused for a minute as if letting the words sink in. "You don't have to be like him if you don't wanna be."

He didn't? So far, he had been.

"I mean, look at what you've done this summer." The ferry arrived and offloaded pedestrian traffic overhead and then vehicle traffic on street level while people returned to the cars in the waiting lanes. "It started out rough, you didn't have our cabin ready for my sis, but then you met the challenge and got it ready. You swallowed your pride and even asked grumpy Burr to join you. You tried to help him. I can't believe you never told me about the tank malfunction when we were in Kauai, by the way. But I'm glad you're okay. And you even started dating Shea—really getting your life together. But then, I call to check in on the family's house, and I get an earful about how you broke Shea's heart." He shook his head and started his engine to join the flow of cars following each other and the directions of the WASHDOT workers onto the boat. "Not cool, Liam."

"I didn't want to hurt her more later. It's better I broke it off now."

He snorted. "*You're* the one who decided to self-destruct. If you hadn't, you'd still be thriving at work and dating Shea. You decided that, Liam. Not Jack, not your genes. You."

Now on the ferry, JP pulled forward as directed, right up near the chain on the lowest deck, dead center. Cars lined up straight back on the left and would soon follow JP's car and then box them in along the right as well. Puget Sound waited in front of them. Liam would climb out, approach the chain, and watch from here if his ankle wasn't killing him. At least they had shade here, and soon, wind, which meant he wouldn't roast during the sail.

JP climbed out, pocketing his keys. "I'm headed upstairs. Don't do anything stupid, okay?"

Engines groaning, the ferry got underway a few minutes later, on time. They'd land in Winslow on Bainbridge in a little over a half hour. JP probably thought Liam would sit here like a scolded child and stew over his words while he was gone.

He'd hung from the fir tree for about forty-five minutes before the crew arrived to cut him down. The ranger had had to tranquilize one of the bears. The other ran off. All while Liam begged God for mercy.

Mercy. Liam had lost hope, given up on himself. He'd believed the voice in his head that told him he couldn't escape his genes, that he was destined to abandon everyone he loved. And then, he'd busted himself up by landing in the trees.

Is that symbolism, God?

Watching the bears root around at the base of the conifers, wishing he could ease the ache in his shoulder, he'd been willing to promise almost anything in order to find relief. Pain blinding him, he'd begged God for mercy and that He'd send help to get him down.

He had made one promise, to reconsider his position on not forgiving Jack.

What if JP was right? What if Liam, and only Liam, was to blame for sabotaging his life? Jack certainly hadn't sent Liam, unprepared, over that cliff's edge. Jack was too broken lately to be a threat.

Maybe the threat was all in Liam's mind, and fear had inflated the lie that he'd always fail and never be good boyfriend or marriage material.

What if all of it was smoke and lies and illusions?

But who would give him another chance now? He certainly wouldn't ask Shea for one.

He'd keep trying to prove himself at his job, and he'd stay out of trouble. But maybe he'd keep to himself more so he wouldn't fail anyone else, wouldn't wound people like Auntie Mat, the Browns, and especially Shea. That way, if he failed, he'd only hurt himself.

CHAPTER FORTY-THREE

Wincing, Liam placed a fence board and held up his drill. This was a simple picket fence, more for looks than practical purposes. But it would update and improve the curb appeal at this Yeomalt beach property on the east side of Bainbridge Island. The Browns had given him time off to heal, but he'd been glad to get back to work after a couple of weeks. Maybe now he'd have less time to think.

After waiting an extra week, the inspector had finally signed off on the Brown's cottage, and Shea had moved next door to Auntie Mat. Shea had been subdued when interacting with Liam, but grateful he'd finished. At one point, he'd caught a glimpse of her smiling face as she hauled out one of her last boxes from upstairs. Yeah, she was happy to be going to her new home. Since he still nursed his injuries, Auntie Mat had grounded him, enlisting JP and a couple of the youth group kids from her church to help her move.

The Brown family's other beach properties needed yard work done. Though there were vacationers, Stephen Brown had asked Liam to fix a fence here and an irrigation system there. He tried to stay out of the guests' way. After all, these properties, right on the water overlooking Puget Sound and with a view of Seattle that lit up like jewels at night, rented for well into the four-digits per week.

Burr had called him the previous night. They'd had twenty minutes because he'd phoned from Jack's office, and Burr had favor with Jack. Burr was no longer cold or harsh. In fact, last night, he'd been all about convincing Liam to follow through with God's directives, especially if he wanted peace.

He'd also asked how Liam was coming with the whole forgiveness thing. As someone who had abandoned his family—Seneca and Breeze—Burr almost sounded like he was pleading with Liam to forgive Jack and give him a chance rather than shut him out of his life. He'd even brought the Bible into the conversation, something about a passage in Matthew.

He'd nursed his grudge against Jack for as long as he could remember. And that grudge had served as a guard that protected him from the man who'd hurt his mom so badly and abandoned him. After securing the slat, he bent for the next board. He spaced it an equal distance from the last one and screwed it into place.

Not forgiving Jack—did that mean Liam's mistakes, his sins, weren't forgiven either? When he couldn't sleep the other night, he'd grabbed his Bible from a shelf. The book flopped open to Matthew five and six, and he'd read about God not pardoning him if he didn't pardon others.

All these years of hating Jack felt like a jail cell. Sure, God hadn't put Liam into an actual prison until he could pay for his own sins, like in Jesus's parables. Liam's choice to hold this grudge, to *nurse* this grudge was his prison. He felt disqualified from God's mercy in his life, barring the forest rescue. And he felt condemned for his mistakes.

Sunlight beat down on him and the meager breeze off the water, passing between the buildings, didn't even rustle the leaves on the trees overhead. These eighty-five-degree temps were rare here, and Liam wished for a cloudy day with a bit of wind to bring relief.

Relief.

Shoulder aching, he placed the next board into position.

What if Liam held the key to his own prison? Would the burdens lift? Would he be able to see both what his aunt saw in him and what God said about him, without fear of failing those he loved?

His image of Jack's character didn't match Liam's accusations, especially now that he'd met the man in person and seen the changes in Burr. Instead, that image evaporated like a marine layer that the sun burned off.

A garter snake slithered by his feet, into the neighbor's yard where it could hide.

And if Jack wasn't who Liam thought, maybe the monster he feared *he'd* become didn't exist either.

Maybe he wasn't as far from a good life, or a strong character, as he feared.

Using the tail of his T-shirt, he wiped sweat from his forehead and checked his watch. He'd been working three hours straight. Time for a break. He strode to his truck and grabbed a water bottle from the cooler. It dripped with ice as he twisted the top off and there, leaning against his truck in the shade, he took a long swig.

Wind swept into the neighborhood on the street side of the properties where a cliff rose behind the road. The air brought cooling relief—and a nudge.

"I hear You, Lord," he murmured. Maybe he was ready to let go. He glanced around and didn't see anyone. The current renters had taken a boat out a few hours ago. For the moment, the narrow road looked empty. He leaned against his truck, closed his eyes. "I need You." He wanted to forgive and get free from this cell. But part of him resisted, still. "Please help me."

An image of Jack from Alki that night and then in the jail came to Liam's mind. He'd been broken, humble, apologetic. If Liam had only recently met him and didn't know of his mistakes, he'd have compassion on him, wouldn't judge him. Even if he learned the man had been in lockup at some point. Because that man didn't seem to deserve hatred or Liam's anger.

How long had Jack been this broken, this changed? This sorry? And how long had Liam pictured him as stuck in time?

He'd been wrong.

"Lord, forgive me for not letting go sooner. I lay it down. Jack isn't what he used to be." Liam wasn't ready to call him anything except his name yet, but this was a start. "I forgive him."

Peace, like that wind that rushed between him and the cliffside, overcame him, followed by a hint of hope.

A memory of his mother greeting him after a collision on the playground came back to him. He'd told the other kid who'd accidently run into him, "Hey, it's okay" and Mom had given him a high five and a big smile. Perhaps, if she was watching from heaven right now, she would do the same again.

"Please help me let myself off the hook." He'd been his own warden, limiting himself, chasing adrenaline highs, risking his life, putting off relationships, disqualifying himself from earning a degree, sometimes giving up and sometimes running away. Releasing Jack, and himself, felt like the first steps toward a good future.

He went back to work on the fence with a lighter step.

Things hadn't ended well with Shea. Still, he wondered if she'd be around later when he stopped by to tell Auntie Mat about today.

Five hours later, Liam pulled into his aunt's driveway. No sign of Shea's car next door. Maybe it was too late for them, and he'd gotten his hopes up—that telling her his revelations might change things between them—for nothing.

His aunt wasn't back from the theater when he arrived, so he let himself in and hit the shower. Auntie Mat had mentioned she had something on her mind. Liam had been watching her closely, to see if she was sick like she'd hinted to Shea. But she'd seemed fine and whenever he asked, she assured him she was well. They had a deal.

The thought of something happening to her still scared him. "Lord, whatever's going on with her, please don't let her be sick." He dipped his head under the cool spray of the shower. The temperature refreshed him after working all day in the heat.

Jack's abandonment and Mom's death left him with several scars. Maybe he shouldn't be so dependent, so worried about being left alone.

I took care of you then. I'll take care of you in the future.

God's words brought comfort.

Plus, Liam, you are not a child anymore.

Shea's counseling stuff, of remembering she wasn't the younger version of herself, came to mind. Liam had changed too.

Whatever happens, I'll get you through. Lean on Me.

One of the reasons Liam hadn't wanted to get into a relationship, besides the issue of his own character, was that he was afraid of being abandoned. He tipped his head down and water ran over his face and dripped off his chin. He couldn't control what others did. His aunt might die—*please, Lord, not for a long, long time.* His mom had died. *Give her a hug for me, will You, Jesus?* And

Jack had left. None of that was under his control.

I will never leave you nor forsake you.

The words brought tears to his eyes. *Jesus.* He would never leave, never let go. And He'd promised to see him through whatever came. Like approaching the edge of a cliff, paraglide in place, he still had to take a leap of faith. Trust everything would work out, that his chute would work as designed.

Armed with the kind of courage God was giving him tonight, maybe one day he could attempt another relationship. He might let himself hope for something with Shea, but hadn't she been through enough? Unless God decided to work a miracle.

CHAPTER FORTY-FOUR

Standing at the ancient window AC unit at his aunt's house, Liam turned the dial to High.

Since the temperature even near the water hovered around ninety, dinner tonight was chicken salad sandwiches, carrot sticks, and grapes. Liam headed over to join her at the table. Hopefully the air conditioner would kick the heat soon. For now, the chill felt good against his back.

Auntie Mat gestured toward the machine. "Thanks for taking such good care of me."

Pausing in his reach for a sandwich, he saw a look in her eye he hadn't seen before. Beyond sincere, it was downright unsettling. Fear hit him. "What's up?"

Liam breathed deeply, trying to remember what God had told him that afternoon. His chest felt less tight as his aunt spoke again.

"I've tried to take good care of you too," she said, looking her age.

"And you have." He swallowed hard.

She reached across the table and patted his hand.

"Thank you." He meant the words, even though they barely came out loud enough to be heard.

"But I've been keeping something from you, and it's time you knew."

"Okay . . ." Here it came—the moment when she told him she was sick, exactly like Shea had said.

She'd put together her plateful of food—a half sandwich, carrots, and a pile of ice-cold grapes. Now she stilled and gave him her full attention. "You knew Jack had been in jail at one time, correct?"

He nodded. She needed to hear everything that had happened lately, but he'd wait until she finished. And the fact she was talking about Jack and not confessing an illness helped ease Liam's worries.

Hearing Jack's name used to make his muscles go tight and his jaw clench. Tonight, his name brought a picture to mind of a humble man who'd asked for forgiveness. A man Liam had forgiven. He didn't need to hold his grudge in order to protect his mom or show loyalty to her. In fact, he pictured her being proud of him for finally letting go of the past. That change felt as good as the cold air filling this corner of the kitchen.

"Well, shortly after he got out the first time, he contacted me."

Liam set down his glass. "He what now?"

"I know you're having a hard time forgiving him, but I wanted you to know he was thinking about you, years ago. He wanted to make sure you were doing okay."

Anger wanted to rise. How dare he? If he cared how Liam was doing, why hadn't he come back to him and Mom? Except, maybe Jack had been right to keep his distance, especially after his first prison sentence. Maybe that was the most protective thing he could do.

Remember your forgiveness.

Auntie Mat's wrinkled brow showed her concern. Liam needed to put her mind at ease. "I forgave him."

Her face lit, and her eyes watered as she clasped her hands together. Calliope startled from her nap near the table leg. "You did? That's wonderful news. Tell me about it."

"It's a long story, but I'm trying. And I want you to know I don't hold anything against you. Even if you were talking to him for years and years and didn't tell me." Though that stung a little.

"Even if I encouraged him to get in touch with you via social media?"

His jaw clenched, and he willed himself to relax. She'd given him so much. "Even if you started it all."

"Even if I knew he was the prison chaplain where they sent Dylan?"

"What? You knew?"

She grimaced and nodded. "I did."

He took a couple of deep breaths, and this time she waited him out. "Even then." He stood and invited her into a hug. She joined him and wrapped her arms around him. "Thanks for protecting me, providing for me, being my second mom." His throat burned. "You are the best."

As they sat down again, he had one more question for her. "So, you're really not sick?"

"I'm not sick."

Now that he and Shea weren't dating, could he ask his aunt about their conversation without ratting Shea out?

Auntie Mat studied him. "I can see you have a question you're not voicing. If this is about Shea, I did have a talk with her where I assumed a role from one of the plays we had at the theater last year. I may have quoted a line from the production about possibly being ill and having a specific request." She feigned innocence while Liam shook his head at her. "And she may have interpreted that to mean I was literally telling her I was unwell." She gave an exaggerated shrug. "I used an accent. I don't know how she could have mistaken my intent." She pressed a hand to her chest and raised her eyebrows.

He scoffed, but he couldn't avoid grinning at her. "You're impossible."

Her expression sobered. "I love you, and I'm glad you two finally found each other."

He wouldn't even address that. "Also, I'm going back to school. Get my degree. For Mom."

"That's beautiful, Son." She gave him one moment's peace before she said, "Now, about this bothersome breakup."

CHAPTER FORTY-FIVE

Her nephew had forgiven Jack? What wonderful news. Matilda studied him now, so proud her chest swelled with joy. But they did need to resolve this pesky relationship issue.

"You knew about that?" From her experience, Liam was seconds away from shaking a finger in her face, but she grinned at him. He'd forgiven his father. Miracles were happening!

"JP told me when you were in the ER." Now to settle things. "Are you going to let her go that easily?"

"Let her go? I'm the one who broke things off. I was in a bad place, you know, ready to jump off a cliff. I'd given up on myself."

"And now?"

"Now, I'm still going to keep my distance."

She eyed him, zeroing in until he squirmed. "You don't trust yourself."

He shrugged. "I don't have the best track record."

"Now that you've forgiven Jack, you can *feel* forgiven. You can delight in God's mercy and live in hope, and dare I say it? Even joy."

"That's a rather optimistic picture."

"But you will have to take a chance in order to have everything God wants for you. A risk, away from the cliffs and sharks. You'll have to pass your Auntie Mat's School of Romance."

His scowl held humor. "We are *not* going there again."

"Oh, yes. Yes, we are. Now," she said before linking her fingers on the table top, food pushed aside. "Have you ever told her how you feel? Do you *know* how you feel?"

He shoved a quarter of his sandwich into his mouth and stared off toward the sunroom.

"Well?"

Bite finished, eyes focused forward, he breathed, "I've loved her since college." He swallowed after his words poured out.

Finally, an admission. She'd take things easy so as not to upset him. "Good. Now, tell her that. A woman can't resist passionate confessions of this nature. Don't hold anything back." How desperately she wanted to see her nephew settled, happy.

He squinted, obviously suspect. "And when she still turns me down?"

Matilda shook her head. "I don't think she will. Either way, you have to try." She gave a definitive nod. "The final step in this phase of my School of Romance is the grand gesture. Think of an act that will help her know you love her—that will show her. Tell her how you feel. She won't be able to resist you after that."

"Auntie Mat, she needs time to heal. She's dealing with all her PTSD issues right now. I'm going to respect that and give her space."

"She seemed fine when she was over here the night you got injured on Tiger Mountain. She said she's had a few appointments, and they've walked through the traumatic event. She's brave, that one." Shea had also seemed very unhappy about the breakup. Yes, she'd respond well, Matilda knew it. "So, can you think of something romantic and personal?"

He stared off behind her for a moment and then met her eyes once more. "Not that I should go along with your School of Romance again, but an idea does come to mind." He thought for another moment. "And you have been right in the past, as painful as that is to admit."

She clapped again, and Pearl flew over, squawking. "School of Romance—squawk."

Liam groaned and covered his eyes with his hands, shaking his head while Matilda laughed. Even Pearl knew the genius in Matilda's ideas. She stroked her cockatiel. "Good bird."

She was doing better. Shea had just come from her latest appointment with Natalie, who'd stated what Shea was beginning to see for herself—she was healing. Natalie promised to put a good word in with Vanessa, Shea's boss. She might be back to work by the beginning of August. Tia had mentioned Shea's previous patient, Liberty Winfield, had stopped by looking for her. Liberty was much older than Shea's usual clients, but they'd clicked after Vanessa suggested they meet. Shea would have to get in touch with her. They'd developed a friendship beyond their patient-counselor roles and with Liberty moving to Whidbey Island soon, Shea wanted to stay in touch.

Outside Natalie's clinic, Shea climbed into her car and pulled out her phone. The cell had vibrated during her appointment, but she hadn't checked it. She found a text from Liam. Seeing his name on her screen accessed a deep place inside. A place of regrets and longing and . . . affection. A place reason couldn't reach. Logic said to let him go. Her heart begged for one more chance.

Why would he contact her? The last they'd spoken, besides the phone call when he'd been in urgent care, was when he'd broken up with her. So, what could he want now? And how *crazy* was she to care?

Letting go of their past and finding a place of healing gave her permission to dream, to hope for a romantic future. But she couldn't force Liam to see the future the way she was beginning to.

She read his text: Hey, are you busy Friday night?

Her heart couldn't take this yo-yo. During her appointment, Natalie had pointed out that Shea was getting a new start and that maybe she should consider Liam on her "keep your distance" list.

Her phone buzzed again as if Liam knew she was reading his text or wanted to clarify his earlier message.

No pressure. I figure after your hard work this week you deserve a break from everything.

Since moving into her house, and unpacking, and more purging, not to mention all her sessions with Natalie, she *could* use a bit of relaxation. His thoughtfulness touched her like soft summer rain. She missed him. *No pressure.* Before she could talk herself out of it, she typed in her response: Thanks for thinking of me. I'm free Friday. What's up?

Could I surprise you?

This sounded familiar. Should she trust him?

MEET ME AT MADISON'S DINER AT SIX FOR DINNER AND WE'LL GO FROM THERE.

She watched people stream past her vehicle as they went from shop to shop along Winslow Way. She'd go this Friday, but she'd keep her hopes locked away.

OK. I'M IN. SEE YOU THEN.

When Friday evening rolled around, Shea spotted Liam's car the moment she passed the diner. There weren't any stalls left, so she parked in an adjacent lot. Madison's metallic silver-and-blue railroad car shone in the summer evening sun. Liam waved to her from under the awning outside, and a breeze greeted her as she approached wearing a gauzy blue sundress.

Liam stood and took her hand. He was early, and that fact wasn't lost on her, especially since his last surprise had ended so badly. His thoughtfulness impressed itself into her heart. *Play it cool. He only asked you out because he feels sorry for you.* Also, tonight was a test to see if they could go forward as friends. She lived next to his beloved great-aunt, so she owed it to Miss Mat to try. Plus, she loved him. Seeing him tonight only strengthened that truth. *Oh, help, Lord. I can't take another broken heart.* Maybe she should leave before the evening progressed too far.

"I'm glad you're here," Liam said. He wore dark Dockers and a button-up black, short-sleeved shirt that brought out his sky-blue eyes. She swallowed at the mesmerizing effect. His gaze took her in, and she forgot about escaping. "You look beautiful."

The compliment felt good, and she wasn't entirely convinced he meant it on a friendship basis. "Thanks. You look rather good yourself."

His face softened at her words and made her heart catch. He didn't seem like Mr. Breakup tonight. What was happening?

They settled at the table and soon had placed their orders. They spent a few minutes getting caught up on each other's news—his chat with his aunt about how she wasn't sick after all, and Shea's hope to return to work soon. She longed to be back serving, helping people like Natalie had helped her.

"So, was this your surprise?" she asked, finishing her Caesar salad with grilled salmon. "I like it here, but we've done this before." She grinned at him and relished the light in his eyes as he smiled back.

"Nope. The surprise is yet to come." He finished his burger and checked his watch. "Shall we?"

After paying their bill, which she vowed to repay, even if he wouldn't accept it, he offered an elbow. They'd broken up, but for one moment, as his friend, she'd take his arm and stroll down the street together. And she'd tell her thumping heart to calm down. "Where are we headed?"

"Well, you know my aunt and her volunteering?"

"Sure."

They approached the crosswalk at the four-way stop. "I thought we'd go see the play she's been working on for the last several months. Tonight is opening night."

A driver waved them on, and they crossed.

"You're taking me to the theater?" The event he'd failed to show up for in college, a night out, turned into a nightmare. And here he was, on time, strolling with her to the playhouse on a peaceful street, arm in arm. What was he up to?

"You still like live shows, right?"

What a great surprise. "I do." She loved them and hadn't seen one in years. The fact he'd think of her and invite her to come ... well, it felt personal. More than friendly. The evening felt like one big "act of service," which he'd probably guessed was her love language. "Liam, what's going on? You broke up with me, remember? Then, you fell off a mountain and suddenly you're taking me on what looks like a date."

He stopped outside the auditorium where a line formed. He pulled her to a semi-private spot. Her guess was the show didn't start for another hour. He stood with his back to the windows of the large building. Behind her, a few cars passed now and then. A loud noise, possibly a car backfiring, shot off behind her and she flinched before spinning around. But she didn't panic. She didn't overreact or nearly hyperventilate.

Liam was right there beside her. "You okay?"

"Of course. Thanks." She stepped away from him, placing the building behind her.

He moved even closer, putting himself between her and the street. "Here's the thing, and I know I blew it, and I said I wouldn't hurt you, but then I did, and you have every right to hate me."

Her pulse skittered but not from fear as she considered his hurried words. "Your sentences are running together." Was it possible he wanted to try again? Her head barked orders of caution, but her heart silenced it with a hopeful sigh as she shoved logic aside.

His grin was delicious. "Are they?"

She nodded.

"I know I don't deserve another shot, but something's changed, and I'd really like to try again." He stopped, blew out a fast breath, and hung his head. "But I'll understand if it's too late."

She used three fingers under his chin to lift his head. "Do you mean that?" She could barely breathe.

His eyebrows rose over amazing blue eyes. "Are you saying you might give me another chance?"

She'd tease him a bit, make him work for this. She tapped her own chin playfully. "I'd like to hear more about the changes you mentioned, but possibly."

Light shone from his gaze like she hadn't seen all summer. "I forgave Jack."

"You did?" Fantastic. "Is this what falling off a mountain does for a person?"

He grunted. "I did not 'fall off a mountain.' I jumped off; thank you very much."

"And the trees bit you on the way down." She gently cupped a hand over the fading scar on his jaw and grimaced.

He placed a palm over her wrist and held on. "I'm fine."

"I'm glad you forgave him. Not to sound like a counselor, but"— she gave him a smart-aleck grin—"how does that make you feel?"

"Counselor Shea." He chuckled, and then his expression sobered. "Before, it was like I was carrying both my paragliding backpack *and* JP's all the time. For years I felt like I owed it to Mom to hold that grudge. And maybe even to Auntie Mat too. But now, those weights are gone."

"You have more faith in yourself too." She didn't ask him; she could see it.

"I do." He lowered their arms and threaded his fingers with hers. "I'm so sorry I hurt you. I wasn't trying to toy with your heart. I was just a mixed-up man with a lot of work to do." He swallowed. "Forgive me?"

"Absolutely. I get it, I always did." She understood that like herself, he needed to deal with his past so he could be free to pursue the future he wanted. "You invited me to the theater."

"Thought I might be able to make up for more than one mistake."

"You don't have to 'make up for' anything anymore. Forgiveness, remember?"

"Yes, but—"

She covered his mouth with her fingers. "Did your lips get scratched when you fell?"

The little lines at the corners of his eyes crinkled with humor. Ever so slightly, he shook his head.

"So, I don't need to kiss them and make them better?"

He wrapped a hand behind her back and tugged her closer. "You are a scamp. I had no idea until we started dating—the second time."

"Then, it makes sense you'd see it, now that we're dating the third time."

He drew her closer, and she gladly stepped toward him. "Let's hope the third time's a charm." His lips touched hers, and applause broke out nearby.

"Now that's how ya skip straigh' to graduation, me beau'iful dearies." Miss Matilda's voice with a cockney accent, but what was she talking about?

Liam broke the kiss to laugh, pressing his forehead to hers. "I love you, Shea."

The applause went quiet as if Auntie Mat held her breath.

"I love you too, Liam." Her heart swelled. *Finally.*

He bent toward her again, and Shea had no trouble getting lost in his next kiss.

More cheering, and perhaps a gathering crowd on this side of the entryway doors, judging by the extra sounds nearby.

"Bravo, you two," Auntie Mat called. "Bravo!"

EPILOGUE

Four Months Later

Dylan's heart thundered. Seneca and Breeze would be here in minutes. She'd finally agreed to let him meet their daughter. He ran his slick palms over his shirt. He could do this. He could be the man he wanted to be. Somewhere, Jack was cheering for him, and that gave him courage. Strange how the man had become like a father figure to Dylan.

For their get-together, Seneca had required that they meet in a neutral place. Then, Liam's aunt had volunteered her home on Bainbridge. Right now, Matilda, Liam, and Shea were over at Shea's house next door. They'd celebrate Thanksgiving here today and the food smelled amazing, nothing like jail chow. If Jack hadn't believed in Dylan, he'd still be in there. But he'd vouched for him and worked a deal to release him until his trial. Every moment Dylan had out of those walls, breathing the wet fall air, walking around free, he thanked God for His mercy.

A car door slammed in the driveway, and Dylan glanced through the window. Seneca's cautious gaze caught his as she moved to the back-passenger seat of her sedan where a little girl slept in her car seat. He bounded outside, unable to hide how eager he was and yet not wanting to scare either of them. *Oh, Lord*. He let the prayer release without adding further words.

"Hey." He stood there wondering how to help while Seneca hefted their dozing daughter into her arms.

"I can't believe she's still sleeping. I must have worn her out at the park earlier."

Dylan studied Breeze's cherub-like face. *Is that what it's called?* Her round cheek pressed into Seneca's shoulder, and Dylan eased the door closed. He pointed to the house. "It's warm inside." He only hoped she'd feel comfortable enough to stay, to let him spend this holiday with her and Breeze.

They had about half an hour before Matilda returned to put the finishing touches on her turkey and the rest of the meal. He swallowed, his throat tight. How could he make up for years' worth of mistakes in thirty minutes?

In the living area, he motioned toward the oversized rocker and Seneca settled in, looking around with a cautious expression. He wouldn't press too close, but he wanted to be where he could study Breeze's face, commit it to memory. Be there, when she opened her eyes. He chose a spot nearby on the sofa. "What have you told her about today?"

Rocking in the chair, Seneca let out a slow breath. "I said we were going to a friend's house for Thanksgiving dinner."

That stung—that she hadn't told Breeze who he was. He nodded, though. "I get it."

Compassion stole over her features. "I don't want to confuse her."

"And I don't want to let her down. You're right. It's probably best not to tell her I'm her dad." Studying the way Breeze's eyelashes fanned her cheek, he kept his voice quiet.

"Smells amazing in here. We haven't had a real Thanksgiving in a long time. Mom always has to work, and I don't really wanna bother when it's just the two of us. Breeze doesn't know the difference."

She was babbling, but Dylan didn't mind. There wasn't another place on earth he'd rather be than here, now.

"I'm rambling." She gave a slight smile, then met his eyes. "I want you to know I forgive you. I don't hold a grudge anymore."

The oxygen was sucked from his lungs, and he hung his head. *Talk about freedom.*

"Of course, I can't even think about the future."

He lifted his face, met her eyes. "I'm not asking you to. But you"—his voice broke, and he took a moment to breathe against the burning in his throat—"being here today, bringing Breeze over . . . I can't tell you what that means. Thank you."

She nodded and looked away.

"And as soon as I can, I will help you, both of you." He wished he had the resources right now, but you couldn't earn money in jail.

Breeze stirred, her eyes blinking open. Eyes like his. Her little fists squeezed her mom when she noticed Dylan.

"You're safe, baby. This is a friend." Seneca's soothing mommy voice even made Dylan feel better.

He gave the toddler a gentle smile. His daughter. "Hi, Breeze." His throat went tight again.

She didn't seem too eager to sit up or interact with him, so he'd take things slow. They had today. After that, he'd carry the memories.

The front door opened off the living room, and Matilda poked her head in. "All right if we come in?"

Seneca moved to stand, but Dylan reassured her. "It's okay. Relax." She settled down in the chair, stroking Breeze's back, and saying hello to the newcomers.

Matilda, Liam, and Shea shuffled in, toeing off shoes and whispering their greetings until Seneca told them the baby had just woke up. No need to be too quiet.

"Listen, you three hang out in here. Enjoy yourselves. I'll take these two into the kitchen and see about getting that turkey carved up. Sound good?" Matilda herded Liam and Shea out of the room, and they cooperated, hand in hand.

Would Dylan ever have a relationship like theirs? Right now, he was grateful for moments with Seneca and the beautiful angel in her arms. And the fact she'd forgiven him? Another Thanksgiving miracle.

In the kitchen, Liam and Shea took turns washing up after Auntie Mat. Liam loved having Shea here. She belonged with them, for holidays, every day. They'd been dating for a few months, and he'd never been happier. She'd returned to work and seemed content with how things were going.

"I probably should have told you earlier," Auntie Mat was saying. "First, could you lift that bird out of the oven? It's heavier than I am."

He chuckled and obliged with a wash of savory heat making his vision blurry. "As long as I get a bite. Worker tax, you understand."

She swatted him with an oven mitt while Shea laughed across the kitchen where she set rolls in rows on a baking sheet.

His aunt tugged him out of the way so Shea could get the rolls into the oven. "Like I was saying, I probably should have warned you, or asked your opinion."

"What are you cooking up now?"

She placed a hand to her chest. "Why, Thanksgiving dinner, my dear." She used her Southern accent, and he squinted at her. "Okay, okay. I may have invited one more guest to the celebration."

Shea stepped over, wrapping an arm behind Liam, and he welcomed her, kissing her temple. She smelled better than the feast aromas.

Back to his aunt. "Spill it."

Hands on her hips, she cocked her head at him.

Oops. "Please."

"That's better. Well, since this is my home, I invited Jack." She brushed her palms together as if all was normal with that confession. "When asked, he mentioned not having a place to go. Couldn't ignore that, you know."

Shea drew him tighter. "What do you think?"

He wanted to be angry. A sense of betrayal crept toward him, but he shoved it out of his thoughts. Then, he gave a nod. "Okay."

Auntie Mat studied him. "Okay?"

"Yeah. We'll see how it goes."

Shea reached up on tiptoes and kissed his cheek, and he held her there. "I'm proud of you, honey."

Baby giggles drifted from the living room before a rap on the kitchen door.

"Jack's here."

"Sounds like Dylan and Breeze are hitting it off," Shea breathed into Liam's ear while Auntie Mat went to the door and let Jack in. "Here's hoping Jack and his kid do too."

Liam gave her a gentle smile. With her beside him, he could do anything. Auntie Mat offered Jack a side hug and pointed toward Shea, introducing her. He lingered near the door as if uncertain, and Liam felt sorry for him. Dylan appeared from the living room, Seneca and Breeze behind him.

"Chaplain." Dylan gave him a hearty handshake and a pat on the shoulder. "I didn't know you'd be here today."

Jack's expression went tender as he took in Dylan's family of three. "Glad to see you, young man. Now, introduce me to these precious people." Dylan did and then Liam felt all eyes on him.

Either he'd forgiven Jack, or he hadn't. He stuck out a hand. "Happy Thanksgiving."

Jack's eyes crinkled. "Same to you, Liam. Thanks for having me."

They settled around the table, and Matilda prayed the blessing. Then, she looked up. "Anyone want to say what you're grateful for?"

Dylan nodded, uncharacteristically animated and assertive. With a wave of his hand, he went first. "Freedom."

Seneca shifted, holding Breeze on her lap. "A daughter." Dylan's eyes shone as he looked on.

Auntie Mat, ever the hostess, glanced at Liam, Shea, and Jack. Letting them consider whether they wanted to participate.

Shea's smile held a hint of mischief. "Auntie Mat's School of—"

"Don't you dare," Liam murmured, chuckling. Yes, he'd told her everything. After telling him how effective they were, she'd delighted in rubbing the lessons in his face.

She sobered, met his gaze. "Okay, how about a hopeful future?"

He couldn't argue with that. Liam studied her bright eyes. "Second chances." She squeezed his hand.

Attention swiveled to the newest addition to the group—Jack. He swallowed. "I'm thankful for restoration." Somehow his sentence almost sounded like a question, as if his hope was showing. He gave Liam a brief glance and then focused on his empty plate.

Liam had forgiven him, but he'd never told Jack, who'd been brave enough to ask him to. Everyone in the room, minus Seneca and Breeze, knew Liam's battle to let go of the past, but was he courageous enough to mention it right now? "Jack?"

The man lifted his head, wearing a guarded expression while he gave Liam his full attention. "Yes?"

"In the jail that day you asked me a question, and I wanted"— he cleared his throat—"to tell you, the answer is yes." *I forgive you.*

And as he'd hoped, Jack must have known what he referred to because his eyes watered, but he no longer looked guilty or unwelcome. Restoration. It was a start.

Across from him, Auntie Mat gave Liam a proud smile, and Shea squeezed his hand again, rubbing his forearm as she leaned close.

Then, presiding over the table, Auntie Mat zeroed in on each person in turn. "Welcome everyone. I'm thankful you're all here," she said as if proud of her meddling that brought them together. Yeah, they'd have a little chat later. But what could Liam do? She was his batty, lovable aunt. And he owed her everything. "Now, let's eat!"

Afterward . . .
Now for a Sneak Peek at book three

*Finding Love on Whidbey
Island, Washington*

As well as author note and contact information

CHAPTER ONE

Stepping in from the evening rain, Liberty Winfield entered the modern church building and followed the other late arrivals down the dim hall. Guitar chord strains mixed with the laughter of the rowdy group ahead of her, so she hung back and let them go into the chapel first. She'd rather enter the room alone, quietly sneak into the last row, and hide there in case she changed her mind and gave up on this mission her therapist had given her.

Try attending a church there, Shea Brown, her counselor-turned-friend from Bainbridge Island had said last month before Liberty moved north to Whidbey Island. *Give God a chance to speak to you, to minister to you. If Sunday morning is too intimidating, simply go during the midweek service.*

The lights were low in the chapel as she passed through the propped-open door. No greeters stood there, and she was glad. Energy didn't exist tonight for playing nice with others.

A tiny redhead in a princess dress shot out in front of Liberty, bumping into her legs. Instinctively, Liberty bent low and steadied the little girl. "Are you all right?" she asked, studying her.

The girl turned wide brown eyes on Liberty and nodded without blinking.

No adults rushed over. Liberty stood and scanned the room, pushing down the searing ache in her stomach. She bent again. "Where's your mommy?"

The child pointed, still not speaking. A redheaded woman stood across the room with her children, occupying one row of seating, midway down the right aisle. She had red, flowing hair, like this little girl and a couple of her sons. Three active boys and a baby on her hip held the woman's attention.

"Let's take you over there." Liberty offered her hand to the girl and swallowed against the burning in her throat when she timidly took her hand.

Together, they approached the woman while the room swayed with the guitar chords. Apparently, the service hadn't officially begun yet. Some folks spoke in soft murmurs, as if respectful of this place and each other.

The woman turned, noticing her daughter who darted to her and threw her arms around her waist. "Oh, Isabella!" the mom said. "You need to stay here with your brothers and me." She gave a sigh of frustration, then she looked up at Liberty. "Thank you."

Liberty could only nod as her own red hair shifted around her face. Isabella was about the right age. But she looked too much like her brown-eyed mother to have been adopted. Liberty gave a weak smile and walked away.

The atmosphere returned to peaceful, but Liberty's heart didn't. *What am I doing here?*

Now that she was back living on Whidbey, it could happen, exactly like that. Liberty running into a little redheaded, blue-eyed girl so much like . . . Except. No. The child tonight had been far too young—probably only four years old.

Why did You let me run into a child like her, God? Do You like tormenting people?

She'd never get over it.

Pivoting, she clutched her purse to her shoulder and readied to escape when a large group of perhaps ten people crowded in, instantly lowering their voices and scurrying down the aisle toward the front. To avoid them, she backed toward the safety of the corner chair at the end of the last row.

Music carried from the front, and her soul stirred with something . . . intangible. Familiar from years ago.

There, on the stage, leading worship on guitar by himself, sat a man in the shadows of the stage. No spotlights. No extra band members. No background singers, though Liberty could hear harmonies in her head the longer she listened. The chords drew her closer, and she inched up the left side aisle until she found a seat on the end of the middle row. All around her, people stood, swayed, bowed, knelt at their chairs, or raised their hands as if they trusted God, or at least wanted to.

Listening to the instrumental music here in this setting, took her back to her teen years. Her foster parents had been thrilled when she volunteered to serve on the youth group's worship team. They felt she could remain grounded and—what, spiritual?—if she stayed involved. And for a while it had worked. But that hole in her heart seemed to connect with the same void in her boyfriend's life.

She shook off thoughts of where that relationship had taken her and zeroed back in on this moment. Her counselor, Shea, had said to stay focused on the present, to take charge of her thoughts whenever possible. And right now, she didn't need any memories of Clay Matthews in her head or heart. Didn't need any regrets surfacing. Or any heartbreak to drag her back to her mistakes. It was enough that she'd returned to Birch Harbor on the northwest coast of the island. She'd do her best to combat the pushy memories.

Words appeared on the far wall, and the leader launched into a song. Sitting there in the shadows, he reminded her of Clay, only older. Except his voice sounded sincere. He seemed open-hearted and genuine—which meant he couldn't be Clay. All Clay ever did was put himself first. He'd never said a sincere thing to her. Not when he told her he loved her, and not when he told her he'd always care for her, no matter what.

But this singer—the one who had the whole room in a peaceful place—he sang and played as if he lived for this. As if this type of atmosphere was the only place he found a sense of calm or value or connection.

She watched him, knowing she should focus on God and the fragrance of anointing oil filling the room, that tenderness surrounding her with such longing she had to gulp and redirect her thoughts to keep from being sucked in.

Now and then, the guy on stage bumped his chest with a closed fist, as if he wanted to knock the lyrics into his heart, or soften it. Or maybe wake it up. Whenever the lingering notes didn't require both hands, he'd thump his ribs again, head tipped back, words flowing that didn't match the stanzas projected onto the wall. She swallowed over the vulnerability in his posture and his voice. Such humility. And a profound passion for the words he sang and their meaning—something about how God's love was unconditional.

Right. Long ago she'd learned the sentiment wasn't true. *No one loved you unconditionally.* But something about this guy, expressing himself through music as if God Himself leaned in to listen… well, that intrigued her. What was his story? Why did he thump his chest as if trying to convince himself?

She looked away from him. She had no room in her life for getting to know someone's story—especially a guy's. Especially one who, like Clay had, led worship.

Nope. She'd never trust someone like him again.

What was she doing? Thinking she could pop into this church building on a Thursday night and walk away without the atmosphere touching her, without questions? She'd only attended so she could tell Shea she tried church and it hadn't worked for her. Big surprise. But Shea was so convinced that if Liberty could resolve some of her spiritual issues from the past, she could find peace, resolution. Worth.

All Liberty felt was a weight of dread, of darkness when she pictured her life going forward in this place. Here she was, back in the city where it had all happened—where she'd made choices that had broken her heart.

And where God stood by and watched the people around her

take away what mattered. Even forced her to relinquish the only fami—

Stop!

The lone worship leader modulated to a higher key and repeated the slow chorus a final time. Then, as the lights rose in the room, the singer welcomed everyone and invited them to go around and shake hands, greeting the fifty or so other attendees.

No thanks. She'd keep to herself. She settled into her chair and dug through her purse, sending a clear message of "leave me alone and go greet someone else." Maybe the sermon would bring relief from the burden she carried; it might be worth staying for a few more minutes. Still feigning an involved purse search, she felt a tap on her shoulder.

"Liberty?"

She peered up toward the man standing in the aisle, not meeting his face. He held a guitar—this was the leader from the stage. Apparently, her aisle was his exit route.

"I can't believe it's you," he added in a careful tone as if he was afraid of frightening her.

She met the man's green eyes. Familiar. Startling as they were the first time she'd seen them as a teenager. And just as startling when she'd seen them in her daughter—*their* redheaded daughter.

"Clay." The name barely emerged. Words had a way of coming out strangled when you couldn't breathe. When you couldn't decide between fleeing or freezing.

The room went quiet around them as another leader took the stage to direct the rest of the service, but Liberty didn't hear what she said. Clutching her purse in a tight fist, Liberty bolted from the room.

"Hey . . ." Clay's voice called from far behind.

He'd better not follow her. If he did, he'd find she had one more option—fighting.

Self-centered Clay Matthews probably had no idea what he'd cost her. Had she been innocent in their relationship? No. But when she'd needed him the most, he'd let her down the hardest.

Barreling out of the church parking lot, all she could think was how not-so-churchy her anger and lack of forgiveness were. And shame pressed on her shoulders like a cloak.

Snapping closed his guitar-case clasps, Clay grimaced. Liberty Winfield. Here. In his church in Birch Harbor. Of all the places to run into her, he'd never expected to find her in church. As if they were going back to the beginning.

How long had it been, ten years? Made him want to fix everything he'd done wrong. Go back in time and say something less selfish, less . . . murderous. Not send her away this time. Draw her close and tell her they'd make it work somehow. That he'd find a way to support her and the baby.

His stomach wrenched into a tight knot.

Oh, Lord. Help me. I can't fix the past.

He wouldn't ask for anything, if she'd agree to talk to him. The only thing he wanted was to tell her how sorry he was for how he'd reacted when she told him her news. All that light in her eyes, mixed with fear.

Clay, I'm pregnant.

His response: *It's not mine.*

Then the hope in her expression faded to pain from his betrayal.

He snatched his guitar case from the row of chairs he'd rested it on in the church's empty lobby. As a teen, he'd known Liberty— Libby—so well. He knew she hadn't dated anyone else. But he'd been self-absorbed. Impossibly self-centered in those days. Ridiculous.

He cringed again on the way to his truck, a cloud of regret swallowing him up like the humid Northwest air pulling in a marine layer from the Salish Sea. Regret and loss. He'd lost her that day. Figured he'd never see her again.

Then today, she attended their Thursday night service. Mid-week and casual and not too well attended, considering how large this church was. But Clay had sensed God in the room with them—His peace and especially His love. Maybe even a taste of His acceptance, except Clay could never grasp that. Sure, he knew the verses. But he also knew his own history, his long list of mistakes, willful and dark. His chest ached with regret.

If she'd stuck around tonight and let him apologize, he could move forward. Instead, he felt the pressure of his sins as if he'd just committed them.

As if God wasn't in the business of forgiveness.

Maybe you were meant to carry some failures forever.

Author Letter

I hope you've enjoyed reading Liam and Shea's story. This novel flowed very quickly for me. I didn't set out to write about an estranged father, but as this book developed during NaNo (National Novel Writing Month—November, where participating authors set out to write 50,000 words in one month), I couldn't slow down long enough to feed any doubts. I believe God led me to this story and these characters. It's my hope that the storyline brings light into any relationship darkened by unforgiveness. I've always puzzled over Jesus's words: unless you forgive others, your Father will not forgive you. (my paraphrase) What could He mean? Were people saved or not when they asked for God's forgiveness?

Then, one day it hit me—perhaps it's not an issue of being saved, but more of *feeling* forgiven by God. Of *experiencing* the joy and peace and relief that comes with forgiveness that we desperately crave. The Message Bible expresses it like this: "In prayer there is a connection between what God does and what you do. You can't get forgiveness from God, for instance, without also forgiving others. If you refuse to do your part, you cut yourself off from God's part." (Matthew 6:14-15) What a gift, and perhaps a confirmation, to find this interpretation after the thought occurred to me.

If we don't extend forgiveness to others, perhaps that choice sentences us to not feeling forgiven for our own sins. But if we do, then we can experience the truth of this verse: *As far as the east is from the west, so far has He removed our transgressions from us.* (See Psalm 103 NKJV.) There's such freedom in that promise.

I've also been fascinated lately by genealogy and family dynamics. As a mother myself, I've certainly seen areas in my life that I could have lived differently. At times, I've felt the burden of needing to ask forgiveness, and more than that, needing to receive forgiveness. But it isn't up to me to make someone else forgive me. I've contemplated the heart of someone (like the father character of Jack Barrett in this story) needing forgiveness, craving it with his whole heart because he's no longer the same type of man he once was, and he can see the damage he's caused and can now own up to his mistakes. I could relate with his deep desire to be pardoned, to feel that sense of peace and relief that comes when someone extends forgiveness to us.

I could also relate with Liam, his son. He had a choice to make—would he forgive? We all get to face that decision at some point. May the grace of God give us the ability to let the past go, knowing we have been the one deeply needing forgiveness at times in our own lives. Then, once we let God have that situation, may peace abound. Here's to reconciled relationships and healed hearts.

I also wanted to mention that I used creative license with my story's location by renaming a real place for my character's cabin. Point Monroe Drive is located on Hedley Spit on Bainbridge Island. I've loved this gorgeous setting for a long time and was thrilled to write about it. Thanks to family friends for the use of their cottage during the writing of this book.

God bless you, dear reader, with more and more revelation of His deep affection.

You can connect with me at the following places:

My website/blog: www.AnnetteIrby.com
Twitter: @annettemirby
My Facebook group:
www.facebook.com/groups/252272708574760/

If you enjoyed my book, I'd love if you'd leave a review online. Thank you!